TRIUMPH TO TRAGEDY

Book Two

The Rise of Toussaint Louverture

DANIEL J.D. BAYARD

Edited by Shawn McAskill

Illustrations by Dian Triyasa

L&D Publishing

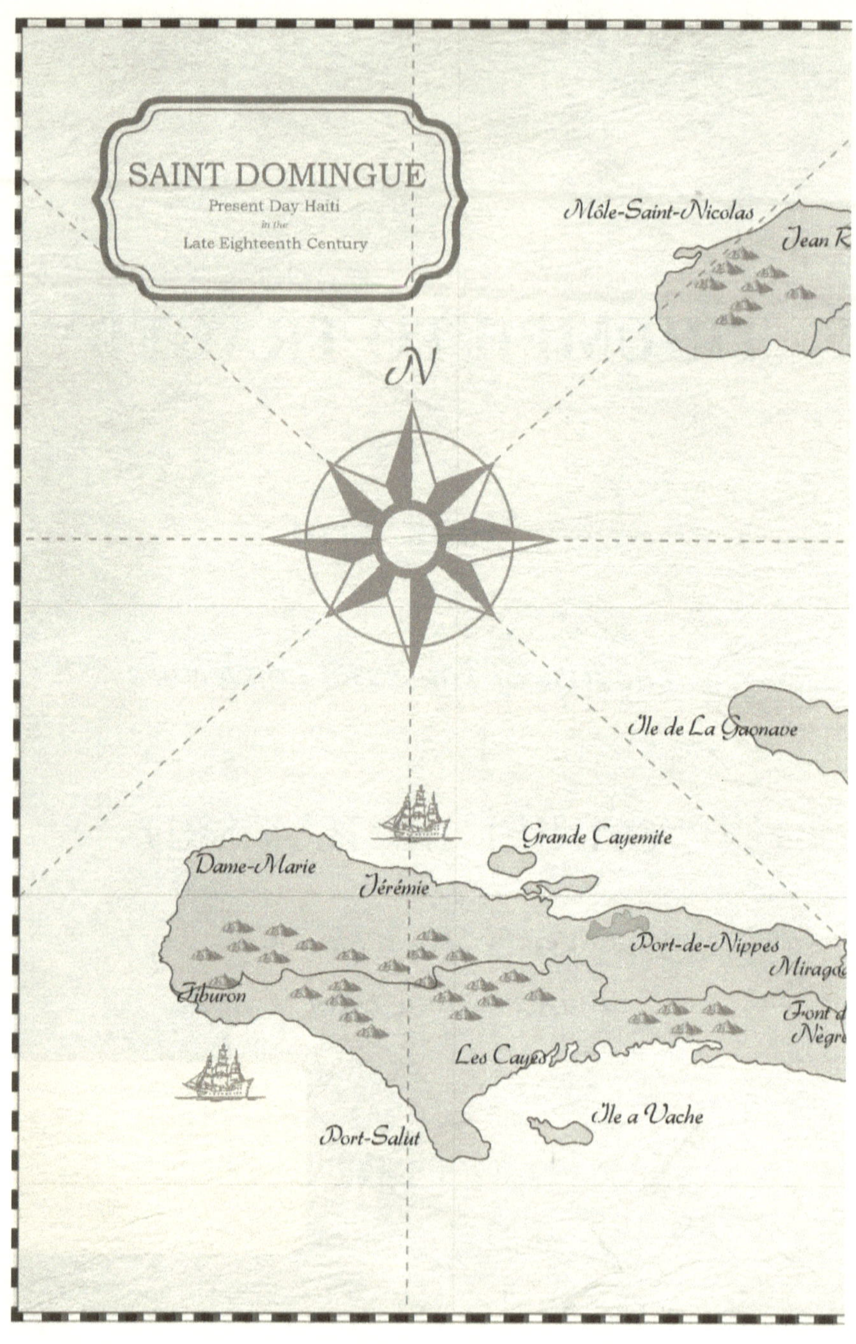

SAINT DOMINGUE
Present Day Haiti
in the
Late Eighteenth Century
N
Môle-Saint-Nicolas
Jean R
Ile de La Gaonave
Grande Cayemite
Dame-Marie
Jérémie
Port-de-Nippes
Mirago
Front d
Tiburon
Nègre
Les Cayes
Ile a Vache
Port-Salut

La Tortue
Port-de-Paix
abel
La Borgne
Limbé
Cap Français
Fort Liberte
Fort Dauphin
Gros Morne
Acul
Plaine du Nord
Plaisance
Dondon
Ferrier Rouge
Ennery
Marmelade
Ouanaminthe
Dajabòn
Gonaïves
Saint Raphael
La Croix
Ravine à Couleuvre
Estêr
Hinche
La Crête a Pierrot
Petit Riviére
Verrettes
Banica
Saint Marc
Artibonite Valley
Mirebalais
Elias Pina
Arcahaie
Sources Puantes
Croix des Bouquets
Port-au-Prince
(Port Républicain)
Plaine de
Cul de Sac
Léogane
Grand-Goâve
Petit-Goâve
ne
es
Jacmel
Bahoruco
Cote Espanol

Daniel J.D. Bayard

Triumph To Tragedy
Book Two

First Edition

First Printing, 2023
L&D Publishing

Email: Author@TriumphToTragedy.com

Paperback ISBN: 978-1-961297-03-6
Hardcover ISBN: 978-1-961297-04-3
eBook ISBN: 978-1-961297-05-0

www.TriumphToTragedy.com

Dedicated to the strong women in my life:

My loving wife Lily
My sisters Marie-Denise and Mica

With Wonderful Memories of Mom, Dad and Jackie

To my children; Laura, Daniel III, Phillippe and Brock
And my Grandchildren; Bianca, Calista, Daniel IV, Andre, and Julien

Special Thanks for Support, Critical Input and Encouragement:

Jean-Bernard Bayard

Frantz Ludecke

Parental Discretion Warning

ADULT SEXUAL CONTENT
GRAPHIC VIOLENCE
Not suited for young readers under 18.

For Young Adults under 18 years of age, refer to:

**TRIUMPH TO TRAGEDY
YOUNG ADULT SERIES**

The Cover Artist

Carl Craig

Style
"Symbolic Expressionism"

*"My Passion Lies in The
Challenge of Capturing the Beauty,
the Delicacy and the Fragility of the
Human Expression"*

Born in Haiti, moved to New York with his family at the age of 15. He served honorably in the U.S. Air Force for more than 5 years. He pursued a Bachelor of Science Degree in Finance and International Business at Florida International University. After a successful career in the financial markets for 16 years, Carl ended his vocation on "Wall Street" and decided to apply his experience and acumen in international consulting.

Despite his successes in the financial markets and as an international consultant, Carl has chosen to walk away from all the power and structure to satisfy his thirst for creativity by unleashing his talent in the arts: painting, photography, and music.

As a self-taught artist, he brilliantly and skillfully projects the inspiration he finds in his models. Since 2008, his work has been constantly displayed on the local and international markets. In 2015 and 2016 Carl was the semi-finalist in the yearly national contest organized by the Bombay Sapphire, The Artisans Series.

Carl is internationally celebrated and has exhibited his works in Mexico by special invitation from Haitian Ambassador in Mexico City. His artworks have also been shown in Cayenne (formerly French Guyana) again, by special invitation of the General Consulate, including many more. Carl's admirers consider him as one of the best Portrait artists of our generation. His critics revere him as the Haitian artist who captures the "Sensuality of the Haitian Woman" like no other. Using Fine Arts By Carl platform, he supports local not-for-profit organizations with the "Philanthropy Through the Arts" program.

LE PREMIER DES NOIRS
By Carl Craig
2023

Carl's belief is that hope lies in the human spirit and, by capturing the balance between delicate facial expressions and body language of his subjects, his message can be conveyed.

Toussaint Louverture was indeed an extraordinary figure in history, especially in the context of the Haitian Revolution. His ability to command respect from both his allies and adversaries was remarkable. His strategic brilliance and pride in his heritage were pivotal in shaping the Haitian Revolution.

His self-identification as "*The First of the Blacks*" in correspondence with Napoleon Bonaparte, who styled himself as "*The First of the Whites*," was a bold statement asserting his authority and the significance of his cause.

Toussaint's military prowess and leadership were undeniable. He was not just a skilled military strategist but also a visionary who laid the cornerstone of the eventual liberation of Haiti. His legacy as a symbol of freedom and resistance against oppression continues to resonate.

The phrase "*Le Premier des Noirs*" encapsulates the strength, determination, and pride that Toussaint Louverture embodied in his fight for liberation and equality. His contributions to history and the Haitian Revolution remain symbolic and inspirational.

LE PREMIER DES NOIRS – Oil on Canvas painting – 20" x 16
www.fineartsbycarl.com
Editing by Marie-Donald Manigat-Craig

TABLE OF CONTENTS

PREFACE

Toussaint Louverture is a Haitian hero—considered one of the most important of the founding fathers of the nation. To understand who he was, we must begin the story with his father in West Africa (present-day Bénin) in the 1720s.

A king had just passed and two brothers were challenging to succeed the throne over the Allada people. The younger brother, named Gaou Guinou—Toussaint's father—went to war against his older brother Hussar for the rightful accession to power.

This resulted in a series of imperialist wars by the Kingdom of Dahomey into Allada territory wherein Dahomean conquerors would remove their political rivals and obtain European trade goods by enslaving captives. Dahomean slavers eventually captured and sold Gaou Guinou and his first wife and children to the crew of the French slave ship *Hermione* which then sailed to the French West Indies.

Gaou Guinou became the property of Comte Louis Pantaléon Noé on the Plantation Bréda near *Cap Français,* the then-capital of Saint-Domingue (present day Haiti). The French Code Noir mandated that slaves brought to the colonies were to be baptized Catholic, stripped of their African names, and given a European one to assimilate into the French plantation system. That is how Gaou Guinou became Hypolite after his catholic baptism.

Many Bossals (newly arrived slaves from Africa) in the slave quarters recognized him as royalty and showed him great respect and reverence. Hypolite received special treatment among the Bossals and was routinely asked to be a peacemaker to appease slaves showing uncontrolled aggression.

Never being reconnected with his original family, in the 1740s Hypolite coupled with a woman by the given name of Pauline and had five children; three boys and two girls. Their firstborn son was named François Dominique Toussaint of Bréda, the future Toussaint Louverture.

Being the offspring of Gaou Guinou—a valuable member of the plantation's workforce—allowed the siblings to work in the manor house and stables, away from the grueling physical labor and deadly corporal punishment of the sugarcane fields. As a youth Toussaint was frail, earning him the nickname *Fatra-Bâton* meaning Feeble Stick, but on the plantation everyone called him Toussaint. As a trained domestic, he was often at the Big House and enjoyed special treatment.

Toussaint developed great skills in natural medicine, eventually becoming a veterinarian, which also saw him act as the health caregiver for the slaves on the plantation. His medical knowledge is attributed to a familiarity with the folk medicine of the African plantation slaves and Creole communities, as well as formal techniques found in the hospitals founded by the Jesuits.

Toussaint proved bright and extremely disciplined, hardening himself physically by becoming a superb equestrian and horse trainer. Toussaint spoke *Fon*, the language of the Allada people, *Kréyòl* the language of Saint-Domingue, and rudimentary French which he was taught by his godfather Pierre Baptiste.

He was an avid reader and eventually became quite fluent in the colonial languages of the time. Toussaint's future letters would demonstrate a moderate familiarity with Epictetus, the Stoic philosopher who had lived as a slave and his public speeches showed a familiarity with Machiavelli and Enlightenment thinker Abbé Raynal, a French critic of slavery.

Toussaint later received a degree of theological education from the Jesuit and Capuchin missionaries through his church attendance and devout Catholicism. His gentle demeanor earned him the trust of his overseer François Antoine Bayon de Libertat who had become steward of the Bréda property after it was inherited by Pantaléon de Bréda Jr., son of the prior *Grands Blancs* owner.

Libertat took a liking to the boy and admired his pride and guts when he would stand firm against members of the *Petits-Blancs* (white commoners) who worked on the plantation as hired help. Toussaint would engage in fights with them or any others who threatened the people or assets of the Bréda plantation. On one occasion, he even threw the plantation attorney Bergé off a Bréda plantation horse when he attempted to take it outside the bounds of the property without permission.

Libertat developed so much confidence in Toussaint that he trained him to become the coachman for his wife and children and granted him *"Liberté de Savanne"* (freedom of plantation restriction). He was allowed to leave the borders of the plantation without fear of retribution.

By his early thirties Toussaint was emancipated by Libertat in the mid-1770s and remained loyal to him his entire life. During the slave uprising of 1791, Toussaint saved the lives of Libertat's family by protecting them from injury and death from marauding slaves.

Upon being freed, Toussaint went from being a slave to becoming a member of the greater community of *Gens de Couleur Libres* (free people of color). This was a diverse group of freed people encompassing Black and mulatto *Affranchis* (meaning freed during their lifetime). The freed Mulatto slaves were often the offspring of French owners and their African slaves. Also in the grouping of *Gens de Couleur* were Black and Mulatto families who had been free for one or multiple generations.

Now enjoying a greater degree of relative freedom, Toussaint dedicated himself to building wealth and gaining further social mobility by emulating the model of the *Grands Blancs* and rich *Gens de Couleur* by becoming a planter. It is believed that Libertat assisted him by renting a small coffee plantation, along with 13 slaves, for Toussaint to manage.

Between 1761 and 1777, Toussaint met and married his first wife, Cécile, in a Catholic ceremony. The couple went on to have two sons, Toussaint Jr. and Gabrielle-Toussaint, as well as a daughter, Marie-Marthe.

During this time, Toussaint purchased several slaves; some to labor on his farm and others in exchange to free the remaining members of his extended family and social circle. Toussaint eventually bought the freedom of Cécile, their children, his sister Marie-Jeanne, his wife's siblings, and a slave named Jean-Baptiste, possibly a child of his godfather.

Toussaint's marriage soon became strained and eventually broke down as his coffee plantation failed to make adequate returns. A few years later, the newly-freed Cécile left him for a wealthy Creole planter.

Due to this economic hardship, Toussaint returned to play an important role as a salaried employee on the Bréda plantation around 1780 and remained there until the outbreak of the revolution, looking after livestock as the veterinarian and training horses. By 1789, his responsibilities expanded to include acting as a muleteer, master miller, and possibly a slave driver, charged with organizing the workforce.

While at Bréda, Toussaint married his second wife, Suzanne. She arrived to the marriage with a son named Placide, considered a mulatto of lighter skin, previously fathered by Seraphim Le Clerc, a Creole planter. Despite this, Placide was adopted by Toussaint and raised lovingly as his own. Toussaint and Suzanne went on to have two more sons: Isaac, born in 1784, and Saint-Jean, born in 1791.

By the early 1790s, Toussaint had accumulated a moderate fortune and was able to buy a small plot of land adjacent to the Bréda property to build a house for his family. Property records also show he purchased or leased multiple plantations during this decade.

At the start of the Haitian revolution, Toussaint was nearly 50 years old. He began his military career as a healer and lieutenant to General Biassou, an early leader of the 1791 War for Freedom in Saint-Domingue. With Generals Biassou and Papillon, he initially allied with the Spaniards of neighboring Santo Domingo against the French.

Toussaint demonstrated strength for military leadership, strategy, logistical operations and fighting capabilities. He trained and mobilized a lethal fighting force encompassing a highly trained and effective honor guard. On behalf of the Spanish in its quest to conquer Saint-Domingue, Toussaint won many battles against the French Colonial Army.

When French Commissioner Léger-Félicité Sonthonax freed the island's slaves in 1793 without any apparent authority from the French Assembly, Toussaint wrote a letter to the population declaring himself a fighter for the people and for the first time used the name Toussaint Louverture, shedding the name of Bréda.

After many military successes, Toussaint switched his allegiance to the French when the new Republican government of France officially abolished slavery in 1794. Spain still legalized the practice. His former comrades, Papillon and Biassou, remained with the Spanish Colonial Army as their Black auxiliaries. Toussaint's army would later engage his old colleagues' armies and defeat them on the battlefield.

Louverture gradually established military and political control over the island and used his influence to gain dominance over his rivals. Throughout his years in power, Toussaint worked to balance the economy and security of Saint-Domingue. The former had stalled due to the constant turmoil, so he restored the plantation system utilizing paid rather than slave labor; negotiated trade agreements with the United Kingdom and the United States and maintained a large and well-trained army.

Economy of Saint-Domingue

As the French Ancien Régime (Old Regime) reached its end between 1788 and 1789, Saint-Domingue, the western part of the island of Hispaniola, was considered the world's most productive and valuable industrial plantation economy; known as the "Pearl of the Antilles" for its wealth.

Saint-Domingue exported 72 million pounds of raw and 51 million pounds of refined sugar which accounted for 50% of all sugar consumed in Europe; plus 1 million pounds of indigo, 2 million pounds of cotton, and 60% of all the coffee consumed across the entire world. The Colony employed 1,587 great vessels and 24,000 sailors. At any given time, over 60 ships could be found in the port of Cap-Français alone.

Saint-Domingue's exports were larger than those of the entirety of the American colonies and worth far more than the gold of Brazil or silver of Mexico. The colony singlehandedly funded France's navy, produced more than all it's colonies combined, and accounted for half of France's GDP. It was the jewel of the French Colonial Empire and the livelihood of countless Europeans depended directly on the colonial trade centered in Saint-Domingue.

Dependent upon half a million African and Creole slaves, its 3,097 indigo, 2,810 coffee, 792 large sugar, and 705 cotton plantations produced today's monetary equivalent of $219 million USD per day, $5.5 billion per month, and $65 billion per year worth of commodities destined for both Continental Europe and the United States of America.

Comparative 2020 GDP numbers of the US would put the colony slightly above Rhode Island ($63 billion) and below Maine ($69 billion). However, considering the colony's small population of 578,000 (inclusive of 500,000 slaves), the per capita GDP would have come to $112,456; nearly double the $65,280 per capita GDP of the United States. This massive wealth was confined to the less than 100,000 free population and would have resulted in an annual per capita income of over half a million dollars per free man, woman, and child.

Between 1763 and 1789, the colony's exports were the driving force behind the French "commercial revolution" in the second half of the 18th century. French plantation owners hailing from Nantes, Bordeaux, Paris, La Rochelle, Bayonne, and the Loire Valley all found dynastic fortunes in Saint-Domingue.

The names of my ancestors and historical figures are real and this series follows an accurate historical timeline of events during the period, however, I cannot confirm their actions exactly as related and attribute personal thoughts as I envision them to be. This is the challenge and reward that comes with filling in the blanks of history.

I do not attempt to be completely accurate, but do intend to utilize these fascinating events as cornerstones of a story and

interject persons of interest within context. I hope you enjoy this enlightening and exciting glimpse of heretofore untold history.

Daniel J.D. Bayard

Daniel J.D. Bayard

Message from the Author

Thank you for reading Triumph To Tragedy – Book Two. The Triumph To Tragedy series is designed to entertain the reader while providing a detailed account of New World history in a manner that has not previously been presented and very much ignored. If you have not yet read Triumph To Tragedy - Book One, I strongly suggest you do so before continuing this journey. Your enjoyment and understanding of the characters and series of events will dramatically increase as a result. However, if you do not have a copy of Book One readily available, or simply desire a refresher, please read on:

In 1771, a young Jean-Baptiste Bayard returned home from his studies in Paris to the Caribbean Island colony of Saint-Domingue (present-day Haiti), unsure whether life on his family's plantation suited him. He had long entertained the idea of joining the French military and touring the New World; so he signed up for a multi-year deployment during which he would earn the title of Captain.

On military leave, he falls in love with the beautiful Marie Jasmine, who also hails from his hometown of *Jeremie* on the island's south side. Marie is a bright and confident woman, with an entrepreneurial spirit, quick wit, and no aversion to risks. In contrast with Jean, she had never ventured far from her small hometown, yet is his perfect complement. Upon completion of his military commitment, the couple begins an exciting life together— launching a successful business venture, beginning a family, and relocating to the bustling city of *Cap Français*—unaware of the drama, societal upheaval, and revolutionary war on the horizon.

In 1779, France interceded in the American Revolution by providing equipment and soldiers. Jean was called up to serve as an army reservist and fought in the bloody battle of Savannah, Georgia. While in the field, he is assigned a slave boy by the name of Henry Christophe, who later assists in rescuing Jean's brother from a grisly fate at the hands of pirates.

Over time, Henry becomes a member of the Bayard family and is freed on his 18th birthday. Jean considers the smart and savvy Henry a younger brother, entrusting him to run a part of the family business; a prosperous hotel.

During this period, both the colony and France were experiencing upheavals. France was in the throes of a revolution which culminated in the execution of King Louis XVI. The colony on the other hand was wrestling with social turmoil between the classes of *Grands Blancs* (white property owners), *Petits Blancs* (white commoners), *Gens de Couleur* (free Blacks and Mulattos), and *Restless Slaves.*

Seeing the chaos unfolding within France and Saint-Domingue, Britain, and Spain conspired to seize the wealthy colony, dubbed *The Pearl of the Antilles',* and readied their armies to invade. The island found itself bracing for these foreign invaders just as a bloody slave rebellion breaks out.

During this time, several new leaders emerged at the forefront of the slave revolt. One of them was Toussaint Breda Louverture—a freed former slave and now property owner. Toussaint enters a confrontation with Léger-Félicité Sonthonax, a powerful French government Commissioner, who soon issues an arrest warrant for Toussaint. Henry assists Toussaint's last-minute escape from the authorities, only to be arrested himself.

Book One concludes with Jean boarding a ship destined for *Port-Républicain*, on the other side of the island, hoping to find Commissioner Sonthonax and plead Henry's release from prison.

Book Two now begins...

BOOK TWO
The Rise of Toussiant Louverture
1793 - 1799

Saint-Domingue
Present-Day Republic of Haiti

Ay-ti
'Land of Mountains'
*The indigenous Taíno-Arawak name
for the entire island of Hispaniola*

*Je suis fidèle à la République
mais ne le servira pas au detriment
de ma conscience et de mon honneur.*

Toussaint Louverture

*I am faithfully devoted to the Republic
but will not serve it at the expense
of my conscience and my honor.*

Toussaint Louverture

One

TRACKING SONTHONAX

Port Républicain
January 1793

Retired Captain Jean-Baptiste Bayard awoke to the waves crashing on the bow of *Laura,* one of his company's cargo ships. He was several days into his mission to track down Léger-Félicité Sonthonax, head of the French Civil Commission—now reported to be touring Port Républicain. Jean had traveled around the island colony of Saint-Domingue to secure the freedom of his quasi-adopted brother and business partner, Henry Christophe, currently incarcerated back in *Cap-Français.*

Henry ran afoul of French forces several weeks prior after facilitating Toussaint Breda's narrow escape from arrest. Toussaint and his family had surely by now rejoined the rebel armies of Générals Francois Papillon and Georges Biassou on the Spanish side of Hispaniola. Jean had promised to do whatever it took to bring Henry home.

The island itself was embroiled in political and international turmoil in the wake of the slave uprising led by Papillon, Biassou, and the voodoo priest Dutty Boukman. The rebellion had been preempted by decades of harsh treatment that the French White planter class—the *Grands Blancs* —had wielded over their Black and mixed-race slave workforce.

However, the simmering embers were fanned into flames when the newly-formed French National Convention indicated that the practice of slavery may be banned. Relying on their considerable wealth and influence in France, the *Grands Blancs* succeeded in pressuring the National Assembly to grant the colony autonomy in their governance—quickly implementing and abusing laws discriminating against the *Gens de Couleur*; the free black and mixed-race residents of the colony. Through an entrepreneurial spirit and prudent financial planning, the *Gens de Couleur* was a growing threat to the ruling class due to their rapid accumulation of wealth, land, and power.

Joining the *Grands Blancs* were the *Petits Blancs;* merchants, artisans, educators, and other middle-class citizens also hailing from France. The *Petits Blancs,* though not as wealthy as some of the *Gens de Couleur*, nonetheless believed themselves superior due to the white color of their skin and European heritage. When the National Assembly granted the *Gens de Couleur* voting rights equal to their own in April of 1792, they too became fearful of waning power and influence.

The alliance was a fragile one, owing mostly to the *Grands Blancs'* air of snobbery over the *Petits Blancs*. It eventually formed a chasm between the two classes of rich and poor Whites. As infighting increased, both groups found their control over Saint-Domingue, considered the richest of France's colonies and arguably the world, slipping away. In their quest for power, dominance, and ultimate rule, the *Grands Blancs* had overplayed their hand.

To regain political control and quell the rebellion, the French Government had been forced to send a Civil Commission to the island led by Léger-Félicité Sonthonax. Accompanying him as second-in-command was Étienne Polverel. Both men's priority was the enforcement of the April decree, a proclamation by the French Assembly granting *Gens de Couleur* equal rights as citizens, which had met staunch resistance from the Whites of the local Colonial Assembly.

Together, Sonthonax and Polverel controlled 7,000 French troops, making them the de facto rulers of Saint-Domingue's non-slave population. Knowing most of Saint-Domingue's White populations were royalists and possibly separatists, they strategically attacked the White-sympathetic Army Regiment at Cap-Français, alienating the group and protecting French rule. Naturally, many *Gens de Couleur* volunteered or were recruited to the cause, forming the military backbone of the colony, and gaining appointments to important positions throughout the colonial bureaucracy. This further angered the White factions.

After an armed confrontation between Mulatto and White troops in December of 1792, Sonthonax began to deport troublemaking White officers and soldiers and relied on *Gens de Couleur* forces for security throughout the colony.

Jean knew Sonthonax well, even having assisted him in procuring lodging at his *Hôtel de la Couronne* in *Cap-Français*. He and Henry both had been instrumental in introducing Sonthonax to prominent *Gens de Couleur* who could assist the Commissioner's mission. Jean had convinced himself that Sonthonax was unaware of Henry's arrest, as well as the charges lodged against him.

Jean had witnessed, the evening before the escape and subsequent arrest, Toussaint Breda and Sonthonax exchanging a heated argument in the *Hôtel de laCouronne's* dining room. Toussaint, a royalist at heart despite his position in the rebel army, adamantly voiced his opposition to the ousting and execution of King Louis XVI. Toussaint, believing the monarchy was best for the colony, loudly and publicly chided Sonthonax for his opposition to the monarchy. He also made a thinly veiled allusion to his contact with the slave army that had been torching the plantation homes and murdering dozens of *Grands Blancs*.

Conversely, Sonthonax supported the French Revolution as a strict nationalist. He felt that anyone who opposed the new movement was an enemy of the state to be dealt with severely. Thus Sonthonax, before his departure to Port Républicain, had issued the arrest order himself on the suspicion that Toussaint was aiding the enemy rebels—a treasonous charge. Henry had unfortunately been caught in the middle by assisting Toussaint and his family to escape town, goaded by his aggressive belief in the emancipation cause.

The early morning breeze coming off the water was crisp, cool, and exactly what Jean needed to shake the fuzziness lingering from the rum he'd consumed the night before. His mind drifted to his wife Marie and their son Jean Junior—who he'd left in *Cap-Français*. He and Marie had grown ever more inseparable since he'd completed his final military assignment back in 1779, fighting for the American Revolution nearly 14 years ago. In the years since, they'd built a successful business portfolio consisting of shipping, importing, exporting, and a thriving hotel and casino. But the prize of their lives together was their son, Jean Junior. The boy was now nearing 18 and growing to become a successful young man in his own right.

Henry, a former slave but now *Affranchi*—a slave freed during their lifetime—was General Manager of the hotel and an integral key to its outstanding success. He had become like family and Jean was determined to secure his release from prison at any cost.

Waiting for the cover of night, ship Captain Marbot expertly navigated the *Laura* past the island of *La Gonave* and into the bay of Port Républicain. By the time they docked, the stars had already risen high in the sky.

As dock workers pulled in the ship and tied her to the pier, Captain Marbot descended the gangway to meet the harbormaster and inform him of his intentions to unload their cargo the following morning. Jean accompanied him to bid him farewell.

"Captain, I'm going to walk into town to secure a room for the night. I will see you in the morning."

"I don't think that is a good idea, my friend" answered the harbormaster, still in listening distance. A hard-working Frenchman, his sunbaked face from years of exposure could be seen in the moonlight.

"Excuse me, sir?" asked Jean, turning in his direction.

"You haven't heard then?" asked the harbormaster.

"Forgive me. I haven't properly introduced myself," Jean said, hoping to build a rapport while extending his hand. "My name is Jean-Baptiste Bayard. And you are..?"

"Lavigne. Harbormaster Robert Lavigne" the man answered, accepting Jean's handshake.

"A pleasure, Harbormaster Lavigne" answered Jean. "And why exactly would I not venture into your lovely city? I have heard it has been partially rebuilt to its original splendor from the fires of '91."

Violence had erupted two years prior when citizen's rights were offered to *Gens de Couleur* by the National Assembly. Angry and fearing disenfranchisement, the *Petits Blancs* rioted. Port Républicain was badly burned and had been rebuilding ever since.

"It's back again—opposition to coloreds like you," answered Lavigne. "Ever since those Commissioners arrived, people think they're here to lift you over the Whites and abolish slavery outright."

"Commissioner Sonthonax has no intention of doing that," answered Jean.

"Perhaps, but that is their perception, *Monsieur* Bayard; and what they believe is their reality" replied Lavigne. "Last week the entire White population—both rich and poor—revolted against the Commissioners at the Assembly House."

"Who would be so bold as to lead a rebellion against the French government?" asked Jean, knowing he might be pushing his luck.

"Some hot-head named Borel. He united the *Grand Blancs* and *Petits Blancs* through their hatred of free *Gens de*

Couleur. The miserable bastard can somehow rile them all into a frenzy" spat Lavigne.

"Where are the Commissioners now?"

"They were chased down here to the docks that night. Luckily, I had a ship I had just unloaded and they jumped on board along with their staff and sailed off—to St. Marc, I think" answered Lavigne. "Lucky to be alive, I tell you."

"This all occurred last week? What has happened since?" inquired Jean, his disappointment in his tardiness becoming apparent.

"*Blancs* have armed their slaves to fight with them and joined forces with the French army's *Artois* regiment, naming themselves masters of Port Républicain. The *Artois* are adamant in resisting the new government; they've even talked of joining the British of all things!" explained Lavigne. "They're already in contact with London, I hear, declaring them ready to join under the Kingdom of Great Britain in exchange for the conservation of racist laws and keeping slavery intact."

"That's treason!" exclaimed Jean.

"Indeed. Still, I suggest you make haste and leave the city, as the animals may be inclined to string you up to the nearest tree for sport," advised Lavigne. "Your skin will betray you here."

Upon hearing this, Captain Marbot deemed it prudent to pay the laborers extra and unload the cargo quickly that night. The *Laura* departed the harbor at 3:00 am, sailing off across the moonlit bay. Jean ordered the captain to chart a course to St. Marc, hoping Sonthonax had reached his destination.

By early evening, the ship had arrived at the port of St. Marc. The air hanging over the town was decidedly different, as Blacks, Whites, and *Gens de Couleur* interacted freely and without any obvious animosity. Jean left the captain and crew to their work and walked into the center of town, finding a quaint hotel and outdoor restaurant on its perimeter.

He entered the lobby to secure a room for the night but decided to grab a table for a meal and perhaps find a server willing to spill some information regarding what exactly was going on in this city—and whether there were any French government emissaries in their midst.

Just then, a professional, well-mannered server arrived to take his order. "Good evening, my name is Jacques. What is your pleasure this evening, sir?" he asked.

"A glass of Merlot would be wonderful," smiled Jean as the server handed him a simple menu.

"I apologize for our current lack of selections, but with the turmoil in the colony, our four pages of delectable selections have dwindled to a handful of choices," informed Jacques. "Allow me to fetch your wine."

Jean scanned the limited menu. The local favorite of chicken and griot—fried lean pork chunks, snapper, and stewed goat— would certainly be a welcome treat compared to the dried fish and smoked meat rations aboard the ship.

"Here is your wine *monsieur*, a delicious specimen from the *Loire* region. Have you decided on a meal?" asked Jacques.

"How is the snapper?" inquired Jean.

"Excellent! It was freshly caught just this evening by a local fisherman. It is filleted and seasoned then slightly broiled over charcoal, before being doused with a tasteful tomato-based sauce and smothered in onions and green peppers. It is accompanied by white rice cooked with peas and paired with sides of malanga and sweet plantains."

Jacques recited the details of the dish as though on stage.

"Sounds delicious, Jacques. I am sold" said Jean.

Jacques nodded, bowed graciously, and left towards the kitchen.

Jean took a moment to look around the restaurant, observing it to be about half capacity. Most of the patrons were men sitting alone such as he—some reading newspapers, others writing notes, and some in the process of enjoying their meals.

Jacques soon returned with a delectable-smelling plate, looking better than even Jean could have imagined. "It looks and smells delicious!" Jean said to Jacques with a smile on his face.

"I guarantee it is, sir" replied Jacques. "The chef does outstanding work, and truly loves the craft."

"How is business at the hotel?" Jean asked before the server could whisk away once more.

"These days it is only business travelers and those who are just passing through, *Monsieur* Bayard. Look around you," said Jacques, gesturing behind him. "The vacation travelers, couples, and families are gone with the upheaval throughout the colony."

Jacques hung his head. "Very disappointing."

"In Cap-Français, we have had an influx of *Grand Blancs* at our hotel," Jean replied.

"Your hotel? Which is that?" inquired Jacques, freshly interested.

"*Hôtel de la Couronne.*"

"Ah, I've heard great things about that place—especially the casino and nightlife," exclaimed Jacques. "I have never traveled that far north myself."

"Then you should! With your skills I guarantee you would find gainful employment if you moved to Cap-Français—I would hire you, surely" stated Jean, finding the perfect opportunity to begin his more in-depth inquiries.

"Jacques, I hear Commissioner Sonthonax has arrived here at St. Marc."

"Yes, he has. It seems the Commissioner was chased out of Port Républicain, barely escaping with his life. He and his companion—Polverel, I believe his name—arrived with only a few men in tow."

"What was this run-in they had with the locals at Port Républicain?" asked Jean, playing naive.

"The *Blancs* have rebelled, sir! They wish to join the British and bring Port Républicain and the southern peninsula under King

George…" His voice started to rise. Jean glanced around the restaurant to see whether they were drawing any unwanted attention.

"Could you imagine that *monsieur* Bayard? The British occupying our fine soil here in Saint-Domingue! *Merde!*"

Jacques paused to regain his composure.

"But why, Jacques? What do they seek to gain by that?" asked Jean. Though he knew the answer, he was curious to hear the opinion of those outside of his home.

"The *Blancs* wish to keep things as they are. The British uphold slavery in Jamaica and their other colonies. They want the Blacks to remain slaves and work the land and keep the *Gens de Couleur* out of power." replied Jacques.

"And what of the Commissioners now?" probed Jean.

"They have settled at the Mayor's office. I hear they've been meeting with government officials since yesterday; through the night and all day today," said Jacques.

"We are supplying their meals. Sonthonax loves to eat—and judging by the size of his belly, I would presume he does a lot of it," Jacques chuckled.

"Indeed he does," agreed Jean. "He is a frequent guest at our hotel and enjoys his food and drink."

The smile suddenly disappeared from the waiter's face. Jean tried to follow his gaze, but Jacques was staring off behind him.

"*Monsieur* Bayard, you have impeccable timing. Look who is standing with the *Maitre d'* now" Jacques said, nodding his head towards the front of the restaurant.

Jean turned around to find none other than both Sonthonax and Polverel—along with three others dressed in formal-looking government-type suits.

Their party was escorted to a table and provided menus. Jacques stepped away to serve his other guests, occasionally returning to provide Jean with tidbits on the other patrons' business or political affiliations. Jean quickly gathered that many were not pleased with the stance of their fellow citizens in Port

Républicain.

Finished with his meal, Jean left twice the customary tip for Jacques and casually approached the table of five. Their conversation quieted as the group noticed his approach.

Jean addressed Sonthonax directly.

"*Léger*? What a coincidence finding you in St. Marc," Jean exclaimed, feigning surprise.

"Jean? What in the world brings you to St. Marc?" Sonthonax replied, placing his utensils down on the table, and rose to greet Jean.

"Well, a possible new port of business here, perhaps. All the trouble in Port Républicain caused by those idiots has me rethinking my shipping routes."

Sonthonax's eyes narrowed. "What have you heard?"

"The *Blancs* have turned treasonous and are courting the British—surely you must have heard?"

Jean waited for the Commissioner to take the bait.

"Your information is accurate Jean. They believe my Commission has arrived to abolish slavery."

Sonthonax glanced down at the table and sighed.

"We only are here to enforce the decree from Paris that grants those like you, the *Gens de Couleur*, equal rights in the colony," replied Sonthonax."The idiot *Petits Blancs* are simply jealous and forging a dangerous alliance that will ultimately not serve them well," he added.

"Well, you of course have my full support, Commissioner," assured Jean.

"And how is Marie, that beautiful wife of yours, Jean?" inquired Sonthonax, attempting to steer the conversation to a lighter topic.

"As beautiful as ever—but rather distraught these days," Jean answered.

"What forever for? You had better not be causing that wonderful woman any strife," joked Sonthonax.

Jean maintained his stoicism. "You haven't heard then,

Commissioner? Captain Renaud of the Garrison of Cap-Français had Henry Christophe arrested and thrown in jail at *la caserne*" Jean replied.

The rest of the party immediately quieted and tensed up, turning their full attention to Sonthonax and Jean.

"Arrested? *Henry*? That accommodating young man that I admire so much?" Sonthonax exclaimed. Jean suspected his surprise was genuine; Henry ran the hotel that Sonthonax had called his second home while at Cap-Français. "Under what charges?" he demanded.

"The Captain claims Henry knowingly aided Toussaint Breda in his escape from the city. However, Henry was unaware an arrest warrant had been issued."

"Jean, I issued that warrant myself after we met the night before I departed for Port Républicain. Breda is counter to the French Revolution—a possible rebel assisting this slave rebellion and favoring the rule of a King over the National Assembly. Yes, I did indeed declare that man a criminal," sneered Sonthonax with unbridled malice.

"Commissioner, Henry was simply accommodating a guest with a special travel request and had no idea anyone had come to arrest him. Not to mention the soldiers laid their hands on my front desk receptionist, who was innocent of any wrongdoing." Jean struggled to maintain his even tone.
"Nathalie—the front desk receptionist? That pretty young woman, Nathalie! This is unconscionable!" Sonthonax said, aghast. "That bastard Renaud and those fresh soldiers from France—arrogant, all of them!"

"They took Henry away in shackles in front of the entire staff. He is now in that wretched dungeon of a prison at the *caserne* and

neither myself nor my attorney have been permitted one word with him!" Jean sighed and held out his hands. "We cannot even

HOTEL
FLORITA
RUE DU COMMERCE ST. MARC

see Henry to assure he is not being mistreated," he protested.

Sonthonax pounded the table, shaking the half-drank glasses sitting upon it.

"A fish rots from the head, and Captain Renaud is rotten to the core!"

Catching his breath—and the eyes of his companions—Sonthonax continued more measured.

"They know little of local politics and less of this colony's finest citizens. You and Henry have sacrificed for France and provided my staff and me with the best of service and accommodations. You both are patriots for the cause of *Liberté, Égalité et Fraternité.*"

Jean nodded. "We are honored to serve you and France, sir."

Sonthonax picked up his glass, swirling and contemplating its contents.

"Come to the Mayor's office tomorrow morning. The day's first order of business will be to execute parole papers for Henry's immediate release under your supervision until my return to Cap-Français. We will clear this matter up one way or the other—even by outright pardon if necessary. I at least owe Henry that much," Sonthonax asserted firmly. "Jean, please give the staff and sweet Nathalie my deep apology for this mishap."

"My sincere thanks, Commissioner. As you know, I consider Henry as a brother," Jean said, giving a slight bow.

"Of course, Jean. Now I must ask that you take your leave, as my fellow administrators and I have much business to discuss, and it is rather sensitive and confidential," Sonthonax finished.

"Yes, Commissioner Sonthonax. Thank you for your kindness and attention."

Jean extended a handshake and a smile before turning to walk away.

He was pleased with the exchange; particularly with how Sonthonax himself had offered the idea of parole and clemency without having to ask the favor himself. While Jean had been prepared to offer the Commissioner anything in return, he was happy to bank such an request for some time in the future.

The following morning, Jean entered the opulent foyer of the mayor's office. Under the high mahogany beams of the ceiling sat a beautiful, exquisitely dressed black woman at a huge desk; the flags of France, the colony, and the standard of St. Marc mounted at attention behind her.

Jean cheerily greeted and informed her he had arrived for an audience with Commissioner Sonthonax. However, his spirits were immediately dashed when he learned both Polverel and Sonthonax had departed early that morning—off to inspect the Mulatto troops garrisoned on the outskirts of the city, according to the receptionist.

"My name is Jean-Baptiste Bayard—perhaps an envelope was left here in my name by the Commissioner?" Jean offered.

"No, there is nothing here, Mr. Bayard. Please wait and let me inquire within."

The woman stood and disappeared into an adjoining room. Jean took a seat on one of the large couches prominently placed on either side of the twelve-foot windows garnished with heavy red curtains.

A uniformed office server came by to inquire whether he would like some café or tea, which Jean gladly accepted; "*café avec du sucre s'il vous plaît*—coffee with sugar, please."

Jean waited for what seemed an eternity; his mind racing with alternative plans should the woman return empty-handed.

"Here you go, Mr. Bayard. Sorry, it took so long. I had to track down Anna, the secretary of Commissioner Sonthonax" said the receptionist. "It must be quite important; Anna said the Commissioner arrived before her this morning specifically to leave this before departing for the countryside."

"Yes, thank you for tracking it down. *Merci et aux revoir*" smiled Jean in response. Leaving the building, he felt relieved and somewhat guilty for doubting the Commissioner's integrity.

The envelope was sealed with melted wax embossed with the official stamp of the Commission. Jean dared not tamper with it lest its validity be questioned when he returned to Cap-Français.

Boarding the *Laura*, he found Captain Marbot anxiously waiting, having already prepared the ship for departure. They immediately set sail under what Jean realized for the first time was a marvelous and sunny morning. As they exited the bay, he gently patted Sonthonax's letter in the breast pocket of his suit to assure it was safe.

Two

THE RELEASE OF
HENRY CHRISTOPHE

Sailing to Cap Français
February 1793

Pelicans dove for their breakfast while breaching dolphins escorted the ship Laura to sea. The distant call of seagulls and the rising sun both warmed Jean's heart on this crisp February morning. Jean breathed in deeply and for the first time in days felt a smile spread across his face.

He glanced at his pocket watch, a Christmas gift from Marie. It read 10:45 am. Jean squeezed it hard, hoping to somehow feel her presence within the golden enclosure. He wondered what she was doing at that moment—imagining her going about her activities in the office; writing in a ledger, directing the warehouse staff, negotiating terms with a hardware store owner, and coming out the better, as always.

"I've calculated our voyage to just under sixteen hours, sir," came the voice of Captain Marbot, interrupting Jean's thoughts. "If the sea stays calm and the winds steady, I estimate arrival at *Cap-*

Français between 4:00 to 5:00 am tomorrow morning."

"Excellent," responded Jean. "Allow me to take this opportunity to commend you on your command of this ship, Captain. I've noted meticulous attention to the equipment by your sailors and all are well-trained and disciplined. A testament to your leadership."

"Thank you, Captain Bayard. That means a lot coming from you" Marbot answered. "Permit me to carry on?"

Jean nodded, and the young Captain moved to attend to his ship duties.

Jean's mind went suddenly to Admiral Charles Henri Hector, the *Comte d'Estaing* whom he served under as Captain of the *Chasseurs-Volontaires de Saint-Domingue* at the Battle of Savannah, Georgia in 1779 during the American Revolution. The Admiral had taught him that recognition and praise of one's men was paramount in leadership.

Unfortunately, in 1793, his mentor was accused of being a reactionary and executed by guillotine during the Reign of Terror. His crime was that he had testifyed in favor of the Queen, Marie Antoinette, at her trial. Before his execution, in a style typical of d'Estaing, he wrote, "After my head falls off, send it to the British as they will pay a good deal for it!"

He was thankful to have learned so much from a truly honorable man.

The *Laura* docked at Cap-Français just past 4:00 am the next morning—just as Captain Marbot had predicted. Having bathed the night before, Jean quickly washed up and excitedly headed for home, hoping to catch Marie before she awoke for the day.

He quietly entered the 1st-floor office and silently made his way upstairs to the second-floor living quarters. Pausing only to remove his boots, he pushed open the unlatched door to Junior's bedroom. He could hear the boy's steady and deep breathing in the dark room. He closed the door and continued down the hall.

Jean slowly cracked the door to the primary bedroom. Marie's presence hit him instantaneously as her flowered perfume dominated the room. The light was just enough for him to make out her silhouette as the moonlight danced upon the complexion of her smooth skin. The mosquito netting of the massive four-post mahogany bed was open as the insects were all but non-existent in the winter air of the island.

Jean heard a slight moan emanate from Marie and his heart began to race. Was she dreaming? If so, was it he she was dreaming of? Could she feel his presence? He quietly undressed and lifted the thick quilted fabric, admiring the rising and falling of her breasts as she breathed.

"*My God*," he thought to himself. She would be forty-three in a few months, yet had the body of a woman half her age. Time had been gracious.

The cool air must have chilled her as Marie shifted to her side, back facing Jean. Her buttocks were firm under her satin dark blue nightgown. This was the same derriere he'd lusted after each time she would venture up the steps of the hardware store back in Jérémie over twenty years ago. He would joke with her every year that if he were to put five twenty-year-old women next to her—all naked with only their backs visible—no one would ever guess she was the oldest of the bunch. Marie would always scold him before sighing and laughing in appreciation.

He crawled into the bed, becoming instantly aroused as he gently ran his arm along the side of her leg. Marie gasped—then, instantly realizing it was Jean—placed her hand atop his. She turned towards him and brought her mouth to him. His tongue met hers and they fell into a long, passionate kiss. Marie slowly guided his hand from her leg up under her nightgown to cup her left breast.

As she took his penis in her hand he stroked and brought her nipple into his mouth. She moaned and whispered in his ear.

"I have just been dreaming of you, my love. Take me. I am

yours, now and forever. Enter me, and make love to me!"

Jean did as commanded, and the two charged into the lovemaking they'd both been longing for since his departure. It was slow, sensual, and profound; each looking deep into the other's eyes and sharing how much they loved the other through each action. Jean dared not look away lest the moment vanish into nothing but a fool's dream.

Marie had been tormented by his absence, overwhelmed by the possibility of harm finding him. At this moment, those fears only served to heighten her emotions into an eruption of ecstasy deeper than she had experienced in years.

He was home. He was safe. She had taken that for granted for far too long. Never again. All that mattered to her was now here, under this roof: both Jean and their son, Junior.

She gulped for air, louder and louder as Jean met her barely controlled moans with his own until they both exploded in mutual orgasm which seemed to last an eternity. Finally collapsing at each other's sides, still panting, he pulled her close. Marie lovingly snuggled into his arms, falling asleep as quickly as she had awoken with a smile still visible on her beautiful lips.

At precisely 6:00 am, three knocks on the door awakened them. A member of their house staff had arrived with a tray of hot coffee, fresh warm cream, and a pitcher of water. Marie looked at Jean who smiled and gave her a nod.

"*Bonjour Odicelle, ou ka antre (You can enter),*" greeted Marie in the language of Creole.

Odicelle pushed open the door with the tray and upon noticing Jean broke into a wide smile.

"*Monsieur Bayard,* you are home!"

"Yes Odicelle, I am—and happy to be," Jean responded as both he and Marie remained under the thick quilt cover so as not to reveal their naked bodies.

"There is enough already in that pot for two, but let me fetch an additional cup," she said, leaving the room.

Jean and Marie looked at each other and laughed heartily. Odicelle soon returned with another coffee cup to serve them both. She added just the right touch of sugar and warm cream, poured two glasses of water, and set them on each of the side tables before turning to leave once more.

"I will go ahead and make a second pot of coffee. Would you like it here, or with breakfast?" she asked.

"We will be down shortly, Odicelle," replied Jean. "I have an early rendezvous with my brother."

She smiled and left the room knowing it was good news about Henry.

"Your trip was a successful one then, my love?" Inquired an excited Marie.

"Indeed it was. Sonthonax graciously prepared the papers for Henry's release."

Marie placed both her hands on her face as her mouth burst into a broad smile.

"You can't imagine how worried I have been, Jean. I tried visiting him the first two days you were gone, but was turned away and warned not to return."

"Then they will not take his pending release very well," Jean quipped. "Let's head down for breakfast so I can visit the garrison prison and secure his release as quickly as possible."

The entire staff awaited Jean at the bottom of the stairs with ear-to-ear grins as the two arrived at the dining room. Next to Odicelle was Madeline, the housekeeper; Robert the coachman, and Pierre the houseboy stood to her other side, giddy in their relief that Jean had returned unscathed and triumphant.

Jean and Marie entered the dining room and found their son, Jean-Baptiste Junior, reading a newspaper at the table with a cup of coffee at hand. He smiled at them, got up, and jumped into Jean's arms, giving the father a bear hug. He then hugged Marie and they simultaneously kissed each other on both cheeks.

"I take it by the chatter of the staff that we have good news to share about Henry, Papa?"

"Very good news indeed. I am going to get him out of prison today," replied Jean.

They enjoyed a hearty breakfast of hard-boiled eggs, smoked herring, boiled plantains, yucca, avocado, and tomato. Once complete, Jean went to leave, but Marie ordered him to wait. "I'm going with you Jean—don't you even think about leaving me behind!" she said, narrowing her eyes as he began to protest.

"Junior, you're going to take care of a few things for me today," Marie said to her son.

"What's that Mama? I already have a full day planned. We are getting a shipment of molasses that needs to be weighed and paid for this morning, the ship Rachel is due into port this afternoon and I have a lunch rendezvous with Marie," Junior said.

"Well, your rendezvous with Marie – you know I still find it bizarre that your lady friend has the same name as I – will need to be postponed," stated Marie. "I need you to meet with Monsieur Lambert, the Dockmaster.

"MAMAN!"

"Don't Maman me. Today is a workday and your lady friend will understand. At least she better or she is not one for this family," Marie responded in finality. "I want you to buy him lunch. Get to know him better to begin to build a relationship and go over this list of what repairs need to be completed at the docks."

"Yes Maman," replied Junior fully understanding that his mother was the boss and there was no sense in putting up an argument that he had no chance of winning. He would tell Marie, his lady friend that is, that he will make it up to her.

"There are two boxes in the foyer to take with you. After, not before but after you take care of business with Mr. Lambert, you will hand him the two boxes."

"What's in them Maman?"

"The latest designer fashion from the House of Pierrot in Paris. Two matching outfits comprising of a printed cotton Pierrot jacket, skirt, and kerchief, plus a bonnet that I understand is the rave of Paris these days 'très à la mode parmi les Républicaines' writes Riberio in this article from La Mode magazine. Here, give him the news article so Dockmaster Lambert realizes the value of the prizes he is receiving for his wife and daughter," stated Marie.

"Marie, you are one subtle woman. I used to grease the likes of Dockmaster Lambert with gold pieces and you do so for half the price with clothes but get double the return. You are a true genius in business," complimented Jean.

"I do not bribe, Jean. I just provide gifts after the fact. I am truly the innocent one and you are the corrupt one, my husband," Marie said with a smile.

Robert steered the carriage with haste to the *caserne*. Upon arrival, Jean helped Marie down from the carriage, and both headed for the stockade where Henry was held prisoner.

"Good morning," said Jean with authority as they entered the office. "I have signed release papers for the prisoner, Henry Christophe."

"Release papers? Under whose authority?" answered the soldier, not yet reaching to grasp the envelope Jean held out to him.

"Commissioner Sonthonax himself" stated Jean, not breaking his gaze from the eyes of the young guard.

After a brief second of consideration, the soldier snatched the envelope from Jean's extended hand. He broke the seal and read the paper out loud:

"You are hereby ordered to release the prisoner, Henry Christophe, to the responsibility of Captain Jean-Baptiste Bayard. He is to be paroled until my return for further evaluation, and or to await trial."

Jean watched the soldier carefully as he finished the note, pleased and grateful at the words that Sonthonax had penned.

"Quite interesting Captain Bayard, but I must seek higher authorization."

Jean was taken aback by the response.

"What higher authorization could there possibly be than the Commissioner?" asked Jean.

"I do not answer to the Commissioners, *monsieur*. I answer to my superior officer. Please wait here" he said, rising to leave the room.

Marie looked up toward Jean with a frown on her face. He put his hand on hers. "It's standard procedure. Let them perform their chain of command and bureaucratic nonsense," Jean reassured her.

The minutes stretched on endlessly. Finally, after what must have been a half hour, the door the soldier had disappeared behind burst open.

"What is the meaning of this, Bayard?" Captain Renaud angrily spit out.

"Captain Renaud, it has been some time," Jean responded in a calm but authoritative manner. "I will forgive your forgetting to address me by my proper title, as Captain. As you may recall, I did honorably serve in the French army prior to my retirement."

Captain Renaud paused briefly before straightening up to meet Jean's eyes.

"With all due respect Captain," Jean went on, "the document should make its direction quite clear. The Commissioner has ordered the release of Henry Christophe, and I am here to receive him."

With fire behind his eyes, Captain Renaud squeezed the decree tightly in his hand.

"*These Gens de Couleur colonists believe they can do whatever they want these days—and the Assembly in Paris and their glorified errand boy Sonthonax are on their side!*" he thought to himself with disgust.

"I know not what tricks you manufactured to obtain this document, but know that it is not the end of this," Renaud seethed. His glare was met with one of equal measure from Jean.

"Christophe refused to confess to his crimes, but I know he is guilty, and he would surely have admitted as such under our more advanced interrogation procedures."

The two continued their stare down for an unknown length of time. Suddenly, Renaud barked, "Lieutenant—fetch the prisoner, Henry Christophe!"

Fifteen minutes of tense silence ensued until the door finally opened once more and Henry walked through the doorway, a uniformed guard on either side. Marie gasped as she saw him. His hands and feet were shackled together and he wore the same clothes he'd been arrested in. He appeared several pounds lighter and his face was unshaven and hair disheveled, but otherwise appeared unharmed.

"Take him and get out of my sight," hissed Captain Renaud. "You, all of you, have not experienced the end of this. Of that, I can assure you."

"Is that a threat, Captain Renaud?" asked Jean, breaking from the embrace he and Marie had smothered Henry in.

"No Bayard, it is a promise."

"Your memory is as limited as your respect for the Army of France. You will address me as Captain Bayard, and extend the same respect as has been bestowed upon me by your country. I will not remind you again—that is MY promise, Captain." Jean's voice had dropped to a low, menacing tone, and somehow sucked all other noise from the room.

Renaud was taken aback. How dare this half-breed *Gens de Couleur* speak to him in such a tone? However, he had no recourse, even though his conduct was ruled by a government he no longer personally recognized. His blood boiling, he turned for the door and spat out over his shoulder, "Good day… Captain

Geôle
NE PAS TOUCHER
AUX PRISONNIERS

Bayard."

Marie was standing next to Henry watching the confrontation. Though she was petrified by Jean's behavior, she'd never felt such admiration and pride in her husband. Marie had never heard a *Gens de Couleur* speak to a *Blanc* like that, much less one who was powerful, armed, and dangerous.

"For a moment I thought you would be exchanging places with Henry and my husband would once again be gone from me," Marie whispered to Jean as they turned to depart the office.

"And what would you have done, my love?"

"Gotten my rifle from home, come back, and shot that bastard Renaud!"

"I do not doubt you would have, Marie. Never underestimate an armed woman," smiled Jean. "Let us take our leave from this wretched place."

"Yes, my love. Come, Henry, let's get you fed and cleaned up."

Marie took Henry's huge left hand in both of hers. She looked up briefly at Henry, now towering more than a foot over her, and caught the sight of a small tear running down his left cheek before he quickly wiped it away.

Marie spent the next week coddling Henry with healthy food, drinks, grooming and caresses until he could no longer take it. Henry had wished to immediately resume his duties at the hotel but, still his superior in the company, Marie had ordered otherwise.

"When you reenter the front doors, you will not be pitied and lamented, but held in awe!" She insisted.

"You survived your ordeal and your appearance will appear no worse for wear. You are the mighty 'Henry Christophe!' You will return at your full weight and your skin will be cleansed and soft as you greet the staff."

Henry looked to Jean expecting support but found none.

"As always, she is right, Henry," reasoned Jean. "A week of preparation will result in years of earned respect. Your workers fear the French soldiers—but when they discover they could not penetrate the armor of your character and determination, they will hold you in even higher esteem."

Nine full days after his release, on the evening of Sunday, February 24th, Marie organized a celebration at the *Hôtel de la Couronne* in Henry's honor. She invited the entire staff, vendors, notable aristocrats, all of Henry and their friends, and anyone else she could find. The gathering was over one hundred strong and included lavish food, premium drinks, and a delightful five-piece musical ensemble.

His arrival was met with great fanfare. Marie was simultaneously proud and annoyed with the fact that the new tailored suit she had commissioned for Henry attracted numerous women of all colors to his side, jostling for attention. She watched him closely, reveling in his laughter, smile, jokes, conversations, and toasts being raised in his honor. Jean found his way to her side at one point.

"When they throw me in the dungeon, I can only hope you nurse me back to health as well as you did Henry, my dear."

Marie turned to playfully scold him, and he was once again captured by her beauty as he caught her eye. Her scent consumed him and his gaze ventured to the skin that was hinting slightly out of her fashionable Victorian gown.

"Your protocol would be slightly different, Jean," she said softly, biting her lower lip in seductive suggestion.

"Oh? How so?" asked Jean, leading her on.

"For one, baths would be administered by me… personally. I would wash every bit of your dirty body with my own lathered and delicate hands from head to toe," she stopped, closing her eyes for added effect.

"And then?" whispered Jean in her ear.

"I would then inspect your wounds on our bed, and rub you

down with one of Madame Karine's healing oils. Perhaps the one you like to use on my body before our lovemaking," she teased. She opened her eyes and looked to her side, making sure no one was within earshot.

"That does sound therapeutic, my love. What would be the next step?"

Jean brought his body close to hers, enveloping her with his essence.

"Well, I would of course have to make sure all the best parts of you were in proper working order."

Marie could feel his arousal through her gown as she simultaneously felt a familiar warm sensation rush up from her abdomen. She looked down at the unsubtle bulge in the front of his trousers and gave a disapproving, though playful look.

"And how would you propose doing that?" Jean said softly, goading her even more.

"You would lie face up on the bed. I would slip off my nightgown, and lower myself to my knees, naked. I would rub oil on my body, spending extra time on my breasts and nipples before taking my hands down to my vagina; making sure to slip a little inside to be prepared for your ultimate test."

"How would you know it was working?" Jean asked, practically panting.

"I would know, because your penis would be hard and erect…just as it is now. I would then take the oil and—"

"Jean! Marie! What a wonderful idea this party was for Henry—such a great gathering!"

The shouting of their business partner, Gabriel Coidavid, discourteously snapped both of them back to reality. Gabriel was approaching their direction with his wife Christiane.

Marie bit her lip once more and whispered to Jean, "I'll give you a sample of my treatment later."

Without skipping a beat, she quickly turned toward the Coidavids and engaged them in small talk. Jean followed Marie's lead, careful at first to position his body behind hers.

The night was both marvelous and therapeutic for Henry, who was grateful to return to work as Général Manager of the *Hôtel de la Couronne* the following morning. By that afternoon, the entire town was abuzz with the story of the young Henry Christophe's ordeal and how he'd emerged from it unfazed. Gossip spread, speculating as to what hidden power or connections he wielded, and the lore of the young Black man who had conquered the soldiers of the French garrison without ever launching a blow, grew quickly.

Three

TOUSSAINT TAKES COMMAND

Hinche
February 1793

Toussaint and his family had ridden for days towards Hinche after their near life-changing arrest in Cap-Français. If it wasn't for Henry Christophe, the General Manager of Hôtel de la Couronne, Toussaint and maybe the entire family would now be in prison.

Upon arrival, he learned that Jean-Jacquess Dessalines, whom he had left in charge during his absence, had procured a comfortable home with enough room to house Suzanne, the boys, and two of the workers that had traveled with them. They would all work together to care for the small plot of land the house offered, growing fruits and vegetables, while Toussaint attended to more pressing matters.

The home itself was located about 20 kilometers northeast of Hinche. This provided comfort and safety far from the theater of military action. Still, Toussaint assigned a contingent of six hand-picked soldiers to guard his family twenty-four hours a day.

The night before he departed for the rebel army base found

him and Suzanne gazing at the stars and romancing long after their boys, Placide now eleven, Isaac seven, Saint-Jean just two, and their nephew Moyse, considered and treated like a son as well who had just turned twenty, had gone to sleep. She knew not whether his upcoming mission would be a successful one, but trusted Toussaint knew well what he was doing. After all, he was the smartest and most savvy man she'd ever met.

"Toussaint, I fear our life will never return to normal," Suzanne whispered as they lay beside each other.

"You are quite intuitive, Suzanne. I do not yet know where this path will lead, but I assure you that I feel it to be the right one. I feel God himself is leading me—it is hard to explain," answered Toussaint.

"I know, my love. And I know that wherever this course takes us, you will do the right thing," she answered, her voice trailing off.

"Please be safe and return to me" she pleaded suddenly, burying her face in his chest.

"Returning to you is the sole mission of my life, Suzanne. That I promise you" Toussaint replied, gripping her tightly.

They spent the remainder of the night together talking of their love and adoration for one another and their family. The next morning, Suzanne kissed him goodbye, and just like that, he was gone. Suzanne, with her boys, was set to begin their new lives in a foreign country without him by their side. She loved him dearly and prayed to God every night to keep him safe.

Upon returning to the encampment, Toussaint was surprised to find an additional 2,000 ex-slaves had joined the burgeoning rebel force and were being trained by Dessalines and his men for the imminent march on Saint-Domingue.

Toussaint's 4,000 troops now nearly equaled the 5,000 combined between Papillon and Biassou's regiments. Many of their original 8,000 had either died in battle or deserted due to bad conditions and poor morale, while Toussaint's numbers swelled—a testament to his superior leadership and organizational skills.

Papillon approached Toussaint shortly after his arrival to request that 1,000 soldiers be transferred to his and Biassou's campaign but was promptly rebuffed by Toussaint.

"These freemen made a free decision to join my army, not yours. Who am I to force them into labor for an army they did not volunteer to join? No, they will stay under my command to not violate their free will!"

Both Papillon and Biassou were angered by this response, but there was little that could be done. Toussaint had built his force brilliantly; his troops were better trained, exhibited higher morale, enjoyed superior leadership, and they dared not test his resolve. The three would have to maintain an amicable relationship if they were to be successful.

Only days after Toussaint's return, Governor de Amora, true to his word, welcomed the black auxiliaries to the Spanish Colonial Army and supplied Spanish uniforms for all officers and enlisted men. de Amora quickly called for a meeting with the Générals at his plush government office building.

Wasting no time, he prompted Général Papillon to reveal his strategy for the conquest of Saint-Domingue.

Papillon hesitated. He was unprepared to provide a sober and comprehensive military attack strategy. He stood momentarily dumbfounded until Toussaint stepped past him to the map, pointed to the city of Gonaïves, and declared; "We must take possession of the Western coast."

"We would lose a great many men in attempting that, Toussaint" de Amora responded, slightly surprised by Toussaint's audacity in bypassing his superior officer. Nonetheless, he was intrigued.

"I will move my forces west, thereby cutting the colony in half—separating the north from the south. We will conquer the towns of Saint Raphael, Marmalade, Pierrot, Dondon, Plaisance, and Ennery."

Toussaint's finger traced a zig-zag pattern as he named each landmark.

"We will then rapidly march upon the port of Gonaïves and take it as well."

He stepped back away from the map and brought his eyes to the Governor.

"This will allow your Navy to resupply our line. We will then control the territory which links the north and south of Saint-Domingue by both land and sea."

"You are quite daring, *señor Toussaint*. It appears you've thought this through—anything else to this strategy?"

"As we conquer each town, we do not kill any hostages or townspeople—unless necessary."

De Amora chuckled. "Enemies must be eliminated, Toussaint."

"They are not our enemies if they join us. We can establish the legitimacy of our government far quicker with the help of the townspeople. We must make them our allies."

The Governor stared at Toussaint, rubbing his chin.

"The colony is in upheaval and its citizens are looking for stability—whether it be under the French *Blancs*, *Blacks*, or *Gens de Couleur*. Why not the Spanish?" concluded Toussaint.

de Amora said nothing, but stood and walked to the map. Papillon and Biassou stared angrily at Toussaint who ignored them. After contemplating the map for an unusually long period, prolonging the awkward silence amongst the group, de Amora turned to face them with a broad smile.

"*Brillante!*" he exclaimed. "*simplemente brillante!* I didn't expect such intellect from a…" De Amora halted mid-sentence as his careless thoughts nearly revealed his inherent prejudice.

"…intellect from a Black?" finished Toussaint. The men stared at each other until the Governor broke his gaze. Papillon and Biassou stood speechless.

"I was going to say 'from a Frenchman" de Amora coyly

offered.

"But of course, you are one no longer," he continued. "You are a soldier in the Spanish Auxiliaries where such intelligence is expected—demanded even. P*erdóname*—forgive me."

The Governor then adjusted his stance to address all three of his charges before him.

"Toussaint, your army will be the tip of the spear for this campaign. Général Papillon; you and Général Biassou will follow behind to secure and occupy each of the towns until the Spanish forces can take control. Do not kill the townspeople. That is an order!" de Amora added.

Toussaint seized his opportunity to further engender himself.

"Once we secure that essential axis line, we can launch our attacks on both the north and south and secure the entire colony for his majesty, the King of Spain!"

"Let us drink to our future successes on the battlefield, gentlemen. All this talk of war and strategy has left me parched."

de Amora poured each a glass of dark liquid from an old bottle.

"I reserve my finest *Amontillado* for special occasions such as this. I secured this fine bottle during my last visit to the Montilla region on my last trip home to Spain."

The four men toasted their campaign. While Biassou preferred it to have been a drink from his ration of rum, Papillon privately steamed over Toussaint's actions but betrayed no obvious hostility.

A few days later, Toussaint's army marched out of Hinche with regal formality; Toussaint and Dessalines led on horseback. Townsfolk gathered and cheered the procession.

4,000 soldiers, dressed brilliantly in their freshly starched Spanish uniforms, marched west with the early morning sun trailing them. Months ago, most had labored as slaves in the sugar cane fields of the *Plaine du Nord*. Now, they were returning to entrench their newfound freedom with pride and ambition.

Officers on horseback barked orders to the troops whose steps thundered upon the ground from their new boots, compliments of the Spanish King Charles IV.

Among the officers was Captain Charles Bélair who had once fought with the famed *Chasseurs-Volontaires de Saint-Domingue* in the American Revolution nearly 15 years prior. He was here now to prosecute his craft and direct the art of warfare across this new battlefield.

The sights and sounds of war were well known and missed, and he was anxious to once again find himself in its theater—this time for a country he could call his own.

He surveyed the soldiers of his regiment as they marched and his chest expanded with pride. 500 he had personally trained for this day. Amongst them were children from as young as twelve to men and women in their fifties. Each had volunteered to give their life for this battle – *their* battle – of life, death, or worse: re-enslavement.

There amidst the crunching of boots over gravel and dust was little Sanité, his youngest soldier having turned twelve only days ago. A young girl so fierce even the older men and women recognized her strength and burning desire for victory. He knew she would fight to her death; destined to be remembered by history—of that, he was sure.

Toussaint's officers and soldiers saluted Governor de Amora in his viewing box on the second-floor veranda of the government office building as they marched. François Papillon stood next to his partner, Georges Biassou. Both had been relegated to the sidelines as the pageantry of the parade passed them by. Papillon felt as though he were watching his reign over their forces depart as well. He nudged Biassou and motioned to Toussaint.

"Look at him, Biassou," he sneered. "I met him as a docile farmer less than two years ago. That butcher Bullet would have strung him up from the nearest tree was it not for me! Now, he has intentions on supreme command—*my* command."

"François; should we not follow those who can lead best?" Biassou responded, chiding his colleague lightly. "I once met a man who was also a farmer turned soldier—Jean-Baptiste Bayard. I followed him and he led me well, even though I was the one with prior military experience. Some men are destined to lead and others are meant to follow. You and I have our role to play; that is why the Gods chose Boukman to inspire the uprising rather than you or me."

He turned away from Papillon to admire the procession once more.

"Look at him and be grateful, for he is a true leader of men," proclaimed Biassou as he motioned with his hand towards Toussaint.

Toussaint waved to the crowd as he cantered his magnificent silver stallion, *Belle Argent*. The beautiful beast whinnied and reared up on its hind legs, driven to showmanship by the roar of the crowd. Toussaint reveled in this newfound feeling of power. He knew it was *his* destiny to not only be a part of whatever the future held but to lead and shape it in *his* vision.

The battle for the colony was finally in front of them. He vowed not to keep their enemies waiting any longer.

Three days into the march, the army found itself encamped several miles southeast of Saint Raphael. Toussaint called a Captain's meeting with Dessalines, Bélair, Grobard, Desbardes, Laguerre, and Sanon. However, their discussion of strategies was interrupted by a commotion outside the tent. Men were shouting and plates were crashing onto the ground. Toussaint looked to the soldier posted at the tent's entrance and nodded for him to investigate the situation while continuing to listen intently to Dessalines's attack plan.

"What is the meaning of this?!" shouted Toussaint to the two soldiers.

"This man claims to know you sir, and demanded to see you at once. We informed him that you were not entertaining visitors, but he pushed past us into the tent" replied the one to Moyse's left. "He states you are his uncle?"

"*Tonton Toussaint*, please do not be vexed. I wanted to join you back in Hinche, but *Matante*—Aunt Suzanne—said you forbid it. I followed the army until I could get an audience with you," cried Moyse. "I belong here!"

The boy had been surviving in the elements for several days and was hungry and dehydrated.

"Take him to the mess tent and have him fed; then down to the stream to wash the stench off and bring him back to me," ordered Toussaint to his men, not addressing or even looking at Moyse.

With that, the meeting resumed and Dessalines wrapped up his proposal. The others made suggestions and offered alternatives, but Toussaint remained silent.

"Dessalines," said Toussaint, standing to address the fray as their discussion died down. "You and Grobard will attack the French at Saint Raphael from the south with a brigade of 1,000 men. Bélair, you and Desbardes will take Marmelade from the south two days later with an equal number. Laguerre and Sanon will take their brigade to reinforce Dessalines if necessary. Then with confirmation that Saint Raphael has been secured, ride to Marmelade to assist Bélair."

He turned to the soldier standing pat to his right. "Send a rider immediately to Biassou with orders to march on Saint Raphael; and for Papillion to set his course to Marmalade."

"I will march the remaining army to Grand Rivière and make camp. I understand that Général Laveaux is engaged with the remnants of the rebellion there and they are lacking proper leadership. We will assist in their fight and the surviving soldiers of that army will join our ranks. I wish to see what this young and of what I hear talented, Etienne Laveaux, has to offer in the theatre of war."

The officers remained silent, nodding along to his instructions.

"Meet me after your campaigns and we will regroup. Any questions?"

"*Non mon Commandant*" came the answer in unison.

"Good. Prepare your regiments to march at first light. Dismissed."

An hour after the meeting concluded, the outside guard reappeared. Opening the panel to the tent he said, "*Mon Commandant*, your nephew is here."

"He can wait," replied Toussaint.

Within earshot of the command, Moyse's shoulders slumped in disappointment. He had come all this way to join the cause and his uncle, but Toussaint offered no acknowledgment, respect, or even an audience. He watched as soldiers entered and left the tent throughout the afternoon, though his invitation never came.

Finally, with the sun low in the sky and darkness creeping across the camp, Toussaint called for his nephew. Moyse entered the room to find Toussaint composing a document behind his desk. His uncle did not look up from his task as Moyse spoke.

"*Tonton Toussaint*, I want to join you and the army. I wish to be a soldier in this great campaign," Moyse began.

"I have not addressed you, Moyse. I suggest you stay quiet and govern yourself accordingly," Toussaint calmly said, continuing his work.

Just then, Dessalines entered the tent.

"Yes, Captain?" asked Toussaint, looking up.

"The men are ready as ordered. But I believe we must adjust the plan," Dessalines said.

"No, the plan is complete," Toussaint replied. "No changes will take place."

"But *mon commandant*—"

Dessalines! That is final!" Toussaint stated again, his voice rising. "Now, this boy wants to join this great army. He has decided to do so of his own free will. He will accompany you tomorrow. His life is now in your hands. You will observe him and decide whether he is honorable and brave enough to join. You are both dismissed."

With a wave of his hand, Toussaint returned to his writing.

Moyse trailed behind Dessalines as they left the tent. He glanced back briefly at his uncle. This was not the same man who had left his family. He did not recognize the person he had seemingly just met.

Moyse had no way of knowing Toussaint's inner transformation. He was now focused on a solitary purpose: conquering his enemy and avoiding the demise of himself and his soldiers. Moyse had never seen him this way before. No one had.

Both Dessalines and Bélair were successful in capturing Saint Raphael and Marmalade. Papillion and Biassou arrived as planned to relieve the conquering forces and take over the occupation of the towns. Dessalines and Bélair then marched to rejoin Toussaint.

Toussaint's scouts had at this time pinpointed where Laveaux was battling the ragtag group of ex-slaves. However, before they could assist, a platoon of Toussaint's men captured nine French army officers patrolling alone south of Grand Rivière. They were quickly escorted to a makeshift jail under a large mahogany tree.

Upon hearing of their capture, Toussaint rushed to question them personally.

"Who is the ranking officer among you?" he asked. "I request the highest-ranking officer to speak for your group."

"We three are Captains, Commandant" stated one in the middle of the scrum, gesturing to the two men behind him. "I am *Capitaine* Alain Bouquin of the National Guard of France, and senior in command."

Captain Bouquin raised his arm in salute, followed by the other eight. Toussaint respectfully returned their salutes.

"I trust you have been treated well by my officers?" Toussaint offered.

"We surrendered honorably with no resistance and were treated with respect, Commandant" stated the young Captain.

"So, *Capitaine* Bouquin, what were officers of the National Guard of France doing patrolling so far from a battle their army is currently engaged in?" Toussaint asked pointedly.

"We are no longer part of the French army," answered Bouquin.

"Have you been retired?"

"Not formally, but we were forced to flee lest we be arrested. Général Desparbes himself was arrested as were most of the officer corps. They were put on ships bound for France. Ruined careers all," Bouquin went on.

"Why?"

"Général Desparbes lost favor with Commissioner Sonthonax, who supported those Jacobin *Petits Blancs* of Cap-Français. After our Général was deported, the *Blancs* turned on Sonthonax when he attempted to integrate the Mulattos into the government. There are no pleasing Jacobins!" Bouquin explained, sighing.

"Then you are deserters!" stated Toussaint, his eyes narrowing.

"Some might call us that. Others would call us loyal patriots to our Colonial Government—or, our past Colonial Government. I do not recognize this colony, the colony I so love, any longer" the young Captain stated. "We wish to stay in this land, and not return to France!"

Toussaint looked at his guards. "Keep them confined until I determine their future. Capitaine; I will trust your word that you will not give us any headaches or make any escape attempts?"

"You have my word, Commandant," Bouquin replied. Satisfied, Toussaint departed.

The next morning, Dessalines roared into town with his horsemen and infantry following close behind. Bringing his forces to a halt, he and two of his Lieutenants moved their horses towards Toussaint who had emerged to greet them in front of his tent.

"*Mon Commandant*, I present to you *le drapeau* – the flag of

Saint Raphael!" Dessalines exclaimed, raising the staff high.

"Well done, Captain Dessalines. Relieve your men and meet me in the command tent" Toussaint said, before re-entering.

Dessalines ordered his lieutenants to dismiss the men and report back in the morning. He then dismounted and followed Toussaint into the tent.

Inside, Toussaint was pouring a cup of rum for the Captain and guava juice for himself. Handing the cup to Dessalines, he toasted; "To a job well done, I have heard."

"*Merci, Mon Commandant.*"

"How many casualties?" Toussaint inquired.

We lost 122 men and return with a little over 300 wounded, *Mon Commandant.*"

"And the enemy?"

"We counted 42 killed and more than 100 wounded," answered Dessalines.

Toussaint turned back to his desk.

"Do you consider yourself effective, Captain?" He asked.

"Indeed," replied Dessalines. "The troops fought well and we secured victory."

"Then why did you sustain so many losses?" demanded Toussaint, his casual demeanor flipping in an instant.

"It was a fierce battle, *Mon Commandant,*" answered Dessalines, taken aback.

"Who was the opposition?"

"Mostly French regulars and Dragoons – a force of 200, sir."

"And you find nothing upsetting with your report, Dessalines?"

"I believe we performed gloriously well, *Mon Commandant.* We accomplished your orders," Dessalines countered.

"And suffered three times their losses!"

"Yes, but we had the greater numbers," protested Dessalines.

"While awaiting your arrival, we captured nine colonial officers that abandoned the French army who are currently our prisoners," Toussaint said, dismissing the argument. "What do you propose we do with them?"

"Kill them! I will do so myself and show our men we have nothing to fear from the French," Dessalines immediately replied.

"And how would you go about that?"

"I will bayonet them—or slit their throats. Whichever you would prefer, *Mon Commandant.*"

"Dessalines… Dessalines… Dessalines," Toussaint sighed and shook his head as he lowered his voice to a whisper with each repeat of his Captain's name. "You are my second in command. I consider you my best officer and yet you present no tactical approaches beyond whatever brutality would amuse you personally."

"*Commandant*?"

Toussaint banged his fist on the desk suddenly. "You need to think more strategically, Jean-Jacquess!"

The silence extended on uncomfortably until Toussaint finally broke it once more, his tone softening to a confused Captain Dessalines.

"You have conveyed that our enemy is better trained and more effective than your men. Their kill rate is three to one! I tell you that we have captured nine experienced but disgruntled French officers who willingly abandoned the French army and you propose we destroy them?"

"They are our enemies. What do you expect me to say, *Mon Commandant*?"

"These French officers are out of favor with their army and have nowhere to go. You will befriend them and build a relationship. They will become trainers for our troops in the art of warfare."

Dessalines stood in silence.

"I expect they will be with us for some time." Toussaint finished.

"Tell me you are not serious *Mon Commandant,*" replied Dessalines. "You know how I hate the Whites for what they have done to me!"

Dessalines angrily ripped off his shirt and turned to display the huge welts on his back from multiple whippings during his lifetime.

"Put your shirt back on Jean-Jacquess. You must leave your past so you can lead your future."

Toussaint went on.

"None of the Whites in our custody have laid a hand on you. We are fighting a rebellion and these Frenchmen will become our allies in that quest. Now come with me to meet our new assets."

Toussaint led Dessalines to the stockade to meet Captain Bouquin. Together, they forged an agreement; in exchange for their lives, protection from the French army, and eventual freedom, they would provide one year of expert training to Toussaint's men.

"You will begin at first light tomorrow," Toussaint said, turning to leave the group. "Dessalines, please come with me."

The two walked away a comfortable distance before Toussaint spoke once more.

"Tell me of my nephew Moyse."

"I didn't have him in the fight, *Mon Commandant*—I feared for his life as he is untrained in weaponry. However, I did engage him in logistics. I like the boy. He carries himself well with the others," Dessalines replied.

"I am still upset that he violated my order and left Suzanne. I do not wish to see him yet. However, assign him as one of the first to be trained under the white officers. I want him training under one directly and fast-tracked to officer status."

"*Oui, Mon Commandant.*"

"Do you believe in Jesus Christ, Dessalines?" asked Toussaint, suddenly.

"No! I do not believe in the white man's God!"

"What if I told you Jesus was not white?"

"Then why do the Whites follow him?" asked Dessalines.

"Because true leadership negates skin color. What year is it, Dessalines?"

"1793, *Mon Commandant.*"

"What does that number mean, Dessalines?" inquired Toussaint.

"The year in the white man's calendar *Mon Commandant*."

"It means that according to the white man's calendar, the non-white Jesus Christ was born 1,793 years ago Dessalines."

"That is what that means? I never knew."

"Yes. And why do you suppose that?" Toussaint went on.

"I do not know, *Mon Commandant*."

"Because he was the greatest leader on earth. Time or should I say the calendar, as we know it, started at his birth," answered Toussaint.

"What made him such a great leader?" asked Dessalines.

"You have finally asked a valuable question, Jean-Jacquess. I will provide you with one trait of his that you can use as a leader: create followers that believe in you. Jesus created thousands which soon became millions over time—but his closest followers he named disciples. They carried forward his mission which has now lasted nearly two thousand years after his death."

"I will create twelve of these disciples myself," Toussaint continued, "And you are my first one. You will then do the same Dessalines, as will the other eleven I so chose. Do you understand?"

"I think I do. You want me to create followers within my ranks, in case something was to ever happen to me?" answered Dessalines.

"Correct. We are an army in training and are doing so on the run and amid battlefields. We must move forward with urgency as we do have not a day to spare. Any questions?" asked Toussaint.

"*Non, Mon Commandant*, I fully understand."

"When I have finished identifying my twelve disciples, and all of you your twelve, we will have created our honor guard – nearly 150 of the most trusted and loyal of our army," concluded Toussaint.

"Understood, *Mon Commandant*."

The following day, Captain Bélair arrived at the camp, another captured flag– his being from Marmalade—in tow. He too was brought up to speed on the white officers' function, as was the entire officer corps. Each received the same lesson, taught by Toussaint, of Jesus's disciples and its application to their cause. Each officer was left charged with developing twelve disciples of their own.

Late that March, skirmishes began in earnest with the troops of Général Laveaux's skilled army. Toussaint and Dessalines were impressed with their soldiers' improvements in such a short time from the training provided by the captured French officers. They saved many of the ex-slaves fighting Laveaux's superior forces, and to their good fortune, Laveaux was summoned back to Cap-Français, abandoning the fight for more pressing issues.

Toussaint took command of the 800 members of the ragtag forces who had been fighting shirtless and shoeless with dull axes and cutlasses. Their call to arms was broadcast through a conch shell, which made a low-pitched vibration that echoed for some distance.

Their commander was lost in battle and they were motivated to join Toussaint when they witnessed his soldiers' superior abilities. Toussaint assigned them under Dessalines, and they began their training.

With Laveaux and his army engaged in other civil disruptions, Toussaint easily conquered the towns of Ouanaminthe, Terrier Rouge, Dondon, Plaisance, Ennery, and finally—just as he had pledged—the prized port city of Gonaïves.

This was dangerously close to the city of St. Marc, where Sonthonax had set up his southern administrative district after Port Républicain had fallen into the hands of the *Artois* regiment seeking to align itself with Great Britain.

His primary objectives completed, Toussaint left a battalion 1,000-strong in Gonaïves and retraced his path to inspect each of the towns and assure order was being maintained and no townspeople were being mistreated by his troops.

At each stop, he left behind between a half to a full battalion in each town, except for Saint Raphael and Marmalade, which were still being administered by Papillion and Biassou's armies.

That June, content with his control of the north-south axis, Toussaint rode back to Hinche to report the conquests to Governor De Aroma. Having already heard of the victories, de Aroma organized a celebration to welcome Toussaint and his army, complete with a parade and lavish parties.

On a glorious and sunny Thursday afternoon, Toussaint entered the main square victoriously.

Atop his great warhorse *Belle Argent*, Toussaint rode ceremoniously up the main street flanked on his left by Captain Dessalines and Captain Bélair on his right. Captains Grobard, Desbardes Laguerre, Sanon, and his nephew Moyse, void of official title, rode directly behind them with 1,000 organized troops marching behind. The crowd cheered their arrival, chanting:

"Tous-saint!"

"Tous-saint!"

"Tous-saint!"

Toussaint raised his right arm, signaling the army to halt in unison. A loud thud echoed forth as all soldiers slapped their right side and the army came to disciplined attention at once.

Toussaint dismounted. The beautiful silver stallion, still excited by the roar of the crowd, continued to dance to and fro as a stable boy fought to gain control of the animal so Toussaint could continue his path to the awaiting Governor.

Toussaint walked gallantly to the viewing stand as the Governor stood to salute him. Toussaint called in a thunderous voice; "I present to you my Captains, Governor deAroma."

"DESSALINES!"

Dessalines came forward on his horse, raising the staff with the *drapeau* of the conquered city, yelling "Saint Raphael!"

"BÉLAIR!"

Bélair rode forward in like form, yelling, "Marmalade!" and raising his *drapeau*.

The rest of the officers did the same with the flags of their conquered cities;

"GROBARD!"

"Ouanaminthe!" yelled Grobard.

"DESBARDES!"

"Terrier Rouge!"

"LAGUERRE!"

"Dondon!"

"SANON!"

"Plaisance!"

"MOYSE!"

"Ennery!"

"And the final triumph for Spain – GONAÏVES!" shouted Toussaint so even the crowd heard him. He then handed the *drapeau* of Gonaïves to the governor with a ceremonious bow.

"On behalf of the great kingdom of Spain, I accept these conquered cities and proclaim them territorial possessions of Charles IV, King of Spain, and admit them into the Spanish Colony of Hispaniola!" bellowed de Aroma.

"All of Spain salutes you *Commandant* Toussaint Breda," de Aroma stated, as the crowd continued to cheer. "You are a man of your word and a victorious commander. Please come forward."

Toussaint approached the stand where de Aroma stood. The governor handed him a flat box. "Toussaint Breda, I hereby award you the *Cruz de Guerra–The War Cross*. Please accept this award for your victories in battle, from his majesty King Charles."

The cheers continued unabated behind them.

"Effective today, you are no longer *Commandant*. Your rank is elevated to that of Brigadier Général Toussaint Breda!"

The men behind him threw their muskets in the air, expertly

catching them on return. The officers on horseback raised their staffs bearing the flags of the conquered cities in the air, and *Belle Argent* reared up on his hind legs in his salute.

Toussaint looked at the crowd and put both arms up in a victory salute. He felt victory and power like never before.

de Aroma invited Toussaint and his officers to a lavish feast in the courtyard of the Governor's mansion. The party was escorted to a long table set for themselves along with an additional six officers of the Governors' entourage. de Aroma walked to his place at the head of the table.

Before sitting, he lifted his glass to Toussaint, saying, "To the great Général Toussaint Breda and his officers. May your conquests on behalf of Spain be many and bountiful. *Salud*!"

The afternoon continued, filled with toasts, grand food, and camaraderie. The soldiers of the army were invited to an open field where roasted pigs, chicken, goats, and accompanying cooked vegetables, rice, beans, cornmeal, and bread awaited them. Unlimited rations of rum were passed to all.

That evening, Toussaint departed for his long-awaited reunion with Suzanne. There he would enjoy a month-long repost before continuing the battle for the colony's dominance.

Four

HENRY MEETS MARIE-LOUISE

Cap Français
March 1793

Cap Français was a city of contrasting paradigms. Business owners of all colors were joyful with the pace at which wealth was transferred from the rich *Grands Blancs'* pockets into their bank accounts. Every square inch of office, residential, and hotel space was at full capacity. Shortages of goods had even created an inflationary spiral of prices that, in some instances, could be considered price gouging.

The *Gens de Couleur* were getting accustomed to the liberties citizenship provided and looked forward to creating political parties and launching candidates for upcoming elections. Conversations and meetings were being held everywhere, from bars to formal meeting halls, with ideas for the colony's transformation flowing freely.

Slaves and abolitionists hoped that emancipation was on the horizon, and plans for compensation systems, land ownership, work schedules, and logistics were being debated.

Of course, there was still the constant threat of the *Maroons*—those runaway slaves camping on the outskirts of the city—and the brigands, those who wished to profit from the insecurity and instability of the colony. Both made it quite dangerous to venture into the countryside. However, it was the Maroons and their threat of violence that was the true genesis of the city's newfound vibrancy and change. Their intimidating drums and history of merciless vengeance accomplished far more than any prior talk or political meetings ever had.

The rebellion of Oge and Chavannes in 1790 captured everyone's attention, particularly the valiant last stand of Jean-Baptiste Chavannes during his execution. What followed was the slave uprising in 1791 led by Boukman, and the continuation of that fighting from the rebel armies of Papillon and Biassou; who were currently menacing the northern plains. Elsewhere outbreaks of violence between Whites and Mulattoes sparked a race rebellion.

There were also whispers of a newly emerging leader by the name of Toussaint Breda who was roaming the mountains of the North directing and winning skirmishes against the French Colonial Army along a westward march toward the coast.

Still, hope for peace was on the horizon; though rumors of peace talks between Sonthonax and the rebels gave no indications of progress, terms, or movement in any meaningful direction, leaving the colony constantly on edge, anticipating more violence at any moment.

In early March of 1793, Jean, Marie, Henry, and Gabriel Coidavid met in Henry's office to discuss the past year's successes and upcoming plans for the hotel and casino. They had leased seven rooms to Sonthonax and his commission for a long-term lease to satisfy the remainder of the note which had financed the casino, removing a large burden from their shoulders.

Henry had been brilliant throughout the crisis, managing the hotel and restaurants at capacity, a fledging food delivery service for guest houses, regular parties at the casino, and increasing revenue from the gambling operations.

They opened a bottle of champagne to celebrate Henry's achievements and their record profits. Henry was the happiest he'd ever been—and was rapidly accumulating wealth through the generous commission and bonus payments included in his employment package.

Suddenly, Mr. Coidavid bowed his head and began to sob, quietly at first, then uncontrollably. The festive air quickly shifted. Marie went to his side.

"Gabriel! What is it? What has you so distressed?"

"My friends, I am dying."

The group caught their collective breath at such news.

"The hotel is grand and I am very impressed," he continued. "I applaud you Henry, but I am afraid I may not see the day when we again toast our successes with champagne next year."

Marie, Jean, and Henry consoled Coidavid as he informed them of his current medical conditions, prognosis, and how much time his physicians believed he had left to live; no more than six months more, according to their assessments.

"Forgive me for raining over what should be a time of celebration, my friends," said Coidavid, drying his cheeks with his handkerchief. "Henry, you have done magnificently well in your management of our hotel. I consider you the son I never had and am grateful you came to *La Couronne*. Do you mind if this old man sits at his old desk just once more to remember the feeling?"

"I would be honored, Mr. Coidavid," responded Henry.

Gabriel Coidavid walked behind the large mahogany desk and took a seat, looking at his partners. He was pleased with what he saw as his succession after the inevitable. He was relieved that the hotel would be in capable hands upon his demise. With the new revenue streams and Henry's stable management, his wife

Christiane and daughter Marie-Louise would have a comfortable income for as long as the island remained profitable—which he hoped would be forever.

"Henry, please take your chair back and let us continue. Excuse this old man's tearful interruption of today's meeting." Coidavid said, regaining his composure.

"No, Mr. Coidavid. You sit right there and enjoy. After all, I consider it yours and only on loan to me. Let me continue from here." replied Henry from across the desk.

Just as they were preparing to resume business matters, the office door flung open and a pretty young Black girl clutching two handfuls of garments entered the room. She did not notice Jean, Marie, and Henry on the other side of the office's wall and instead marched straight up to Mr. Coidavid, excitedly launching into a dramatic and animated speech about how impressed she was with the locally-designed clothing in the stores in downtown Cap-Français. She began holding up garments, taking a pretty yellow imitation peasant dress—the latest style from a local fashion designer of Saint-Domingue—and placing it in front of her as she sashayed about the office in an exaggerated waltz.

Henry froze at the sight of her as if he'd suddenly realized men were not the only inhabitants of the planet. Her shiny ebony skin glistened and her short-cropped afro was well-groomed and feminine. Her eyes were large and framed her wide, distinguished, and elegant nose. Her lips were plump with a larger lower half that gave her a seductively pouty, albeit innocent, expression. Her breasts were large and pointed with a slim waistline. It was love at first sight.

"Marie-Louise!" shouted Coidavid to his daughter as she continued her catwalk of modeling. "Marie-Louise! I am in a meeting and you were to wait for me in the lobby!"

The 14-year-old Marie-Louise stopped dead in her tracks, utterly embarrassed by her theatrically-staged immaturity. She had deliberately dramatized the girlish act in an attempt to smooth over the lavish purchases she had just completed, courtesy of his

numerous store accounts throughout the town and unknowing of the business meeting taking place.

"Oh, my gosh! Excuse me, Papa!" she embarrassingly proclaimed.

"Please excuse my daughter. She has just arrived from her schooling in France and cannot contain her excitement to be back in Saint-Domingue," intoned Coidavid. "Marie-Louise, this is Jean-Baptiste and Marie Bayard, and this young man is Henry Christophe—practically a Bayard himself—and the General Manager of *La Couronne*."

"It is a pleasure to meet all of you," replied Marie-Louise as she curtsied. "Forgive me for barging in. I am just so happy to be home that excitement seems to have gotten the best of me. Please excuse me. See you later, Papa!" she said before hastily exiting the room.

Henry was convinced he had just met the most magnificent woman walking the earth. It was all he could do to concentrate on the group's final business conversations, and his head was still swimming with images of her skin against the bright yellow fabric as they bid each other adieu and dispersed.

The Coidavid family lived in a two-story home across town from the hotel. Gabriel was madly in love with both his wife and daughter. He and Christiane had been born slaves but were now *Afranchi*, the designation of a freed slave in the French colonial caste system. Marie-Louise however was a free *Gens de Couleur*.

Being that he and Christiane had limited schooling, they both wished their daughter to have the very best education money could buy. She was sent to study in Paris for basic scholastic and art — particularly in music and oil painting.

Marie-Louise had a wonderful personality. She took after her father, inheriting his easygoing disposition. Gabriel Coidavid was certainly successful, but that success hadn't spoiled him or put a chip on his shoulder as he could converse with any class throughout the colony.

Marie-Louise grew up as a small child in a hotel and interacted with a wide variety of the town's children. She played on the palm-shaded streets in the richest sections of the city with the upper class; with the *Petits Blancs* in *Cap Français's* pretty main square at the *Place d'Armes;* and with ragged-clothed Black slave girls in the clay-baked alleyways of the town. As such, the station of one's life and the color of their skin made little difference to her.

Growing up around the hotel provided her with a priceless and well-rounded reality. When home from her studies abroad, she would listen to the stories passed down from the slaves who scrubbed the floors, cleaned the rooms, or had other duties at the hotel. They would recount ancestral tales of West Africa, which they called Guinée, believing there to be an island below the sea where they would eventually return to upon death for eventual perpetual happiness. They told stories of kings, queens, warriors, tribes, wild animals, different customs, and lost dialects from home. She wondered whether her ancestors shared similar stories, but none were ever spoken of by her parents.

Some of the more scandalous stories were told by Avril, a free colored woman who brought gossip of theft, corruption, fraud, and deceit throughout the white-owned plantations of the *Plaine du Nord* where she sold her vegetables and fruits to the head chefs of plantations.

Then there were the unhappy French white women who frequented the hotel's restaurant. They complained of their husbands, and the mistresses they knew they maintained. They felt it ghastly that a white man could love a Creole Gens de Couleur – Mulatto or Negro, and insisted a white woman would never think of taking a colored lover to their bed—knowing full well that some among them did. There were also stories of France, and it seemed these women constantly longed to soothe their loneliness by reminiscing about the times they lived there.

Marie-Louise much enjoyed meeting visitors from France, especially during the years she studied abroad, as some became friends she would visit while in school there. She found Parisians to be less prejudiced than the Whites in the colony, even if only slightly.

Thus, Marie-Louise gained an education unavailable from public schools and historical knowledge not found in her academic textbooks. At only 14, she was a poised and mature young woman with experience far in advance of girls her age. She was beloved by all who encountered her.

Several days after her faux pas in the office, Marie-Louise was sitting on a bench under a palm in the hotel's courtyard when Henry approached her.

"I see you are wearing one of the dresses you showed your father the other day. I must confess that I like it very much," he offered.

"Do you?" she replied, her eyebrows lifting ever so slightly as she studied him.

"May I get you something to drink, Mademoiselle Coidavid?" Henry asked. "Lemonade, tea, coffee, Guava juice?"

"No, thank you, and you can call me Marie-Louise," she replied. "But you can tell me a little about yourself. I am particularly interested in that English accent of yours. Where does it come from?"

The prompt began a long conversation about Henry's past home, bondage, adventures, and appreciation for where his life had brought him. Their hours-long conversation stretched over the coming days as the two spoke as often as possible. During Henry's time off he would expand on his stories—so many for a young man of only twenty-six—and she would impart her academic knowledge to him, plentiful for a girl of fourteen.

Henry soon approached their talks as outright lessons, eager to learn all he'd missed after being thrust into the arenas of war and work so early in his life. He would devour math, science, history, foreign cultures, and other subjects with gusto, much to Marie-Louise's delight. They would spend hours together among their books.

They became close friends, now and then flirting at the idea of a relationship; but Henry was keenly aware of her age and his respect for Mr. Coidavid. He pledged not to entertain any personal romantic interest until Marie-Louise reached the age of sixteen.

That May was Marie-Louise's fifteenth birthday, and the Coidavids came to dine and celebrate at the hotel. Mr. Coidavid invited Henry to dine with them as he genuinely enjoyed his company, and knew he had been kind to his daughter.

The evening began well, but as the hours went by, Mr. Coidavid became visibly tired and withdrawn. He and Christiane asked Henry to escort Marie-Louise home by midnight to allow her to enjoy the hotel a bit longer under his supervision. Henry agreed and the Coidavids quickly left in their carriage.

Marie-Louise looked at Henry as they disappeared.

"So what do you have in store for me, Henry?"

"What is it that you would be pleased to do on your birthday, Marie-Louise?"

"If I were one of your women friends, what is it we would do?" she asked, a flirtatious look spreading across her face.

"We would drink some liqueur and cognac and maybe dance a little," answered Henry honestly.

"Then *that* is what I want to do!"

"I believe the tongues would wag if people saw the owner's daughter dancing with his employee, Marie-Louise," Henry replied, smiling despite himself.

"Then let's go somewhere—anywhere besides here. Please, Henry! That is what I want from you for my birthday. Take me somewhere no one would know us or care," she said, puckering her lower lip in a sensual pout.

"Alright then; one birthday wish coming up."

Henry stood and extended his hand to Marie-Louise. She felt a shiver go through her body she had never felt before. Henry guided her to the front of the hotel, hailed a carriage, and off they went into the night.

They arrived at a small, cozy nightclub named *Les Rochers*. Both the floor and building were made of dark blue stone and the candlelight cast a warm, dim glow and soft ambiance. There were about fifty people in the club, mostly young couples, and a three-piece ensemble led by a female Creole vocalist played soft ballads.

The two were escorted to a table made of old rum barrels and cushioned chairs with carved frames.

"What may I offer you to drink, Marie-Louise?" asked Henry.

"At home, I drink wine with dinner. Since it is after dinner, what would you suggest?" she asked.

"Have you ever tried *Chartreuse*?"

"No. I have not. What is *Chartreuse*, Henry?"

"*Chartreuse* is a French liqueur produced with over one hundred herbs and botanicals. It was first produced by Carthusian Monks back at the turn of this century and is known as one of the few liqueurs that get better with age."

"How does it taste?"

"It has a sweet, spicy, though smooth flavor with an herbal finish. You'll experience mint, sage, gentian, apple, vanilla—and a hint of cinnamon."

"I see I am definitely in the company of a master of gastronomy," Marie-Louise teased lightly. "Yes, I will try it as it sounds delicious!"

Henry ordered *Chartreuse* for her and cognac for himself. They spent a lovely night listening to music, conversing, and laughing amid the ambiance of lovers. Though Henry wished to treat her as an older woman, he refrained. Marie-Louise was still far too young for him, regardless of her maturity.

At precisely 11:30 p.m. Henry hailed a carriage and escorted

Marie-Louise home. They arrived just before midnight and Henry assumed the Coidavids were awake and awaiting the safe return of their daughter. He caught the closing of drapes as her mother and father quickly headed upstairs before she entered so Marie-Louise would not think they were spying on her.

"It was a wonderful birthday Henry," began Marie-Louise. "Thank you for being the one to help me enjoy it."

She reached up to hug him and kiss his cheek, but Henry moved to expose his opposite cheek for the incoming kiss, awkwardly heading in different directions and accidentally bringing their lips to meet. They both immediately pulled away, looked at each other, and regrouped for a proper peck on the cheeks before saying goodnight.

Though unplanned, the brief touch made apparent to them both that they were destined to be a part of each other, age difference be damned. It was as pure and obvious as anything either had ever believed. They simply didn't know how or when— but time would reveal all.

FIVE

THE GALBAUD AFFAIR
& SLAVE EMANCIPATION

Port Républicain
May 1793

The French Commissioners had finally succeeded in wresting
back control of Port Républicain with the aid of the Mulatto militia
stationed in St. Marc.

Both Polvérel and Sonthonax were of equal minds but
overseeing operations in different parts of the country; Polvérel
with his headquarters in Port Républicain, and Sonthonax
headquartered west in St. Marc. They agreed to govern those
sections somewhat autonomously to see which of their strategies
worked best while remaining in constant communication regarding
any major decisions.

On May 5th of 1793, Polvérel issued a proclamation that
demanded enforcement of the French *Code Noir*. The *Code Noir*
was a series of laws, enacted over 100 years' earlier stating slaves
be treated with respect and not abused. Although passed in 1685,

the *Code Noir* was never respected by most colonists—who routinely abused their slaves, often with extreme harshness and violence—which would have been considered criminal under the law.

Polvérel's proclamation added that slaves be given basic provisions and a small plot of land to cultivate food for themselves and their families. To ensure all slaves were aware of the proclamation, Polvérel had it translated into Creole—a mixture of French and a variety of African languages and dialects perfected in the colony for over a century into a broad-based common language spoken by all slaves, their overseers, and most seasoned colonists throughout the colony—and read aloud to slaves at all plantations by representatives of the colonial government..

This enraged the plantation owners immensely, particularly since many already detested the newly minted French First Republic. The Commissioners' attempts to gain more control through such a mandate was quite vexing to them. Many of these property owners were now secretly seeking independence from France and making overtures to ally with the British authorities stationed in Jamaica. In exchange, they believed the British would protect their current abusive status quo.

Two days after Polvérel's proclamation was issued, a new Governor-Général by the name of François-Thomas Galbaud du Fort arrived to the island. Galbaud was a strong military commander with a specific mission provided by the French National Convention: obedience to the Commissioners in all political matters and absolute military authority. Though standing only 5 feet tall, he projected a forceful personality and presence.

He was married to a Creole woman named Marie-Alexis Tobin de Saint-Aubin—a French Creole Blanc born in Saint-Domingue and the two's eighteen-year marriage had born three sons. She possessed an equally strong personality and aristocratic air. Together, they made a formidable force.

Marie-Alexis' family owned a vast plantation in the colony, and they both were avid proponents of the slavery system. As such, he distrusted, and even fostered hatred towards both commissioners. For reasons unknown—perhaps through bribery or deception, Galbaud was appointed to his current post.

Soon after his arrival, Galbaud called a meeting with several wealthy planters from the Northern Plaine, wherein they expressed loyalty to each other and their determination to govern the colony in spite of the Commissioners from France.

On June 10th, Polvérel and Sonthonax both finally arrived in Cap Français to greet the new Governor, and immediately headed to check in at the *Hôtel de la Couronne*.

"Commissioner, welcome back to your home here at the *Hôtel*," greeted Henry Christophe at the door. "I want to once again thank you for interceding on my behalf and ordering my release from prison."

"Henry, I apologize for the mistreatment you received on behalf of France. I will personally deal with those officers who had you incarcerated."

Jean joined Henry and extended his own greeting to both Commissioners.

"I have assembled a small reception in your honor, Commissioners. The guests are all powerful members of the *Gens de Couleur* community," stated Jean. "You will need their support, as you may be discontent by the immediate movements of our new Governor-Général."

"Unfortunately, with what I have read and heard, you are correct Jean-Baptiste," replied Sonthonax.

At the reception, Polvérel and Sonthonax were warmly welcomed by the *Gens de Couleur* and the Commissioners were able to clearly articulate their supportive intentions for the community. The successful and productive reception was the least Jean could do to repay Sonthonax for his kindness toward Henry.

As expected, however, the Commissioners received a cold reception from the plantation-owning *Grands Blancs* and *Petits Blancs* the following day.

In an act of good faith, Sonthonax requested that Henry prepare a lavish dinner in Galbaud's honor and booked the entire banquet hall at the *Hôtel de la Couronne* for that purpose, The goal was threefold; potentially mend fences with the White citizens, welcome the new Governor-Général, and present the idea of a collaborative relationship between the *Blancs* and *Gens de Couleur* moving forward.

The dinner was attended by 200 of *Cap-Français's* high society. Also in attendance were members of the colonial government and republican forces, specifically Général Étienne Laveaux, the Chief Commander, who had arrived with Polvérel and Sonthonax as an enforcement arm of the Commission.

All had heard of Galbaud's shared hostility towards the Commission, and Sonthonax's intelligence sources reported of his intentions towards disobedience. Towards that end, the Commissioners had readied a plan to deal with such insubordination should the need arise.

During the dinner, all parties displayed their best behavior. *Blancs* and *Gens de Couleur* feigned civility and engaged in light conversation, albeit of non-political topics and with neutral tension.

When the servers clanged their glasses in the customary announcement of toasts, a silence fell over the room. Sonthonax raised his glass first.

"On behalf of the distinguished Commissioner Etienne Polvérel and the accomplished Général Etienne Laveaux, I wish to welcome our new Governor-Général to Saint-Domingue; the honorable François-Thomas Galbaud du Fort. May we all wish him Godspeed with his mission here in the colony."

Everyone raised a glass and Galbaud himself rose to speak.

Despite the whispers of where his true sentiments lay, his forthcoming tirade shocked nearly all in attendance. Galbaud immediately began insulting Polvérel and Sonthonax, spouting pro-slavery rhetoric, criticizing the attempts to designate *Gens de Couleur* as property owners equal to *Blancs*, and scolding the Commissioners on their ignorance of the wants and needs of the colonists.

The room exploded. *Blancs* were cheering Galbaud while the *Gens de Couleur* faction viciously cursed him. Polvérel, Sonthonax, and Laveaux glanced at each other briefly before sprinting into action with their pre-conceived plan. The three made their way to Galbaud and Sonthonax raised his voice over the din of the arguments.

"François-Thomas Galbaud du Fort, you are hereby placed under arrest and ordered to board the ship *Normande* for immediate deportation to France. You are officially dismissed from your duties as Governor of Saint-Domingue and exiled from this colony!"

"How dare you, Sonthonax!" cried Galbaud as the *Blancs* scurried to back him.

"Your words are treasonous and incite violence. Any man or woman that speaks the same shall be exiled as well" announced Sonthonax to the crowd. "Général Laveaux will be installed as acting Governor-Général of Saint-Domingue, effective immediately," he announced.

News of the uproarious dinner and subsequent decree spread quickly, and by morning, Sonthonax and Polvérel were requisitioning ships and packing the harbor for a mass exodus of their political enemies. Galbaud's official termination papers were drawn up and handed to the captain of the *Normande,* along with orders to set sail for France no later than the following day.

Galbaud was a cunning strategist, and despite his more recent arrival, had a much better understanding of the simmering tensions and loyalties of certain citizens than either of the Commissioners. Once aboard the ship, he quickly convinced the captain to call a meeting of his officers to discuss the legality of his dismissal as the duly appointed Governor of Saint-Domingue by the French Assembly in Paris.

After much debate between the officer corps, they sided with Galbaud. Preparing for a potential confrontation, the group went about recruiting sailors who were disgruntled with the Mulatto regiment, customs authorities, and bureaucrats.

They quickly raised an army of 2,000 sailors and volunteers, both naval and merchant. Most regular troops of *Cap-Français*'s garrison also aligned with the growing White forces, swelling their ranks to nearly 3,000.

On the 20th of June, a general riot—spurred by the perceived illegality of the Colonial Commission—broke out in the city, with the *Petits Blancs* citizens fighting alongside Galbaud's forces. Though outnumbered, the Mulatto and Blacks fought solidly in support of the Commission. However, the Commission's forces were eventually driven back to the outskirts of the city where Laveaux had established a fortified line to protect it from attacks by the rebel slaves of the countryside.

Sonthonax, Polvérel, and Laveaux were in a precarious position. The day after the riot began, the three gathered within a makeshift command tent, discussing their next strategic move.

"We are badly outnumbered," announced Laveaux. "I had not anticipated the garrison's ranks to side with Galbaud."

Sonthonax spotted Henry, who had taken up with the Commission in the wake of the chaos, and called him over.

"Henry, I want you to set up a meeting with that rebel leader Macaya; you had mentioned his name to me in the past."

"For what?" inquired Henry, believing this to be a dangerous gamble.

"We need the help of his forces. I will offer them freedom in exchange for their military intervention," stated Sonthonax.

"You do not want to do that, Commissioner. These *Bosals* and *Brigands* are angry and dangerous. They are mostly fierce 1st-generation African warriors from Senegambia, Igbo, and Dahomean," warned Henry. "They are able fighters but angry and have turned into killers and seek revenge."

"It is a risk I am willing to take. We have no choice—set the meeting, Henry."

Three hours later, Henry and Sonthonax found themselves flanked by six men holding torches in the outdoor camp of Macaya, the leader of the rebel tribe who had been terrorizing the outskirts of *Cap Français*. Menacing warriors—unruly, drunk and disorderly—were armed with makeshift spears, axes, machetes, and cutlasses. Sonthonax's white skin and Henry's clean and polished appearance seemed to further agitate them.

Their six escorts had a hard time elbowing through the crowd of men pushing at them and wielding fists in serious attempts to hit either Sonthonax or Henry. Occasionally one would land home on the face of one of their temporary protectors. The men pressed on regardless, tightly surrounding their charges and insulating them from the worst of the horde.

After what seemed an eternity, the party finally entered a clearing, where they were led to three men sitting cross-legged on the ground in front of a fire. The man at the center was of equal height to Sonthonax but could not have weighed even half of his body weight. His large biceps seemed out of proportion with the tight and wirily muscles of his physique. Sonthonax and Henry were pushed to sit down.

The man at the center spoke in Creole.

"*Mwen se Macaya. Kisa ou vle.*"

Translating for Sonthonax, Henry explained; "*I am Macaya. What do you want?*"

Macaya was born in the Kingdom of Kongo, located in West-Central Africa. In his teenage years, he was captured by a warring tribe, sold to the Portuguese and brought to the French colony of Saint-Domingue as a slave. When the 1791 slave rebellion began, Macaya escaped and became a lieutenant under an elderly rebel commander named Pierrot. Pierrot's rebel forces established a base near the Bréda plantation in the hills outside of *Cap-Français* by 1793.

"Tell him I come in peace—and that we share a common goal," Sonthonax replied.

"*Mwen vini ak kè poze epi mwen vle sa ou vle,*" Henry translated.

Macaya erupted in laughter, as did the two men next to him. Both Sonthonax and Henry were puzzled as to why. They suddenly stopped as quickly as they began.

"*Ou pa ka ban mwen sa mwen vle Blanc.*"

"He says *'You cannot give me what I want, White Man'*" Henry said.

"*Èske ou ka mete m 'ak pèp mwen an sou yon bato epi mennen nou tounen nan Lafrik?*" Macaya went on.

"He asks, *'Can you put me and my people on a boat and take us back to Africa?'*" Henry said.

"I cannot do that, but I can grant him and his army freedom," Sonthonax said to Henry, while meeting Macaya's eyes.

"*Blanc di li pa ka fè sa men li ka ba ou ak pèp ou a libète,*" Henry translated.

Again, came a hearty laugh.

"*Nou gen libète deja. Se konsa, nou ka koupe gòj ou.*"

Suddenly two of the six men brought huge knives to each of Sonthonax's and Henry's throats.

"He said, *'We already have freedom. So much so that we can slit your throats,'*" said Henry, straining against the dull, blood-stained blade pressed against his Adam's apple.

After a tense moment in which both men considered their lives forfeit, Macaya gestured for the men to lower their weapons.

"*Ankò, Kisa ou vle Blanc?*"

"He asks again, *'What do you want?'*" Henry said, hoping his steady tone belied his racing heart.

With Henry's help, Sonthonax explained that he had been sent to the colony by the French government, and tasked with ensuring the rights of Blacks—including current and former slaves—as well as the uprising of Whites who are opposed to his mission. He finished by asking for aid as their forces are overwhelmed.

Macaya was a shrewd negotiator, offering Sonthonax what amounted to a deal with the devil over several hours of talks; in exchange for driving the White opposition from the city, Macaya's warriors would be permitted to plunder the city, with all of the atrocities it would entail, for a period of 5-days.

"Do not do this," Henry pleaded, leaning in close to Sonthonax. "Once this begins, it will not end."

"This is the only way to save the colony, Henry" concluded a somber and exhausted Sonthonax.

Macaya was untrusting of Whites, but knew they respected the written word. He demanded Sonthonax write the proclamation on paper, which stated:

We declare that the will of the French Republic, and its delegates, is to give freedom to all the Negro warriors who will fight for the Republic under the orders of the Civil Commissars, against Spain or other enemies, whether they are interior or exterior... All declared slaves freed by the Republic shall be equal to all free men and they will have the rights of French citizens.

Macaya accepted the proposition, and immediately mobilized more than 10,000 *maroon* and *bosal* rebels to converge on the city like a swarm of ants. It was a surprising and incredibly violent attack marked by atrocities of heretofore unseen proportions. Men were brutally hacked to death, women were repeatedly gang-raped, children were decapitated and their bodies mutilated.

Years of pent-up rage were suddenly reflected unto their perpetrators and the results were grisly. Henry, mortified, watched the events taking place on the streets below from the balcony of the

HÔTEL DE LA COURONNE

Hôtel de la Couronne. His security team and several of Macaya's men—whom he dispatched without prompting—stood guard at the main doors of the hotel.

Four more of Macaya's men were positioned at each corner of the establishment; barefoot, barrel-chested, clothed only in a loincloth and armed with either a machete or a lance. However, none of the marauding warriors dared overstep their line and the guardsmen's weapons saw no action during the siege.

At *Place d'Armes, Cap Français's* beautiful main square, Macaya stood holding a spear and directing his mob by simply pointing toward one location or another as drummers beat their instruments in front of a raging fire. Some of the other merchant shops, warehouses, and buildings were spared, but Henry knew not why.

Jean, Marie, Junior, their staff, and many friends received warning prior to the attack and had boarded a ship to escape the violence. They remained at sea for several days until the agreed-upon period of anarchy concluded. Galbaud and his army were soundly defeated and forced to retreat, but the aftermath saw over 1,000 soldiers, sailors, and citizens lying dead in the city's streets—and more than half of its beautiful buildings reduced to smoldering rubble.

Macaya's army pillaged every home, business, and warehouse from morning to night. Bands of rebels drank themselves into a frenzy, amusing themselves with anything they desired, even raiding local theaters and donning costumes and make-up in a macabre comedy of their own.

After the 5 days allotted to them, the soldiers retreated to the hills once again, their spoils loaded onto stolen horses, wagons, and backs. Some attempted to drag White, Black, and Mulatto women with them as prizes, but Sonthonax quickly appealed to Macaya. Honoring the agreement, Macaya declared his warriors release the women, who collapsed in gratitude for being saved from even more horrors.

The riot of *Cap-Français* was over.

After Macaya's troops left the city in ruins, the Commissioners—now in a position of strength—sent Polverel's son Richard to negotiate with Galbaud, who had taken refuge aboard the docked ship *Jupiter*. However, Galbaud refused any discussions, and instead held Polvérel's son as prisoner. In response, Galbaud's brother Ernest, living in *Cap-Français*, was taken by men loyal to the Commissioners and offered in exchange for Polvérel's son.

Though Sonthonax approved the prisoner exchange, Polvérel refused it.

"No, my son cannot be exchanged for this or any culprit," he stated, with tears in his eyes.

Galbaud fled, setting a course for Baltimore with Polvérel's son onboard. During the voyage, Rear Admiral Joseph de Cambis regained authority over the crew of the ship and arrested Galbaud. However, soon after reaching the United States Galbaud spurred another revolt, forcing Cambis to flee the ship and seek safety at the French consulate in Baltimore.

Over the next several weeks, Sonthonax allowed a fleet of 120 ships, carrying 10,000 refugees who had aligned with Galbaud, to leave the colony. It was the largest mass exodus in history, with passengers escaping to the United States, France, and other colonies.

During the uprising, Galbaud's troops depleted the arsenal of weapons and munitions, utterly destroying most of *Cap Français's* defenses and leaving the city and its citizens vulnerable to a Spanish or British attack.

In a letter dated July 10, 1793, the Commissioners wrote to the National Convention describing what had happened, including how Galbaud had left the Northern Province defenseless. Galbaud and his fellow agitators were accused of allying themselves "…*during the federalist period, with all of the aristocratic and royalist planters and merchants, in our principal commercial city.*"

In response to Sonthonax's radical proclamation of freedom to male slaves who agreed to fight rather than general emancipation for all slaves, Toussaint again entered the fray, hoping to lure any remaining rebels to the Spanish side by promising protection under the King of Spain.

Sonthonax's 10,000 citizen-rebels were an asset as well as a problem. Most of these men had wives and children who remained slaves and began demanding their freedom—claiming to the Commissioners that their family's freedom was a part of the original bargain. With no leverage at his disposal, Sonthonax acquiesced, freeing the families of the rebels to prevent further violence. It also proved a deft move in countering Toussaint's attempts to lure the new soldiers to the Spanish forces.

Still, the Commissioner understood how fragile his position was. There was no hope of reinforcements or supplies from France, as the European war with Spain and Great Britain still raged. The colony was isolated and it was forced to fend for itself by whatever means imaginable.

Toussaint, Papillon, and Biassou had a well-armed, well-trained army in Santo Domingo and they were on the march. The rest of the island's slaves—500,000 of them—seemed his only hope of lasting stability and protection from invasion. While the colony's slaves were not armed or trained, their sheer numbers might provide some defense.

Would they fight to defend France? Certainly, not. Would they fight to achieve their freedom though? It was another gamble Sonthonax felt was necessary.

On August 29, 1793, Commissioner Léger-Félicité Sonthonax unilaterally decreed the emancipation of all slaves in Saint-Domingue. It was by far the most radical step yet of the colonial government and perhaps the entire French Revolution and he could only wait and see how the newly-freed citizens would respond.

Toussaint and the other rebel leaders knew that Sonthonax had exceeded the authority granted him by the French National Assembly. The decree, he argued, would be soon annulled by the government in France. This message was put into a proclamation and widely broadcast in an attempt to sew distrust and win loyalty for their own means.

Simultaneously, Toussaint changed his name from Toussaint Breda to Toussaint Louverture and issued his own, brief, proclamation:

Brothers and Friends,

I am Toussaint Louverture; perhaps my name has made itself known to you. I have undertaken vengeance. I want Liberty and Equality to reign in Saint-Domingue. I am working to make that happen. Unite yourselves with us, brothers, and fight with us for the same cause.

Toussaint Louverture.
Général of the armies of the King, for the public good
August 1793

After the uprising in *Cap-Français*, many French army officers had deserted across the border to the Spanish side. Spanish military leadership permitted Toussaint to recruit from the deserters, who he immediately began tapping, to train his widely-dispersed army. Over the next several months, Toussaint's army transformed itself into a lethal fighting force, combining rebel African tribal war tactics with synchronized French army protocols. The startling results were both lethal and effective.

Thus, the battle of political wit and military engagement between the French Colonial Forces under Général Laveaux and the Black Spanish Auxiliaries under Toussaint Louverture were set in place to launch many long and violent confrontations.

Six

THE WEDDING OF
HENRY AND MARIE-LOUISE

Cap Français
September 1793

Through a combination of purposeful protection and sheer luck, *Hôtel de La Couronne* sustained no damage during the siege and plunders of Cap-Français by the rebel army of Macaya—yet the luxurious hotel now stood surrounded by a city in ruins. Jean and Henry had worked hard to prepare and arm their staff as well as assemble a small security force to guard the property and other Bayard family assets amid the skirmishes.

Macaya also ordered his men to steer clear of the building as a show of gratitude toward Henry for arranging the fateful meeting with the Commissioner as well as many other Gens de Couleur establishments. He and his men now enjoyed freedom as well as a small fortune from their pillaging of the city.

Henry and Marie-Louise maintained a somewhat strained though cordial relationship since her birthday. Each was aware of their feelings for the other, but the wall of age was an obstacle to anything further. Still, they occasionally caught themselves lovingly looking at the other, felt the fleeting jolt of electricity arising from a mistaken touch, or lustily dreamed of one another when alone at night.

One evening shortly after the conclusion of the horrific fighting, the Bayards and Coidavids dined together for the first time without the sounds of gunfire and cannon. The food of course excellent, and the conversation was kept light.

The dinner was a pleasurable gathering until Gabriel Coidavid suddenly grabbed his chest and a painful grimace crossed his face. Henry and Jean hurried to his side to catch him as he fell from his chair. Christiane rushed to her husband's side with Marie-Louise in tow.

"Send for the doctor!" Henry shouted to one of the servers. The other guests in the dining room paused from their meals, looking over with concern and trepidation. The Coidavids were one of the city's most prominent and philanthropic families, well known to and loved by all.

Henry called for the servers to assist him and Jean as they carried Mr. Coidavid to the General Manager's office couch to ensure his comfort and privacy. Mr. Coidavid soon regained his composure and was provided some water. He looked exhausted and spoke slowly, but was in much better condition than he'd been only moments earlier. Marie-Louise held cold compresses to his head.

Mr. Coidavid then lifted a hand to summon Henry to his side.

"I am an old man, Henry—an old man without much time left," he began with a soft and steady voice. "I have seen the way you look at my daughter."

Both Marie-Louise and Henry looked at each other with shock, confusion, and embarrassment on their faces.

"Children, do not deny it. You are in love with each other, yes?" he went on, looking at them both.

"Papa, this is not the time or the place to be discussing such things," inserted Marie-Louise, unable to meet her father's gaze.

"This is exactly the time and the place, Marie-Louise. It is urgent that we discuss such matters," Coidavid replied, his hoarse voice fading. He cleared his throat and looked directly at Henry.

"Henry, do you love my daughter, yes or no?"

"I do, sir" replied Henry without hesitation—knowing he was venturing into unknown territory.

Marie-Louise covered her mouth with both hands as Coidavid looked at her.

"Do you love this man, Marie-Louise?"

"I do, Papa," Marie-Louise said as she looked at Henry, relieved to finally proclaim her feelings out loud. "Yes, I do love him—and have since the day I met him."

"Your mother and I have spoken about this subject. My days are numbered, and this could be my last opportunity to speak seriously with you both," said Coidavid before looking to his wife who smiled and nodded.

"Non, Papa. You are not leaving us—" protested Marie-Louise, her voice catching. Her tone then changed to one of authority. "I forbid it! Do you hear me, Papa? I forbid you to even have these thoughts of leaving us!"

Mr. Coidavid could not help but smile. He looked at Christiane.

"There she is, Christiane. There is our daughter. She is poised, confident, and forthright! Stubborn as a mule—and quite commanding when she wishes to be," he said, almost as if he'd forgotten others were in the room with them.

"Papa!" cried Marie-Louse, a smile breaking out between her tear-stained cheeks.

"Listen to me, Marie-Louise; and you as well, Henry."

He beckoned them both closer as his voice was soft and coarse. Henry knelt next to the couch and Coidavid placed a hand on his shoulder.

"If you so desire, Christiane and I grant you permission to wed our daughter. Though she is far younger than you, she is years beyond her age. We have seen the way you look at each other and recognize it as true love—for it reminds us of our own," Coidavid said, as Henry and Marie-Louise stole a glance.

"We are pleased for you both" he added.

"So there. I have said my piece on the matter with time to spare. God can take me now, Christiane. In the meantime, you can take me home please."

"The doctor is here now, Gabriel," Christiane responded as Doctor Bosico entered the room. "Please let him examine you!"

After fifteen minutes of examination, Coidavid was pronounced fit to leave.

"No more drinking, Gabriel, and no unnecessary excitement. We have been over this many times before—please curtail your activities!" lectured Dr. Bosico, a longtime friend and physician of Coidavid. "Especially your champagne, red meat, and wine— you are on borrowed time, my friend."

"If you wish me to live that way, inject me with poison now and get it over with, Bosico! I'd rather die living than live as though I am dead already."

This drew a light bit of laughter from those assembled, but Coidavid remained stoic.

"Christiane, take me home. I have had enough excitement for one evening and I have made enough of a spectacle of myself," he concluded.

"Yes, Gabriel. Let me tuck you into bed for the night" joked Christiane. It would have been comical if it weren't ever so tragic. Everyone knew Coidavid would depart for good soon but bravely feigned ignorance.

"Henry, Marie-Louise; stay behind. You will make plans for the wedding before I am unable to attend. You young people move so slowly these days. Be more urgent! You only have one life to live!" Coidavid ordered as he walked out with his wife on one side and Jean on the other to assist him.

"Gabriel! *Enough!* Pierre, please summon my coach. I need to get this loudmouth home before he works himself into another medical incident," Christiane retorted.

The Maître d' immediately left to do as instructed.

Henry and Marie-Louise were overjoyed with their gift of freedom and truth. They were ready to be in love with each other for the rest of their lives. Hastily, and with much excitement, the two made plans for an October wedding—only four weeks hence.

The wedding was a lavish affair at the Cathedral and the reception was held in the Casino's ballroom and attended by over 500 guests on Saturday, October 19, 1793. Jean-Baptiste Bayard was Henry's best man, and Marie-Louise's maid of honor was her best friend Lilian.

Mr. Coidavid thought his heart might burst with joy as he watched the proceedings. Here he was; born a slave, had purchased his freedom and that of his wife, and today marrying off a daughter educated in France's best schools at a hotel under his ownership with family and friends in attendance.

His heart lasted not only through the night of the wedding but for another nine months allowing him to witness the birth of his first grandchild, François Ferdinand Christophe, in July of 1794. At the pinnacle of his life, Gabriel Coidavid who had beat the odds in so many ways, passed away peacefully six months later as a happy grandfather.

The Catholic Cathédrale de Notre-Dame de l'Assomption is located in downtown Cap-Français and is the same church where Henry and Marie-Louise exchanged their vows to each other nearly two years ago in marriage. The ornate building dates from 1670 and is a hallmark of the city.

In the Place d'Armes, the square of this famous cathedral, the liberation of the first slaves in the country of France was officially

proclaimed on the 29th of August in 1793. It is here that the once-enslaved Gabriel Coidavid, who would have never been allowed inside the cathedral while a slave, was now celebrated by the highest-ranking member of the Saint-Domingue clergy during his funeral mass.

It was a warm day in March and it appeared that the entire population of Cap-Français had arrived to be in attendance and participate in the service performed by Bishop Max Leroy Mésidor. The church overflowed with people onto the main square.

"There is sacredness in tears," announced the Bishop as his voice began to rise. "They are not the mark of weakness, but of power. They speak more eloquently than ten thousand tongues. They are the messengers of overwhelming grief, of deep contrition, and of unspeakable love," he bellowed. "We celebrate and now mourn the loss of our brother, the great Gabriel Coidavid, who has now departed to meet his creator in the garden of heaven."

Towards the rear of the church, the Mamboo Priestess of Vodou, Cecile Fatiman, bowed her head and brought her veil closer to her face to go unnoticed by the audience. There was still an official arrest warrant on her head for murder charges stemming from the now famous voodoo ceremony at Bois Caïman that had sparked the brutal slave revolt in 1791. Tears flowed easily from her green eyes as she whispered a voodoo prayer of her own to celebrate the life of this man, her father, Gabriel Coidavid.

She looked towards the front of the church where his now widowed wife Christiane and daughter Marie-Louise accompanied by Henry Christophe and their child, all dressed in black, ceremoniously chanted Catholic prayers and participated in their customary rituals in front of the casket that encased her father.

Yes, Marie-Louise was her half-sister and the daughter of their shared father, Gabriel Coidavid. She knew very much of the man by reputation, but very little by way of his affection. She was the outside child, cast away long ago and deprived of his love. It was her mother's doing who refused to allow her to have a relationship with the man as she stole her away in the middle of the night long ago.

Her mother was a scorned woman that went into hiding high and deep into the mountains with Cecile. She taught her the craft of voodou, passed down from ancient ancestors from the Kingdom of Dahomey. She also taught Cecile the Dohemey language of Fon, and potions, herbs and healing techniques handed down from one generation to the other. Her mother was a light-skinned mulatto, lighter than her, with the same beautiful green eyes as she that made them unique amongst others.

After her mother's death, Cecile descended to the city nearly five years ago. Then twenty, she was seven years older than Marie-Louise but it was far too late to now begin a relationship with her father, she thought. She quickly left to begin the ancient practice of her mother's legacy in the hills surrounding Cap-Français. It was better that this family not know of her existence.

After the funeral, and after celebrations and visits had been completed and all citizens had gone home in grief, Henry took Marie-Louise and her mother back to their home, not wanting to leave Christiane, who under protest, agreed to spend several days with them. They felt that the presence of her grandchild François would be a calming distraction to assist with the loss of her husband.

When Henry and Marie-Louise were finally alone and the house was quietly settled in bed, they toasted the life of her father with a Cognac for him and *Chartreuse,* that French liqueur that Henry had introduced her to, for Marie-Louise.

Later that evening as the city retired for the night and all was calm and quiet, they could hear drums far in the hills pounding their rhythms long after they dozed off. The drums were not invasive but brought them an air of calm and serenity after the long rituals of the day.

Little did they know that it was Cecile who, far in the hills, performed a send-off of her own for her long-lost father. Within that ceremony, Cecile found the affection she so desperately longed for somewhere between life and after-life as her father and she embraced deeply and emotionally, sharing their love amidst the fire, the drums, the rum, the dance, the chants, and whales of her followers, and the intoxicating trance she had succumbed to.

When she awoke in the morning, after the fires had died and the drums were made silent, an unbreakable smile remained on her face. She had finally united with her father. She had found inner peace as gentle tears suddenly exited each of her beautiful green eyes and then wandered to her lips so she could taste the salty fluid of her body's creation.

Cecile then burst into an uncontrolled sob, like a demon deep inside was suddenly set free, that she had waited years to do. She was her father's daughter after all. He had told her so last night as she continued to sob uncontrollably.

Seven

THE BRITISH INVASION & FRENCH EMANCIPATION

Jérémie
September 1793

Sonthonax's prediction that the British would plan to invade the richest colony in the world soon proved prescient. Their numbers slowly built over the years, and the British navy now controlled most access to the Caribbean, making the French colony of Saint-Domingue a natural target.

One morning in early September, Jean-Baptiste's brother René was conversing with Gustav Jasmine in his family's hardware store in downtown Jérémie. A young man suddenly interrupted them, pushing his way to a tall post, and nailing a piece of parchment to it.

PUBLIC MEETING
OF THE CONFEDERATION OF THE GRANDE ANSE
Your presence is requested for an important meeting
Tuesday, September 3, 1793, at 6:00 PM
Jérémie Town Square

"What is this about?" René asked Gustav.

"I don't know," Gustav replied. "But this *Blanc* Confederation has been up to no good ever since the *Gens de Couleur* like us finally received rights as citizens."

"Will you attend?"

"Absolutely. This is the first non-secret meeting they have held. I want to see what they are up to," Gustav said. "I would suggest you come as well—and get as many *Gens de Couleur* there as possible."

On Tuesday, René arrived at the meeting with his younger brother Julian in tow. Outside the square they met Gustav and several friends; mostly merchants and planters. They were clearly in the minority, as nearly every *Blanc* family from miles around was represented; the group even learned that local hotels were filled to capacity with attendees from as far as Port Républicain to the east and Jacmel and Les Cayes to the south.

Even the local Jewish community turned out in droves, though no one quite knew which side they favored.

"Oh, Jesus" proclaimed Julian. "Look who is chairing the meeting; It's Charles Garnier, a real hothead for independence, indeed."

"My brother Jean-Baptiste used to tell me horrid stories about the mistreatment of their slaves," René said as he glanced around at the square, counting more than 200 people, mostly *Blancs* of the planter class. "There must be something going on that we don't know about. Why such a big turnout?"

René felt out of place and his instincts were beginning to make him nervous.

Garnier approached the podium and cleared his throat. "I call this meeting of the Confederation of Grande Anse to order," he shouted over the dying conversations. "We have one order of business on the agenda this evening—but I would first like to introduce our distinguished guest of honor."

A murmur spread through the crowd.

"Please welcome his excellency, Sir Adam Williamson, Governor of the colony of Jamaica!"

All the *Blancs* roared with cheers as if they'd been expecting the Governor. René, Julian, Gustav, and the rest of the *Gens de Couleur* were caught off guard—looking at each other in bewilderment. The British Governor stood, bowed gracefully to the crowd, and strode to the podium.

"Citizens of Saint-Domingue," the Governor began, in perfect French. "It is with great honor and respect that I stand here before you on this fine evening. You have invested your lives and pledged your treasures, your properties, and loyalties to the crown of France. Yet in return, you have been dealt a severe injustice which cannot be held to stand!"

Several whoops erupted from the gathered crowd.

"Your beloved King Louis XVI has been murdered; your benevolent monarchy has been destroyed, while an illegitimate government has inserted itself and stolen your country. Unfair laws are flagrantly enacted which infringe upon your rights, your properties have been seized, and life as you know it, destroyed."

René began to feel eyes on him and his brother. He straightened up slightly, feigning courage for Julian's sake.

"We in Great Britain feel your pain," Williamson continued. "I am here as an official representative of His Majesty, King George, to extend his warm salutations and an invitation of assistance to ameliorate your plight.

"With me is a signed proclamation from our King, sovereign ruler of England and all its colonies, territories, and possessions, to protect all peoples of Saint-Domingue, including their properties, re-establish all just laws nullified by the rogue French Assembly, dissolution of all laws prejudicing you and causing strife, recognition and enforcement of the institution of commercial and agricultural slavery, and return of all former slaves in the colony to their rightful, legal owners as they are your property."

The crowd erupted in cheer. Shouts of slurs could be heard over the din.

"I invite the elected head of the Confederation of the Grand Anse to call a vote to this proposition and if passed, to affix his signature next to his majesty's to officiate ratification of the agreement."

With that said, the Governor turned and took his seat as the *Blancs* continued to celebrate.

"I wish to voice my opposition to this invitation for England to occupy our land!"

René barely recognized his own voice. Something deep within him had burst forth and he found himself fighting through the crowd toward the stage.

"You are not recognized as a member of the Confederation, sir," responded Garnier. "You may take your seat or leave the area."

"You have no authority to negotiate with the British government!" Another *Gens de Couleur* yelled from behind René.

"Throw them out!" yelled a *Blanc*, a refrain that quickly built into chants that echoed through the town square.

"Throw them out!"

"Throw them out!"

"THROW THEM OUT!"

René, possessed by patriotic passion, continued to approach Garnier and the podium but was violently halted by members of the Confederation.

"Clear the square of all non-members of the Confederation of Grand Anse!" shouted Garnier.

The *Blancs* suddenly converged on any man deemed a *Gens de Couleur*. Fists began flying and men started wrestling on the ground, but ultimately the outnumbered *Gens de Couleur;* both Black and Mulatto were overpowered and removed from the town square. Beaten and bloodied, René, Julian, Gustav, and the others could do nothing but watch and listen as Garnier called for a vote on the British offer.

It was immediately accepted without opposition or discussion and the document to transfer allegiance to the British Crown was signed.

The truth was the British had been preparing their conquest of Saint-Domingue long before the town square meeting. The whole facade was simply a formality under the veil of appearing official. Their strategy could finally move forward.

On September 19, 1793, the British landed in Jérémie with a force of 1,000 soldiers. More troops under Irish Major O'Farrel of the Dillon regiment also landed and took the Northern peninsula all the way East to *Port-de-Paix,* where Général Laveaux and a small force of fewer than 700 troops found themselves defending a tiny garrison. Laveaux was now threatened by the British to his West and the Spanish from the East.

Another British force landed just west of *Port Républicain* in *Léogâne* and marched across to the *Artibonite* valley; welcomed along the way by the *Blancs*. Within a month, the British controlled portions of the north, west, and southern peninsula. Polverel and Sonthonax, now in *Port Républicain*, were surrounded.

The *Blanc* property owners celebrated each strategic victory, fully anticipating Saint-Domingue to become a British colony and slavery reinstated. *Gens de Couleur* would be marginalized and stripped of citizenship, and the Crown's economic policies would favor the colonists more than France's *Exclusif* system of trade.

Jean, Marie and their families were shocked and outraged by how quickly the *Blanc* planters abandoned the new French Republic and turned the colony over to the British. They rallied their fellow *Gens de Couleur,* leading to explosive meetings at the town's assembly that were continuous and downright dangerous. Soon after, such gatherings were outlawed by the puppet British government: the *Confederation of Grande Anse.*

The British continued to consolidate their presence and

extinguished pockets of resistance where found. Anyone deemed unsupportive of their cause was outlawed from venturing into any towns, participating in public gatherings, and restricted to their residences. Blacks who had been freed were ordered to return to their former owners and take up plantation work. Many fled the region, but others went back to work for their survival. Another 7,500 were recruited by the British military to form a local militia.

The Bayards were quarantined at their plantation, only venturing out for food and supplies—a government-imposed house arrest.

Elsewhere, in the northern region of the colony, a black officer by the name of Jean-Baptiste Belley was running to become *député congressman* to the French National Convention. He had distinguished himself by supporting Sonthonax and the Commission at the battle for *Cap-Français* against Galbaud. At the time, he was Captain of the infantry and fought valiantly despite being wounded six times. Sonthonax himself campaigned for his election, which proved successful.

Belley, who at the age of two was sold to slavers sailing for the French colony of Saint-Domingue, had endured a lifetime of hard labor until he finally bought his freedom after years of saving his wages earned from extra work and tips from his masters. Now, here he was—the first black *Député* in French history.

There were three *Deputés* to the French National Convention in the northern region. Jean-Baptiste Mills, a Mulatto, and Louis-Pierre Dufaÿ, a European White, were seated at the Convention the following year.

On February 4, 1794, Belley gave an eloquent address, moving the French revolutionary government to proclaim the abolition of slavery in all of France and its colonies, thus ratifying the emancipation decree that Sonthonax had issued a year prior.

Polverel and Sonthonax established a new work code for the

ex-slaves, with a new title of 'Cultivator'. Among other things, it required owners to provide Cultivators with a plot of land and an additional free day to work the land so they could grow their food and sell their surplus crops on the open market. In exchange, Cultivators were to provide their labor to the plantations at government-set low minimum wages.

Despite this progressive mandate, the ex-slaves of Saint-Domingue, now known as Cultivators, were still largely unaffected by the changes. France's version of emancipation, in which little changed on the plantations themselves, was unacceptable to the Cultivators and incompatible with their values.

They believed that freedom was the ability to own a piece of land, grow their food and live a peaceful life with their family, free of work requirements on the plantations. This system of forced labor, whether they wanted to work or not, was not their idea of freedom. Further, should they return to work, it would be under the employment of their previous slave masters!

As a result, widespread resistance continued, with many slaves appropriating abandoned land from vacant plantations for themselves, to accomplish their goals. Tensions and outbreaks of violence continued throughout the colony unabated.

The fight towards freedom was far from finished.

Eight

LA VOLTE-FACE
OF TOUSSAINT LOUVERTURE

Ouanaminthe
April 1794

In the north, Toussaint's Spanish forces were finding great success. His regiment was solely responsible for more than half of all Spanish gains north of the *Artibonite* Valley and had captured the port town of *Gonaïves*.

After learning of the official emancipation of slavery by the French Convention in Paris, Toussaint initiated a discreet diplomatic channel with French Général Ettiene Laveaux. Despite their gains on the battlefield, tensions had emerged between Toussaint and the Spanish higher-ups. His original superior, Governor Matías de Armona, with whom he enjoyed a good relationship, was replaced with Juan de Lleonart—who was unapologetically racist and vocal in his pro-slavery politics.

In addition to these obvious differences in beliefs, Toussaint's near-autonomous control of a large and strategically important region in the *Cahos* Mountains was making his Spanish superiors anxious; they also suspected his loyalty was waning. Meanwhile, his military successes continued to foster jealousy among his peers; Papillon and Biassou. Toussaint could tell that his power and support might soon disappear completely.

In April of 1794, the Spanish garrison at *Gonaïves* was suddenly attacked by a Black contingent of troops demanding surrender in the name of *"The King of the French."* Approximately 150 men were killed, and much of the city's population fled. Spanish guardsmen in the surrounding area had also been murdered, and Spanish patrols sent into the area never returned.

Lleonart sparked suspicions that Toussaint and his troops were behind the attack, even though the latter was not present at the garrison and there was no evidence to tie him to the violence. Toussaint had lost trust in Lleonart as well, so when the two met at Commander Lleonart's camp in late April, Toussaint arrived with 150 mounted and armed men, his honor guard, as opposed to his usual 25. Lleonart was quick to note Toussaint's lack of usual modesty or deference.

"I am not happy with the King of Spain and the Spanish Government in Santo Domingo, " Toussaint stated sharply as soon as Lleonart was within earshot. "I am allowing the Spanish government one week to match France's total abolition of slavery per the French government's proclamation in February."

"Has your mind left you, Toussaint?" Lleonart angrily shouted. "I should have you arrested right here on the spot for insubordination and sedition!"

Armed Spanish soldiers began to surround Toussaint's horse. The troops that had accompanied him immediately drew their swords in response. Each side anxiously awaited orders from their respective commanders.

"One week, Lleonart. One week is all you Spanish get to do the right thing," Toussaint said. Bel Argent, his mount, lifted his huge body onto his hind legs before turning and speeding off—his

150 horsemen kicking up a storm cloud of dust as they closely followed.

Toussaint knew his ultimatum would prove an impossible bureaucratic feat. The local administration would not have the authority to make such a decession and communication with Spain would take far longer than one week. But he was convinced the Spanish government had never been inclined to abolish slavery in the first place. They had no intention of advancing his cause; only to use the Black army to do the fighting and dying for them in their quest to conquer the French colony for their financial gains.

Indeed, he'd had enough of the Spanish.

Toussaint sent a messenger to advise Générals Papillon and Biassou that he wished to meet with them on the last Sunday of April. That afternoon, Toussaint arrived accompanied by his 150 horsemen. All were well received by Papillon and Biassou. The three interacted like brothers who had not seen each other in years—the two Général's jealous notions quickly faded. They spent an hour talking families, and other pleasantries, and drinking rum. The aroma of a roasting goat over charcoal and the promise of a delicious afternoon supper further lifted Toussaint's spirits.

In the wake of a delightful meal, Toussaint finally broached the subject he'd come to address.

"Gentlemen, what are your future intentions with the Spanish in Santo Domingo?"

"I gave my word a year ago that I would fight alongside the Spanish Colonial Army and swore an oath of loyalty to the Spanish King in my name and that of my soldiers," Papillon replied. "That has not changed."

"Our allegiance was always to Louis XVI, King of France— before this cursed republic chopped off his head," replied Toussaint.

"My men are aware the Spanish are but a means to seek

freedom and avenge our French King," replied Papillon. "Our Spanish King Charles, after all, is our sovereign's cousin," he added.

Biassou then joined in.

"Toussaint, we have made important progress in *Hispaniola* against the French. We have conquered *Gonaïves*, *Gros-Morne*, *Plaisance*, *Acul*, *Limbé*, *Borgne*, *Petit-Saint-Louis*, and *Terre-Neuve*. The French hate us and the Spanish respect us as their Black auxiliaries."

"Have you and Papillon buried the hatchet regarding your differences?" Toussaint asked, pivoting the conversation suddenly. "I heard your two armies had an armed confrontation last September. The French took advantage and re-conquered the Tannerie Fort."

"Yes, we were fools—vying for the attention of our Spanish superiors," offered Biassou in his typical mindful fashion. "I think we are beyond that now, right Francois?"

"For the twentieth time Georges, yes we are beyond that silly dispute," answered Papillon before turning back to Toussaint. "It took Governor de Armona persuading us to meet in *Dondon* to come to an agreement—which we did before the year ended," he said.

"And, we went on to achieve many victories in the service of Spain," interjected Biassou proudly. "Especially the conquest of Port Margot which earned us several gold and silver medals from the Spanish Crown!"

Biassou smiled at Papillon while showing off his medals to Toussaint.

"You two have become an old married couple!" roared Toussaint as the three chuckled amongst themselves. He allowed the snickering to gradually die down before again changing the subject swiftly.

"Men, I want you to leave the Spanish and rejoin the French with me."

Papillon and Biassou sat in stunned silence. Toussaint

continued.

"I have been in touch with Général Laveaux and he is willing to grant pardons and welcome our armies back under the French flag. Britain is on the attack and it is time to kick those bastards off of our island."

"Toussaint, we swore an oath to the Spanish," Biassou said. "We are part of their army now."

"You will never be a part of their forces as you are not White," Toussaint shot back. "Only Whites can be members of the Spanish Colonial Army and as we can see, you are far from White!"

"But we are free citizens and they respect us," insisted Papillon.

"They only respect your ability to die for them," stated Toussaint. "Slavery is still legal in Spain and her colonies, and I strongly suspect that will remain the case. However, it has now been eliminated in France and her colonies."

The two Générals again remained silent and contemplative.

"I have given the Spanish an ultimatum: abolish slavery, at least in Santo Domingo, or we will become enemies," Toussaint went on.

"I am a man of my word, Toussaint," Biassou said, after a long moment. "I remain with the Spanish. You, Francois?

"I stay with the Spanish as well" answered Papillon.

Toussaint sighed and raised his glass in a toast. "Then gentlemen, let us enjoy one final evening as friends; as by this time next week, we may find ourselves across from each other on the battlefield."

Papillon and Biassou raised their glasses as well. The three sat in solitude as they finished their drinks, and Toussaint walked out of the tent.

A few days after that fateful meeting, Lleonart arrived at Biassou's encampment flanked by a dozen horsemen. After retreating within the tent, Lleonart began, "You and I have done good business together, Biassou."

"Yet I remain not in favor of this arrangement, Lleonart, as I have told you numerous times before," Biassou spat back in response.

"Why not Général? You are unsatisfied with some of your soldiers—and instead of ending their life by the firing squad or worse, you sell them to me, and their lives are spared," responded Lleonart.

"Turning these men into slaves is not saving their lives," Biassou retorted. "To some, it is a fate far worse than death. I would rather kill traitors than re-enslave them."

"You are paid handsomely Général, and you purge your ranks of the disloyal," said Lleonart, unfazed. "Think of their families; they would never survive without their men. As slaves they have a roof over their heads and food to consume, no? My conscience is as clear as yours should be, Biassou. But you seem to consider yourself equivalent to a Judas Iscariot for selling them. Why?"

Biassou seemed to only get more irate and provided no answer to this veiled insult as he stared down Lleonart who continued "Now, how many do you have for shipment today?"

"32. 14 men, 10 women, and 8 children under the age of 15," replied Biassou through gritted teeth. "They are near the ravine under guard. All are in good health, no disease."

"Good," Lleonart said as he counted out and put gold coins in a sack and tossed it to Biassou. "There are an extra 10 coins in there, Général."

Biassou paused and looked up at Lleonart, afraid of what might come next.

"I need Toussaint to go away. Kill him before he gets to Camp *Barade*."

"That is not a job for me, Lleonart. Toussaint was once my friend—and I still consider him one."

"Then make his death painless. That is what friends do for one another," counseled Lleonart. "Either way, he does not reach

Limbe."

With that, Lleonart mounted his horse and departed to fetch the newly minted slaves.

Toussaint, accompanied by a small regiment arrived at the temporary home that Suzanne and his sons Placide, Isaac, and Saint-Jean—now 12, 8, and 3—were living in on the outskirts of *Hinche*. Moyse rode in first, jumping off his horse and running to Suzanne whom he hadn't seen since stealing away in the middle of the night to join his uncle and the rebel army.

"I'm so sorry *Tante Suzanne*. I had to do it—I had to join! Please forgive me, I knew you wouldn't let me leave," Moyse said, standing before her with his eyes cast down.

Suzanne looked at him with a stern face for a long time, before suddenly pulling him close for a profound hug of affection. Toussaint could see tears running down her cheeks even from his mount several yards away.

Unfortunately, the happy reunion was short-lived. After briefing Suzanne on his defection back to the French and the danger they were now in, the family's belongings were loaded into wagons and they departed before daylight the following morning. Toussaint's honor guard was present to escort them back to the French side of the island.

Several miles outside Camp *Barade* in the *Limbe* province, the caravan fell under attack by a lightly armed group of bandits. Though quickly defeated, three men were lost, including his beloved brother Jean-Pierre. Toussaint had no doubt the thieves had been tipped off by the Spanish.

They arrived at their plantation at *Sancey* still mourning the loss of Jean-Pierre. Toussaint tasked 100 soldiers with keeping Suzanne and the children safe. Despite their circumstances, Suzanne was delighted to be home and find their overseer Orthello had performed an excellent job maintaining the production of crops. He'd even kept Suzanne's prized gardens in splendid and bountiful condition. Her home was as good a place as any to greet what would come.

As expected, the Spanish government rebuffed Toussaint's demands for emancipation, and a week later, on May 6, 1794, Toussaint and his followers officially deserted the Spanish army.

Toussaint still controlled a heavily armed and well-disciplined Black army, the best of the Spanish Colonial Army Auxiliaries, with more than 4,000 troops and an Honor Guard of lethal warriors waiting on his commands.

He launched a blitzkrieg campaign through the mountains, retaking each of the towns and cities he had previously conquered for Spain. He raised the French flag over *Gros Morne, Ennery, Plaisance, Marmelade, Dondon, Acul, Limbe*, and the port city of *Gonaïves*. Spain's influence in the French colony was virtually snuffed out in one rapid swoop.

Toussaint always led from the front, which heartened the foot soldiers and the cavalry. He took to wearing a mauve *mouchwa tèt,* a head scarf that he tightly bound over his hair when preparing for and in battle, before exchanging it for a yellow version when not engaged. His troops always knew when a fight was on the horizon, and that their fearless leader would be by their side.

Just after the conquest of *Marmelade* Toussaint received word from a scout that the British were marching toward the city. Unbeknownst to him prior, the Spanish and British had forged a pact to collaborate in their shared conquest of the colony—and later split up the spoils.

Toussaint was very angry that the Spanish had, behind his back, reached such an accord while he was still previously fighting for them. However, he felt somewhat vindicated that he had made the right decision to turn his back on the Spanish. Well, he thought, *I did to them what they did to me.*

However, he now found himself in a predicament for which he hadn't planned. He'd split up his army in order to attack simultaneously across several fronts. Dessalines, Moyse, Belair, Maurepas, and their associated brigades were spread among different towns leaving him with only 80 cavalry and 220 infantry under his command.

He waited anxiously for the British to arrive in order to assess their full strength.

The next day, the British army appeared on the horizon. Toussaint ordered the Spanish flags to remain flown so as not to tip off the incoming force. Toussaint looked through his spyglass and counted column after column of British redcoats. By his estimation, around 1,200 troops were descending upon them.

Toussaint ordered the cannons to the edge of the city and aimed at the approaching army. The infantry and cavalry stood at the ready.

The British continued to advance, yet the command for the attack did not come. The soldiers looked at each other apprehensively but trusted Toussaint with their lives. The British continued forward, close enough to hear the thunder of boots on the ground.

Toussaint removed his yellow *mouchwa tèt* and carefully folded it into his right vest pocket. He then tied the mauve *mouchwa tèt* tightly around his head and donned his tricorn hat. The soldiers, diligently watching his every move, turned and passed the word that the Général was ready for battle.

His mount, Bel Argent, snorted in anticipation. The horse understood Toussaint's habits and precision; the way he tightly gripped the reins with his left hand, the slight squeeze he exerted in his legs, and the sound of the sword hilt lifting from its sheath. The animal knew what would come next.

Toussaint looked to both sides. He was centered in the cavalry with 40 of his best horsemen to each flank. He knew they would either prevail or die without surrender. He looked out over his infantry. They were battle-tested, trained, and eager to eliminate the wall of red marching toward them on the ground of their homeland.

Toussaint looked up. Huge buzzards circled above. He believed the huge black birds, called Griffon on the island, were one of God's finest creatures created; cleansers of the earth. They too were eager for war—prepared to pick the battlefield clean for days afterward. Within weeks, grass and brush would overtake the bones and before long there would be no clues left of the death and mayhem that was about to commence.

Toussaint heard a British officer call to halt. He must have perceived something was not as it should have been. Certainly, he was not expecting to find cannons and cavalry in battle positions.

The British Captain had seen the Spanish flag in his spyglass, accompanied by what he thought to be the legendary Black auxiliaries of the Spanish colonial army. Perhaps the soldiers assembled were a welcoming gesture of their newfound alliance? His years of experience in the field however had the hair on the back of his neck standing up and his senses on alert. Of what was his gut attempting to warn him?

Watching through his own spyglass, Toussaint saw another officer ride up to the British Captain and exchange words. The second officer took the spyglass from the captain and set its sight directly on Toussaint.

They were near enough. No more waiting. Toussaint pulled out his sword, pointed it to the sky, and bellowed, *"LOUVRI DIFE! LOUVRI DIFE!* OPEN FIRE! OPEN FIRE!"

Six cannons discharged their bellies simultaneously toward the British line.

"CHAJE! CHAJE! CHARGE! CHARGE!" He yelled out to his honor guard

. Horses lunged forward past the front line, charging the British Grenadiers a hundred yards away. The infantry began a mad dash at full speed, ferociously screaming, surprising, and confusing the British.

"Vive la France!"

"Ready the front battle line!" commanded the British officer as the troops lined themselves up for a full frontal attack. "Load your weapons and ready for fire!" shouted the second officer. The first line crouched and began the process of loading while the rear line loaded standing upright as Toussaint's cavalry closed the distance to 25 yards.

Bel Argent was running as swiftly as he ever had, his mane hare flapping wildly in the wind.

"*CHAJ! CHAJ! CHAJ!*" Yelled Toussaint as he steered Bel Argent straight at the two officers, one of which was pointing his pistol straight at him.

The first officer sent out a shot that whizzed by as Toussaint brought his head down low behind Bel Argent's neck. The second had no time to squeeze the trigger of his pistol before Toussaint's sword hit his neck with such force as to send his head three feet into the air before landing a dozen yards away.

Bel Argent felt the pull of his reins and dug his hind legs into the earth, skidding to a stop. Toussaint then gave the second command, and Bel Argent kicked his front legs high and turned around to launch toward the second officer who had by now unsheathed his sword. However, the huge horse was too fast and Toussaint slashed a red line down the officer's torso, throwing him from his mount. He was dead before hitting the ground.

The British line could not get off a single shot before being mowed down by the cavalry. Though Toussaint's forces were outnumbered three to one, the surprise attack and their superior tactics quickly gave them the upper hand. Just as they had practiced countless times, the cavalry would ram the front line and continue their gallop before halting after 20 yards, turning, and charging the line from the rear.

The British, having immediately lost their two top officers were in a state of absolute confusion. A lower-ranking sergeant attempted to regroup the troops and form a defensive box, but they were quickly enveloped by the infantry. Meanwhile, Toussaint and his cavalry continued slashing them up and down the line from behind. The battle was over in less than an hour. 500 redcoats lay dead in the field while the remainder of the detachment retreated from whence they came.

A horseman from Toussaint's honor guard came to him and asked, *"Mon Jeneral, èske nou ta dwe kouri dèyè yo?* - My Général, should we chase them?" *"Non, kite yo ale* – No, let them go," responded Toussaint.

"Reinforce the city instead. They may return for a proper attack if more British are waiting in the forest beyond. Get me a casualty report and make sure all are tended to."

"Mon Jeneral, ou blese wap senyen! – My Général, you've been wounded. You're bleeding!" shouted the cavalry officer.

Toussaint looked down at his bleeding leg which had entirely soaked his trouser in red.

"Sound the signal. Get back to camp," ordered Toussaint as three nearby soldiers brought conch shells to their lips and trumpeted the order for reassembly.

A female horseman by the name of Marie-Jeanne Lamartiniére arrived and convinced Toussaint to follow her to the field infirmary. Upon arrival, he was helped onto a cot while Marie-Jeanne elevated his leg and cut away his trouser to reveal the extent of the wound.

"Yo tire w Mon Jeneral — You've been shot, My Général."
She immediately began to address the wound.

Nine

TOUSSAINT MEETS LAVEAUX

Marmelade
May 1794

Fresh from victory but nursing his wound, Toussaint's mind raced as he impatiently sat in the medical tent. Though he was physically weakened, he knew his army had secured a position of strength. His adrenaline spiking, he believed the time had come to contact Général Laveaux.

He called in one of the French lieutenants serving as a trainer and informed him that he intended to dictate a letter. The officer quickly left, returning with a quill, ink, and parchment paper.

While watching Marie-Jeanne as she worked efficiently but gently on his leg, he began to speak. Those in the room were shocked by his steady voice even amid the obvious painful treatment.

"Marmelade, 18 May 1794
From Toussaint L'Ouverture, Général of the Western Army,
To Etienne Laveaux, interim Governor Général

It is true, Général, that I have been led into error by the enemies of the Republic and humanity, but what man can flatter himself to have avoided all the traps of evil men? In truth, I fell into their nets, not without knowing what I was doing; you will remember that my goal was only that we unite to combat the enemies of France and to bring an end to an internal war among the French of this colony."

Just then, Toussaint winced once again in pain and clenched his jaw as Marie-Jeanne probed ever deeper, obviously hitting a tender portion of his wounded leg. She stopped until Toussaint took a deep breath, gave her a nod to continue, and began speaking again.

"Unfortunately for all concerned, the paths toward reconciliation that I suggested were rejected. My heart bled and I shed tears over the unfortunate fate of my country, foreseeing the misfortunes that would follow, and in this, I was not mistaken. Fatal experience has shown the truth of my predictions..."

Toussaint hoped Laveaux would recall the rejected overture he'd made years ago, and realize that this was now a different time.

"You need to remain still *Mon Jeneral*," said Marie-Jeanne, probing his muscle with her pincers. "You have a musket ball deeper in your leg which must be extracted."

Toussaint was undeterred and continued to dictate his message. The officer dipped his quill pen back into the ink bottle and the scratches on the parchment became a background soundtrack in the otherwise silent room.

"At the time, the Spanish offered me their protection and freedom for all those who fought for the cause of kings. Having always fought to achieve this same liberty, I accepted their offer, seeing myself abandoned by the French, my brothers. But a somewhat late experience opened my eyes to these perfidious protectors. Having perceived their treachery, I saw clearly that they intended for us to set upon each other to diminish our number and to enchain those who remained to return them to their former slavery…"

Toussaint winced in pain but did not stop speaking until Marie-Jeanne looked up and asked, "Can I get you a goblet of rum, *Mon Jeneral?"*

"No, Marie-Jeanne; please continue your work and I will continue mine," Toussaint replied with a tense tone in his voice. The officer struggled to keep the quill matched to Toussaint's pace.

"No, never would they achieve their infamous goal! And we will have revenge on these contemptible beings in our turn in every way. Let us unite forever, therefore, and, forgetting the past, let us seek henceforth only to crush our enemies and to avenge ourselves against our treacherous neighbors."

Toussaint closed his eyes momentarily and went back to dictating.

"It is true that the national flag flies over Gonaïves and its surroundings, and that I have routed the Spanish and emigrants from the area. But my heart is broken to contemplate the event that occurred against a few unfortunate whites who were victims of this affair. I am utterly unlike many others who witness scenes of horror in cold blood. I have always held humanity in common with all, and I suffer whenever I cannot prevent evil…"

Besides Toussaint, Marie-Jeanne, and the French officer scribing the dictation were two honor guardsmen. They sat in silent disbelief, occasionally stealing a glance at each other, at their leader's constant tone and clear mind while remembering how many French White civilians were caught in the crossfire of recent battles.

Toussaint then switched the tone of the letter to one of a subordinate reporting to his superior officer, as if he had already received the blessing of Laveaux to come back into the fold of the French Army under his command.

"...There were also several uprisings in the workshops, but I rapidly returned things to order and all are working as before. Gonaïves, Gros-Morne, the canton of Ennery, Marmelade, Plaisance, Dondon, Acul, and all of Limbé are under my orders, and I count four thousand armed men in these areas, without counting the citizens of Gros-Morne, who number six hundred. As to war munitions, I am entirely bereft, having consumed them in the various attacks that I made against the enemy.

Salvation in the Fatherland,
Toussaint"

"Should it not be signed *Toussaint Louverture, Général of the Western Army*?" asked the officer.

"*Non.* This is as much a personal letter as an official one. Send a courier and have it delivered at once to Governor Général Laveaux. Have this room guarded until I command otherwise," Toussaint said before falling unconscious into a deep slumber.

A few days later, the courier arrived at Général Laveaux's garrison in *Port-de-Paix* with Toussaint's letter. Sitting in his small tent behind a once ornate but now rundown desk, the General read Toussaint's words in disbelief: '*Gonaïves, Gros-Morne, the canton of Ennery, Marmelade, Plaisance, Dondon, Acul, and all of Limbé are under my orders…*'

"How is this possible?" he asked Montblanc, his top officer. "How has he retaken so much territory so quickly? No army can move that fast!"

"I do not know, *Mon Général*," replied Montblanc.

"If we'd agreed to his offer last year, none of this territory would have been lost to the enemy in the first place," Laveaux sighed. "In any case, Toussaint flies the French flag now—and with 4,000 armed soldiers under his command, he claims!"

In the North, Toussaint's rejoining made all the difference. His army fought ferociously and with lightning-fast attacks, covering territory at seemingly impossible speed. The Northern Plaines had become Toussaint's domain, with his soldiers acting as a quasi-police force for the area.

Such was Toussaint's success that Général Laveaux was now able to leave the *Port-de-Paix* garrison and travel to *Dondon*, unthreatened by either the Spanish or British.

Along the way Laveaux noted that the area appeared to be experiencing a period of calm and cultivation was on the rebound—evidenced by the planting of fresh crops. Gone were the maroons and brigands; those troublemakers who had wrought such death, destruction and plundering.

Arriving at *Dondon*'s outskirts, the organized tent city of Toussaint's army could be seen clearly in the distance. Laveaux quizzically looked at Montblanc as Laveaux's small procession continued toward the town. Toussaint's soldiers began to appear, standing at attention for the final mile, holding salutes for the incoming army. Once passed, the soldiers formed orderly columns and marched in step behind Laveaux's troops.

The contingent entered town via the main street, while every side street to the right and left was blocked by Toussaint's soldiers four men wide. Toussaint came into view mounted on top of his

magnificent war horse, Bel Argent, with 2,000 soldiers behind him at attention. Most were uniformed, but many stood shirtless toward the rear. Some carried conventional arms but most proudly held the only weapons they had machetes and axes.

Laveaux could identify Toussaint's officers by their pronounced dress uniforms and demeanor; Dessalines, Moyse, Belair, and Maurepas.

Toussaint dismounted and Laveaux raised his arm to halt his followers. The Governor General also departed his mount and the two men approached each other.

Toussaint removed his bicorn hat to reveal the yellow *mouchwa tèt* tightly tied over the growth of his afro. Laveaux had pictured Toussaint being taller, as he towered nearly a foot over him. Toussaint's legs were slightly bowed from years of horsemanship, his hair was graying at the tips, and his jaw protruded outward.

Toussaint saluted Laveaux and greeted him in perfect formal French.

"Mon Général, je me place ainsi que l'Armée de l'Ouest sous vos ordres" – 'My Général, I place myself and the Army of the West under your orders.'

Laveaux was nearly overcome with emotion. For months he'd been isolated and walled up with the remainder of his troops—less than 700—living like prisoners at the *Port-de-Paix* garrison. Life was a worried existence under the fear that they might meet a painful demise at any moment at the hands of either the Spanish or British. Sleepless nights, anxiety, tensions, and a host of other maladies were a reality he and his men were forced to endure.

Yet here the answer to their prayers, the man responsible for their liberation, stood in front of him. How could he not be affected?

Laveaux quickly saluted Toussaint and approached with his hand outstretched. They shook hands while smiling at each other enthusiastically. Laveaux couldn't resist taking his left hand and placing it affectionately on his comrade's right shoulder—where it remained as he addressed him.

"Général Toussaint, together we will do great things for the colony and for France. Of that, I can assure you."

Toussaint returned the warm greeting, and hat in hand, turned to his army.

"Sòlda yo; mwen prezante nou kòmandan nou an; Gouvènè Jeneral Sen Domeng: Jeneral Laveaux!—*Soldiers, I present to you, our Commander; The Governor General of Saint-Domingue: Général Laveaux!*"

4,000 soldiers roared a collective cheer. The connection between these two men—one white and one black—was obvious. This guaranteed them an uncertain future, though one that would hopefully bring an end to the past few years of deadly struggle and sacrifice.

Over the ensuing months, Toussaint's army began to confront the inevitable engagements with the Spanish battalions of Papillon and Biassou. All through the mountains of the *Cordon de l'Ouest,* Toussaint dispatched and scattered their forces, leading to a hasty retreat to the Spanish colony of Santo Domingo to remobilize and rearm.

Elsewhere, at the end of May 1794, the British launched a major offensive on the capital city of *Port-Républicain,* which forced Commissioners Sonthonax and Polverel to evacuate to *Jacmel* and join Rigaud at his stronghold there.

The British now held many of the port towns from *Môle St. Nicholas* to *Jérémie.* With little support from France, as the country was entangled in its own war back in Europe, the colonial cause was dangerously close to being lost. The Spanish and British onslaught continued on multiple fronts.

The situation did not improve the following month as Commissioners Sonthonax and Polverel received a recall order from the French Convention. They were ordered back to France to face charges stemming from the myriad of disasters that took place under their administration, including the sacking and burning of Cap-Français. Governor Galbaud, who they'd arrested and sent back to France had also pulled his connections to protest their leadership and was still backed by the political influence of *Grands Blancs* of the colony who had emigrated to Paris.

Before his voyage home, Commissioner Polverel appointed André Rigaud as General in charge of the Southern Region. A native of Saint-Domingue, Rigaud had been born to a wealthy French planter and a black slave woman in *Les Cayes*. His mother was of the Allada tribe of Benin, coincidentally the same as Toussaint's mother. Rigaud however, unlike Toussaint, wanted nothing to do with any part of his African lineage.

Acknowledging the Mulatto boy at a young age, his father sent him to France for an education. Upon returning, Rigaud became active in politics. He was a successor in the vein of Vincent Ogé and Julien Raimond—a champion of the interests of the *Gens de Couleur*. He aligned with revolutionary France and the interpretation of the Declaration of the Rights of Man and Citizens that ensured the civil equality of all free people but held contempt for the Blacks as he felt their superior even though his mother was a Black woman.

The newly-appointed handsome, articulate, 33-year-old Rigaud began consolidating the colony's leadership in the South. Rigaud's power came from the relationships and influence he wielded among the free Black and Mulatto planters from his hometown of *Les Cayes* in the Southern peninsula. This initial power consolidation led to a period of relative peace, with markedly fewer protest movements from ex-slave laborers—now known as the Cultivators.

4 months after Polverel's departure, Rigaud enthusiastically wrote:

Étienne,

The southern province is finally tranquil and in a reasonably good state of defense . . . Work is going well; your proclamations on agricultural production are having the full effect that you anticipated. I will keep you apprised of our improvements.

André.

Meanwhile, Toussaint turned his ire and army toward the British—in particular the army of a certain British Major by the name of Brisbane. A series of skirmishes followed, but despite inflicting multiple casualties, Toussaint failed to dislodge the British from the coastal towns they held. A counter-offensive led by Brisbane in June of 1794 likewise failed to break Toussaint's control of *Cordon de l'Ouest.*

That October, Brisbane devised a campaign in the Artibonite Valley along with Papillon and Biassou from the Spanish Auxiliaries. The British would attack from the west, while Toussaint's two former colleagues would ride in from the east, effectively trapping Toussaint in the middle.

Toussaint was based on a small sugar plantation at the time. The owners provided food and lodging for him and his military entourage in exchange for protection and modest fees from the army. However, the relative comfort belied their precarious position between the congregating forces—which Toussaint soon learned of through his spies.

One cool fall night, Toussaint invited his top Commanders; Dessalines, Moyse, Belair, and Maurepas to a strategy dinner wherein each of the commanders reported on their troop strength, equipment, and munitions amid the traditional dish of *mayi moulen ak pwa*—steaming hot cornmeal topped with black beans.

"Gentlemen, we have made great progress with the troops regarding training and how far they have come," Toussaint said, addressing those gathered. "But this alliance between the British and the Spanish has us at a crossroads."

The commanders all looked at each other, solemnly nodding.

"Brisbane is sly as a fox, and now Papillon and Biassou are on their side. You all know those two are quite familiar with the terrain and population."

"It is time we shift our tactics," he went on. "I know we have learned much on the art of European warfare from our White officers, and have also benefited from the knowledge of jungle warfare imparted by our African *bosal* brothers. We will now combine the two."

The officers looked up from their plates to eye him directly with heightened interest.

"Look down at your plates and tell me what you see," implored Toussaint.

Each looked at their plates and at each other, somewhat confused by the order.

"Dessalines, compare your plate to Belair's."

"It appears to be the same, unless…" Dessalines offered. "…unless I got more than Belair and am the faster eater!" Dessalines finished to the laughter of the group.

Unfazed, Toussaint continued. "And you, Maurepas, compared with Moyse?"

"It looks like we eat at the same rate, as he has as much left as I," Maurepas responded.

"Anyone else?" asked Toussaint.

"The cornmeal is hot," said Moyse, softly. "We all ate from the outside of the plate and worked our way in?"

"Brilliant, nephew!" shouted Toussaint. "The dish contains hot cornmeal—so as not to burn your tongues, each of you has done what you always have since childhood."

More confused faces greeted this revelation.

"You circle your plate with your spoon, and eat the outer

bands before working to the middle, is it not so?"

"Yes, it appears we all do the same," stated Belair. The others nodded.

"That is how we will defeat our enemies," declared Toussaint triumphantly. "Eat them from the outside first, and then proceed to destroy the middle."

He stood, reached for a paintbrush, and dipped it into an indigo container. Drawing a circle on the canvas to illustrate his point, he said "You may continue your dinner as I draw this out."

Toussaint slowly drew trees, hills, and dots of soldiers and horsemen. Finally, he began to speak again.

"Divide your men into small bands of 50 to 60 each. The first group will pick off the enemy at a fast pace on their perimeters, and just like you consumed your food tonight, another will encircle them and work towards the center – the heat of the battle."

Wave after wave you will launch the subsequent group, then the next, and the next, and continue circling the enemy just as your spoons have circled your plates. Eat them in spoonfuls as each of your attackers pass; the enemy's eyes and attention will follow the first group as the second presses down on them in surprise. Continue to repeat this until—well, take a look at your plates," finished Toussaint.

All looked down to find each had eaten every last bit of the corn and bean mixture except for the still piping-hot center. One by one smiles spread across their faces.

"We will call this *Encirclement Warfare*," Toussaint said, as he picked up his spoon and walked over to Moyse's plate. Gracefully scooping up the remaining corn and beans in the center of the plate and placing it in his mouth, he smiled.

"Mmmm…I taste victory. Now taste yours; just as it is cool enough now to eat so the enemy will soon be cool enough to destroy."

The men did so, sharing their hushed acknowledgments at the brilliance of the plan.

"Assemble your soldiers tomorrow for a meal exactly as the

one we have enjoyed tonight," Toussaint ordered. "They have all had this meal before, the same way their entire lives, so the concept should prove easy. Begin training and have your men prepared for battle within the week!"

The entire army quickly took to the battle plan. Several of the men chose to discard their shirts and boots in order to attack the enemy in stealth. The plan was launched in waves, with regiments dispatched both to the east and west. The results were immediate, effective and lethal. As quickly as the attackers arrived they prosecuted their destruction, and just as quickly disappeared; the pattern repeating over and over.

Toussaint ordered brigades to attack at all hours of the night and early morning while the cavalry picked up the onslaught during the daylight hours. The British were besieged relentlessly 24 hours a day. He rotated men with reinforcements replacing the small 50-60 man groups every four hours, leaving Toussaint's troops rested and hungry for the next battle.

After months of this encirclement warfare and heavy casualties; the strength, effectiveness, and morale of the mighty British army waned deeply.

The British soldiers would tell tales of Toussaint in battle, brilliantly leading the cavalry charge atop *Bel Argent*. So quickly and thoroughly did these stories circulate that it became forbidden to even mention Toussaint's name.

One commander wrote to his General Brisbane "Louverture appears and attacks, disappears and flies away, and as if by magic he reappears again where he is least expected. He seems to be ubiquitous. One never knows where his army is, what it subsists on, or how he manages his supplies and his treasury. He, on the other hand, seems perfectly informed concerning everything that goes on in our camp."

Toussaint was simultaneously fighting the Spanish

Auxiliaries. He drove Papillon's and Biassou's soldiers out of *Saint Michel* and *Saint Raphael* and razed the towns to prevent the Spanish from reusing them.

He then attacked *Saint Marc*, capturing the outlying Fort Belair and establishing a battery on *Morne Diamant* above the town. However, the British quickly arrived in force, driving him from his new position. Outmanned, Toussaint retreated to *Gonaïves* for a much-needed respite.

Six months after the campaign had begun, Général Laveaux traveled to *Gonaïves* in November to host a celebratory dinner for Toussaint and his officers. It was a lavish affair in which Laveaux and Toussaint both congratulated each other as successful brothers in arms.

The wine was plentiful and within a short time all the officers; White, Mulatto, and Black, were laughing, cheering, toasting, singing, and genuinely partaking and enjoying each other in the spirit of '*liberté, égalité, et fraternité!*'

The following day, the entire army assembled in a large field for inspection by the Governor General. One by one, Toussaint's officers; Dessalines, Bélair, Grobard, Desbardes, Laguerre, Moyse, Mornet, Desrouleaux, Dumenil, Clervaux, Maurepas, and Bonaventure, presented their troops and came forward to receive their official promotions.

The Governor General took the time to praise each one as if he had known them for decades.

Unprompted, each officer bent their knee as they had read of the knighting of men by a King or Queen. Toussaint looked upon them brimming with pride; here were his 12 handpicked disciples before him, and every last one of the 4,000 soldiers who watched the ceremony would shed their last drop of blood to serve them and this cause.

Governor Général Étienne Maynaud de Bizefranc de Laveaux

looked up to the sky and issued a brief prayer, as he felt truly blessed with how things had turned around in a rather short time.

After touring the *Cordon de l'Ouest,* Laveaux reported to his superiors in France that Toussaint had brilliantly enacted the new cultivation system, with more than 15,000 Cultivators returning to work in the region.

He also reported that White colonists had begun to return to their plantations from the cities in which they sought refuge, making peace with Toussaint in the process. The properties started to re-establish themselves as agriculturally solvent.

Despite the bloodshed of the past several years, the region had now turned into a model for the re-establishment of commercial agricultural production throughout the rest of the colony.

Could this be the beginning of a new era, Laveaux thought?

Ten

JUNIOR, PÉTION
& THE END OF THE SPANISH

Cap Français
September 1794

The *volte-face* - flip-flop - of Toussaint Louverture and former slaves who were now fighting for the French instead of the Spanish, hastened the withdrawal of the Spanish from the battlefield. As a result, the colony's violence took on lesser proportions, and relative calm was welcomed by everyone during the latter part of 1794.

Toussaint's attempts to re-establish the plantations and bolster the economy were seeing limited success though slowly gaining traction. His constant invitations to emigres to return to the colony were aided by his old friend Bayon de Libertat. Bayon had convinced Toussaint that real stabilization of the economy required the expertise, skills, and investment of rehabilitated *Grands Blancs*.

These emigres had fled to the United States, France, and other colonial settlements throughout the Caribbean, and to New

Orleans. Toussaint provided assurances, by way of Bayon, that they and their property would be protected from further violence or destruction. Furthermore, Polverel's work code being implemented by Rigaud was being fairly respected by the Cultivators—or ex-slaves in the south.

Jean-Baptiste Bayard Junior was home during what would have been the school year, as violence in Paris precluded him from attending his father's alma mater, *Louis-le-Grand Université*. Jean and Marie decided to enroll him in real-time business studies by putting him to work in the Bayard family businesses.

A lavish party was planned for Jean Junior's twentieth birthday celebration on the first Saturday in October of 1794. The boy was allowed to extend invites to anyone he wished. Junior thus invited his entire graduating class from Notre Dame Catholic School of Saint-Domingue, several non-scholastic friends, and nearly a dozen others who had attended university with him in France.

One of the invitees was Alexandre Pétion—who was 5 years his elder. Junior had met him while studying in Paris, when Pétion had addressed the university students about *gens de couleur* in the French Military and opportunities for advancement. Like Junior, Pétion was a Mulatto—born to a wealthy French father and a free Mulatto woman. He'd been sent to France at the age of 18 to study at the Military Academy of Paris and began his military service immediately following the completion of his academics.

Pétion's birth name was Alexandre Sabès, He adopted the Pétion surname out of admiration for the Mayor of Paris from 1791-1792 named Jérôme Pétion de Villeneuve. The mayor made a huge impression on the young man as he was a staunch abolitionist and extremely vocal about his opposition to slavery.

After the lecture, Junior invited Pétion to an outdoor café for coffee. They spent hours sharing their experiences in Saint-Domingue and France; quickly becoming friends. Pétion hailed from the western capital of *Port-Républicain* while Jean-Baptiste Junior had arrived from *Le Cap* in the north.

The two vowed to keep in touch as best they could while in France and back home. Thus, Pétion was ecstatic to receive the invitation to his dear friend's party; even as he and his family were staying at his uncle's house in *St. Marc* due to the ongoing British occupation of *Port-Républicain*.

Meanwhile, at the *Hôtel de la Couronne*, Henry had worked hard to plan a lavish party for Junior, whom he considered a younger brother. The celebration was a grand affair featuring singers, a dance troupe, jugglers, entertainment of all sorts, and dancing well past 3:00 in the morning.

With his parent's blessing, Junior invited Pétion to spend a few days at the Bayard residence rather than at the hotel, having made plans to show his friend the sights of *Cap Français* during his stay.

The day after the party, the entire family gathered for a grand late-morning breakfast. Jean and Marie were impressed with the maturity of Pétion and both endorsed the close friendship the boys had, despite Pétion's more advanced age.

"What are your plans, Alexandre, now that you are home?" asked Jean as eggs, ham, plantains, Malanga, cheeses, warm rolls, and butter were passed around the table.

"I've been assigned to Général André Rigaud in the South. Our mission is to kick the cursed British out of the Southern Peninsula. I can't believe that the British occupy my hometown of *Port-au-Prince,* or I should get accustomed to calling it by its new name of *Port Républicain* since that French Commissioner Polverel renamed it that! My parents and I were driven out of our home because of the British!"

"When do you report for duty? asked Jean.

"Next Sunday, here in *Le Cap* to General Jean-Louis Villatte. We will march and join General Rigaud with about a thousand men I am told."

Jean took a bite of his eggs.

"I know how you feel Alexandre," he began. "The redcoats occupy our hometown of *Jérémie* as well. We are constantly in fear for our parents who remain there, but we understand the British are more concerned with outbreaks of yellow fever and do not travel to areas they do not fully control. Still, our families are virtually under house arrest."

"Don't you worry, Mr. Bayard. We will soon kick them out of the colony for good—mark my words," Pétion responded passionately.

"Of that I'm certain, but not quickly enough to save our annual visit for Christmas," chuckled Jean, before sighing. "Perhaps by next year."

"No—you can make your plans now, Mr. Bayard. It will be done!" Pétion said, his smile brimming with the confidence of youth. He then took several more gulps of the hot dark coffee and scooped up another mouthful of the delicious meal.

Immediately after breakfast, Junior and Pétion excused themselves to do what young men do; visit girls, go to the beach, roam about town, play dominoes, hit the local taverns, and eventually come home to sleep it all off. Jean and Marie thoroughly enjoyed Pétion's well-mannered company and Junior was overjoyed to have a partner in crime.

One day while drinking and toasting at Club Dominos, a local tavern, Junior asked his friend; "What do you think about the prospects of a permanent peace in the colony after the British are sent packing on their ships?" asked Junior while the two relaxed in front of a café.

Pétion considered the question deeply before taking a long drag off his cheroot, allowing the smoke to linger as it released a unique profile of smoked almonds and creamy espresso notes.

"Alexandre, that cigarillo smells better than any other I have seen you smoke," proclaimed Junior.

"It is fine indeed. Want one?"

"No, thank you. They give me a headache—either by the

Club Domínos'

smoke or my mother's hand on the back of my head!" Junior scoffed. "Where did you get it?"

"An American smuggler out of *St. Marc* knows a family by the name of *Rencurrel* in Havana. He smuggles them from Cuba and sells them here and in the American Carolinas. I like these best—when I can get my hands on them."

"But back to your question;" Pétion continued. "We will not find peace, I am afraid. The British must be ousted, but besides that, the Mulattos are concerned with the Blacks—they significantly outnumber us when all the ex-slaves are added together. Meanwhile, the *Grands Blancs* want a return to slavery and will make any deal with the devil to make it happen.

"The *Petits Blancs* hate us *Gens de Couleur* because we own more businesses and property than they do, and they still see us adjacent to slaves. We are their competitors for the land and riches of this colony. How in the world could there ever be peace in this land?"

Junior could find no argument to parlay, and the two sat in silence for several moments before heading out to their afternoon dates on the beach.

The following Sunday, Pétion reported to Général Villatte and the regiment began their march toward *Léogâne* the very next day.

Upon arriving at Rigaud's main camp, Pétion and his battalion were placed under the orders of Commander Rigaud's army. Pétion came to admire Rigaud immensely while in his stead. Rigaud led a professionally-trained, multi-racial, lethal force of Blacks, Whites, and Mulattos. In December, they attacked the British at *Port Républicain* but were ultimately unsuccessful. However, the battalion did manage to capture the town of *Léogâne*, the most important and strategic town to be captured in the South.

In December of 1794, Toussaint led five brigades to engage Biassou and Papillon in the valley of *Grande-Rivière-du-Nord*. His new tactics again proving victorious, he set his sights on the northeastern town of *Petite Riviere* occupied by British Major Brisbane—ultimately driving their forces away.

Weeks later, in the early days of 1795, Toussaint led a successful cavalry charge against British artillery at *Grande Saline* and continued to chase his British adversaries southwest towards *St. Marc*. Two months later, Toussaint learned that his nemesis Brisbane had finally succumbed to injuries he received in battle.

Upon news of these successes, General Laveaux promoted Toussaint to Commander of the *Cordon de l'Ouest,* in March of 1795.

That July, the French Convention named Laveaux the permanent Governor General of Saint-Domingue. Toussaint, Rigaud, and Beauvais were promoted to the ranks of Brigadier General. With Laveaux's nod of approval, Toussaint launched a diplomatic maneuver to unite and fold into his forces the remaining maroon rebels periodically menacing the countryside. This both strengthened Toussaint's army and finally brought peace to the plantations throughout the countryside.

Laveaux also ordered Generals Rigaud and Toussaint to coordinate their future efforts together. Within a few months, they began launching simultaneous attacks against the British.

By the end of 1795, the news of the peace Treaty of Basel between France and Spain reached Saint-Domingue. By this treaty, Spain stunned the world by ceding its eastern portion of the island, the Spanish colony of Santo Domingo, to France. They deferred transfer *'until the French Republic should be in a position to*

defend its new territory from attack.'

Papillon had lost favor with the Spanish due to his massacre in the town of *Bayajá* which was captured by the French and renamed Fort Dauphin.

The residents had warned the Spanish against letting Papillion's army into the town, as many of the soldiers were former slaves of its residents. However, Papillon marched his army forward, and revenge-seeking troops massacred the French inhabitants who had previously mistreated them. Many Spaniards also died in the episode.

The Spanish garrison did not interfere to halt the killing and was greatly criticized and accused of complicity by foreign governments around the world. The incident had deeply embarrassed the Spanish crown and Papillon's direct involvement in the incident had snuffed out any remaining goodwill.

The General and his collaborators were escorted to Havana for disciplinary action. However, the Cuban governor, Luis de las Casas, was so frightened that punishment would provoke an insurrection across the island, that he pressured the Spanish government to remove them from his colony.

In March of 1796, Papillion and his party arrived in Cádiz, Spain—where they were, for all intents and purposes, kept as prisoners. The officers lost their military ranks and rights to economic compensation after their retirement. Papillon had to use his few remaining resources to assist his family and those of his companions. Once one of the great generals of The Spanish Colonial Army's Auxiliary Forces, he died a pauper in 1805.

General Biassou had tried talking Papillon out of entering the town and was thereafter praised by the Spanish for his attempts to mitigate the affair. As a reward, he was allowed his choice of any Spanish colony in which to relocate that he and his officers desired.

Before his final departure, Biassou received a message from Toussaint requesting a peaceful meeting. Toussaint arrived to Biassou's camp with his honor guard in tow. Tensions were initially high; Biassou feared Toussaint had learned of the murder plot Biassou had loosely engineered against him, but it quickly became obvious Toussaint remained ignorant of his involvement.

"Welcome, General Louverture—please accept my compliments on a war well fought, and my congratulations on your promotion to Brigadier General of the French Colonial Army," saluted Biassou.

Toussaint returned the salute and offered a smile to his old colleague.

"George, you kept me awake each night in anticipation of your next move. It was very interesting indeed," replied Toussaint.

"Yet you still managed to rake us over the coals, Toussaint. Brilliant execution," Biassou stated, a tinge of bitterness in his voice stemming from his wounded ego.

"Enough of the praise. Let us talk," said Toussaint.

"Of course. May I offer you a coffee, water…rum?"

"Just water, thank you" replied Toussaint as he followed Biassou into his tent.

"The Spanish are finished here," began Toussaint. "I need someone I can trust on this side of the island. Join me and let us work to integrate the Spanish East and the French West, together."

"I am flattered, Toussaint. But I need a change of scenery. I now have far too many enemies throughout the island," deferred Biassou. "My sights are on Spanish Florida."

"Florida, Biassou? You cannot be serious. There is nothing there! It is nothing but swamp, I am told."

"I know Governor de Quesada in St. Augustine. He has extended a personal invitation and has a mission awaiting me."

"A mission? It is a foreign land! You have a mission here with your people, Biassou. What could be more important or exciting in the far-off colony of Spanish Florida?"

"Chasing Indians. A savage tribe called the Seminoles are giving him and his new settlers hell."

"Florida is a strange land Biassou. It is even one with ancient monsters—they call them alligators and say they have called it home for all of history. Stay here! Work for the benefit of France, and your home, instead."

"My mind is made-up, my friend. I do appreciate your trust, but I cannot accept," Biassou replied with a bit of reservation. "I would ask a favor though; that you pardon my soldiers of any wrongdoing and consider folding them into your army. I have 1,800 or so good men ready to follow you. Papillion has also departed, and his army is now at your disposal – another 1,200, I suppose."

Toussaint eventually accepted the request and folded the troops into his armies. He bid farewell to Georges Biassou, knowing he would likely never see him again. The following week, Biassou departed for the Spanish colony of Florida, where he continued a distinguished career with the Spanish military, bought a home—and later plantation—where he lived until he died in a drunken bar brawl in 1801.

Eleven

THE COUP
OF JEAN-LOUIS VILLATTE

Léogâne
January 1796

Although Général Rigaud had reluctantly acquiesced to Toussaint's superior rank in the French Army and his role as the lead general of the Black former slaves in the North, he dared not concede any power in the South. Rigaud strongly believed Commissioner Polverel upon his departure from the colony had entrusted the region to him and him alone.

Rigaud also believed in Saint-Domingue's race-based caste system, which placed Mulattoes just below Whites, and left Blacks, like Toussaint, at the bottom of the social classes. That was incompatible with him being subordinate to a Black superior officer such as Toussaint.

When Général Jean-Louis Villatte, commander of the *Cap-Français* garrison, and Rigaud finally met, both men concluded that Toussaint Louverture and Governor Général Laveaux had grown far too close in friendship and professional proximity. They felt that the French White Général preferred the commander and his Black troops over their Mulatto regiment.

The fact that Toussaint had achieved the most success engaging the British was none of their concern. Of course,

Toussaint's professional relationship with Governor Général Laveaux had developed over years of battles, compromises, and mutual respect for one another's capabilities. Frankly speaking, Rigaud and Villatte were jealous.

Nonetheless, the two felt the time had arrived for a move on Toussaint. The British forces had developed grave difficulties in maintaining morale and strength due to an outbreak of Yellow Fever and military needs spread elsewhere. When a rebellion broke out in Jamaica, the British ceased their offensive in Saint-Domingue altogether, settling on merely holding the coastal towns, particularly the capital of *Port Républicain.*

It was the perfect opportunity for Rigaud and Villatte to conspire together and eliminate Toussaint. They enlisted the diabolical services of a cunning political operative by the name of Pierre Pinchinat. A light-skinned metropolitan lawyer educated in France, Pinchinat was one of André Rigaud's most trusted agents—albeit an altogether different type of fellow than his colleagues.

He was a brilliant but unprincipled man who combined aspirations of power with a relaxed sexual license toward women. Rumors and outright accusations of molestation and even rape were whispered, but he was never brought to justice.

Though considered a genius by his peers, his vicious personal life created animosities and fostered a lack of faith among those who would have otherwise wholeheartedly admired him. He possessed a savvy grasp and control of any political situation, though his diplomatic actions were dubious.

He'd eventually outgrown his welcome in the southern region of the colony, and Rigaud now had just the perfect assignment for him and his talents as an instrument against Toussaint in the north.

Pinchinat arrived at *Cap-Français* two months ahead of Governor Général Laveaux and quickly set to work spreading rumors of Laveaux's intention to reinstitute slavery, remove the rights of the *gens de couleur,* and effectively return the colony to its previous state of affairs before the French Revolution.

So successful was his subterfuge that by early March *Cap Français* was festering with agitation and rumors against the Governor Général and his sinister plot. The Blacks feared slavery, the free *Gens de Couleur* were upset at the reported revocation of their rights, and yet all of it was created out of thin air by Pinchinat and his cohorts.

They further falsified reports and produced fake invoices and bills of lading showing the importation of slave shackles and whips that were stored in secret warehouses along the docks. They provided stories and falsified documents to the local *Gazette* newspaper of Laveaux having written proclamations that terminated citizens' rights. Laveaux of course was unaware, absent, and helpless to defend himself against these accusations.

Upon his return to *Cap Français* from *Port-de-Paix*—where he had established the temporary seat of government on March 20, 1796, Général Villatte immediately placed Laveaux under arrest on charges of conspiracy against the citizens of Saint-Domingue, as well as a charge of treason against the French Revolutionary Government. He was imprisoned in the city's jail and Villatte appointed himself Acting Governor Général.

Laveaux was showing signs of fever when arrested but was provided no medical treatment. His cell was cold, damp, and dark, with palm fronds thrown on the ground for bedding. There was an infestation of scurrying rats and insects which he could hear and feel but do nothing about. He could hardly tell whether it was day or night; only when the outer door of the stockade opened and a small sliver of light crept through could he discern any sense of the passage of time.

He was served days-old bread and cold soup of green leaves in a watery and flavorless broth. Water was rationed with a cup each day. The Governor Général was convinced he would not survive long under such conditions.

Villatte anxiously monitored his prisoners' well-being or lack of. If the Governor died in prison of fever, dysentery, or other illness, he would not be blamed for his killing. His original murderous plot had become unnecessary. The days ticked away, and the new Governor Général felt the hold on his power grow.

Toussaint was in *Gonaïves* and unaware of the happenings in Cap-Français during this time, successfully incorporating the forces of a rebel leader by the name of Dieudonné. Dieudonné was an African-born slave who had become the chief of some 3,000 ex-slave rebels. He had control of the mountains above *Port Républicain* and was increasingly reluctant to submit to both his direct commanders, Général Louis Jacques Bauvais, or Général André Rigaud.

Perhaps resenting the discrimination he perceived from the two, Dieudonné had begun negotiations with the British to join them several months prior. Toussaint penned a personal letter on behalf of Dieudonné's superiors in an attempt to persuade him from the alliance. It read in part:

'Believe me, my dear friend, forget all individual animosity, and reunite with our brothers Rigaud and Bauvais. They are brave defenders of general liberty who love their fatherland too much not to desire with all their heart to be friends of you and all whom you command.'

Ever the tactician, Toussaint devised an alternative plan should Dieudonné not be swayed back into the fold. Knowing he could not read, Toussaint arranged for his representative to read the letter out loud to Dieudonné in the company of his top lieutenants. When Dieudonné responded with a refusal, as they expected, he was immediately overthrown by a subordinate, Captain Laplume, with pre-planned support of his other officers.

Laplume turned Dieudonné over to Rigaud who promptly threw him in prison. However, rather than joining Riguad, Laplume and Toussaint arranged for Dieudonné's men to be absorbed into the latter's ranks—a brilliant ploy by Toussaint.

As Toussaint and Captain Laplume were finally meeting to congratulate each other on the implementation of their successful plan, Jean-Jacquess Dessalines entered the room with anxiety.

"Forgive me, *Mon Général*. I have important news to report," he hastily offered. It wasn't like Dessalines to appear so agitated.

"Go ahead, Dessalines," Toussaint replied.

Dessalines glanced over at Laplume before continuing.

"It is alright Dessalines; Laplume is now one of us and will be an important member of our officer corps moving forward. He may hear what you have to say."

"Do you remember my Aunt Gran Toya I have spoken of many times?" began Dessalines.

"Yes, a Mrs. Victoria Montou; you met her as a child on the *Duclos* plantation. She taught you her fierce fighting skills and the art of combat. How could I forget?" replied Toussaint. "I dare say I owe her a debt of gratitude."

"Yes, *Mon Général*." Said Dessalines.

Toussaint turned to address Laplume and continued.

"She was a great warrior back in the Dahomey Empire of our African homeland before she was captured, enslaved, and shipped to this colony, *non*?"

"Yes *Mon Général*," Dessalines added.

"Imagine; an army so fierce the invading Europeans were terrified of them—comparing them to the Greek Amazons for their bravery and brutal tactics in protecting their king."

"She is the same—and she is here and she wants an audience with you," Dessalines interjected, no longer able to contain his excitement.

"Here?!" Toussaint exclaimed. "Please bring her in so I may meet this great woman!"

Toussaint and Laplume both rose to greet her. Dessalines

turned back to open the door of the room and gestured for his Aunt Toya to enter. Toussaint was shocked by her appearance. He knew she was born a few years before him, but the woman before him looked decades younger than his 52 years.

Her complexion was smooth and clear. Her eyes were large with dark brown pupils. Her hair was black, mostly hidden by her red *mouchwa tèt* scarf—and her teeth were straight and white. She wore a pair of long earrings, a necklace of beads, and a loose blouse that revealed the upper portion of her still-firm breasts.

Toussaint could only attribute her good health to her famed powers of herbal healing, which Dessalines had previously conveyed in length.

"Madame Montou, it is a great honor and pleasure to meet you," Toussaint said as he extended his hand. "Jean-Jacques has spoken such warm words on your behalf."

Victoria Montou accepted Toussaint's hand in a firm grip, smiled, and addressed him curtly.

"Général, I have ridden through the night to inform Jean-Jacquess of terrible things happening in *Le Cap*."

Montou proceeded to give a full account of the activity leading up to the arrest of the Governor Général. Toussaint listened with a growing mix of anxiety and anger. His rivalry for power with Villatte—whom he believed to be an unapologetic bigot—had now reached its apex.

"This will not stand!" shouted Toussaint. "Dessalines, prepare the army to march the day after tomorrow. The 8th and the 9th brigades are to remain at *Gonaïves*—but the rest should prepare for battle!"

He then turned to his messenger.

"Madame Montou, please rest your mind and body here as our guest. I will have a room prepared for your stay and food and refreshments brought immediately."

"*Merci Général,* but I will ride with you to *Le Cap*."

"So be it. But I must insist you refresh and rest for the ride. My secretary will see to your accommodations and nourishment.

Dessalines, bring me the officers after informing them of the march."

With that, the camp burst alive with activity and preparations for war.

Two days hence, the army left *Gonaïves* bound for *Cap-Français* with 10,000 men strong. On March 27th, only one week since Laveaux's arrest, the menacing sight of the advancing army caused the smaller Mulatto forces under the command of Joseph Flaville to capitulate and remain hidden in their barracks. The city fell quickly under Toussaint's command, but Jean-Louis Villatte, Pierre Pinchinat, and their remaining supporters fled to the southern part of the colony to evade capture.

Toussaint entered the city in triumph, marching directly to the jail and releasing Laveaux—who he found in a desperate condition. A huge crowd of citizens had assembled to meet them as they departed, chanting:

"Death to Laveaux!"
"Death to Laveaux!"
"Death to Laveaux!"

Toussaint formed a protective escort to take Laveaux to the army's encampment for treatment of his wounds and fever. His friend safely transported from the area, Toussaint walked to the front of the crowd and addressed them;

"Everything you have been told concerning our great Governor-Général is a lie!" he shouted. "This great man of France, and loyal servant to the great colony of Saint-Domingue, is a patriot who has been slandered by Villatte and his band of liars headed by Pierre Pinchinat. This Governor has done more for your freedom and rights than any besides Commissioner Sonthonax!"

The crowd began to quiet and the chants gave way to confused murmurs.

"He imported chains to enslave us. They are in warehouses at the docks!" shouted one man.

"Take me to this warehouse immediately and show them to me!" replied Toussaint sharply.

The crowd and Toussaint's honor guard promptly walked to the docks and began opening warehouse after warehouse—but no such chains of bondage were found. The lead instigator, a plump man by the name of Fevrier Cherisme insisted upon the existence of the chains and continued to open door after door.

One after another, the inspections turned up nothing. By the time the last warehouse was declared clean, a crowd of several hundred had gathered.

"All of you owe our great governor an apology and shall forever pledge your loyalty to him," stated Toussaint in a resounding voice. "The entire city has been duped—thinking him a traitor rather than a great patriot serving the citizens of Saint-Domingue!"

"Cherisme, you have lied to us!" shouted a woman from the crowd.

"He is an agent of that man Pinchinat!" shouted another man.

"Traitor!" Came yet another voice.

"Seize him!"

"That is *enough!*" shouted Toussaint. He turned to address his lead officer. "Take this man into custody and get a statement from him."

With that, Cherisme was arrested, detained, and interrogated, ultimately providing valuable information about Pinchinat's plot and his success in manipulating the people of *Cap Français*.

On the morning of April 1st, 1796, Toussaint's honor guard rode down *Rue Espagnol*. They halted their horses at attention in front of the Governor's Mansion. On command, the two columns, in great ceremony, split with the horsemen facing each other, leaving a corridor a dozen feet wide down the center. Toussaint, followed by Dessalines, Moyse, Belair, and Maurepas slowly walked their horses forward from behind the lines through the gates, stopping at the steps of the entrance.

A crowd of over 1,000 looked on as a rested and refreshed Governor Général Laveaux, accompanied by other dignitaries of the government stood awaiting Toussaint's arrival. Laveaux saluted Toussaint, walked down the several steps, and the two dear friends informally greeted each other with a kiss on each cheek.

They turned back toward the soldiers and the crowd, Laveaux holding Toussaint's hand in his, and both men raised their hands in a show of victory and solidarity. The crowd erupted in cheers.

Laveaux then stepped up to address those gathered before him.

"Citizens of *Cap Français*; I, Étienne Laveaux, do hereby proclaim the fulfillment of Guillaume-Thomas Raynal's prediction that a Black Spartacus would rise to free you from your chains and protect your freedoms from all those who come to challenge it. I proclaim that Black Spartacus as Général Toussaint Louverture!" he finished as the crowd roared in response.

"By the power vested in me by the French Convention and Assembly, I, Governor Général Étienne Maynaud de Bizefranc de Laveaux, do hereby declare Général Toussaint Louverture as the lawful Lieutenant-Governor of the colony of Saint-Domingue from this day forward, and grant him all the vested authority and power this title affords!" Laveaux shouted.

Toussaint stood at attention behind him, a twinkle of moisture building at the corner of his eye, but not falling.

"I further hereby pledge to our Lieutenant-Governor that I shall not create or execute an order without his full consultation and agreement!"

The crowd cheered ever louder as Laveaux handed Toussaint a rolled, wax sealed, and bound written decree.

Toussaint accepted the gift and approached the crowd.

"Citizens of Saint-Domingue. I, Toussaint Louverture accept this honor and the responsibility to guard and protect this colony,

on behalf of France, until my death."

"I further hereby pledge to our Lieutenant-Governor that I shall not create or execute an order without his full consultation and agreement!"

The crowd cheered ever louder as Laveaux handed Toussaint a rolled, wax sealed, and bound written decree.

Toussaint accepted the gift and approached the crowd.

"Citizens of Saint-Domingue. I, Toussaint Louverture accept this honor and the responsibility to guard and protect this colony, on behalf of France, until my death."

The crowd quieted to hear his every word.

"I pledge my life, my liberty, my army, and my honor to you and Governor Général Laveaux!" bellowed Toussaint, raising the decree in his fist and shouting *"APRE BONDYE SE LAVO!"* — *AFTER GOD IT IS LAVEAUX!*

The crowd exploded, chanting in Creole, *"APRE BONDYE SE LAVO - APRE BONDYE SE LAVO - APRE BONDYE SE LAVO!"*

Laveaux and Toussaint waived to the mêlée of people once more before retreating into the Mansion, prepared to enjoy the waiting feast in their honor.

Twelve

TOUSSAINT LOUVERTURE AND HENRY CHRISTOPHE

Cap-Français
May 1796

One evening following the daring rescue of the Governor Général and the triumphant announcement of Toussaint's elevation in rank, they together found themselves dining with several of Toussaint's officers at the *Hotel de La Couronne*. After polishing off a delicious feast, and bidding their farewells, Toussaint requested their evening's server bring him the General Manager, Henry Christophe.

Henry soon approached Toussaint's table.

"Henry Christophe, the great hotelier, it is so nice to return to your fine establishment," said the General, rising to greet him.

"The pleasure is ours, *Général*. Has your meal been to your satisfaction?" offered Henry.

"Superb as always, as was the service," Toussaint mused with a smile. "My party and I very much enjoyed ourselves, mixing a little business with pleasure."

"Wonderful. How are your children and lovely wife, Suzanne?"

"Much better than when you last saw them. They are back at *Habitation Sansay* in *Ennery*. My nephew Moyse, whom you recall, is in the army—and assigned to me."

"Please forward my salutations to them all," replied Henry.

"Henry," Toussaint began, taking a more serious tone. "I never thanked you for assisting my departure—or rather my escape—from this fine city all those years ago."

"It was my pleasure to serve, *Général*," answered Henry. "You had committed no crime here. Commissioner Sonthonax had no reason to issue that warrant."

The two men exchanged small smiles.

"May I offer you an after-dinner cognac—or anything else you may desire—compliments of the house, of course?" Henry inquired.

"A cognac would be very nice but I shall only accept if you join me," Toussaint replied.

Henry took a seat at the table, waved over a server, and provided him with their order.

"I was pleased to hear that scoundrel Sonthonax was recalled to France to stand trial," Toussaint stated. "However, I have heard he is destined to shortly return with a new commission."

The server arrived with their drinks. Each took a sip before Toussaint continued.

"I have heard nothing but good things of you, Henry. The same is said of this wonderful establishment you oversee."

"*Merci, Général*. I have an excellent staff."

"Have you heard of the Governor *Général* and I's plan to entice back the *Grands Blancs* and thus reestablish our colony's flourishing economy?"

"Yes," replied Henry. "I learned of it from my brother—well, as close to one as I've ever had—Jean-Baptiste Bayard. He is in full agreement with you."

"Go on," encouraged Toussaint.

"If the plantation owners and Cultivators can move past the issue of slavery and accept your proposed system of compensation for production, this colony will once again become the agricultural powerhouse of the world," Henry finished passionately.

Toussaint could not help but smile at the young man's fire.

"The lack of production is undoubtedly putting pressure on Mr. Bayard's import and export business, no?" he asked.

"Certainly. The Bayard companies and employees are suffering immensely. They may soon be forced to liquidate half their fleet."

Toussaint nodded knowingly and offered his glass up before taking a respectful sip. The two men sat in silence for several minutes contemplating the consequences the past several years of upheaval had brought upon the colony. Toussaint finally spoke again:

"Speaking of business, excellent staffs—like loyal soldiers—do not appear out of thin air. They are nurtured and coaxed towards being a cohesive unit."

Henry nodded his agreement.

"Before this war and the invasion on our soil, I'd never considered joining the army. Were you ever a military man, Henry?"

"I was in the French force of the *Chasseurs-Volontaires de Saint-Domingue* at the battle of Savannah under the command of Jean-Baptiste Bayard. I was but a child—just turned twelve. That is actually how I came to Saint-Domingue," Henry replied. "I was a slave in St. Christophe for eleven years until I fled the British island, stowing away on a French military vessel not knowing it was bound for a war in America."

"I now understand the English spelling and pronunciation of your name," said Toussaint, bemused. "Even the slight English accent you sport today—I'd long wondered. Now, what are you doing these days Henry?"

"Assuming you keep the peace *Général* I will continue to enjoy life here in *Cap Français* with my lovely wife, children, and this magnificent hotel."

"Your wife and children?" asked Toussaint, somewhat surprised. "Please do tell!"

"The love of my life is Marie-Louise. She is the daughter of the hotel's founder, the late Gabriel Coidavid. Mr. Coidavid passed a year and a half ago, but Mrs. Coidavid is still quite active, especially with her grandchildren. She is wonderful with them and we are blessed to have her."

"My condolences to you and Marie-Louise, Henry," stated Toussaint, raising his glass once more.

"Thank you, I will pass that along to Marie-Louise," said Henry, bowing his head slightly. "Gabriele was able to see our oldest child, his grandson, Francois born. He just turned two. We also have a daughter Françoise who is almost one—and hopefully soon another, who knows?" Henry beamed with pride.

"A family man that has a stake in this land. There is nothing more important than that. I could use someone like you, Henry."

Henry was taken aback by Toussaint's sudden suggestion.

"In the—the army?" Henry stuttered slightly. "My military days were brief and quite long ago *Général*. My true expertise is in running this hotel and casino."

"You possess the exact military skills our cause needs, Henry. You have organizational traits, leadership qualities, procurement abilities, and the motivational aptitude to keep your staff engaged," Toussaint's voice quickened as he listed Henry's credentials. "All of these are the qualities of a great military leader. I am charged with a huge army full of followers—but very few leaders."

"I cannot leave my family *Général,*" Henry shook his head. "Besides, the French government has now emancipated the slaves and the colony is more autonomous than ever. Non-French trade routes are even being established, especially with the Americans. What enemy do you intend to fight?"

"The British have an appetite for this colony's riches and still hold the capital city of *Port Républicain*. The time may soon come to forcefully eject them and bid '*au revoir'* as their mighty ships leave for the long journey home," replied Toussaint before taking another sip from his glass.

"Do not underestimate the troublemakers within our colony, either," Toussaint went on. "Many of the ex-slaves have no desire to return to the plantations; the *Maroons* have a taste for killing and pillaging and still roam the countryside; the constant agitation between Blacks and Mulattos continues, and if the colony is not productive at any time, the French government may once again attempt re-enslavement," Toussaint added, passion sneaking back into his voice. "There is much which threatens the future of your children."

Henry slowly nodded. He could not deny the General's logic. So what say you, Henry? Join us for the good of the colony."

"I need to think this through, *Général*" replied Henry in a measured tone.

"I can see you are motivated to join, Henry. You believe in our cause—in our homeland; what holds you back is your family. I can respect that." offered Toussaint.

"It is complicated," Henry agreed.

"Henry, what is complicated is what may happen to this land's future if men like us do not prevail," said Toussaint matter-of-factly. With that, he finished off the last drops of liquor and stood to leave.

"I will be at *Ennery* for the holidays and remain through January fifteenth of next year. Due to your past military and current managerial experience, I will immediately enlist you at the rank of Captain and provide you hundreds of men to lead, should you join me there."

Toussaint locked eyes with Henry.

"I need you, Henry. Of that I am certain."

On the carriage ride home, Henry replayed what *Général* Toussaint Louverture had said over and over. The thought of leading and managing a force of several hundred soldiers was enticing—but was he truly willing to give up his dream life in *Cap Français*? He was manager of the most successful hotel and casino in the colony, had a beautiful young wife awaiting him each evening, and the two most joyous parts of his life; François and Françoise.

He entered his two-story home on *Rue de la Reine* and was greeted by Jerome, his loyal butler, who took his cape and offered him a drink, to which he nodded his agreement and reminded Jerome to bring one for his wife, Marie-Louise. She was in the sitting room reading a book, having already put the children to bed when he saw her. She rose to him and they embraced with a hug and kiss.

"I am so fortunate to have you here every night I come home," said Henry.

"Always," she replied with a smile. "How was your day my love?"

Henry took a seat in his large leather chair and looked admiringly around him. The luxuriously-appointed room was brightly lit with lanterns on the tables and walls. In the center was an ornate rug from Persia—a wedding gift from Jean and Marie. Solid mahogany bookcases housed an assortment of books and a beautiful clock, a small writing desk charmingly sat against a wall, and assorted artwork and decorations were arranged neatly with fresh flowers everywhere. He often marveled at his good fortune and took none of it for granted.

"My day went well, though it ended with an interesting visitor," replied Henry. "Général Toussaint Louverture himself— along with an entourage which included the Governor Général and six top commanders."

"What is he still doing in *Le Cap*?" asked Marie-Louise, surprised. "It's been over a month since he squashed the coup and liberated the Governor Général from prison."

"Having a wonderful meal, to hear him tell it," said Henry as he settled more into his favorite chair. "Of what I understand, the two were discussing how to further attract the *Grands Blancs*

Émigrés back to their plantations and the colony."

"Oh, he also wants me to join his army as an officer," Henry added, purposefully nonchalant.

Henry and Marie-Louise enjoyed a relationship in which neither felt the need to filter themselves. It was perhaps what they both loved most about the other—but Marie-Louise remained silent at the presentation of this information. Truth be told, she would have preferred that Henry kept this to himself a while longer rather than being so forthright.

Jerome arrived with a sniffer of cognac for Henry and a glass of Chartreuse for Marie-Louise—the same drink Henry had introduced her to on their first night on the town together.

"May I get you anything else *Monsieur et Madame*?" Asked Jerome. "Claire is still in the kitchen but will soon be closing for the night."

"That will be all for tonight, Jerome. Have a good evening and we will take care of the glasses" Marie-Louise replied for them both.

"You need not trouble yourself, *Madame*. I also need to turn off the lanterns," Jerome answered.

"No, Jerome, thank you. Take the night off—I will take care of the glasses and *Monsieur* Christophe will handle the lanterns. Good night." Marie-Louise repeated more forcefully.

Jerome looked at Henry who shrugged his shoulders. "Lady's orders, Jerome. Good night."

Jerome smiled and bowed his head before bidding both goodnight and leaving the room.

"So, what do you think of Général Louverture's offer, Henry?" asked Marie-Louise, pointedly.

"I think my life is full and splendid, my love. You have given me the best and most precious gifts in our children. To leave you and them would weigh heavily on my spirits" replied Henry, honestly.

"That is not what I asked, Henry. Tell me how you feel about what the General proposed."

"To lead men in the military would be a great challenge—one I would have jumped at five years ago. Now, I have much too much to lose…"

"And what then if you do not accept?"

"I will stay here with my family and continue our wonderful lives together."

"Is that what you want, though my dear? Is that what you need?" she pressed.

"I think it is Marie-Louise. No—I am *sure* that it is."

They dropped the subject and instead stayed awake talking of the children and gossiping about friends, business, and politics around the colony. However, that night Henry tossed and turned with nightmares. He saw visions of a destroyed *Cap-Français*; his children driven away in chains with dozens of other slaves; Marie-Louise in soiled clothes on the back of a horse-drawn wagon with other women, screaming his name as the rest of the city burned behind her.

He saw himself seated in his restaurant, smoking a cigar with a cognac in his hand, surrounded by rich white people he did not know, all laughing and cavorting together. Turning away from the festivities, he was confronted by the face of Chavannes on the day of his execution. His old friend returned Henry's gaze staring deep into his soul as his tear dropped in slow motion to the ground in the town square. As it hit, the ground turned to sand and dust as the laughing *Grands Blancs* disappeared, leaving behind Chavannes standing alone in front of the rack that had torn him limb from limb.

Henry awoke with a gasp; sweating, fearful, and no longer wishing to close his eyes. He went downstairs for a glass of water, where the clock showed four in the morning. He spent the rest of the early morning in silent contemplation.

Marie-Louise softly arrived by his side two hours later. She wrapped her arms around him and whispered in his ear.

"You must join *Général Louverture*, Henry. I dreamt of disaster should you decide not. It was horrible! We were separated and the children and I were in chains. I lost you and could not find you anywhere. It was horrible I tell you—"

She began to sob in his arms. "This colony needs you. You must not think of us now, you must think of our future and the future of our children."

She continued to cry in his arms.

"You are right, Marie-Louise. I shared your dream exactly as you described. I must do this—" Henry felt his own voice catch in his throat. He swallowed before steadily continuing so as not to further upset his wife.

"We have several months before I leave in January. Let us live like we never have before."

The Christophe family did much together over the next several months, enjoying a grand holiday season, intent on forging a lifetime's worth of memories in a few precious months.

The following January of 1797, Henry left for *Ennery* to join the army of *Général Toussaint Louverture* and a future with only time to reveal its chain-reactive outcomes.

Thirteen

THE RETURN OF SONTHONAX

Cap-Français
May 1796

It was a brilliant sunny morning on the 11th of May, 1796 when a crowd of nearly 200 Black ex-slaves gathered near the harbor to await the arrival of a French warship. The vessel docked at the waterfront, its two tall-masted escorts anchoring just outside the inlet. They had assembled to welcome their liberator, the great White Frenchman Léger-Félicité Sonthonax back to Saint-Domingue.

The 180-foot *Wattignies,* a 74-gun French Naval ship, lowered its gangplank. Two dozen uniformed soldiers descended, clearing a pathway for its occupants.

The crowd excitedly cheered, *"Papa libète nou! Papa libète nou! Papa libète nou!*—Father of our Liberty!"

A small, overweight White man dressed in a tan suit appeared at the ship's railing. His long, ruby-tinted brown hair flowed behind his collar, and his red, white, and blue sash sporting numerous medals hung around his shoulders. There was no

DAUPHIN ROYAL

mistaking the now famous great Commissioner. Sonthonax lifted his hand to wave at the crowd, who erupted in cheers; men tore off their straw hats and threw them into the air, while women raised their hands to the heavens, shaking them

as if in a hypnotic trance. They continued to chant; *"Papa libète nou! Papa libète nou! Papa libète nou!"*

Four other men quickly joined Sonthonax—his fellow commissioners Roume, Giraud, and Leblanc—all white men from France—and Julien Raimond, a wealthy *Gens de Couleurs* of the planter class from the town of Aquin in the south. They, too, wore similar sashes equally equipped with medals.

Sonthonax began to walk down the gangplank, greeted by fresh refrains of his name; *"Son-Ton-Nax! Son-Ton-Nax! Son-Ton-Nax!"*

He quickly descended the gangplank, smiling and waving to the crowd with his fellow commissioners in tow. They followed four sentries through a corridor of soldiers which kept the pressing crowd, still chanting Sonthonax's name, at bay.

The procession continued to Government House with more citizens coming out of shops to monitor the commotion. Onlookers' reactions were split between excitement and anger at his presence. Sonthonax stopped the cavalcade at the front of Government House before offering a final wave and entering the building. He had come to reclaim the power bestowed upon him by the Legislature of France.

Sonthonax had been cleared of all charges from his assignment in 1793. He'd argued that most of the Mulattos, a portion of the *Gens de Couleur* who were his original mission and biggest allies, were no longer loyal to France and the Republic and should instead place their faith with the freed slaves and Black rebel army. Newly vindicated and politically rehabilitated, he returned to Saint-Domingue for a second time, carrying the title of Head Commissioner of the Third Commission sent by the French *Directoire*.

The new commission brought with them 900 European

soldiers under the capable command of the Generals Donatien Rochambeau and Edme-Ettienne Desfourneaux. The force also imported 30,000 muskets to reinforce the colonial army.

One of the commission's first proclamations targeted the colonists who had fled Saint-Domingue and were currently residing elsewhere as *'émigrés'*. They were to be considered disloyal to France and their properties thereby subject to sequestration.

This created a direct issue for Toussaint's old friend Bayon de Libertat. The two shared nearly a lifetime of history; Toussaint was once owned by Bayon, but it was he who freed the former and set him up with his first plantation as full owner.

Bayon had recently lobbied for an olive branch policy that enticed these absentee colonists to return without being tagged guilty of any crimes. The strategy had been sanctioned by Governor Général Laveaux in the hopes of revitalizing the waning economy.

The French Whites who had escaped to other colonies—including the United States—were needed for their agricultural expertise, investment capital, and properties. They were guaranteed safety and inexpensive labor in exchange for their return.

These labor work codes were originally implemented by Sonthonax and Polvérel in 1793 and were presently being enforced by Toussaint in the North and Rigaud in the South. The ex-slaves—now "Cultivators"—were allocated a plot of land on former plantations in which to grow crops both for their consumption and to sell. In exchange, they provided five days of labor to the landowners at a rate set by the government. Landowners could elect to offer additional compensation or none at all.

This made for an uneasy arrangement. Many of the Cultivators were working on the same properties and for the same masters they'd previously toiled under or suffered from as slaves. In addition, the policies and labor responsibilities were strictly enforced by Toussaint and Rigaud's armies.

Four weeks after the new proclamation essentially reneged the assurances to the *émigrés* from Governor Général Laveaux and Toussaint, Laveaux found himself alone in a private office at the *Hôtel de la Couronne* with Sonthonax; who had again leased several rooms and office space from Henry Christophe upon his arrival back to the colony.

The Governor Général was in St. Marc with Toussaint meeting with city officials and both were not present to receive the new commissioners upon their arrival a month prior. However, upon hearing news of the new commission, both set out for *Cap-Français* to offer a proper welcome.

During their journey to *Cap Français,* Sonthonax—forever impulsive—made several public decrees unbeknownst to the Governor Général, including the émigrés policy. However, by this time many that had previously fled had returned and reactivated their previously dormant properties. Others were presently on ships bound to do so as well, and even more were making travel preparations.

Sonthonax was in the process of arranging a luncheon for Toussaint and Laveaux to persuade them to endorse his new policy. First, though, he wished to consult with the Governor General alone.

"Étienne, these *Grands Blancs* are nothing but trouble. Do you not remember the disorder they caused with the traitor Galbaud back in 1793?" asked Sonthonax, after the two briefly shared pleasantries.

"Indeed Commissioner, I remember it well," Laveaux replied, his eyes remaining on the proclamation document.

"They nearly burnt the entire damned city to the ground!"

Laveaux looked up, locking eyes with Sonthonax.

"As I recall, Commissioner, it was the rebels of *Macaya* that you collaborated with who ransacked the town and burned our city."

Sonthonax pivoted adeptly.

"But why was it necessary? Because of the treacherous

Grands Blancs who are now *Émigres*! I was forced to make a deal with the devil to save the colony."

"Blame can be attributed to many sides, Sonthonax. For example, I am to blame for not having a force strong enough to quell the violence at the time," Laveaux responded. "However, the *Grands Blancs* lost a vast number of lives and properties and wish to leave that atrocity in the past."

"Do not forget the *Petits Blancs* were as, if not more culpable for much of the destruction," he added.

"And the next time they believe their wishes are not met?" Sonthonax shot back. "Another revolt? A new insurrection? More destruction in the name of equality?"

"The *Grand Blancs* are responsible for building half of this colony," answered Laveaux matter-of-factly. "Most of the *Gens de Couleurs* owe their success to them. Many were financed, freed from slavery, and even sired by a *Blanc, non*?"

Sonthonax nodded his head slightly—a small concession.

"And what does Bayon de Libertat wish to gain?" he asked, pushing the conversation forward.

"He is the link between the *Émigrés* and the colonial government. His word holds these agreements together, as they trust him—not you, nor I, nor our government. After all, can you not fault them after this new proclamation which directly works against their interests and that of the colony?" responded Laveaux.

"But what is the profit to this Bayon de Libertat?"

"Toussaint Louverture," stated Laveaux.

"Toussaint Louverture?" asked Sonthonax, confused.

"He loves him as a son. He was once Toussaint's owner before setting him free and investing in his first plantation. He wishes Toussaint to succeed in returning this colony to its former glory."

Sonthonax pondered this information for several moments.

"What are your sentiments toward the great Lieutenant Governor General Toussaint Louverture, Étienne?" Sonthonax asked, his sarcasm obvious.

"I owe my life to the man," replied Laveaux, a spark igniting behind his eyes. "France owes this colony, or what remains of it, to him. Toussaint is this colony's future!"

He paused, attempting to reign in his passionate tone.

"I consider him a brother, not only in arms."

"Your immense affection for him is apparent," responded Sonthonax, unfazed by the Governor's sudden fire. "That makes you blind, my friend. He is a dangerous man, Étienne."

"Pray tell, how so?"

"He is cunning, ambitious, calculating, and resourceful," responded Sonthonax.

"Exactly the skills that render him qualified for his current position," answered Laveaux.

"He will remove any obstacle in his path to get what he wants!"

"You are not appreciative of what he has done for this colony, Commissioner?"

"For the colony—or for himself?" Sonthonax quipped.

"Lay your thoughts out for me, Commissioner," said Laveaux, shifting in his seat. "What is it about Toussaint you consider so dangerous?"

"You are a brilliant military mind, Laveaux. So skilled in your craft you could win a battle with any army in the world. A strong tactician, weapons expert, strategist, logistical master, lethal warrior, and able to march men to their death for any cause you deem worthy for them to die for," began Sonthonax. "But you are not a politician."

"I thank God for that every day," replied Laveaux, a smile flashing across his face.

"I, on the other hand, am no Général. I cannot lead men into battle. I cannot load a rifle, swing a sword, or punch a man. I vanquish my opponents by debating in the halls of the National Assembly; by convincing intelligent men to see an issue as I do. I navigate the machinations of hooligans and hypocrites with ease. I am a politician."

"I can certainly agree that your military experience is lacking and your political ones are keen," Laveaux replied with a sarcastic tone of his own. "What is your point, Commissioner?"

"Toussaint is you and I combined—don't you see?" Sonthonax implored. "He is a master politician and able warrior. A truly lethal combination. The man was a planter and healer before skillfully assembling an army, joining the Spanish, winning battles against us, the French, then coming back to us and destroying the Spanish! As we speak, he is routing those red-coated British—all while being hailed by the public."

"So, is it not for the best that he is our ally and loyal to the French Republic?"

"Mark my words, Étienne. He will find a way to eliminate both of us. That, I can guarantee, because you and I are in his way," Sonthonax concluded.

"You are paranoid, Léger," Laveaux chuckled, dismissing the topic with a wave of his hand. "Tell me now, what is the purpose of this meeting you have called? Your bloody proclamations have already stirred up a hornet's nest."

"I wish to discover whether Toussaint will support them…," Sonthonax paused. "And me."

Laveaux remained silent.

"You do know that I almost had him arrested for a loose tongue a while back?"

"I had heard something of that nature. Not a particularly wise political move on your part," Laveaux replied.

"Well, rather than chains, I have a gift for him today," answered Sonthonax.

"A gift?"

"Scholarships to a prestigious Parisian school for his two elder sons, Placide and Isaac," replied Sonthonax with a smile.

"You do not shower gifts without reason, Commissioner. As you said, you are a politician."

"If I hold his—I mean, 'host'—his two sons in France, I maintain some leverage over the great Toussaint Louverture. As a loving father and husband, he would allow no harm come to them."

Laveaux felt his stomach churn. "Commissioner, I—"

Two knocks on the door interrupted their conversation.

"Enter," called Sonthonax.

A well-dressed staff member opened the door and stated, "General Toussaint Louverture is here for his lunch appointment with you, Commissioner."

"Very well. Inform him that I am on my way to the table now."

As the young man shut the door once more, Sonthonax turned to address Laveaux.

"Étienne, wait 5 minutes before arriving at the table. I do not wish for the general to have the impression that we are colluding or plotting against him."

He stood to leave, throwing a final comment over his shoulder.

" A mere *political* precaution, I assure you."

Laveaux arrived at the table several minutes after Sonthonax, greeting Toussaint warmly as Sonthonax looked on.

"You two are quite fond of each other," Sonthonax offered.

"We have accomplished great things for this colony, Commissioner," replied Laveaux, smiling at Toussaint.

"I am hopeful you will allow us to continue that mission Commissioner," said Toussaint, taking his seat.

"Ah, yes. I do commend you on helping to stabilize the situation here. You have greatly assisted our Governor Général," Sonthonax replied. "France is eternally grateful for your service, Lieutenant Governor Général."

"I am a servant of the French Republic," stated Toussaint. "It is my honor and duty to have been instrumental in the cause."

"Of course, you were once devoted to King Louis the

Sixteenth—or rather, Citizen Louis Capet," replied Sonthonax, referring to the name given to the former French King executed by guillotine back in 1793.

"Indeed I was then and always will be a servant of France. At one time, the ruler and sovereign of my beloved country was the King," Toussaint shot back, agitated at the implied questioning of his integrity. "I served the King because I served France!"

"Do you now denounce the monarchy, Général? Do you embrace the French Revolution and many advances it has provided your people?" pushed Sonthonax.

"Are you referring to emancipation?" asked Toussaint.

"Among other things, yes."

"It is not a liberty of circumstance, conceded to us alone, that we wish; it is the adoption of the absolute principle that no man, born Black or White, can be the property of his fellow man. Is this what you speak of, Commissioner?"

"I am held in high regard by our fellow citizens as the Frenchman who granted them their freedom—and I am grateful for your help in quelling the violence in the colony that resulted, Général."

"The revolution of Saint-Domingue was taking its course. I saw that the Whites could not endure because they were divided and overpowered by our numbers; I congratulated myself that I was a Black man," replied Toussaint.

"I intend to proclaim it a crime for any man, Black, White, or mixed, to threaten that the freedom of former Black slaves can ever be revoked or that one man can ever own another," Sonthonax proudly asserted.

"We are only free today because we are the stronger; we will again become slaves when the government regains the upper hand," countered Toussaint.

Laveaux's head moved back and forth between Sonthonax and Toussaint, enthralled by both men's clever wit. Clearly, there was no love lost between the two. Laveaux could not help but imagine that they despised each other. He was bearing witness to a battle of intellects, veiled accusations volleyed about under the guise of normal conversation. Attempting to gain some control, he issued a statement.

"I understand you have brought 30,000 muskets for our army, Commissioner."

"Yes—a large stock of muskets has been purchased and is now being loaded into warehouses at the docks, Governor Général. I am authorizing Général Donatien Rochambeau to use his discretion on the appropriate distribution, but I do intend for some to be given to ex-slaves."

"That is not wise, Commissioner," Toussaint stated. "These weapons should be consigned to the Governor Général who shall order their distribution where he feels necessary."

"Is that your wish as well, Governor Général?" Sonthonax asked, turning to Laveaux.

"It is the most orderly protocol," replied Laveaux.

"How would you handle these arms, Governor?"

"I'd hand them over to my Lieutenant Governor, for distribution."

Sonthonax eyed Laveaux and Toussaint. This particular battle was not worth confronting them both, he decided.

"Done," Sonthonax said, clapping his hands. "Général Louverture, you will receive the munitions for distribution, provided I participate and can ensure a portion reaches the Cultivators as an act of solidarity."

"Solidarity with the Cultivators or I?" asked Toussaint suspiciously.

"Both!" Sonthonax replied quickly. "Now, with regards to Général Donatien Rochambeau, I am assigning him the responsibility of the Spanish colony ceded in the treaty of Basel and placed under French protection and control. He has come with 900 European soldiers to aid in this task."

"More than enough," answered Toussaint.

"Indeed," added Laveaux.

Two uniformed servers arrived, one with a pitcher of water to fill their glasses.

"May I interrupt your meeting, Gentlemen, to recite the special dishes available for lunch?" asked the first of the servers.

"Please do. I am ready to enjoy another delightful lunch at this fine establishment!" replied Sonthonax. The tension at the table instantly eased.

The server recited an assortment of appetizers, entrées, and desserts, while his cohort continued to pour water and offer each of them wine. With their orders quickly recorded, business resumed.

"Now, Commissioner. Let us address the sensitive issue of the *Émigrés*," Toussaint began. "You issued this proclamation without any input from either the Governor Général or myself."

"There was no need for consultation. The proclamation is just and right. The *Émigrés* are traitors to France and thus are not welcome in this colony," answered Sonthonax.

"How are we to restart our economy without the investment and expertise of the *Grands Blancs*, Commissioner?"

"Oh, I trust you will think of something, *Mon Général*. Our citizens are quite capable of stimulating the economy without them," replied Sonthonax slyly. "Confiscate the traitors' lands and distribute the acreage to capable planters or the Cultivators. Lease it to them and fill the coffers of the government!" Sonthonax's voice began to rise in volume. "Divide it and pay your soldiers—I don't care. But the original owners are not coming back to work them!"

Toussaint looked over to Laveaux, who only shook his head and closed his eyes.

"What of the *Grands Blancs* who have already arrived? Bayon de Libertat assured them the return of their properties and my protection. I gave him my word! To make these promises on behalf of our government, of myself, and the Governor Général —" Toussaint protested.

"A small blemish on your record, General," Sonthonax cut Toussaint off. "Your reputation will survive it."

"I am faithfully devoted to the Republic Commissioner, but

not at the expense of my conscience or my honor," Toussaint responded angrily.

"Commissioner; General, we can certainly find common ground here," inserted Laveaux before tempers could flare any further. "Commissioner, consider allowing the *Grands Blancs* who have already returned and begun their operations to continue. Assure them in writing that they are protected."

He then turned to Toussaint. "In exchange, consider advising all future *Émigrés* that their return is no longer welcome due to their choice of abandoning the colony at its weakest. Can we agree on that, gentlemen?"

"What of those currently en route to the colony? They have already applied and been approved for visas, Governor Général," asked Toussaint.

"They would be considered as already engaged and should be reinstated, I would reason," answered Laveaux, watching carefully for Sonthonax's reaction before forging ahead. "Can you sell this to Bayon, Toussaint?"

"I have not yet agreed to any of this nonsense, Governor Général," began Sonthonax.

"Well, what say you?" Laveaux asked, shooting him a stern look. "If Toussaint agrees to tarnish his word, do we not have a compromise?"

"Général?" Sonthonax offered, turning to Toussaint.

"In the pursuit of peace in this colony, then yes, I agree," replied Toussaint, meeting the Commissioner's eyes.

"Well, then, we have an agreement," said Sonthonax, slapping his palm against the table. "Have the papers drawn for my signature; any *Émigrés* already here or in the process of traveling to the colony are exempt from the new decree. Those without approved visas as of today are not welcome."

As if on cue, three servers arrived with a delicious selection of appetizers, presented in a synchronized theatrical method.

Sonthonax's disposition always softened with food, and with the negotiations complete he freely dug into his plates with abandon.

Toussaint was a light eater, on the other hand, picking at his food and consuming little as the conversation continued over an array of personal subjects. With the precision of a cobra, Sonthonax found the perfect opportunity to enact his secondary scheme as the talk turned to families.

"General, you and I got off to a rocky start years ago—right here in this very restaurant," Sonthonax offered.

"To say the least, Commissioner," Toussaint snapped back. "You issued a warrant for my arrest."

"Those were difficult times. With the revolution back home, many were testing the resolve of the new government, Général," replied Sonthonax. A small smile tugged at the edges of his mouth. "After all, was I not accurate to foresee you becoming rebellious toward France, eh?"

Before Toussaint could retort, Laveaux jumped in once more.

"Commissioner, I recall that you greatly enjoyed your time at the université back in France. Toussaint has expressed to me in the past that he is remiss to have missed such an opportunity himself."

It was a delicate ploy; Laveaux was desperate to keep the conversation civil, but could not let on to his friend that he had any idea of what was to come next.

"Ah, I did indeed, Étienne. It was one of the greatest experiences of my life; and one that I actually wish to offer to our dear friend Toussaint," Sonthonax instantly responded. "Général, I have secured two prestigious scholarships for your sons, Placide and Issac."

"Scholarships? Whatever for?" asked Toussaint, taken aback.

"To help secure the future of *Saint-Domingue, Mon Général*," replied Sonthonax. "Your youth—Black youth—all the youth of this colony, are its future. They must achieve the best education possible so they may one day govern this colony themselves."

Toussaint was disarmed and had to calculate his next response. He was no longer an accomplished military leader in this moment; he was a father. His sons, 15-year-old Placide and 10-

year-old Isaac, both possessed a good understanding of several subjects. They could read and write, had been taught basic arithmetic, spoke and could write the French language, and knew its history. They excelled in farming, horsemanship, and veterinary practices learned from their work and chores around the plantation.

Toussaint had also taught them the holy scripture and imparted his understanding of natural philosophy and the healing medicines of herbs and roots found across the island. But none of these skills would be enough for the prominent roles in running the colony which he envisioned for them.

"How exactly would these arrangements work?" he asked. Sonthonax realized he'd taken the bait.

"I have secured several qualified tutors who would room and board your sons. The boys would attend the *lycée* during the day and, for two hours after school and on Saturdays, be tutored by these qualified mentors. On Sunday, they would attend church and be enrolled in the study of theology," Sonthonax pointedly emphasized the latter, understanding Toussaint's deep-rooted Catholicism.

"What are the tuition and boarding costs?" asked Toussaint.

"Both will be government subsidized, of course. France must have her children of government officials properly educated. Your sons' tuition will be fully funded by the colonial treasury," Sonthonax stated drinking the final remnants of his wine.

"I trust France also wishes my children safe passage en route to their studies?" asked Toussaint.

"The *Wattignies* will be here in early July. She is large, fast, and powerful enough to ram any British blockade she may encounter," replied Sonthonax nonchalantly. "Her captain is a friend of mine, and highly competent. I trust him immensely."

Sonthonax sat up straight and met Toussaint's eyes. This was his final appeal.

"Toussaint, this is an incredible opportunity for your boys. To be schooled in the best institutions of France is to take the final step toward a more equal world."

The three men raised their glasses in a toast.

Toussaint was convinced that sending Placide and Isaac to France for their education was for the best. Suzanne reluctantly agreed after several conversations. When presented to both boys, Isaac reacted with enthusiasm; Placide however, was initially against the idea.

Placide loved the colony—the plantations, his relationships with the workers, his ability to be one with his horse, and the stature he had gained from his father's role as the primary general of the colony all held great allure.

"Father, why do I need to be educated in France? The government men I see are less knowledgeable than you, and you have never been to France," Placide said with conviction in his tone.

"This is true, my son. The difference is I have had a lifetime to study the French Whites. Your White uncle Bayon de Libertat was my teacher. I was tutored by his brother Jerome in my studies, including the teachings of Jesuit theology. I have studied the Whites who have had dealings with the Breda plantation. I have been exposed to the ways of the Whites—but only here in the colony," counseled Toussaint. "What has been your learnings of the Whites, Placide?"

"Limited in that aspect, Father," Placide conceded. "You are right; I have not had many experiences with the Whites from France. But if I stay here, I can begin, just as you did!"

Placide's tone was desperate and he struggled to keep his eyes dry. Toussaint placed a reassuring hand on his shoulder.

"My son, times are rapidly changing. What I learned in my time was quite different than what your education should be today. France has changed. The new government is not as straightforward as the monarchy. There is not one king, but many men who seek to shape the laws and ways of the Republic. Each with their own conflicting and selfish interests, debating on a decree's validity. To protect our interests and those of this colony, you must understand and be able to excel in their court," Toussaint explained.

"But I do not want to leave you, Maman, and the island. I will miss you so if I am far away in a distant land!"

"I will one day need a successor, Placide. You are my eldest son. You must be ready, and this is a necessary sacrifice to prepare you for the challenge. You must accept this as your destiny," Toussaint replied, a balance of firmness and love in his voice. "Do you understand me, my son?"

"I suppose it is the right thing to do if you say it is so, Father" replied Placide.

"Time will pass quickly, Placide, and you will soon return home. But during this time, you will have the opportunity to absorb France and all of its splendor, as I have never been able."

Toussaint pulled Placide tightly to him and embraced him as a child.

"I need you to look after Issac as he admires, respects, and listens to you. You will be the elder in the land of France."

"Yes, Father. I will."

The family began making preparations for the boys' trip, all in agreement that it was for the greater good of themselves and the colony.

As promised, Sonthonax had arranged for Placide and Issac to depart for France aboard the warship *Wattignies* in July. The boys were excited, as they'd never been on a ship of such size and power before. Sonthonax briefed the captain on who the boys were and their importance. He asked that he provide them with his time and explanations during the voyage to keep them entertained. Thus, Placide and Issac embarked on an adventure that would span the remainder of their adolescent lives.

The same month of Placide and Isaac's departure, Sonthonax

found Général Donatien Rochambeau in contempt for his refusal to march into Santo Domingo. The colonial army was holding territory from the British during this time, and could not provide additional soldiers without weakening their position in the colony. Rochambeau had tried to warn Sonthonax that his European force numbering less than 1,000, was not adequate for such a campaign.

Général Rochambeau and Sonthonax argued passionately and as a result, the Commissioner stripped the Général of his rank and ordered his deportation to France—a worrying trend that spoke to the Commissioner's growingly impulsive nature.

Watching these events unfold, Toussaint realized that his future, and that of the colony, would not be in his hands until Sonthonax and Laveaux were no longer the primary decision-makers. While he trusted Laveaux with his life, his friend was a military man to his core and thus an instrument of the state. In Laveaux's mind, France came first, the colony second, and friendships were contingent on oaths of service. He would always dutifully follow orders given by any of his superiors, no matter the personal consequences.

As for Sonthonax, Toussaint believed him a scoundrel in pursuit of absolute power and control. He rallied the Black former slaves to follow and worship him as their savior and supreme leader—which they did, believing to owe him their loyalty for emancipation.

However, those same souls viewed Toussaint as the man who protected them from re-enslavement—who had picked up the torch of Sonthonax when the Commissioner was recalled to France for his trial. Some even began calling Toussaint '*Papa Toussaint*'.

Toussaint resolved that the power wielded by Sonthonax would need to be won back without drama and conflict. If Sonthonax could easily dislodge a man as capable as Général Donatien Rochambeau, destroying a career without so much as a second thought, he could attempt to do the same to him.

The removal of these two Frenchmen would become Toussaint's mission, albeit an extremely delicate one. Sonthonax had extreme leverage over him, after all, as he held the health, safety, and well-being of his children in his hands.

Political care would be of the utmost importance going forward.

Fourteen

SONTHONAX AND RIGAUD

Les Cayes
August 1796

In August of 1796, primary electoral assemblies in Saint-Domingue were formed to elect colonial representatives to the legislative body in France. Through careful maneuvering, Toussaint managed to engineer the results so that both Sonthonax and Laveaux were elected to return to France and represent Saint-Domingue in the National Assembly. Though done without their consent, this still represented prestigious and important roles for the two to play.

For Toussaint, this presented the perfect opportunity to wrest control of the colony and shape its future in his vision, not that of Whites who had grown up far away from its beauty and culture. There was much work to do, but this would be a good first step and the other Commissioners remaining on the island posed no threat, in his opinion.

Toussaint wrote to Laveaux urging him to attack the serious work ahead necessary for the colony. He pleaded with his friend to fight the growing pro-slavery lobby in Paris. He also included a personal note, which read;

As I foresee, and with chagrin, what unpleasantness is likely to happen to you in this unfortunate country, for whose inhabitants you have sacrificed your life, your wife, and your children, as I would not like to be witness to such unhappiness. I wished for you to be named deputy so that you can have the satisfaction to see your own country once again and be safe from the factions that are gestating in Saint-Domingue.

- Toussaint

Laveaux left the island that October. In the *Conseil des Anciens*, he would become an active promoter of Neo-Jacobin ideas within the framework of the bourgeois Republic. He believed in equal rights for all and advocated for the French constitution to apply equally to its colonies.

Sonthonax, on the other hand, resisted his calling to the delegation, instead insisting on completing the remainder of his 18-month term as Commissioner. However, politically backing only the freed slaves and rallying against both the *Blancs* and Mulattos only increased the number of his enemies during this period.

He attempted to rein in André Rigaud—who by then was acting leader of the nearly autonomous state in the South of the colony. Rigaud was intent on refusing any direction in governance from the French colonial authorities—which Sonthonax naturally represented.

André Rigaud was a proud Mulatto and part of the Southern oligarchy of the region. The son of a rich planter and a freed black woman, he'd led a privileged life; educated in Bordeaux and a goldsmith by trade. Though he had money, he'd always been inclined toward the army. He adopted Vincent Oge's ideologies and greatly admired the uprising that followed Oge's and Jean-Baptiste Chavanne's execution years ago, although he was not a believer in emancipation. He at one point had fought with the French army in the American War of Independence.

Experience and charisma made him a brilliant soldier, while his great courage and intelligence won him respect—but he ultimately lacked the advanced qualities of a great leader.

Rigaud was a bad-tempered narcissist and did not possess the willpower to overcome the violence in his character. Narrow-minded, he never succeeded in stifling his feelings of prejudice against the Blacks, nor could he square the disdain the Whites held for him. He also possessed a weakness for drinking, and when inebriated his behavior worsened causing him to act out in outrageous ways. He was power-hungry, with few close friends, and preferred frivolous and shallow relationships over deeper connections.

He considered the South his domain to control and ruled as such. He resented the fact that French commissioners—who knew nothing of the colony—would dare order him to be their partner, or rather puppet, in governance.

Rigaud was now 35 years old and wielded tremendous power, granted to him by the rich and powerful *Gens de Couleurs* who had chosen him as their defender and maintainer of the status quo.

Sonthonax despised Rigaud's arrogance and felt it was his duty to keep him under control. He devised several intrigues to throw Rigaud off balance and force him into critical mistakes. To that end, Sonthonax sent four delegates—Roger LaFontaine, Elias Kerverseau, Patrick Leborgne, and Olivier Rey—to the south with clear directives:

LaFontaine would attack his military power structure; Kerverseau would find and arrest Rigaud's friend Pinchinat, the political scoundrel behind Général Jean-Louis Villatte's uprising, and bring him to *Cap-Français* for trial; Rey would rally the local *Petits Blancs* and fuel their natural prejudice against the Mulattos; Leborgne would endeavor to discredit Rigaud personally—the more embarrassing, the better;

Their mission established, the four set out immediately for *Les Cayes*—Rigaud's stronghold in the South.

That summer, around the time the elections were being held in the North, Rigaud invited his top officers to a celebration at the Club Copa Cabana in downtown *Les Cayes*. He wished to build camaraderie among his commanders for future campaigns against the British across the peninsula. All flocked from their stations spread among the many towns of the South.

The Copa Cabana was a two-story white-washed masonry structure. Entertainment inside the busy nightclub was supplied by musicians and scantily-clad women. Rigaud booked the second floor of the club and arranged for a troop of 'women of the night' to be on hand for his entourage.

Among the guests was Alexandre Pétion, who brought his younger sidekick, Jean-Pierrre Boyer. While Pétion and Boyer were roaming the town earlier that day, they happened into Jean-Baptise Bayard Junior—promptly inviting him to cavort with them at the evening's celebration.

Pétion greatly admired Général Rigaud and wished to impress his friends with an introduction. The evening was exciting for the young guests, who drank, socialized, and cheerfully played with the hired women. At one point Pétion, a Cheroot clenched in his mouth, spotted Rigaud and quickly grabbed Boyer and Junior to lead them toward the *Général*.

Rigaud was resplendent, brandished in a brand new dress uniform. He was of medium height and build, sported short curly hair, and wore a gold earring in his left ear. He was a dark Mulatto with bronze-colored skin seemingly tanned by the sun, a strong sculptured jaw, and dark eyes. The *Général* was handsome and charismatic with a strong presence—of which he was well aware. Two beautiful women stood to either side of him, smiling and laughing; the trophied accessories complimenting his military glamour.

Several Mulatto officers surrounded them at the center of the smoke-filled, rum-perfumed room. The uniforms of the attending officers appeared nearly as brilliant as the *Général's*. In contrast,

Pétion's was faded from washing and its cuffs were frayed at the edges, leaving him feeling rather self-conscious. Rigaud was engaged in the retelling of some old battle story, the group mesmerized and clinging to his every word.

Uproarious laughter signaled that the story had reached its conclusion. Pétion took the moment to approach Rigaud and salute.

"At ease, soldier," commanded Rigaud with a wave of his hand. "Pétion is your name, correct?"

"*Oui, mon* Général, Alexandre Pétion" he replied, lowering his hand. "I wanted to thank you for the invitation to tonight's festivities—as well as my recent promotion."

"Well deserved, Lieutenant—excuse me— *Capitaine* Pétion; Very well deserved indeed," replied Rigaud, raising his glass. "I heard of your heroics while pinned down by the British outside *Léogâne.* In your brilliant escape, all of your men survived—as well as all of my cannon, shot, and powder! Well done!" Rigaud had steadily raised his voice so that his officers could hear. All smiled, cheered, and vigorously patted Pétion on the back.

"You will go far in my army at this pace," added Rigaud. Looking past Pétion, he noticed Junior and Boyer. "Tell me, who are the soldiers in your company—one appears out of uniform?"

"This *mon Général*, is Jean-Pierre Boyer," said Pétion, pulling Boyer to his side. "He is a grenadier in my regiment and an excellent marksman. He was with me at *Léogâne* and proved fearless."

Boyer saluted the General, who returned the gesture.

"My other comrade is not a soldier—he is my good friend Jean-Baptiste Bayard Junior of *Cap-Français*. He is in town scouting the docks for possible business. He represents his family's shipping company," stated Pétion.

"Welcome to *Les Cayes*, young Bayard," Rigaud said, extending his hand towards Junior. "Where is your family's company based, may I ask?"

"Our main headquarters is in *Cap-Français*, sir, and it is

where I reside as well," Junior responded.

A Captain suddenly pushed through the crowd to approach Rigaud.

"*Mon Général*, A gentleman who is a representative of Commissioner Sonthonax has arrived with an urgent dispatch for you."

"We are at a party, Captain," Rigaud replied, his brow furrowed. "Have him report to headquarters tomorrow at 11 am."

With that, Rigaud turned back to the woman on his left, never acknowledging the White Frenchman standing behind the Captain. However, the raised voice of the man instantly caught the General's ear.

"*Général Rigaud*! Commissioner Sonthonax is your superior and I am his emissary. The message in my possession is of the utmost importance and begs an audience this evening—not tomorrow—as ordered by the Commissioner."

Rigaud motioned over one of his officers and whispered something in his ear. The officer left the group and Rigaud moved forward to address the emissary.

"You dare interrupt my festive evening honoring my officers and their sacrifices for their country without even a formal introduction? Do you even have a name you lousy scamp?"

The air was seemingly sucked out of the room. The distant noises of celebration in other areas of the club subsided as all within earshot were now paying rapt attention to the exchange unfolding before them. The emissary appeared stunned and embarrassed at the public indignity he was now suffering at the hands of this Mulatto.

"My name is Roger LaFontaine, Emissary to the Saint-Domingue Commission," he replied.

"Newly arrived from Paris I presume, *Monsieur LaFontaine*?"

"Three weeks ago."

"So, *Monsieur LaFontaine*, are you here to show the niggers and half-breeds of France's colony the ways of servitude?" demanded Rigaud with a sharpness in his voice.

"You have no right to speak with me in that tone," LaFontaine shot back.

"Give me the dispatch," ordered Rigaud before rapidly finishing the remainder of rum in his goblet. LaFontaine began to hand him the wax-sealed envelope before Rigaud snatched it from him. Without opening it, Rigaud stared at him and inquired; "And what does the dispatch say, *Monsieur LaFontaine*?"

"It is an order outlining the reorganization of the Southern Army and designating new assignments for your officers."

The officer Rigaud had sent away returned to whisper in the General's ear. Rigaud nodded and the officer turned and left once more. Pétion, Boyer, and Junior watched with astonishment and shot puzzled looks at each other at the political game playing out before their very eyes.

"You think your lily-white complexion gives you the authority to come to our island and tell me how to manage my army? How to manage our colony?" Rigaud's voice continued to rise with each question.

"This dispatch was meant to be confidential, as evidenced by its seal—yet you know what it says. Why is that, *Monsieur LaFontaine*?"

Unfazed, LaFontaine produced a wry smile.

"Because I am the architect of the pen, *Général*. Should it be known, I consider all you of African blood in need of management—whether fully Black or *Gens de Couleurs* like yourself," he replied, slowing his pronunciation of the latter; an indication of his privileged Parisian upbringing.

Rigaud adhered strictly to the race-based caste system of the island, finding great insult in being aligned in any way with Blacks.

"Is that so?" he asked, anger quickly boiling under his still-calm face.

"You are all Africans in my eyes," LaFontaine continued. It was unclear whether he was aware of the personal danger he was constructing. "I imagine you and Toussaint Louverture could be brothers. After all, both your mothers are from the Allada tribe of the kingdom of Dahomey back in Africa, *non*?"

Rigaud's temporal vein began to pulsate and a small droplet of sweat formed on his forehead from the tension of keeping his temper under control.

"Of course, he is your superior in command," LaFontaine said, a mocking smile spreading across his face. "How does it feel to be in the service of a Black, some would say even a *Nèg Kay* - House Nigger?"

"I would mind the wagging of that tongue of yours," warned Rigaud, feeling the eyes of his entourage looking to him for a response to the insults of the Frenchman.

"What do the *Petits Blancs* in the colony say with such eloquence, *Général*? *Le 'Colon guette ta Mère'*—or the niggers in Creole, *'Koulan gèt Manman w'*?—*The colonist is watching your mother?*"

Rigaud was at his boiling point. He stared daggers at LaFontaine, who in turn wrongly interpreted his silence as servitude and obedience. After all, who did these savages think they were?

Believing to have established the upper hand, LaFontaine couldn't resist venturing further in his performance for the crowd gathered.

"Tell me *Général*; was your mother held down for your conception or did the shrew seek out a White father on purpose. Many Black women love French love, non?"

Utter silence engulfed the room. Rigaud's entire entourage looked at him with a mixture of shock and rage; several gasps escaped open mouths, and the women began to slowly shift away toward the walls. Rigaud turned his back to the Frenchman and glanced beyond the rear doors to the veranda and its charming wrought iron railing. He inhaled deeply and turned back to face his adversary.

"Walk with me," Rigaud said to the group as he exited the crowded salon of the second floor and out onto the covered veranda. "LaFontaine, let me show you something,"

Rigaud's entourage followed him out, as did LaFontaine. The air was thick and heavy with the evening's humidity. The August heat still clung from the day and a light breeze from the ocean gave the air a salty scent.

Others from the club were also moved out to the veranda, whispering and sensing a potential altercation.

"Well then, I shall open this urgent dispatch to learn what our esteemed Commissioner has ordered—as penned expertly by the architect before us, *Monsieur Roger LaFontaine*."

Rigaud held it with two fingers as if it were diseased, and handed it to an officer on his right. "Unseal this and read it to me," he ordered.

The officer carefully opened the document. It was everything that LaFontaine had said; orders in detail for every commander's new station, assignment, and how many men they would retain.

"So, *Monsieur LaFontaine*, the architect; I do not hear where my command is to be in this official dispatch. Tell me, where am I to be stationed?"

"Commissioner Sonthonax has ordered your transfer to a regiment in Guadeloupe, where you will oversee the adherence and discipline of the new cultivation work codes in that colony," LaFontaine responded.

A server arrived with a tray of rum for the entourage. Rigaud motioned over the two women who had been standing with him. The first took a goblet from the tray, sipped a taste, and handed the goblet to Rigaud. The General took the goblet, put an arm around her waist, and brought her face to his to give a light and gentle kiss on her cheek. He then turned to the second, placed his left hand on her buttock, and pulled her close for a brief kiss on her lips. He then lifted the goblet and looked at his officers.

"Drink up, my mighty warriors. You are the very best France has to offer and this evening is to your honor!" he ordered.

The men in unison shouted, *"AU SUD!—'To the South!'"* and took swigs from their goblets.

Suddenly, Rigaud swiftly covered the distance between himself and LaFontaine, bringing his face inches from the White man's.

"Here is what I think of you, the Commissioner, and your fucking orders!"

He threw the contents of his goblet into LaFontaine's eyes, who yelped in surprise. Before the Frenchman could react further, Rigaurd violently seized him by the waist and hoisted him over the railing. LaFontaine's legs kicked fruitlessly as he fell over the side, crashing ten feet down to the street below, his scream of pain the lone sound to break the stunned silence of the crowd.

"There, *Monsieur LaFontaine*—the architect! Take that as my answer to your Commissioner!" Rigaud yelled down as the man writhed in pain. Rigaud then tossed the dispatch off, which floated slowly to the street below.

The officer Rigaud had whispered to earlier was waiting below and retrieved the papers. A donkey was walked to him by two shirtless boys dressed in ragged cut-off trousers. The officer took some twine from his pocket and tied the three pages of the dispatch to the tail of the awaiting donkey. A roped plank of wood with the freshly-painted words 'Commissioner Sonthonax - The Jackass' was then tied to the donkey's neck.

The two boys led the animal down the street as Rigaud turned and shouted to the crowd; "Observe the Commissioner from France. The intelligent Ass!"

The crowd roared with laughter. Pétion looked upon Rigaud in awe. He appeared like a king holding court with his top officers at his side, all in impeccable dress uniforms as if actors in a stage play.

Rigaud made his way back inside, a woman on each arm. Passing Pétion he offered; "Come sit with the big boys, young Pétion. I hear you have become quite the artillery expert. Come school me on your craft and bring young Boyer along and that

Bayard fellow too. The government of the South may require a new inter-island shipping company after today.

COPA CABANA

Daniel J.D. Bayard

"Pétion, Boyer, and Junior looked at each other and smiled broadly as they followed Rigaud and his entourage into the club.

An officer approached Rigaud as he entered and pulled him aside.

"What shall I do with the Frenchman, m*on Général*?" whispered the officer.

"Have his wounds cleaned and dressed—to show him we are not the savages he claims," replied a smiling Rigaud, before narrowing his eyes and cutting his tone. "Then, to show him we are not to be trifled with, cut his tongue from his mouth for insulting my parents—particularly my dear mother—and cut off his index fingers to make it more difficult to author such useless and vile proclamations."

"*Oui, mon Général*. Anything further?"

"Hire a wagon to deliver him to the Government House in *Cap-Français*. He can deliver my response in person to Commissioner Sonthonax," laughed Rigaud. "Do this and return quickly. I have a feast prepared and I want you to be a part of it."

The officer smiled and saluted as he left the room to dispatch the emissary to *Cap-Français*.

Pétion, Boyer, and Junior spent the evening drinking, eating, joking, dancing, and romancing with girls until the morning daylight concluded the party.

Later that following day, two more ragged-dressed boys replaced the ones from the night before, continuing to parade the donkey around town for all to see. The tired donkey clip-clopped down one street and up the other with its head lowered as citizens either laughed at the humor or shook their heads in disgust upon seeing Sonthonax's sign around the animal's neck, and the pages of the decree tied to its tail.

Les Cayes was divided on the occurrences of the night before, and by that afternoon townsfolk were arguing amongst themselves in saloons, the town square, workplaces, and the streets. Smack in the middle of the discussions and arguments was Olivier Rey—another official sent by Sonthonax.

The *Petits Blancs* and *Gens de Couleur* hated each other, so it wasn't at all difficult for Rey to stir up several groups with his twisted stories, downright lies, and potty conspiracy theories. As he told it, the *Petits Blancs* were purposefully kept poor and hardworking by the Mulattos. He reminded the *Petits Blancs* that they were *'les nobles de la peau'* — *'the noblemen of the skin'*.

Most Mulattos in the southern region were richer and more well-educated than their *Petits Blancs* peers; many surpassed even a sizable percentage of *Grands Blancs* in their prosperity. The *Petits Blancs* resented working side by side with the slaves—now-paid ex-slave laborers—in shipbuilding, housing construction, and other work formerly their sole domain. The tense racial situation in the South was potentially explosive and the local militia had their hands full mediating the constant clashes. Rey used all of this to his tactical advantage.

Violence soon erupted in the town, fueled by Rey's machinations and Rigaud's outrageous donkey stunt. Both knowingly and not, the two served as sparks to a powder keg of acrimony.

Riots enveloped the streets with the torching of homes, businesses, and even murders perpetrated by both Mulattos and *Petits Blancs*. The darker-skinned and Black *Gens de Couleurs* suffered as well, despite their attempts to remain above the fray. The militia was called to control the unruly mobs over the days that followed in an attempt to return *Les Cayes* to order. Rey naturally took the opportunity to spread the word far and wide that the blame for the chaos all fell on the arrogant and uncontrollable Général Rigaud.

Days later in *Cap-Français*, a wagon arrived at the front of

Government House. A battered LaFontaine stumbled out, his cheeks swollen from a cloth in his tongue-less mouth and both hands wrapped in bandages. The driver helped him to the guardhouse and informed the soldier to take him to Commissioner Sonthonax at once.

Sonthonax was seated at the Governor's desk when LaFontaine was brought in. Unable to speak, LaFontaine wrote his report on the events in *Les Cayes* as best he could. Without the benefit of his index finger, the transcribed report was nearly illegible.

There was no mention of his insults toward Rigaud, only of the latter's behavior, insubordination, and stated disdain towards the Commissioners—in particular Sonthonax himself.

Elsewhere, Sonthonax's third agent, Elias Kerverseau, arrived at the home of Pierre Pinchinat with six soldiers from the *Cap-Français* garrison and an arrest warrant. They took him with little resistance other than his demands to see Général Rigaud. His requests were refused, and Pinchinat was scurried out of the city.

Before leaving, false information was provided to the household staff alleging that Pinchinat had provided a wealth of damaging information; most scandalously the accusation that Rigaud had orchestrated the *Villatte* rebellion. Pinchinat was supposedly distraught by his actions during that treasonous ordeal and was only acting under grave threat by Rigaud. They told the staff he had left voluntarily and under the protection of soldiers to give a full accounting to Commissioner Sonthonax at *Cap Français*.

Rigaud was furious upon hearing the news, shocked by how easily his friend Pinchinat would betray him.

However, it would be Sonthonax's final emissary, Patrick LeBorgne, who would plunge the proverbial dagger deepest into Rigaud's heart.

Rigaud spoiled his women with extravagance. His wife, Marie Anne Villeneuve, was utterly devoted to her husband, bearing him four children. But this was hardly enough to keep him from freely roaming the bedrooms of others. The General maintained three quasi-marital relationships with mistresses who sired five children.

The women were well taken care of as long as they refused the affections of other men and remained at his disposal any time he wished. Should they ever stray, both the mistress and children were forever cut off from any financial assistance. Rigaud managed to develop good partner and paternal relations with them all, however bizarre and unconventional the entire charade.

A year before that fateful night at the Copa Cabana, Rigaud had taken on a new mistress by the name of Nathalie Moulin. At 23, she was twelve years his junior and the most fetching of them all. He spent much of his free time with her and showered the girl with affection, admiration, and treasure.

Of all the women of *Les Cayes*, she was arguably one of the most beautiful. A Creole Mulatto with soft shiny skin, long black hair, mesmerizing blue eyes, a physique admired by any man or woman who beheld her, and a commanding personality that caused even the hardened Rigaud to swoon.

She was the center of attention in any room she entered, and Rigaud's ego loved it. Every man wanted her, but she was his alone. He was powerless to refuse any of her desires and she very well stretched that weakness to the limit. She was completely spoiled, receiving jewels, money, attention, and everything else she asked for or demanded from him.

Patrick LeBorgne was a strapping twenty-eight-year-old Frenchman who resembled a Greek God. He was muscular with porcelain white skin and an imposing jaw. His fashion was impeccable and his mastery of the French language and its ballads of love easily captivated any woman in his presence. LeBorgne was also a loyal and intelligent bureauocrat, who fully investigated the entire love quandary of André Rigaud—his twisted love entanglements, children both in and out of wedlock, and the particularly frivolous nature of his latest mistress, the young Nathalie Moulin.

Nathalie was staying with her friend Annette on the outskirts of *Les Cayes* that summer while the *Général* was making preparations for his upcoming campaigns against the British. LeBorgne spied on her entourage and eventually befriended Richard, one of Annette's brothers. He fed Richard rumors that Rigaud had acquired another mistress during his planning, sure that this false information would quickly reach Nathalie. With her status as the apple of her lover's eye and the extravagant lifestyle it afforded under threat, Nathalie was furious.

LeBorgne orchestrated a Saturday afternoon luncheon at the town's Government House several days later and invited Richard to bring his friends, family, and any others he thought would enjoy the event. LeBorgne prepared his most regal suit with the sash of the Commission in red, white, and blue on loan to him from Sonthonax.

He greeted all who entered with lavish praise and compliments; the townspeople adored him. The only person in attendance to whom he withheld his massive charisma was Nathalie, who received minimal attention. Upon their *'au revoir'* LeBorgne appeared aloof—which infuriated her. She had never been ignored like this, causing her to desperately crave this man's affection.

The following day Richard invited LeBorgne to the family's plantation for an afternoon game of croquet. The statuesque Frenchman continued to ignore Nathalie throughout the afternoon until the young girl could bear it no longer. She marched up to him in full view of the party and demanded the two have a private conversation. By the end of the afternoon, she had borne him her soul. Within the week, at the prompting of her broken heart, she'd seduced him into her bed.

The two became obvious lovers, inseparable and in plain sight of her hosts. Toward the end of their third week together, he'd convinced her to sail with him to Paris to continue, as he called it, 'the love affair of the century'.

That same week, Rigaud traveled to the small hamlet, a 2-hour ride from *Les Cayes*. He'd not received any of Nathalie's letters in weeks. Upon arrival, he interrogated Annette, who quickly confessed to the love affair between Nathalie and a gallant White man, as well as their shared plans of escape. Rigaud was devastated which manifested into a rage; he mounted his horse and immediately left, terrified of what destruction his heart might wreak should he hear anything further.

The night before their supposed departure from *Le Cap*, LeBorgne stole away to the docks, abandoning Nathalie and setting sail for home. The young girl dutifully awaited him in their hotel room for two days before she realized that he had disappeared forever.

Nathalie remained at the hotel crying for LeBorgne and mourning her foolish loss of Rigaud for ten more days until she was forced to leave. Having no money to pay the bill for room and food at the expensive Grand Hotel, she was arrested, found guilty of fraud, and thrown into the local jail for 90 days.

She was not permitted to return to *Les Cayes* after her release until she satisfied her debt to the hotel and paid the legal fines from her conviction. She'd lost everything, most especially her dignity. It was rumored that she began a career in prostitution to pay her fines, restitution to the hotel, and food and boarding at the brothel owned by Madame Babet. With her natural beauty and grace, Nathalie found the profession lucrative, though distasteful, and in the coming years, she resigned to her fate.

LeBorgne had succeeded in his mission to inflict as much personal pain, insult, humiliation, and embarrassment as possible on Rigaud. Sonthonax toasted his success and rewarded LeBorgne with a letter of commendation and recommendation for promotion to a higher post back home in Paris.

Thus were the despicable intrigues engineered by both Sonthonax and Rigaud—who remained bitter enemies from that summer forward. Rather than finding a diplomatic solution to the problem of Riguad, Sonthonax opted to make the situation far more hostile.

Sometime after Nathalie's betrayal, Pinchinat escaped from his captors while en route to *Cap-Français.* He ran immediately to Rigaud in an effort to explain what happened. Rigaud, fortunately, spared his life, and now knew of the Commissioner's reprehensible behavior and tactics of deceit. He also quickly learned of Olivier Rey's treachery and manipulation in the city on behalf of Sonthonax. Finally, he received news that the lover whom Nathalie took was Patrick LeBorgne—yet another emissary of Sonthonax.

The battle lines had been drawn.

In early October of 1796, Sonthonax, with the full backing of his fellow commissioners, wrote a letter to the French *Directoire* concerning the behavior of André Rigaud. He described mutiny, treason, and separatist actions intended to provoke a reaction— namely the incident involving the donkey and LaFontaine.

The letter also voiced their concerns for the blind loyalty that the Black troops maintained for Toussaint Louverture and their suspicion that this loyalty may override their duty to France. They made no recommendations for change, only wishing to make notes in the official record in the case of future ramifications.

Thus was the turbulent year of return for Commissioner Léger-Félicité Sonthonax in 1796.

FIFTEEN

TOUSSAINT GOES BACK
TO ENNERY

Ennery
December 1796

With two hundred horsemen, including his honor guard of 25 of the best soldiers under his command, Toussaint and his troops arrived at the Sancey Plantation at Ennery in the early dawn hours the Saturday before Christmas. As the party entered the plantation's main road, they were immediately stopped at a heavily fortified gate—which satisfied Toussaint immensely. He had stationed one-thousand troops on the outskirts of Sancey to await further deployment orders and act as a security force in his absence.

Their identities confirmed, Toussaint allowed his tired troops to retire and rest and requested four of his most trusted honor guard to escort him to the main house. As it came into view, he closed his eyes, breathing deep the rich scent of roasting coffee beans that had cooled during the night. It was good to be home.

Daylight was just breaking as the riders approached the front yard of the *gwo kay* – the big main house. A loud click of a rifle being cocked greeted them, accompanied by a deep voice.

"*Kanpe! Ki moun ki ap vini la* - Halt! Who goes there?!"

Toussaint smiled instantly at the voice of his trusted right-hand man.

"It is I, Othello. We have returned!" shouted Toussaint.

"Thank God Master Breda—ah, I mean—Mr. Louverture; I mean, *Général* Breda, no, I mean *Général* Louverture!" stuttered Othello. "Please excuse me, Master. I mean excuse me, *Général*."

"Come, Othello, shake my hand and forget the titles. You and I have been together far too long for all of that," Toussaint said, grasping Othello's huge hand while waving his other. "You have performed your duties exactly as I asked. This plantation is a fortress!"

"Just as you ordered, Sir. Ordering me to stay here, even though I wished to go with you, was a wise move. Our lives have been threatened countless times," Othello replied.

Toussaint lowered his voice and whispered, "Where is Madame Breda?"

"She will be down momentarily if not already. She still enjoys her coffee each morning in the same rocking chair she used to do with you on the back porch. If you head back, you will probably find her there now," Othello whispered back.

Toussaint snuck around to the back kitchen where he knew the servants would be brewing coffee and preparing breakfast. He peeked into the dimly lit room and two of the women saw him, they raised their hands to their faces and burst into broad grins. Toussaint placed his finger over his lips to silence them.

He picked up the tray with the pot, sugar, and warm goat milk and added a second cup. He took a cloth, placed it over his arm, and pantomimed as a server approaching the porch. Suzanne was just exiting the main house to take her chair—completely unaware of his presence as he moved behind her. He loved this woman so much and had missed her tremendously.

"Your coffee Madame, straight from the best beans of the *Roufittier* plantation just to the north."

Instantly recognizing his voice, Suzanne stood and whipped around with a huge smile as tears began pouring from her eyes.

"Toussaint! Thank God you are safe! Come to me, my love."

They embraced for several minutes before falling right into their morning coffee routine as if he'd never left. Suzanne demanded to know everything Toussaint had accomplished and experienced since they were last together six months prior, bidding *au revoir* to Placide and Isaac. Toussaint took his time regaling her with updates; it was as if no time had been lost between them.

Christmas at Sancey was a vacation Toussaint needed immensely. As a devout Christian, this was the holiest of times for him and Suzanne. The colony remained in relative calm during the holidays as well; Whites, Blacks, and Mulattos—citizens, government employees, or soldiers alike—all seemed to ease their tensions with respect for the season.

Assisting in this undeclared cease of hostilities, the British campaign had stalled due to a lack of munitions, as the English parliament had grown impatient with the lack of progress in conquering Saint-Domingue.

The victorious capture of the capital of *Port Républicain, Saint-Marc*, a swath of the Southern peninsula, and the Northwest Territory failed to be enough to satisfy the policymakers back home in London who demanded a rapid return on their investment.

Also dividing the politicians' attention was an ongoing uprising in Jamaica by the Maroons. This superseded the Saint-Domingue expenditures as the Jamaican colony was a working tax base already, albeit minuscule compared to the potential in Saint-Domingue, which required the army's more immediate attention.

At the end of the second week of January, Henry Christophe arrived at the plantation and was escorted into the Sancey library by

Othello.

"You have come, Henry! I am so pleased you are here," greeted Toussaint. "I see that you have already met my right-hand man; Othello, this is the hotel manager I told you about."

Othello looked to Henry and offered, "The *Général* says you make excellent shrimp. We do not have any shrimp here, but I will serve some local fish from our rivers during your stay, *Monsieur* Christophe. I will grill it on charcoal myself. Anyone who takes care of our *Général* is welcome in this home."

"Thank you for your hospitality, Othello," replied Henry, genuinely humbled. "*Général*, thank you for the invitation. I see that your security is quite impressive and effective. I would hate to think what could have happened to me if my name was not provided to them!"

"I see you waited until the last minute to accept," replied Toussaint. "Tomorrow is the fifteenth you know—but I am sure you wished to spend every moment possible with your family and that warms my heart immensely"

"You already know me well, *Général.*"

"Othello, have the guest room readied. Henry will be our guest here in the *gwo kay* until he has his assignment. Send for Yolande to take measurements for an officer's uniform. I want it stitched immediately."

"Thank you *Général,* I am at your duty for any assignment you deem appropriate," Henry remarked.

Toussaint and Henry spoke for several hours before he was shown to his room. The two spent even more time together over the coming days, and the more Toussaint was with him, the more he believed Henry would become instrumental in his vision for the colony's future.

A week after his arrival, Henry departed Sancey along with Toussaint and 200 men—including the honor guard—toward the town of *Plaisance*. They were to meet Toussaint's men and

Sonthonax who would soon arrive from *Cap-Français* to begin the distribution of the 30,000 muskets, one million balls of ammunition, and 400,000 pounds of gunpowder that had arrived from France nearly a year prior.

Toussaint and his honor guard entered the town early on a Wednesday morning. Children ran behind the regiment, marveling at the two dozen honor guards on horseback. They were all Black like them but wore fancy uniforms and shiny helmets. The young boys had never seen soldiers who looked like them before.

When they saw Toussaint, both children and adults alike cheered and chanted his name:

"Papa Toussaint, Li la, li la - Father Toussaint, He's here, he's here."

Toussaint waved to the crowd, truly grateful for the affection he was receiving.

He had sent word earlier in the week requesting to meet with the elders of the town. During these meetings, Toussaint advised them of the planned distribution of munitions and wanted their feedback on who the most responsible persons to entrust the muskets and supplies of ammunition might be. The town elders were invaluable as they knew every individual and family. They all quickly determined the safeguarding of the munitions to a trusted member of each village. Those would in turn be monitored by the towns' elders, whom Toussaint greatly trusted.

He instructed his soldiers to accompany the elders to assure they pass word that it was Toussaint's arms being distributed—and they were to be stored and not to be used until ordered.

The following day, Sonthonax arrived from *Cap-Français* with Toussaint's men and wagons filled with muskets, gunshot, and powder. Sonthonax wished to also be involved in their distribution and attempt to take credit for arming the peasants and Cultivators— even though the population already accredited the arms to Toussaint.

They traveled from village to village where Toussaint would uncover the wagon tarps to expose the weapons. Sonthonax would then take a musket, fire it into the air as a show of its use, and hand it to one of the men eagerly standing by to receive one.

During each visit, Sonthonax would declare, *"Zam sa a se libète w"* - *This weapon is your freedom,"* to the cheers of the crowd, repeating the phrase over and over and placing another musket into the next outstretched hand.

"He's amusing himself to believe these people would fight for him," said a smiling Toussaint to Henry during one of the presentations. "He has no clue that it is us they will follow—even to fight against him if need be!"

Henry smiled back, recognizing the genius of Toussaint. The General had selected and screened the citizens in advance for the most qualified and responsible to receive the arms. He'd established a relationship with the elders and made sure it was his men who oversaw their storage and security. It was his soldiers who had arrived with the arms first. It appeared to the population that it was Toussaint who was the owner of the arms and fully in charge of their distribution; He was after all the one unveiling them on the wagons and seemingly allowing Sonthonax to hand them out—almost as if Sonthonax was *his Subalterne-his subordinate* and doing the manual labor.

They repeated the show throughout the Northern plains from *Plaisance* to *Limbe, Le Borgne, Acule, Dondon, Terre Rouge, Saint Raphael*, and the entire *Plaine du Nord*. When finally emptied, the wagons were sent back with Sonthonax to *Cap-Français* for more. Toussaint waited a week in *Hinche* for their return, however, Sonthonax had tired and had had enough of the action, declining to make the second journey.

The second load of 8,000 muskets soon arrived in *Hinch*. Half of the haul was distributed between *Banica, Crête-à-Pierrot*, and *Verrettes*. The remaining 4,000 along with a stockpile of shot and powder were secretly stored at three locations surrounding the fort at *Crête-à-Pierro*t.

Sonthonax was unaware of the true number of inventory, nor where they went. Toussaint of course kept an accurate accounting of each town's deployment and had his men record the names and

addresses of their recipients. He also sent several more wagons to remote locations in the mountains to be stockpiled for future needs.powder were secretly stored at three locations surrounding the fort at *Crête-à-Pierrot*.

Sonthonax was unaware of the true number of inventory, nor where they went. Toussaint of course kept an accurate accounting of each town's deployment and had his men record the names and addresses of their recipients. He also sent several more wagons to remote locations in the mountains to be stockpiled for future needs.

Their distribution mission complete, Henry and Toussaint traveled to *Gonaives* where Henry would undertake his first assignment. He was to be placed in charge of a five-company battalion, each composed of two-hundred men and headed by a Captain. Henry was bestowed the title of Major.

Henry was introduced personally to each of the five captains to establish Général Louverture's respect for him. Each was impressed to learn Henry had fought in the American revolutionary war alongside the famed *Chasseurs de Saint-Domingue* back in 1779.

Still, Henry hoped to further earn the respect, loyalty, and trust of his captains by meeting with each separately and ascertaining their positions on various subjects; the needs of their troops, and the battle capabilities of their companies. With these separate meetings, he was also able to gauge their attitudes, have more intimate conversations, and compare each of their leadership styles away from the larger group.

He then met with all the captains together to determine who was the informal leader of the group. As a test, Henry feigned having forgotten a map in his quarters. As he got up to leave, he said; "Gentlemen, continue this discussion without me. Who should lead the conversation in my absence?"

Four immediately pointed to Captain François Capois. With that, Henry knew he had his leader.

"Captain Capois, you are now in charge. Carry on."

Capois' military career began in 1793, assigned under Colonel Jacques Maurepas of the 9th brigade at *Port-de-Paix*. His rank advanced quickly—first to Lieutenant, then Captain of a company in the 3rd Battalion. He led under Maurepas against all expeditions and invasions in the northeastern region of the colony until reassigned to the West. In his current role, the battalion was charged with maintaining peace in a rather large swath of territory—east to *Saint Raphael*, south to *Hinche*, and northwest towards *Estere*, skirting the line near *St. Marc* that was adjacent to territory held by the British.

Over the next several weeks, Henry had the Captains meet together without him present. He charged Capois with leading the meetings. Capois and Henry also began to meet together more frequently. This was the former's way to groom the person he would designate as his second in command, just as he had done back at the hotel he managed.

Henry and Capois assessed that the current funding for the battalion was far short of what would be required to keep control of such a large area. They would have to devise a solution to move forward in their mission. Henry set out with Capois' company to survey the territory and meet with the local citizens, plantation owners, and business people in the towns.

They quickly devised a bartering system to improve his battalion's sphere of influence. The area's residents needed certain commodities that were only available in larger cities—such as hardware, fertilizers, tools, and other equipment. On the other hand, the rural towns were plentiful in agricultural products, including sugar, coffee, corn, beans, an abundance of produce, and rice which could be sold at markets in the larger cities.

Seeing a potential opportunity, Henry contacted Jean-Baptiste Bayard. They quickly made a deal for the company's ships, already traveling to *Gonaives*, to export agricultural products to *Cap-Français*. In turn, they would import hard goods ordered by the planters and business people from *Cap-Français*. Using their military wagons, Henry's army would deliver the merchandise while on patrols to the citizens and bring the agricultural products back to the ships.

The army's payment for these services was ten percent of either inbound or outbound merchandise, paid in the form of food products for their troops and also included feeding his troops in the field if in the vicinity.

Conquering such a logistical milestone enriched Henry's standing immensely—all troops now ate adequate meals, which led to increased morale and performance. In addition, he scheduled additional training to bolster the men's warfare, horsemanship, marksmanship, and an array of other skills. Creative and fun war games were run between the five companies with rewards consisting of additional time off, special meals, and other benefits.

Henry increased field deployments—which the troops enjoyed since food was now available at various farms or merchants throughout the area. As a result, the army became more familiar with the territory and its citizens leading to reduced crime and increased security.

After hearing reports of these ingenious strategies and training regiments, Henry had proven an excellent leader in Toussaint's mind. That March, the General sent a message to Henry requesting a meeting at the fort of *La Crête-à-Pierrot,* along with half of his men.

Henry arrived that spring at *Petite Riviere de L'Artibonite* with three companies—roughly 600 men. The fort imposingly stood on a peak above the town. It was the first time Henry had traveled to this area, and he was taken aback by the magnificent fertile green valley irrigated by the *Artibonite River,* which curled like a snake across the land.

Before he and his men set up camp, a rider arrived with orders to meet *Général* Louverture at *Verrettes,* a day's ride south. The next afternoon, Henry and his regiment found the *Général* already mounted and ready to move out once more; this time across the river towards the mountains. Exhausted, the party finally reached the town of *Desarmes* by midnight and marched again before 7:00 am.

They arrived a few miles outside *Mirebalais* just after nightfall. Toussaint sent numerous scouts to spy on the territory and neutralize any British or Spanish patrols that may have been active in the area. He then ordered an artillery brigade to disassemble the cannons from their carriages and reassemble them in the hills in preparation for an attack.

Toussaint then took the remainder of the army and split them among the surrounding towns of *Dubon, La Marre, Haut Saut d'Eau, and Trou Chouchou.* Henry was charged with overtaking *Docan.*

Toussaint avoided *Mirebalais* as it was well fortified with 2,000 redcoat soldiers and commanded by the capable Vicompte de Bruges. His spies had reported that they were well-armed and supplied. Toussaint's strategy instead was to conquer the outlying towns and tighten the noose on the main city of *Mirebalais.*

Henry marched his three companies through the lush and fertile hills and among herds of grazing livestock. They passed numerous plantations, mostly of coffee, which were all well stocked and manicured. These plantations were managed by *Gens de Couleurs* as well as a small number of *Blanc Émigrés* who had returned.

As Henry progressed with his army to *Docan*, he would encounter many citizens curious and puzzled by their presence—though none appeared hostile. The citizens did not fear Toussaint's army, as he had once occupied the area before the British conquest and they knew his soldiers were well-disciplined.

The company arrived about a mile from *Docan* in the middle of the night. Henry's strategy required encirclement with a surprise attack from every corner of the town at first light. His plan worked brilliantly—within a few short hours the British were either on the run towards *Port Républicain* and *Mirebalais* or had surrendered themselves. As ordered, Henry and his men secured the town for three days, making new friendships with the townspeople and leaving a contingent of 25 men to guard their prisoners of war.

Four days after their success, Henry and the rest of his soldiers rejoined Toussaint on the outskirts of *Marceline*. Arriving at the same time was a ragtag group of 300 *Maroons* with new muskets,—gifts from the Sonthonax cachet—which had been hidden in the hills by Toussaint.

They were a bare-chested, rough-looking bunch with bodies built of wiry muscles under tight flesh; equipped with only a goatskin pouch that held a goblet of water, their assigned musket, and another pouch of shot and powder.

Toussaint approached Henry and the other officers; "These men are fast runners and will flank the town. We will attack from this west side. They will run down any of the British or Spanish who escape to the east or south. Dessalines will attack from the North."

The battle proceeded as planned, and the garrison was quickly overpowered. The sounds of conch shells and high-pitched war cries continued in the distance as the band of *Maroons* chased the enemy for the kill as they exited the town. By noon, the battle concluded again in victory.

That evening in the camp, Toussaint invited Dessalines to meet Henry over a dinner of chicken, rice, and beans. Henry was accustomed to more sophisticated dishes, but in the field, this meal was admittedly delicious. Dessalines said little throughout the meal and appeared agitated with the attention Toussaint was paying the much younger Henry.

During a lull in the conversation, Dessalines could not help himself. Without looking up from his plate, he said;

"*Mwen tande ou renmen moun blan—I've heard you are in love with white people.*"

"*Mwen renmen tout pèp toutotan yo respekte mwen—I love all peoples as long as they respect me,*" replied Henry. "That goes for you as well, Captain."

Itching for a fight, Dessalines bolted to his feet.

"What do you mean by that, boy?"

The older Captain towered over Henry. He was nearly ten years his senior and his aggression was intended to demonstrate himself as Henry's superior.

Henry responded once more in a measured tone.

"Exactly as I said. If you respect me, I will respect you. Who knows, we may be friends one day."

"You and I can never be friends *Nèg Kay—House Nigger!*" spat Dessalines.

Toussaint quietly studied the exchange between his two officers. He had suspicions that Dessalines might explode in this way and wished to observe Henry's reaction under intense personal pressure.

"Insults do not sway me either to hate or love you; they only serve for me to understand your prejudice. Are you upset because I served the *Blancs* in my business, Captain Dessalines? Is that what you are implying?"

Dessalines was boiling and turned to walk out. Toussaint suddenly yelled, *"DESSALINES! Chita—Sit down!"*

Dessalines did as he was told, but grabbed his goblet of rum and drank deeply from it. The heavy breathing coming from his mouth between swigs indicated to Henry they wouldn't be friends anytime soon.

"Now, we will go over the plans for tomorrow, before we depart," stated Toussaint, as he laid out the plans for the upcoming campaign to *Mirebalais*. No further incidents interrupted their meeting.

The sounds of cannons in the distance abruptly awoke Henry at 4:00 am. The bombing Toussaint had ordered from the hills was already pounding the town of *Mirebalais*. At daylight Toussaint's assault was launched into motion. The army arrived at the outskirts of *Mirebalais* that afternoon—all while the cannons continued to relentlessly punish the town.

They made camp as the cannonballs rained down unabated until early the next morning. *Mirebalais* was on fire by the time Toussaint's army attacked. The 2,000 British had gone nearly mad from the bombardment and by noon the Vicomte de Bruges had ordered an evacuation of the town with hardly any fight. Not wanting to hold more prisoners than they already had, Toussaint allowed the British forces to escape; with their abandoned small arms, powder, munitions, and cannons all quickly reappropriated by Toussaint.

He took up residence and set up his headquarters in the main Government house. It was a stately old building, well preserved with a shaded wrap-around balcony that became a favorite hangout of his officers as they awaited an audience with the General.

That following morning, Henry had barely arrived for an appointment of his own when he heard a commotion nearby. Walking over to investigate the noise, Henry found Dessalines with a knife to the neck of a white man in the courtyard. Toussaint appeared as well, also having heard the sounds of a struggle.

"What's going on here?" demanded Toussaint.

"This man is a supplier of arms and supplies to the British, *Mon Général*," snarled Dessalines. "I will slit his throat right here on the spot!"

"No, Dessalines. Bring him to my office," ordered Toussaint. "Henry, you come as well."

Dessalines stared daggers at Henry as they both followed Toussaint into his headquarters; Dessalines roughly dragged the man behind him.

Dessalines' shirt was wet with sweat and he'd opened three buttons from the neck by the time they reached the office. Here, Henry caught his first sight of the huge welts crossing his comrade's lower neck and upper chest from the whippings he'd endured as a field slave. He could only imagine what the rest of his tortured body looked like under his clothing.

"This man is a traitor, *Mon Général*. He deserves to die!" barked Dessalines.

"To what end would that serve, may I ask?" replied Toussaint.

"One less *Blanc* in this colony, for starters."

"Henry—what would you have us do with this man?" asked Toussaint.

The White man before them was utterly terrified and did not utter a single word. He stood motionless before the trio with his head down, staring at the floor.

"I would first ask his name, *Mon Général*," replied Henry.

"Hmm. Proceed with your questioning, Henry. Dessalines and I will observe," said Toussaint. He then motioned over toward two chairs in front of the office's desk. "Jean-Jacquess, come sit with me."

Dessalines began to walk across the office but turned his head back; "What is that stench? Is that shit I smell?"

Their captive closed his eyes and seemed to lower his head even lower to the floor.

"You fucking stinking *Blanc*! Did you shit your pants? Is it you who smells so foul?" demanded Dessalines.

"The f—figs I ate…they, the figs—which did not agree with me…" answered the man, his voice trembling and tears in his eyes.

Dessalines violently lunged toward the cowering man with his huge hand lifted when Henry suddenly blocked him.

"Get out of my way, *Nèg Kay*! I will put this animal out of his misery."

"ENOUGH! Dessalines!" roared Toussaint. "You have scared this man half to death. His bowels have given way. *You* are the reason for this smell that now engulfs my office. You don't seem to understand the effect your brutality can have on those unaccustomed to it."

Dessalines dropped himself heavily down on the chair alongside Toussaint, his long legs spread wide. He dramatically took his *mouchwa tèt* from his pocket and placed it over his nose.

Toussaint glanced at Dessalines and smiled at him. He also placed his *mouchwa tèt* over his nose. Before him, Henry was playing the consummate diplomat; polished through years of providing service, negotiating deals, and supplying happiness to others. He had discovered that through the act of giving he would receive tenfold, so much so that he was able to purchase his freedom with the very money the *Blancs* would gladly give him during employment at the hotel.

Dessalines on the other hand was forced into servitude and required whips to finally coerce his grudging obligation. He never sought to serve but rather to fight those who had made him subservient. His spirit could never be broken and he was greatly feared by any who dared try.

Each of these men served Toussaint with loyalty. Differently to be sure, but equally competent in their respective roles. Dessalines would willingly march into hell and slay any dragon Toussaint deemed necessary; requiring neither explanation nor conscience. Alternatively, Henry would negotiate situations that could be won through diplomacy and act as an experienced sounding board when Toussaint was in need.

The two men would never think alike—nor care to—or ever be friends, but would always be useful and willing to sacrifice their lives for him. They were two of his most trusted and valued assets.

"Sit and tell me your name, *Monsieur*," began Henry.

"Maurice Allard," answered the man in a French accent.

"And what are you doing here, Mr. Allard?"

"I sell supplies to the army, sir."

"You know it is against the law to sell to the British?" asked Henry, narrowing his eyes.

"With respect, it is not, sir. *Général* Rigaud has allowed it. The money I collect from the British is passed to the planters and used to purchase their coffee and sugar."

"What do you supply the British with?" asked Henry.

"Beef, rum, grain, some guns, and powder," answered Allard.

"You will immediately cease supplying the British and instead provide for the army of Toussaint Louverture. Is that clear?" asked Henry.

"Yes sir. How…well, will I be paid?" asked Allard.

"You will have your life," replied Henry slyly before meeting the man's eyes. "We will work out those details. Where do you get your beef?"

"I have 500 head of cattle hidden and guarded in a valley to the north."

"And the guns?"

"Smugglers from the United States Carolinas. They dock in *Saint-Marc*."

"What do you do with the coffee that is traded?"

"Trade it to the Americans for the guns."

"Anything else?" prompted Henry.

"I have a good Cuban brand of cigars," Allard offered with a tense and awkward smile. He then reached into his vest pocket producing three *Cheroots* as an offering to gain favor and perhaps save his life.

"Go wait outside the door and do not leave," Henry ordered.

After Allard left, Henry turned to Toussaint with a triumphant smile.

"It appears we may have a new Quartermaster, General."

"We should confiscate his cargo, slit his throat, and be done with him," interrupted Dessalines. "Why pay him anything at all?"

"Would you like to answer the Captain here?" asked Toussaint to Henry.

"If we kill him, we have also eliminated any further supply. If we pay him, he will come back again and again. He's simply a merchant seeking to earn a profit and feed his family, if he has one," replied Henry.

The argument won out. Maurice Allard was paid out of the town's treasury and allowed to go on his way—with strict instructions to trade only with Toussaint's army. Dessalines was vexed but Toussaint was rather pleased with the arrangement.

Henry ran into Dessalines later that evening and promptly handed him a box of cigars.

"Compliments of *Monsieur* Allard for not killing him."

Dessalines shot Henry a dangerous look before a sinister smile spread across his face.

"I will kill you if you ever betray *Papa Toussaint*—even if I ever suspect anything of the sort," Dessalines growled. He turned on his heel and walked away, box of cigars clutched under his arm.

That evening, Toussaint wrote a letter bound for France to proudly inform Étienne Laveaux of his progress in conquering *Mirebalais* and the surrounding towns. He dearly missed his friend and confidant, yet felt guilty over being the one who had arranged his departure from the colony. Alas, Laveaux did not fit into his plan of governance.

Though the two agreed on nearly all aspects of management, he knew Laveaux was loyal to France first and the colony second. However, he also needed him in Paris to protect the colony's interests amid the winds of change; a new generation of politicians was hungry to re-establish the slavery economy and increase the revenue coffers of the government. The absentee Grands Blancs who owned vast tracks of land in the colony were enthusiastically in support.

To that end, he also reported that the production of the plantations was on the rise, and the farms around *Mirebalais* were still in working order.

As he was composing the letter, a messenger arrived with a dispatch. Toussaint read over the message and placed it on the portable writing desk he carried in the field. His officers were mingling about, waiting for a briefing. He stood and went outside to the courtyard and announced;

"Gentlemen; the British General Simcoe is marching here with freshly arrived troops from Britain. I am told nearly 30,000 of them."

The officers looked at one another. All told, they commanded 10,000 troops at best. They were outnumbered three to one. Toussaint calmly continued.

"We march to *Saint Marc* within the hour. Strike camp and burn the town before we leave."

The officers scurried to their regiments and within the hour *Mirebalais* was in flames, leaving no prize for Simcoe to claim.

Toussaint's army marched relentlessly towards *Saint Marc* through the afternoon rains. They stopped only for a couple of hours to start a fire, eat, and dry their clothes before beginning to march again.

They arrived soon at *Saint Marc*, the very place where General Simcoe had launched his expedition the day prior. Toussaint's army passed Simcoe's, undetected, moving in the opposite direction on the northern flank. The British had left a force of four brigades numbering about 2,000 troops.

Toussaint's army quickly attacked *Saint Marc*, nearly destroying the entire regiment. Simcoe received word of the disaster and turned back to *Saint Marc*, arriving two days later to a defeated army. He had lost *Mirebalais*—effectively burned to the ground—and now *Saint Marc,* without even engaging in battle himself!

He cursed Toussaint's trickery and vowed not to leave *Saint Marc* so vulnerable again. He wondered why Toussaint hadn't simply massacred the remainder of his men and taken complete control of the town. He could not square the decision.

Toussaint's officers were wondering the same. They were tired, hungry, and hoping to have the town to themselves for some much-needed rest after their recent campaigns.

Sensing the discontent and confusion, Toussaint gathered his men in his tent.

"What happens after the rains in April?" he prompted them.

They looked at each other and back to Toussaint.

"*Lafyèv Jòn—Yellow Fever*," he went on. "I predict the British will remain here so their newest military disaster is not repeated. However, they will then face an equally or even more dangerous enemy; *Lafyèv Jòn. Saint Marc* is already inundated with it. I saw it for myself."

The men smiled at the thought.

"We must find ways to keep them bottled in," stated Toussaint.

"The fever will do much of our work for us without losing any of our men or wasting our powder and shot. Keeping them in the tight restrictions of the city will lead to a higher infection rate."

For the next several weeks, one battalion remained in the vicinity of *Saint Marc* alongside the horde of *Maroons* inflicting guerilla warfare upon the British faction. The redcoat soldiers would march out of the city to patrol the countryside and inevitably suffer an attack by Toussaint's men.

They would line up for the firing line under typical British formation, and Toussaint's men would encircle, picking them off from the flanks. The British would complain of the unorthodox, unorganized, and undisciplined form of engagement, all while being slaughtered in their gentlemanly fashion of fighting.

As Toussaint had predicted, an epidemic of Yellow Fever soon swept *Saint Marc*, felling Simcoe's newly arrived soldiers quickly. The local townspeople had built-up an immunity to the disease, but the recruits were prone to catch it, suffer, and succumb without the British physicians knowing what to do.

Simcoe had now suffered a third defeat without ever laying sight on Toussaint or his army. This would turn out to be the final British attempt to conquer the colony's interior.

Sixteen

THE DEPARTURE OF SONTHONAX

Cap Français
May 1797

Word had reached Cap Français of Toussaint's victorious campaigns against the British in Mirebalais and Saint-Marc.

Also of news was the disgraceful performance of Général Desfourneaux, a White French career officer, who together with Moyse was supposed to engage the enemy in the valley of Grande Rivière, take over Valliere, and join Toussaint in Banica or Las Cahobas.

However, Moyse and Desfourneaux disliked and distrusted each other resulting in no coordinated attack ever materializing. Sonthonax was no fan of Desfourneaux either and upon his return to Cap-Français, the White French General was relieved of his command, arrested, and deported from the colony.

Sonthonax then named Toussaint Louverture Commander-in-Chief of the French Republican Army on May 8th, 1797

In a ceremony filled with pomp and circumstance, Toussaint was given his promotion along with gifts of two beautiful pistols manufactured at the House of Versailles arms maker and an ornate saber as appreciation from the French Directoire for his service to the colony.

In addressing the crowd, Toussaint was humble, and courteous and proclaimed that the honor bestowed upon him was too much of an honor.

"Let the sacred flame of liberty that we have won lead all our acts.

Let us go forth to plant the tree of liberty, breaking the chains of those of our brothers still held captive under the shameful yoke of slavery.

Let us bring them under the compass of our rights, the imprescriptible and inalienable rights of free men.

Let us overcome the barriers that separate nations and unite the human species into a single brotherhood.

We seek only to bring to men the liberty that God has given them, and that other men have taken from them only by transgressing His immutable will."

The crowd cheered as Toussaint looked out at them. He wished his friend Étienne Laveaux could be here with him, as a partner. Unlike this scoundrel who now pretended to honor him, Toussaint knew it would serve only the Commissioner's selfish means.

At the state dinner in his honor, Toussaint ate nothing but cheese and bread, refused wine, drank only water, and consumed only a piece of fruit for dessert. That evening after the dinner, Toussaint retired early with an entourage of his most trusted officers.

The following week, Sonthonax called Toussaint into his office and shut the door. He nervously peered out the window and shut the curtain and looked back towards Toussaint as he took his seat.

"With you as Commander-in-Chief, do you know what we are going to do first?" asked Sonthonax. The Blacks are worried about their freedom. We have here colonists of whom they are suspicious. They must all be slaughtered. Everything is ready. You only must agree with me.

"What?" blurted a confused Toussaint with his mouth wide open. "You want to slaughter all the Whites? Aren't you White yourself?"

"Yes, but not all of them. Only those who are enemies of freedom."

Toussaint could not believe what he was hearing. He looked at Sonthonax who was evidently sober, but had he gone mad? "Let's talk of other things," said Toussaint to move off this subject. "We'll talk about this tomorrow."

"Alright. That's enough for now," Sonthonax said.

Sonthonax attempted to bring the conversation back to the last military campaign in the south, but Toussaint feigned a headache and said he needed to leave.

The next morning, Sonthonax asked Toussaint to come to his house. Upon his arrival, he was let in by the butler and escorted to the main parlor where he was greeted by Marie Bleigeat Sonthonax, unquestionably one of the most beautiful women of the colony and now the wife of the Commissioner. She was magnificently dressed in a gorgeously ornate Victorian gown and her face and hair were made up as if she was ready to attend an opera.

The stunning Creole woman had soft and delicate brown skin and a blondish wig of curly hair. She was the daughter of a wealthy French Blanc father and Mulatto mother. She was widowed two years earlier to a wealthy Mulatto Gens de Couleurs gentleman named Villevaleix who had accumulated properties in the northern plains.

At twenty-seven, she was younger than Sonthonax by seven years. She was well-traveled and sophisticated and arrived with two toddlers; a three and a five-year-old, from her previous marriage. With Sonthonax, she birthed a new baby, now a little over 3 months old.

A wet nurse, Toussaint presumed, entered the room with the baby in her arms. She brought the child to her who, as Toussaint could see, Mrs. Sonthonax was accustomed to caring for a child. She appeared to have warm motherly instincts and the child settled comfortably in her arms, obviously having fulfilled her appetite from the black woman who had just nursed her.

"My apologies from the Commissioner, Général Louverture or should I now call you Commander-in-Chief?" Marie Bleigeat said when the baby was settled. "And this is our son Jules-Pierre-Isidore Sonthonax. Say hello to the Général, Jules-Pierre."

"Oh, let us not be so formal Madame Sonthonax. You may call me Toussaint if the informal address does not cause you awkwardness," answered Toussaint.

"Well thank you, Général Louverture," casually ignoring his invitation to be informal. "Please have a seat as my husband shalt not be long. May I offer you some coffee?"

"That would be wonderful," Toussaint responded.

"Clarice; please have some coffee brought in for Général Louverture. And that will be all for now, thank you," she commanded of the wet nurse who scurried for her wishes.

"Your new son brings you much pleasure, I can see," Toussaint said.

Marie Bleigeat smiled and said "Yes. Jules-Pierre is such a good baby, never making a fuss."

"I had not the opportunity to congratulate you on your wedding day as my military obligations prevented my attendance. Please accept my sincerest best wishes, as I hope the Commissioner has conveyed them already to you on my behalf from our previous conversations," Toussaint said.

"Yes, he has. He has also expressed much confidence and trust in you, Général. I am certain you will not disappoint him," Marie Bleigeat said with her right eyebrow slightly pointing up as if the

conversation had suddenly turned into an inquisition.

"I can promise you that I will never intentionally disappoint my commissioner, albeit at times we may disagree on some matters," Toussaint said with neutrality in his voice.

Just then, Sonthonax burst into the room. "Mon Général, the Commander-in-Chief. Please forgive my depravity for the tardy arrival. Business in the colony, as you well know, can put one behind their schedule and well-meaning intentions."

"Of that, I am very familiar," responded Toussaint.

"I see that you have made the acquaintance of my love, Madame Marie Bleigeit, and our new arrival Jules-Pierre-Isidore Sonthonax."

"Yes Commissioner, we have been acquainted and very well engaged in conversation," Toussaint said with a slight glance and smile towards Sonthonax's wife.

"Excellent. But without further ado, please forgive us, my love. The Général and I have much business to discuss. Please excuse our dismissal."

Marie Bleigeit smiled as Sonthonax, without sitting, turned to leave. Toussaint got up and excused himself as Sonthonax led him to his office and congratulated Toussaint once more for his promotion. He asked Toussaint to sit in the chair next to him. "Let's talk about the affair."

"What affair? asked Toussaint.

"That which we broached yesterday evening. I am very happy to see you are head of the armed forces of the colony. We are in a perfect position to do all we want. You have much influence over the inhabitants. We must carry off our project; it is the perfect moment. The circumstances have never been more favorable, and there's no one better than you to act together with me."

Toussaint looked at Sonthonax and thought how Sonthonax was a practiced and unrepentant liar, living in a world of fantasy in which he could conjure up plots and counterplots and eventually deceive even himself. He even lies when it was unnecessary, which is always foolish.

"You mean, Commissioner, that you want to ruin me... Kill the

Whites? Take our independence? Did you not promise me that you'd never again talk of these projects?"

"Yes, but you see it's indispensable. No, it's to chase them out, these Grands Blancs émigrés. We won't kill them."

Sonthonax wasn't making any sense. Has this man gone completely mad, thought Toussaint? "Today you say you want to chase them out, but yesterday you said they had to be killed. But if a White was killed here it is I who would be held responsible and it is I who would be blamed! I'm leaving, Commissioner!" Toussaint said as he took his hat to leave and went through the door of the office.

He heard Sonthonax running behind him. "Toussaint. Please return and let us finish this unsettled business," pleaded Sonthonax

"Commissioner, I am very angry with you," Toussaint said as he passed the parlor where he had been sitting and glanced through the doorway to see Marie Bleigeit staring at the door, stunned at his tone. He continued towards the front door.

"Well, if you are angry, let's talk about anything."

"You have already given me your word of honor not to talk any more about this, yet you still bother me, you persecute me. I am angry. Very angry," replied Toussaint.

"It is over. I thought you would have joined me, but since you take this ill, I'll no longer speak to you about anything. Do you promise not to tell anyone about this?"

"I have often promised you many things that I've fulfilled, but this time I cannot promise you anything."

"I swear to you that I won't ever talk about this ever again. Promise me you'll say nothing."

"No, because of the past promises you have made to me but didn't keep, one can't count on your word. I'm leaving. My thought is to gather my officers and make known to them your projects so that if I were to die, they could be on their guard against you and my memory wouldn't be dishonored."

Sonthonax became increasingly agitated; "I give you my word of honor. I swear to you that I will never speak of this again. But promise me that you'll keep this secret. This isn't something your officers should know about. Give me your word of honor that you won't speak of this to anyone."

"Alright then. I give you my word that I will contemplate your request. Farewell," replied Toussaint, disappointed at the notion of what the Commissioner had proposed. Toussaint abruptly left and mounted his horse.

"Where are you going, Général," asked Sonthonax.

"I go to Gonaïves," Toussaint responded.

Toussaint left but instead made a trip to visit Bayon de Libertat at the Breda plantation on the outskirts of Cap-Français. In confidence, he briefed his trusted friend on what had transpired.

"Sonthonax is not to be trusted, Toussaint. I do not say this lightly and I know in my heart it is I who he would first have killed, but I also worry for you," Bayon said.

"I made it known to him that I would tell my officers of our conversation so that if there is an attempt on my life, others would know of this treachery. Why does he hate the Whites so?" asked Toussaint. "After all, he is White!"

"Things are very fluid in France, Toussaint. I believe the commissioner fancies a colony without Royalists, managed by Revolutionaries, and living in concert with the former slaves with him as the ultimate ruler.

If it was for him, all Mulattos would be executed along with the Whites as well as any Blacks who crossed him in the past. He is a very delusional, deceptive, fanatical, and dangerous man, Toussaint. You have every right to fear him as he is unpredictable, impulsive, and wields immense resources."

"What should I do, Bayon? How would you proceed?" asked Toussaint.

"When was your last correspondence with your confidant, Étienne Laveaux?"

"I have sent him three previous letters, all unanswered. I believe him to be vexed by my insistence that he departs the colony and represent us in France. He was very fond of this island's beauty and it's people."

"I would write him again before Sonthonax can spew hatred at the legislature in Paris. He has many supporters there as well as many enemies. You have Étienne."

Toussaint stayed the night at Breda and left the following morning for Gonaïves. Once there, he assembled his officers and briefed them on the 'project' that Sonthonax had spoken of.

Although immensely loyal to Toussaint, many had affection for Sonthonax, especially if they were former slaves, as it was he who initially declared emancipation on behalf of the French government and who had stood with them against the Grands Blancs who sought to enslave them.

However, in the end, Toussaint convinced them to remain solidly behind him as he sought to peacefully move Sonthonax to France to represent them in the legislature against those aligned with slavery, especially the group headed by the pro-slavery royalist Vincent-Marie Viénot, Count of Vaublanc who supported the reinstitution of slavery in the colonies.

In the following days, he drafted the components of his letter to his friend Laveaux. With each draft, he attempted to limit his words to the most poignant as to sway any reader to see that he was a true patriot and interested in only serving the French Republic. Components included words and phrases, such as…

... We shall soon purge the French territory of the tyrannical hordes who have infested the colony for too long and soon we will form a single, unified family of friends and brothers.

... Please convey to the Legislature the nature of my efforts and my sincere attachment,

... The colony's preservation, let me repeat, is assured, and France can count upon my irrevocable zeal as its true defender.

... My time and attention will be fully occupied in seeking to merit the support of the Legislature and my fellow citizens.

... France may be certain that so long as the blood flows in our veins, we shall only strive for the defense of the colony and liberty, and to cast away all agitators and enemies.

When the outline was complete, he completed the composition of a two-page letter and addressed it as...

Gonaïves, 4 Prairial, year 5 of the French Republic,
From: One and indivisible Toussaint Louverture
To: Étienne Laveaux, Representative of the People, Deputy of St-Domingue in the Legislature

And as a closing, he signed it as a friend, fully knowing that more formal eyes would be reading the letter and interpreting the friendship of the two men...

Greetings and friendship
Toussaint Louverture

The letter was quickly dispatched to France by courier on a frigate from Gonaïves.

While still in Gonaïves, Toussaint was visited by a delegation from Général Rigaud. The delegation met with Toussaint in private with Rigaud's assurances to lend support towards the removal of Sonthonax from the colony.

Rigaud, of course, despised Sonthonax for his moves against him and though he and Toussaint were not nearly the strongest of allies, the alliance served Toussaint's interests as he had decided that Sonthonax must go. He was a danger to himself, the Whites, and the stability of the colony.

Additionally, his army was desperately in need of funding.

Sonthonax had decreed that the army would not participate in any tax revenue derived from exports at the largest productive port; Cap Français. All taxes were the purview of the Commission.

Meanwhile, Sonthonax further damaged his case by allowing French privateers to operate against American shipping, expecting that he would received profits as a result. This hurt everyone, including the black freed slave commerce that was just beginning to be born at a time when most people were sympathetic to Toussaint's pro-American trade stance and his opposition to French privateers attempting to disrupt and steal from it.

Toussaint, during the summer of 1797 tried several times to coax Sonthonax to step down as Commissioner and assume his elected role as a legislative representative from the colony to the legislature in Paris.

Sonthonax continued to evade providing a date of departure, alluding to his desire to be at the 4-year celebration of his famed declaration of emancipation from slavery on Sunday, August 20th. He alluded to the idea of making a grand announcement of departure during the celebrations.

On that day of celebration, Cap Français was alive and enjoying a huge festival at the city's center named the Champs de Mars where citizens rejoiced, music was played and cannons blasted from forts and ships to mark the occasion.

Sonthonax gave a resounding speech to mark the occasion and publicly questioned why Toussaint was not present by his side. He however made no mention of stepping down or of his planned departure to attend to his duties at the legislature to the citizens.

The following day, after the evening parties and festivities had died down, Toussaint, mounted on Bel Argent, and accompanied by his 24-member honor guard barreled into town and headed towards Government House at a fast gallop.

By the thunder of the horses, the shine of the honor guard, and the fact that festivities had ended the day prior, the citizens knew that a political showdown was going to take place.

The gates were immediately opened by the compound's soldiers on his arrival at Government House. Four of his Honor Guard remained at the front gate, twelve others on the steps in front of the building, four at the main doorway, and the remaining four at the entrance to the Commissioner's offices. Toussaint passed the offices of Sonthonax's fellow commissioners, Pascal and Roume, and barged into Sonthonax's office.

"So, Toussaint, you have finally decided to arrive for the anniversary of the emancipation of slavery, albeit late," Sonthonax stated with a sharp tone in his voice.

"You have once again given me your word and dishonored yourself by not being true to it. You were to make a public announcement of your glorious return to France and your assumption of the role as a legislator on behalf of the citizens who elected you. Why did you not make the announcement yesterday?"

"Général, I do not serve you as Commissioner. It is you who serve me," Sonthonax stated matter of fact.

"Commissioner, here is my final letter to you on this subject." Toussaint handed him the wax-sealed envelope which contained a letter praising Sonthonax for his successes in the colony, in being instrumental in the defeat of its enemies and the restoration of peace, stability, and prosperity to its citizens. The letter ended with…

'May you always be the defender of the cause we have embraced of which we will be eternally soldiers. Vive la République!'

"I will have it published in every newspaper in the colony, in your honor, Commissioner."

Sonthonax read the letter and handed it back to Toussaint. "Thank you Général for such a thoughtful composition. Maybe it is you who should depart for France, eh?"

Toussaint had arrived at the end of his patience. "You have 48 hours to depart on the ship awaiting you in the harbor. Otherwise, I will have you arrested for your plot to kill the Whites and send a report to France concerning the same. That is my final conversation with you on this subject." Toussaint then stormed out of the room followed by his honor guard.

Sonthonax, accompanied by his wife Marie Bleigeat, beautifully dressed in a petite coat with a silk scarf hiding her face, and an entourage of twelve departed on the frigate *Indien* on August 23rd, exactly as Toussaint had wished. They would never return to their beloved Saint-Domingue.

As Commissioner Sonthonax was not fully endorsed by the remaining civil commissioners, Roume and Pascal, they chose to defer to Toussaint, reaffirming that he is now the most powerful figure in Saint-Domingue.

Seventeen

PEACE WITH THE BRITISH

Cap-Français
October 1797

Toussaint Louverture was now the unequivocal main leader and power broker in Saint-Domingue. With the departure of Commissioner Léger-Félicité Sonthonax, the remaining two Commissioners— Philippe Roume and Julien Raimond—along with the Black military and mass of citizens recognized this openly. However, spats of class and race-based power struggles continued to ignite throughout the colony. The Mulattos were at constant odds with the Blacks; in turn, the Whites detested the Mulattos. Even within the Whites, there arose conflicts between the *Grands Blancs* property owners and *Petits Blancs* commoners.

Toussaint took up residence at Government House and used the Governor General's office, previously occupied by Sonthonax. He requested that Commissioner Roume establish himself in Santo Domingo—now a French possession—and report his findings since the Spanish ceded the colony to the French. He moved his top officers and staff not assigned at the *Caserne* to assist in administrative duties at his new home base.

He also began planning social events. Government House was a beautiful structure, rebuilt a little over five years prior into a magnificent home and office building. Housing over a dozen bedrooms, multiple offices, conference parlors, support staff housing, and kitchens in separate wings; with the crown jewel being the Grand Ballroom where Toussaint would host extravagant parties and events.

These events did not particularly impress, nor were they held in high regard by Toussaint, but the politician in him knew they were the inevitable sacrifice required by his role. An invitation to one of these Grandes Soirées was not a privilege to be taken lightly by the elite of *Cap-Français* and its surrounding hamlets.

On one such evening, Jean-Baptiste and Marie Bayard found themselves on the guest list by way of Henry Christophe. The couple was honored to be included and Marie appeared ravishing as ever in her newest evening gown. It was the latest from the runways of Paris called The Mantua; an open-fronted silk and fine wool gown with a matching train and petticoat. She wore the train looped up over her hips to reveal the petticoat in a vibrant new color called Dragon Blood. Jean much admired the view.

As she and Jean joined the line of invitees awaiting entry into *La Grande Salle de Bal - the Grand Ballroom*, they engaged in small talk with others in the line. During these events, talk of politics, business, gossip from around the colony, and news from France would circulate amongst the guests. After several moments, Henry arrived and Marie looked admiringly upon him as he strolled up to them. He had grown into a handsome man and filled out his regal uniform perfectly. She was immensely proud of who he had become; husband, father, and now an officer in the Colonial Army of France and close confidant to Governor General Toussaint Louverture himself.

"Marie, you look exquisite this evening," Henry stated as they exchanged kisses on both cheeks and turned to Jean-Baptiste and said. "Jean-Baptiste, my brother, you are a lucky man."

"For the life of me, I cannot fathom what this remarkable woman sees in a lowly soldier like myself; my brother—soon to be *Général*, rumor has it?" greeted Jean.

"Not yet, my family. But one day soon perhaps," replied Henry with a proud smile.

"The Commander in Chief would be a fool not to elect you for such an honor," interjected Marie. "Many thanks to both my handsome men for the flattery you have bestowed upon me."

"Come with me," Henry said, escorting them out of line and toward La Grande Salle de Bal.

"So, you do have some clout in this place, after all" laughed Marie as Henry nodded to the guard at the front of the line, who stood aside.

"*Monsieur et Madame Bayard*," Henry announced to the guard. "I am going to find Marie-Louise and will return with her," he told Jean and Marie, before disappearing back into the crowd. The guard then turned to the open room and announced in a baritone formal French voice; *Général Toussaint Louverture, Mesdames et Messieurs. J'ai le plaisir de vous présenter Monsieur et Madame Jean-Baptiste Bayard.*"

Jean and Marie entered and approached Toussaint and Suzanne Louverture, who were waiting to receive every guest who arrived.

"Ahhh, *Monsieur* Bayard; what a pleasure to see you once more," Toussaint said as he extended his hand in greeting. "How long has it been, almost five years now?"

"Yes, you have a keen memory *Général*. We originally met at our hotel in 1793," Jean replied, shaking Toussaint's hand. "Thank you for the invitation this evening. It is a pleasure to be here. Please allow me to introduce my astonishing wife, and love of my life, Marie Jasmine-Bayard."

"*Madame* Bayard, you are certainly as beautiful as I've been told. The wisest men of Saint-Domingue understand that their woman is their center—and the one who truly manages our households. I am lucky to have Suzanne at my side," replied

Toussaint. "Enjoy your evening and thank you for coming." With that, Toussaint turned to greet the next pair of guests as Suzanne offered a warm smile.

Jean and Marie continued into the ballroom, which was already filled with over 100 guests. An orchestra played a classic waltz to a large crowd swinging on the dance floor. Jean and Marie wasted no time joining them.

Suzanne Louverture attempted to support her husband in these endeavors and had moved their son, Saint-Jean, to Government House to help impose structure and management of the home and staff. Not long after, however, she felt out of place and thought that it was not a good environment in which to raise the boy. With much pain, she departed *Cap-Français* a mere two months after their arrival and returned to Ennery and her comfortable, easy-going, life on the plantation.

That fall, Toussaint's intelligence service learned that the revolt against Governor Laveaux was a partnership between Villatte and Rigaud. He now felt that only the British and the traitor Rigaud were standing in the way of his absolute dominance of the colony, and utmost diplomacy would be required to progress toward his goals. He needed Rigaud's cooperation to conquer the British and show France he could unite the colony—both North and South.

In a conversation with Henry Christophe, Toussaint emphatically said 'I have need of Rigaud. He is violent. I want him for carrying on war; and that war is necessary to me to remove the British.

In November of 1797, he composed two eloquent letters to the French Directoire; one in which he reported successful negotiations with *Général* Rigaud, and that the two would soon be coordinating attacks on the British. The second letter was to be a response to the increasing conservatism of the *Directoire*, and in particular, the attacks against Toussaint by the arch-racist, proslavery representative, Vincent-Marie Viénot, the Count of Vaublanc.

Toussaint asked Commissioner Julien Raimond and his trusted confidant Henry to assist him in a draft of the letter and what it should contain. It was decided that Raimond should scribe the letter with all three collaborating on its contents.

"I suppose that we should begin with, '*Toussaint Louverture, to the French Directoire*—simple and straight to the point," stated Raimond. He did not wait for acknowledgment or permission to dip his quill into an ink bottle and scratch the line onto the parchment.

Toussaint began his dictation with a brief history on the injustices of slavery; the revolts that had taken place; and the wise decision of the French government to abolish the evil practice. He then moved on to the current appearance of the threat of slavery's return. The three men debated throughout the session, arguing over what should or should not be included in the letter and their reasoning.

"I want this line emphasized," Toussaint said, gesturing. "*… the greatest enemy of the colony's prosperity and our happiness is still to dare to threaten us with the return of slavery.*"

"Yes, that is a perfect beginning. We should add how we have... '*tasted the fruit of liberty that they hold from the equity of France*'" Henry added, flowing with Toussaint's last line.

"Yes, Henry. That speaks volumes. We will not go back into bondage and are praising France for that freedom," Toussaint replied. "Add a line about the pain we have felt, Raimond "... *colony had too long suffered,*' and this too, in a question form '...*still to dare to threaten us with the return of slavery?*"

"Yes. that works well," answered Raimond. "Now, we should get to the root of the matter!"

Toussaint immediately rattled off an eloquent paragraph, ending with "...*the impolitic and incendiary speech of Vaublanc...*"

"Yes, that is very good, *Général*. I think we must demonstrate our love for France—all of us," added Henry.

"You are correct, Henry. Raimond, add '...*my attachment to*

*France, the gratitude that all the Blacks conserve for
her...,"* continued Toussaint in his dictation.

"Call them to action, *Général,*" Raimond insisted. "Make it a
personal mission for them. We should be political and hold them
accountable to take action for our people."

"How would you do this Raimond? You know politics the best
of us in this room," said Toussaint.

"I would say…'*It is for you, Citizen Directors, to remove from
over our heads the storm that the eternal enemies of our liberty are
preparing in the shades of silence.*'"

"Perfect, Raimond. That forces them to confront these slave
masters," Toussaint agreed. "Now, acknowledge that I have sent my
two sons to France for their education and that I of course separate
these honorable legislators from the colonists who are conspiring
with Vaublanc; "*It is to the solicitude of the French government that
I have confided my children. I would tremble with horror if it was
into the hands of the colonists that I had sent them as hostages.*"

"That strikes at the heart, General," Henry stated. "You have
vested your children into their care."

"Very powerful!" agreed Raimond. "Now, we must include a
veiled threat as to what might happen if Vaublanc is allowed to
continue this horrible path."

"I agree, *Général*. At this letter's conclusion, they should see
you as a loyal servant devoted to the Republic, and Vaublanc as the
one trying to unravel it. They must understand the violence that will
ensue if they decide to side with those who seek to re-enslave our
people," finished Henry with a passion in his voice.

Toussaint nodded as he turned to Raimond and said *"But if to
reestablish servitude in St-Domingue was to be done, I declare to
you that this would be to attempt the impossible. We have known how
to confront danger to obtain our liberty, and we will know how to
confront death to preserve it."*

"*Oui, Mon Général.* That is perfect!" exclaimed Henry. "I would
finish with a simple line speaking to the unity here in the colony."

"Raimond, finish with this;" Toussaint began, looking to the sky in contemplation and concentration.

"'*This, Citizens and Directors, is the morality of the people of St-Domingue, these are the principles I transmit to you on their behalf.*'"

Toussaint once again looked at Raimond and said with an authoritative tone; "Now end the letter here. I want them to contemplate that last warning of caution over and over."

"Then do so with simply *Greetings and respect, next line Toussaint Louverture,*" said Raimond.

With the outline of the letter complete, the next two hours were used to fill in details and complete the two-and-a-half-page document. The letter was copied twice; once more to be perfect and the other for an official record in the colonies archives. It was then sealed, placed in a diplomatic pouch, and sent by courier on the next ship bound for France.

The letter was well received in Paris and the Vaublanc faction lost the entirety of its influence due to its radical position on the reinstitution of slavery. Royalist and colonial pro-slavery elements were thus purged from the government. They thought that it would signal the final ending of a dark era of slavery in all of France.

In December of 1797, Toussaint sent word to Rigaud to begin coordinated attacks on British installations in the southern peninsula. Toussaint meanwhile would attack the western region of *Las Cohobas*, *Grand Bois*, and surrounding plains. For the assignment, he sent Generals Dessalines, Mornet, and his nephew Moyse.

As Toussaint's army sacked the towns, the British retreated to *Archaie* but lost nearly half of their troops during the battles in their retreat. With the area clear of the British, Toussaint ordered the army to set about rebuilding *Mirebalais* which very much pleased the city's inhabitants. Their homes and businesses were restored to a far better condition than they were before the destructive battles.

By March of the following year, Toussaint's army had

conquered most of British-occupied western Saint-Domingue and was re-arming and beginning to stage the siege of *Archaie* with nearly 20,000 troops, led by *Général* Dessalines. The British knew they were outnumbered and outmaneuvered. With Dessalines' ruthless reputation for savagery, they were staring down an inevitable bloodbath. Meanwhile, in the south, Rigaud's army laid siege to the redcoat faction at *Jérémie*.

In late March, British General Thomas Maitland arrived on the island to review the situation and chart a course forward. After receiving reports from his commanders at *Port Républicain, Archaie, Jérémie, Saint-Marc*, and *Môle-Saint-Nicolas*, he understood that remaining in Saint-Domingue was unsustainable. He understood the British political ramifications well from having served as a member of Parliament from 1790-1796.

The British army was defeated here. He decided on and had the autonomous power to agree to, an honorable surrender and negotiation of peace with Toussaint, who had proven himself a brilliant strategist, military leader, and worthy adversary. He sent a message to Toussaint in *Cap-Français* requesting a cease-fire so the two could negotiate a treaty.

Toussaint appointed a skilled negotiator by the name of Huin, a savvy political strategist whom he trusted for his judgment and common sense. General Maitland entrusted the talks to a British officer named Nightingale. Within a month, the two sides reached an agreement for the abandonment of *Port Républicain, St. Marc, Archaie*, and later *Môle Saint Nicolas,* as well as all other territories occupied by the British—except for *Jérémie*.

Upon retreat, the towns were to be unharmed and the forts restocked with all munitions they had found upon arrival.

The British wished to negotiate separately with *Général* Rigaud for *Jérémie* as they knew that he was the supreme power broker in the Southern region and there were stark differences of opinion between the two French leaders on the subject of Émigrés who had cooperated with the British. Maitland knew that Rigaud would make their lives miserable at the very least and probably destroy them as a worst-case scenario. Toussaint, however, would protect and incorporate them back into the colony as he understood their productive capabilities.

The British insisted on the protection of the colonists who had sided with them, and the non-confiscation of their properties. Huin agreed, knowing this violated the law Sonthonax had enacted against these *Émigrés*, but understood Toussaint's wishes. Huin added the condition that these property owners would voluntarily free all slaves in their possession per French laws in contradiction to enslavement under the current British law.

The agreement reached was sound, with each party making compromises. Once completed, the draft agreement was sent to Toussaint and Maitland for their approval.

The treaty was signed on May 2, 1798, and a week later the British ceded *Port Républicain* and embarked their soldiers and any French citizens who wished to leave the colony on board the British warships Thunderer, Abergavenny, and others. The flotilla sailed to *Môle Saint Nicolas*, where the troops and French refugees safely disembarked to await further transport off the island.

Toussaint left *Cap-Français* shortly after, journeying to *Port Républicain*—but decided to take his time for the tensions and shock of the British departure to sink in with residents. This also allowed him the opportunity to further inspect the current state of cultivation in the countryside.

He appointed Captain Christophe Mornet to enter the city of *Port Républicain* and assure that the troops under the command of Captain LaPlume did not sack the city or terrorize its citizens. Most of LaPlume's troops were *Maroons* from the army that had been previously led by Dieudonné; who had been imprisoned by Rigaud and died while incarcerated. Rumor had it that Rigaud had ordered his death.

LaPlume reported to Pétion, who had risen to the rank of

Général under Rigaud thanks to his effective menacing of the British. Pétion, not one to be trifled with, ordered LaPlume to ensure none of his troops step out of line with the citizenry, which all strictly obeyed.

Mornet was reassured by this, and slowly found the citizens beginning to trust that the French Colonial Army troops were not there to terrorize them. The city slowly returned to normal, with crops shipped to the docks for export and schools and stores reopening.

Toussaint progressed toward the city with his army of 10,000, stopping frequently at towns along the way to study their activity in the wake of the British departure and assure citizens of a lasting peace. Drawing on his agricultural experience and background, he also evaluated everything from the condition of the soil to the crops, pests, and the state of the cultivation equipment.

Captain Bouquin, the French White soldier who Toussaint had appointed as a trainer nearly five years prior, had elected to remain with Toussaint after his one-year commitment. Six of the eight other White officers also remained and were now integrated into different divisions of the army—all with Black officers as their superiors.

Henry and four honor guards awaited at the Plantation Auberge's wellhead, supervising the collection of water for the troops as Captain Bouquin rapidly rode up and dismounted.

"Why do we keep stopping at almost every plantation?" the captain inquired.

Henry turned to Bouquin, whose horse was restlessly dancing from right to left beside him.

"The *Général* wishes to assure the citizens that the livelihood of the colony remains viable," answered Henry.

"These constant stops are slowing our progress to *Port Républicain*," barked Bouquin.

Unbeknown to Bouquin, Toussaint had approached the conversation from behind.

"It's about the land, Captain, not the cities," stated Toussaint with authority, startling the captain. "Without the commodities produced by the land, the cities are worth nothing. The colony without the cultivation of these places will die. This is the most important part of our trip."

He then turned to the broader group.

"Mount up!"

Bouquin watched as Toussaint mounted Bel Argent and galloped towards the direction of the next plantation with Henry and the honor guard following, leaving the remaining men to continue to load water into barrels and onto the awaiting wagons.

Three days hence, the army arrived at the outskirts of *Port Républicain* and made camp with 1,000 tents neatly erected in 10 rows of 100, mimicking a small city. The army consisted mostly of shirtless soldiers—lean with wry muscles under tight skin, and legs that could run swiftly for miles at a time. They subsisted on daily rations of a single mango, banana, or plantain which they would forage themselves.

Toussaint called an officers-only meeting and stressed the importance of troop behavior when entering the city. He had learned that before his arrival, a group of his army's soldiers had terrorized the residents of a nearby plantation. Three of the soldiers had raped the daughters of the horrified owner.

When a young Captain Deschamps arrived at the scene, he was so enraged by their despicable behavior that he shot the three perpetrators right on the spot and had the remaining men of the company arrested and thrown into the stockade.

Toussaint gave the order that no soldier would be executed without due process, however; "Any soldier who steps out of line with either man or woman will be severely court-martialed, to the extent of finding themselves in front of a firing squad!"

Toussaint's tone demanded compliance. There were no further incidents.

The following morning, Toussaint's 24 honor guards, along with 100 of the army's best horsemen, galloped into the city in a show of pageantry and flair. Townspeople came out in droves and cheered as the legendary Toussaint Louverture, feared by the redcoats, entered the city on his way to Government House.

Once there, the horsemen encircled the building and Toussaint entered it with his honor guard in tow. He went straight to the mayor's office and opened the door to find the man seated behind his desk. Mayor Bernard Borgella was a *Gens de Couleur* businessman of about forty, with a medium build and the personality of a true politician.

"Welcome to the city of *Port Républicain, Mon Général*," he said, slightly bowing to Toussaint.

"Thank you, Mr. Mayor. I am sure we have much business to discuss," said Toussaint in a measured tone. "Let us begin with a full accounting of the situation of the city with the departure of the British."

The two men engaged in a detailed accounting of the current affairs of the city, port activity, necessary infrastructure repairs, fiscal health, population census, and improvements implemented by the British during their multi-year occupation. The meeting lasted well into the night and Toussaint accepted the hospitality of the mayor to stay overnight at the residence, albeit with two of his honor guards posted outside his bedroom door.

The following morning, Toussaint was awakened by the noise of a crowd, already over 100 in attendance. He quickly cleaned and dressed.

By 7:00 am, he was seated at the mayor's desk. Henry entered shortly thereafter.

"What is going on outside, Henry?"

"They are petitioners, *Mon Général*. They want to see you. I have had the men line them up in order of arrival," Henry replied.

"For what, may I ask?

"Each has a request, a grievance, a land dispute, or some other business that requires government intervention. There is a woman who is asking that her husband be reinstated to his government post as he was terminated by the British for insubordination to them and a pregnant woman who wants you to be the Godfather of her child. There is more, need I continue?" Henry answered.

"Where is Mayor Borgella?"

"I do not know of any politician who enters his office before noon, *Mon Général*," quipped Henry.

"Bring in the first of these citizens and send two men to rouse the mayor. Inform him that there is a new schedule now being implemented at Government House."

The first of the petitioners was let into the office to dispute land taken from him for a British encampment. Toussaint quickly approved the request. The next wanted his confiscated slaves taken from him by the British military returned. Toussaint denied this request and explained that going forward, all slaves would be freed. If they elected to return to the plantation, they would require compensation as provided by the colony's work codes.

And so it went continuously over the next seven days—with Toussaint insisting that Mayor Borgella sit in and observe his rulings. At the end of the last day of these ordeals, Toussaint said, "You should now see my standards for the rulings on the issues of the day, Mayor."

"I have," Borgella responded.

"Then you now must tend to the needs of our citizens. I trust you will rule as you have witnessed me do so. I will leave an appeals process so if you do not satisfy their wishes, the citizens will be invited to appeal directly to me, and I shall have the final say. Do we agree that this should not be necessary?"

"I agree it should not," answered the Mayor.

"Then I bid you *au revoir*, Mr. Mayor; I have other matters in the colony which require my immediate attention."

Toussaint exited the office to a Mayor who was relieved to have command of both his office and city again.

As agreed, the British continued their retreat from *Archaie, Saint-Marc*, and other strongholds, amassing themselves at *Môle Saint Nicolas* in the north for their final departure. However, they remained in *Jérémie* where Rigaud was still besieging the town, certain that if they left, a massacre of the *Émigrés* would ensue. Maitland wrote to Toussaint asking him to intercede and negotiate a safe surrender of the town with Rigaud on his behalf and awaited his reply.

Toussaint was pleased with the results of his trip to *Port Républicain* and concluded that the British were true to their word. The town was in good shape and the fort was not pillaged—but in fact, restocked with arms as it had been when the British arrived. He was also confident that Mayor Borgella would carry out the business of the town as he had instructed. Confident, he made his way south to meet with Rigaud.

Eighteen

THE ARRIVAL OF
FRENCH AGENT HÉDOUVILLE

Spanish Santo Domingo
June 1798

The following April a special agent of the French *Directoire* by the name of *Général* Gabriel comte d'Hédouville arrived on the Spanish side of Santo Domingo. His orders included the arrest and deportation of André Rigaud to face charges filed by Commissioner Sonthonax.

Hédouville's mission also required the assessment of Toussaint Louverture's power over the colony, and the direction to ease him out if necessary. The French National Assembly had become increasingly worried about the extent of Toussaint's influence and his tendencies toward independence from France—as reported by Sonthonax upon his return to Paris.

Hédouville met first with Commissioner Julien Roume to gain intelligence on the General, so he could better understand the myth

and the truths behind the tails of the so-called Great Toussaint
Louverture. Unbeknownst to Toussaint and British General
Maitland, he also began independently negotiating the departure of
the British outside of their newly-consummated agreement.

Hédouville dispatched an officer named Dalton to *Môle-Saint
Nicolas* to represent him in negotiations with his British counterpart,
Colonel Stewart. They discussed the evacuation only of their current
outpost at *Môle* —whereas Toussaint and Maitland's treaty had
included many ports in the South—and other conditions more
deferential to the British strategy.

Upon learning of this, General Maitland immediately interrupted
the talks and invited Hédouville's agent as his guest on the
ship *Abergavenny,* at the time moored in *Môle's* harbor. The
clandestine agreement did not provide for the safety of the colonists
currently under British protection, nor encompass a universal peace
plan involving British departure from all territories held. Dalton
would later call his time with the British incarceration rather than
hosting, though he admitted to being treated with great hospitality
during his visit. Still, he was not permitted to depart the ship.

A week later, Hédouville arrived in *Cap-Français* and
summoned both *Générals* Toussaint and Rigaud to meet him. This
was on the heels of Toussaint concluding his business in *Port
Républicain,* so after leaving the 6th Battalion in place on the
outskirts of town, he departed for *Cap-Français.*

He arrived at the 4th Battalion encampment under the leadership
of Jean-Jacquess Dessalines just outside the city. Dessalines had
maintained order well; all was peaceful and to Toussaint's approval.
He then sent ahead the French Captain Bouquin to announce his
arrival at Government House in *Cap-Français* and request an
appointment with the new French Agent.

When Captain Bouquin arrived at the outer gates of the building,
he realized he didn't recognize any of the soldiers present; and

observed that their uniforms were of a different fabric and quality from his own. These soldiers had only recently arrived from France.

"I am seeking an audience with *Général* Hédouville" Bouquin announced at the gate.

"Who are you?" questioned the guard.

"I am Captain Bouquin of the Colonial Army and you will address me by my visible title, soldier. I have arrived on behalf of my commander, *Général* Toussaint Louverture. Take me to the offices of Commissioner Hédouville at once," Bouquin replied in a commanding tone.

Six other soldiers appeared just beyond the gate's entrance, sensing a growing tension. The senior officer approached quickly.

"What is the situation here?"

Bouquin stood at attention and saluted his counterpart. The newly arrived Captain looked at and studied Bouquin to consider whether he should return the gesture. After an awkward silence, the Captain lazily put up his hand and produced a lackluster return salute.

"This man seeks an audience with *Général* Hédouville," interrupted the guard. "He claims to have come on *Général* Louverture's behalf."

"I warn you again that I am an officer of the Colonial Army of France and demand you address me by the title I have honorably earned!" Bouquin said with venom in his voice.

Several of the other soldiers murmured to each other, which Bouquin interpreted as derogatory remarks toward Toussaint Louverture and his army of Black soldiers. Having fought alongside those men for the past five years and despite his admitted initial prejudices, Bouquin now considered them to be the most committed and disciplined he'd ever had the privilege of leading.

More than that, Toussaint Louverture could have easily had him killed the day the two met. If not for him, Dessalines would have slit his throat without a second thought. But Toussaint had brilliantly recruited him and his fellow officers—yes, forcibly at first—to train his troops.

Over time, each willingly stayed with the *Général* as a result of the loyalty, respect, and camaraderie they'd found under him. Bouquin struggled mightily to contain his anger at the disrespect shown by the young white officers who'd likely never seen a drop of blood stain their immaculate uniforms.

"Accept my apologies for the misunderstanding of our young soldiers here. This is their first time in the colony, and they are not accustomed to negs having superior positions of power than a White Captain such as yourself," replied the Captain with a condescending attitude, though stepping aside and allowing the gate to open. "I understand you wish to have an audience with *Général* Hédouville, but unfortunately that will not be possible at this time. I will escort you to his secretary to request a meeting on his schedule."

"Thank you—but just a moment Captain," Bouquin growled. He walked up to the soldiers who were still whispering to themselves with snide expressions.

"I didn't hear what was so funny just then. Repeat it so I can take part in the comedy."

His tone indicated a command more than a query. The largest of the group, a private with red rust hair, a burly moustache, and seething of a bad attitude stepped forward.

"I said the British are weak and cowardly, so that is why they are being defeated by this nigger army. It would hardly be a fair fight if true French soldiers such as ourselves had gone against the nigger army of savages from the jungle," stated the man, smiling.

Bouquin returned a grin of his own and replied; "Of that you are correct, boy. It would only take one of them to gut you like a pig, slice off your tongue, shove it up your ass, and replace it with your balls."

"How dare you regard us soldiers with that contempt!"

The French soldier had lost his smile, but Bouquin's grin remained.

"I assure you, should I ever see you in such a state, I will have the same smile I do now, as I will remember your arrogance today."

He then took a step back and addressed the group; "Be careful in this colony, young children. Your darkest nightmares are but a premonition of the reality you appear so eager to experience."

Bouquin began to make his way back to the Captain, a smirk still on his face.

"Shall we see the secretary now, Captain?" Bouquin prompted.

The Captain looked at his men who had seemingly lost their spirit, though he heard not a word of the brief exchange. Both men turned and walked away towards Government House.

Bouquin secured word that Hédouville would entertain Toussaint two days hence at 11:00 am. Once back at camp, he also reported on the exchanges he'd had with Hédouville's staff and their lack of respect for the Colonial Army.

Two days later, Toussaint rode into *Cap-Français* accompanied by Bouquin, Dessalines, and his honor guard—each splendidly dressed in helmets shining under the morning sun. They were met by Henry Christophe, who had been charged with security within the city. Henry briefly explained that the security forces he had left at Government House were relieved of their duties and replaced with a personal detail by the new *Général* Hédouville upon arrival.

The three officers followed Henry to the closed gates, stopping just outside of them. Henry dismounted and announced their arrival.

"*Général* Toussaint Louverture to meet with *Général* Hédouville."

"The General may enter, but the rest of you are to wait outside," replied the French guard.

"That will not be so," replied Henry. "The *Général* does not enter without his officers and honor guard. Open the gates at once— that is an order, soldier."

"Our orders are only to allow the *Général* entry," replied the guard with a sneer. Bouquin recognized the soldier as one of the group that had been present upon his initial visit.

"This compound is the seat of the Colonial Government of

Saint-Domingue, and *Général* Louverture is the highest-ranking officer of that government. As such, he is also your Commander in Chief. You are hereby ordered by him, through me, his representative, Colonel Henry Christophe, to open these gates!"

"*Non*," replied the French soldier. "I do not take orders from the Colonial Military. I am assigned to the security detail of *Général* Hédouville."

"*Monte miray la epi louvri pòtay yo! - Scale the wall and open the gates!*" Henry shouted to the commander of the honor guard, who turned and nodded the affirmation as an order to his men.

Eight horsemen immediately galloped to the surrounding iron fence, throwing their ropes upward and scaling the fences quicker than the soldiers on the other side could react. Six tied up the three guards present, and stood back to await further orders as two others swung open the gates for Toussaint's party.

As all galloped their horses through the gates, they took hold of the ropes tied around the soldiers and dragged them behind. The soldiers struggled to keep up with the horses as they were dragged down the long road toward the main building. They arrived at the grand building moments later to the soldiers' captain barreling down the front steps.

"What is the meaning of this?" he thundered, as the captives fell to their knees, struggling to catch their breath.

The soldiers of Toussaint's honor guard encircled the building and stood at attention as Toussaint, Dessalines, Christophe, and Bouquin approached on their horses.

"These men are to be court-martialed for insubordination to the Commander in Chief," stated Henry in a commanding tone.

"Under whose orders?" demanded the bewildered Captain.

"Those of the Commander in Chief of the French Colonial Army of Saint-Domingue," responded Toussaint, gracefully dismounting from Bel Argent. "I have important business with *Général* Hédouville and these soldiers have obstructed my timely arrival."

"These men do not report to the Colonial Army. They are separate—," began the French Captain.

"They are on the grounds of the Government House of Saint-Domingue, so they report to me," Toussaint interrupted. "Those who disagree shall be removed from this property at once!"

"That will be decided by *Général* Hédouville" growled the Captain. "I will show you the way to his office."

"I can find the way myself," Toussaint said as he quickly brushed past, walked up the steps with Christophe, Dessalines, and Bouquin in tow, and left the Captain to remove the ropes from his men.

Toussaint knocked twice at the door of the office of Governor *Général* in which Hédouville had taken residence. It was the same office Toussaint had occupied himself months prior. He opened the door to the familiar office and allowed himself entrance without awaiting a response. His three officers remained in the corridor outside.

"We have not had the opportunity for a personal introduction, but I presume you to be Toussaint Louverture," Hédouville said without standing.

Toussaint stood at attention and offered a salute.

"*Général* Toussaint Louverture, Commander in Chief of the Colonial Army of Saint-Domingue."

Hédouville stood to acknowledge and returned the salute.

"Please sit *Général*; we have much to discuss; you signed a treaty with the British without my approval. Explain," he began, without preamble.

"The treaty was negotiated and ratified before you arrived in the colony, *Général*. You were not available for consultation. As I am the highest-ranking military officer in Saint-Domingue, it was my duty to lead the negotiations for the expulsion of the British from our land. However, I will have a copy of the document transcribed for your records," replied Toussaint.

"I see. If you would, please lay out the conditions for me now, *Général*."

"The British have surrendered the cities of *Port Républicain, Saint-Marc*, and *Archaie* and have amassed themselves at *Môle Saint*

Nicolas for their final departure. The cities have been secured by our army and are in good standing. However, the town of *Jérémie* is surrounded by *Général* Rigaud's force which has led to certain complications wherein the British General requires additional stipulations. I will revisit that later."

"And what of the *Émigrés*—illegal in this colony—as well as those who fought for the British?" inquired Hédouville.

"*Émigrés* who did not take up arms against us and continued to harvest produce will be protected. They will also retain ownership of their lands, but they will free their slaves as required by French law."

"I do not want these *Émigrés* in the colony!" snapped Hédouville.

"It is a *fait accompli, Général*."

"You are not to sign treaties without my authorization in the future."

"Duly noted," responded Toussaint, though he had no intent on honoring such a request.

"Now, I will be issuing an arrest warrant for the outlaw *Général* André Rigaud. I have already requested his presence here and upon his arrival, you are to execute the warrant."

"I will do no such thing," responded Toussaint. "*Général* Rigaud is a loyal servant of France and this colony. He continues to wage war on France's enemies in *Jérémie*, as I have just reported. Arresting Général Rigaud would be akin to arresting myself. Besides, I have need of Rigaud. He is violent. I want him for carrying on war, and that war is necessary to me so the British have no spirit to return."

Surprisingly, Hédouville did not push back. Instead, he turned to gaze out the window. Toussaint wondered what he might be thinking.

"Very well. I understand your position," replied Hédouville. "I would very much like for you to see France, *Général*. You have served her well without ever even setting foot on her soil."

"I embrace her soil every day, here in French Saint-Domingue. I cannot leave, however, as I have much still to accomplish. Though I do hope to one day bless my lungs with her divine air.”

"Nonsense. The colony can operate just fine without you while you explore the homeland. The ship *Nantes* is anchored in the harbor waiting to escort you to France. It is quite comfortable. You may even take your wife and baby and reunite with your sons in Paris.”

"That ship is far too small for me, *Général*. When I visit France, it should be on a much grander vessel. If there is nothing else, I shall take my leave,” stated Toussaint with a finality in his voice. Without Hédouville's dismissal, Toussaint bowed his head and turned to leave.

Hédouville stood, mouth slightly agape at the exchange which had just transpired. Had Toussaint implied the ship he'd arrived in himself was not to his standard? As if this Gilded African would expect a higher status, larger ship to transport him? How dare he!

The General stewed in his office for quite some time afterward.

Three days later, a horse galloped into one of the army's encampments and headed straight for Dessalines' tent. The guard, recognizing the rider as a Lieutenant immediately allowed him in.

"*Lame milat yo la—The army of the Mulatos is here,*” he stated to Colonel Dessalines.

"*Ki kote? Montre mwen—Where? Show me,*” replied Dessalines, as he followed the man outside the tent. He quickly mounted his stallion, Gallipòt, and gave the steed a hard kick with the heels of his boots which launched the animal swiftly behind the lieutenant's horse. They soon arrived at the intersection for the road to *Limbe*. The lieutenant stopped and pointed into the distance. Peering through his spyglass, Dessalines could see the trail of the Mulatto army, approximately 300 strong, slowly marching toward them, leaving a trail of dust in their wake.

"Go to the camp of *Général* Louverture and inform him of this development. It could be the party of Rigaud.”

The lieutenant jumped back on his horse and took off in

Toussaint's direction. Dessalines returned to his camp and ordered his 30 men to be prepared for a reception.

Two hours later, the advance detail of the Mulatto army reached the intersection. Knowing of the friction between the two armies, a crowd had assembled to watch the proceedings. Leading the soldiers was a Mullato Captain named Rochelle. He was a formidable man— the same height as Dessalines, well-dressed, and accompanied by a dozen uniformed horsemen. The bulk of the army followed about 50 yards behind.

The captain paused and dismounted. He looked over Dessalines, turned and looked at the crowd, and then back to Dessalines and his men behind him.

"Clear the road. I have an army to pass this way," he said. It was less a request—more an order.

Dessalines firmly stood his ground.

"I have no instructions to allow you passage. Do you possess papers signed by *Général* Toussaint Louverture to move an army within striking distance of the city of *Cap-Français*? Dessalines asked. "I am responsible for the security of this region and only the Commander-in-Chief, *Général* Louverture, can approve a march further than this intersection."

"Do not let me repeat my order, Colonel," replied Rochelle.

"I do not take my orders from you—and never will," Dessalines shot back. He dug his heels into the damp earth as his hand instinctively traveled to the hilt of his sword. The crowd became agitated knowing full well who Dessalines was—and the terror he could rein down on any adversary.

The Mulatto looked curiously at Dessalines and cocked his head.

"Tell me *Nèg*; are you Kongo or Dahome—so I may retrieve the appropriate whip best suited to your hide."

The crowd let out a unified gasp. Dessalines however did not move nor register a response as he stared the Mulatto down.

The bulk of the approaching army was now a mere ten yards away. Rochelle gripped his sword hilt and Dessalines now moved his entire hand over his weapon as well. The surrounding soldiers of both parties prepared for a confrontation and the crowd jostled to get a better sight of the potential action.

Just then, the lieutenant from earlier galloped towards them with Toussaint by his side.

"Colonel, allow them passage," commanded Toussaint from atop Bel Argent.

Dessalines turned towards Toussaint and saluted. With total obedience and without protest, he replied, *"Oui mon Général."*

Général Rigaud appeared behind the Mulatto Captain and dismounted; followed by Toussaint. The two men approached each other and exchanged a friendly handshake—diffusing the tension between the soldiers who, seconds earlier, were ready to die if necessary.

Toussaint gestured toward the side of the road out of listening range from the others.

"I have met with Hédouville," stated Toussaint to Rigaud.

"Of what sort is he?" asked Rigaud.

"A bureaucrat with a military title. Pompous and condescending if allowed," replied Toussaint.

"Have you seen his orders or has he told you his mission?"

"He demanded I arrest you, which I refused. Do watch yourself when you meet him—but he is in no position of power here. We control the military, and my men will pose no threat. He only has a small security detachment under his command," Toussaint explained.

"That comforts me greatly, *Général,*" Rigaud replied, bowing slightly in respect.

"You are a servant of France and fighting her enemies. After all, I need your help to finally expel the British, and on that front we are very near."

"It is clear that their days are numbered; in *Jérémie* and the entire south," Rigaud agreed.

"Are you staying long at *Cap-Français, Général?*"

"Only long enough to appease the bureaucrat. I plan to leave immediately after," Rigaud replied.

"Break up your journey and join Suzanne and me at our

residence in Ennery. I already plan to stop by home on my way to *Gonaïves*," invited Toussaint.

"It would distress me to interfere with your family time, *Général…*"

"Nonsense—I insist. It would be our pleasure to host you for an evening and overnight at the Grand Batisse at my plantation of Sansay."

"Thank you, *Général* I accept. Now, I must be off to see his majesty who has summoned me," Rigaud said with a slight smile.

"*Au revoir*. Send word the day prior to your arrival; plan on dinner and we will also set plates for two of your senior officers."

"Thank you for your kindness. I will do so," Rigaud said mounting his horse and leading his officers toward the city, his mixture of Mulatto, Black and White soldiers marching behind.

Hédouville had initiated a dangerous game pitting Toussaint and Rigaud against each other with hopes of exploiting the inherent distrust and animosity between the two. He hoped to distract them, thus freeing him to maneuver the policies he felt necessary for the colony.

He attempted to plant the seed first with Toussaint, implying that Rigaud should be arrested and deported to answer the charges lodged by Sonthonax. Perplexingly, Toussaint had not seized on the opportunity to eliminate his powerful rival. As a result, Hédouville took a different tactic in his meeting with Rigaud, instead suggesting Rigaud become autonomous from Toussaint's control and administer the Southern region of the colony as he deemed fit. He even offered to support such a proposition to the French *Directorie* in Paris. This idea enticed Rigaud immensely.

When Rigaud left *Cap-Français* for Ennery he was more confused than ever. Was Toussaint attempting to trick him into agitation toward Hédouville in suggestions that he was to arrest him? Had he hoped Riguad would be abrasive, thus instantly losing favor with the new agent from France? Or was it Toussaint who was telling the truth and Hédouville the deceiver?

He would quickly need to solve this riddle.

A week later a Mulatto horseman arrived at the Breda plantation to announce Rigaud's scheduled arrival the following afternoon. Toussaint was in a good mood and unexpectedly excited to host *Général* Rigaud in his home.

The servants were busy spot-cleaning the already pristine home, adorning it with flower vases, spraying sweet scents, and preparing the *Général's* accommodations. Suzanne went about planning a 5-course feast of fine foods while one of Toussaint's secretaries prepared elegantly transcribed menus on fine linen for each guest.

Le menu du Soir

Appetizer of Fresh Anguille (Eel)
on Biscuit with Beet and Avocado Cream
Soup of Crème of Citrouille (Pumpkin)
with Coconut Shavings
Suzanne's Garden Salad of Lettuce, Tomato, Avocado,
And Mango Dressing
A main course of Filet de Boeuf,
Potatoes, Sweet Peas

Desert of Oeufs Au Lait (Egg Custard)

Général Rigaud arrived with a detail of one dozen horsemen and two of his most senior officers. Toussaint had also invited Dessalines and Moyse to join them after a severe warning to be on their best diplomatic behavior.

Rigaud was dressed in a striking new uniform, complete with all of his medals and gold *Epaulettes* on his shoulders. He greeted

Toussaint and Suzanne with warmth and respect, complimenting on her gardens, home, and articles of interest throughout—which she greatly appreciated.

Trained in the art of flattery, Rigaud spoke lovingly of his wife—Marie Anne—and four children, which pleased Suzanne. He of course failed to mention any of his three mistresses nor the five children he'd conceived with them. He would occasionally marvel at some piece of furniture or work of art knowing he was building a solid ally in Toussaint's wife.

Toussaint wore his best dress uniform as well. Suzanne was the only woman present along with their son, 7-year-old Saint-Jean, who was also invited to the table. Rigaud had invited two young officers—one by the name of Fombrun, a Mulatto, and the other named Fontaine, a Black. He wisely kept Captain Rochelle, who'd had an altercation with Dessalines, far from the plantation.

The dinner was a welcomed *détente* from the friction between the Black and Mulatto armies and all participants enjoyed the evening to the fullest. Suzanne presided like a queen in her castle, receiving compliment after compliment from Rigaud, who also engaged with young Saint-Jean. The officers appeared at ease with one another and were genuinely pleased by the food and relaxed atmosphere.

After dinner, Suzanne excused herself to tend to Saint-Jean while the staff removed the last of the dessert plates. The conversation shifted to the military campaign against the British and the siege at *Jérémie*. Nothing was spoken of the conversations with Hédouville, and before long all retired to their quarters.

After coffee and a light breakfast the following morning, Rigaud departed for *Jacmel*. Both Rigaud and Toussaint felt they'd come a long way in mending their relationship.

Negotiations for the surrender of *Jérémie* and *Môle* with British

General Maitland continued. Maitland was anxious to put a wedge between France and Toussaint, now the most powerful man in the colony. Thus, he was deferential toward Toussaint, even as Hédouville made constant overtures to negotiate peace without the *Général*. Maitland was determined to protect the planters who had cooperated with the British and knew Toussaint would guarantee that security—whereas Hédouville and Rigaud opposed it.

Hédouville began sending letters of reprimand to Toussaint regarding the latter's ignorance of his requests, but they fell on deaf ears. Toussaint eventually convinced Rigaud to respect the protection of the French planters upon the British departure, assuring them of a swift evacuation from the colony.

Toussaint finally wrote a letter in reply to Hédouville, dismissing the French agent of nearly all his requests. Hédouville had now had enough of Toussaint's arrogance and considered him the true problem in the colony—far more serious than Rigaud. He soon initiated a private channel of conversation with Rigaud through various emissaries to plan his ousting and elevate Rigaud to Supreme Commander of the Southern Region.

At the end of August 1798, Toussaint arrived at *Môle Saint Nicolas* to personally meet with General Maitland and take possession of the town. With the peace treaty already signed, the trip was a mere formality. He arrived with 10,000 men and had them prepare a victorious parade march through town.

On the morning of August 31st, Toussaint put on his dress uniform and requested Dessalines, Moyse, Bouquin, and Henry Christophe lead with him. As they entered the town, the road was lined with their former adversaries; British redcoats, dressed in their best parade uniforms, standing at attention.

Toussaint and his officers marched to the center of town as cannons from ships and batteries saluted their arrival. The churches rang their bells and dispatched clergy to briskly walk ahead of the procession with incense and prayers. At the *Place d'Armes* at the center of town, General Maitland waited with six officers ready to greet Toussaint and his entourage. Toussaint turned Bel Argent 10 yards before reaching the group to look back and watch his army arrive.

He remembered a familiar feeling from when he first marched out of *Ouanaminthe* back in 1793; and marveled at how far had he come and the power he had gained. He was proud of these men—once slaves and now a formidable fighting force. They did not disappoint as they paraded in discipline and pageantry, instantly gaining the respect and pride of the townspeople.

No longer British, *Môle Saint Nicolas* was returning as a colony of France. The British had not mistreated the inhabitants, but the citizens always knew they were a people occupied by a foreign power and speaking a different tongue.

When the last of the troops stopped at attention, all gave a unified salute and yell of "*La France!*" before all went quiet. There were 10,000 men stretched down the road and jammed down every side street. Toussaint looked among them, and with great ceremony returned their salute.

"At Ease!"

Toussaint turned and walked to Maitland with his officers in tow. He stopped a yard from the British General, who remained at attention. It was the first meeting of the two men and Maitland was certain that Toussaint would have been taller – larger from the numerous accounts of invincibility he had received from his officers.

In unison, the two formerly saluted each other, as did the officers of both armies. "I congratulate you and your formidable army on this day, and turn the city of *Môle Saint Nicolas* over to you," began General Maitland, breaking the silence. "Please allow us the honor of hosting your first meal in the city."

He turned and gestured toward an elaborate open-air tent wherein a feast had been prepared for the group.

Amidst the food and wine, toasts of formal, and later, informal nature rolled off the officers' tongues as all relaxed and enjoyed each other. The war had officially ended, and the British soldiers were excited to depart for home. Both sides were happy to still be alive.

General Maitland presented Toussaint with two bronze culverin cannons, a cadre of guns, and all the formal silver dishes and furniture with which they'd equipped their government headquarters. Two hours afterward, they exited the tent to find Toussaint's army still standing with unwavering discipline under the hot sun. The townspeople were in awe; pointing to one after the other and offering words of praise as the men stood still, refusing to acknowledge any of the flattery showered upon them.

The British army meanwhile had been at recess and needed to be reassembled. It was clear they were finished in Saint-Domingue and were motivated to leave with honor and dignity. Of the 8,000 in uniform, only 2,000 soldiers were indeed English. The rest were Creole colonists. These would later volunteer into service with Toussaint's army or depart for their homes or farms.

Toussaint marched out of town that afternoon to their encampment while the British began the process of loading their ships over the next few days. About a week later, General Maitland sent word requesting a meeting with Toussaint to officially bid him farewell. He arrived at the camp with three of his officers shortly afterward and was greeted by Toussaint outside his tent.

"Thank you for the courtesy of your time, *Général*," Maitland said.

"It is my honor, General," replied Toussaint. "You may have interest in this order I received two days back."

Toussaint handed a letter to Maitland bearing the broken wax seal of the Commission. Maitland read the letter, composed by Commissioner Roume at the behest of General Hédouville. It encouraged Toussaint to arrest General Maitland 'at his earliest opportunity.'

The General's face grew dark as he looked up at Toussaint.

"I suppose this order cannot be ignored by you, sir? As an officer, I would not hold its execution against you, but know that I would damn the French—all of them!"

"You may also be interested in my response—to be dispatched upon your safe departure," Toussaint said, smiling and extending a piece of parchment addressed to Commissioner Roume. It read:

Commissioner,

What? Have I not given my word to the English Général? How could you suppose that I would cover myself with infamy for violating that promise? The confidence that he has in my good faith engages him to deliver himself to me, and I would be dishonored forever, were I to follow your advice.

I am wholly devoted to the cause of the Republic, but I shall never serve it at the expense of my conscience and my honor.

Toussaint Louverture

Maitland passed the note to his junior officer, returned Toussaint's smile, and briefly nodded as a show of gratitude. Toussaint turned to the curtain of his tent and invited Maitland inside.

The men discussed future trade relations, with Toussaint agreeing to trade with British merchants anywhere he controlled in the colony. Maitland suggested Toussaint was now in a position to proclaim himself King, and went so far as to promise the assistance of the British fleet if ever necessary, provided that Great Britain received the assurance that Toussaint would not expand his influence, especially igniting a slave rebellion, into Jamaica.

Toussaint's sound common sense put him on guard against the proposal of royalty but deemed it wise to maintain good relations with those he was expelling from the colony.

The British army departed a few days later, ending their failed multi-year expedition to conquer Saint-Domingue. Toussaint now felt that the time had come for Hédouville to exit as well. The man was a schemer of massive proportions and a politically dangerous individual to the fragile peace throughout the colony.

An opportunity arose when Hédouville finally made a strategic error. He'd decreed that plantation workers contract themselves for three-year periods at the same plantations at which they were formerly enslaved. This aroused suspicion in the freed slaves; wary that this Frenchman was planning to systematically restore the practice.

Toussaint plotted with Moyse to foment further discontent in the hills, spreading the rumor that Hédouville was indeed planning the reinstatement of slavery. The Cultivators quickly became restless, nervous, and angry.

Toussaint then released 5,000 soldiers from his army and ordered them to act as Cultivators and had rumors circulate that this was Hédouville's doing.

Through his nephew Moyse, Toussaint was also able to convince the masses that Hédouville planned to unseat him. In love and support for their leader, a huge mob assembled, storming the city of *Cap-Français* in search of Hédouville to murder him.

After multiple assassination attempts, Hédouville feared it was no longer safe nor feasible to remain in the colony. He and his security forces fled on ships destined for France in October of 1798, never to return to the colony.

However, before leaving the colony Hédouville, in a final dastardly deed, wrote a letter to *Général* Rigaud relieving him from his duty as a subordinate to Toussaint Louverture. Hédouville criticized Toussaint thoroughly, writing in part;

"... I deplore the perfidy of Général Toussaint Louverture! As a result, Général Rigaud, you are hereby officially absolved of Général Toussaint Louverture's authority upon you as Général-in-Chief. I encourage and implore you to take full command of the Department of the South."

Despite their tenuous good standing, the seeds of new confrontation and civil strife had been sown; and they would soon propel the colony into a new period of conflict, war, and destruction.

Nineteen

THE TOUSSAINT CLAUSE

Cap Français
October 1798

Government House in *Cap-Français* was thriving with energy. It was a Saturday evening, and Toussaint was hosting a dinner for the local business community as well as those visiting from other towns.

Jean and Marie were in attendance, seated apart from each other at the long mahogany table, alongside 16 other guests. Jean was adjacent to a sugar broker from *Gonaïves* named Stéphane Allard. Next to Allard was Caroline Cartier, a well-known local fashion designer, and Véronique Duplantier—wife of Roland Duplantier, a construction tycoon.

To Jean's right, a stunning woman by the name of Micheline Georges—wife of Claude Georges, an influential hardware importer, and retailer—was leading a conversation regarding her delightful experience at an opera in Paris. Beyond her was Marie Hypolite, the mistress of Paul Loussaint, though Jean didn't know much about either of them.

All erupted in laughter at the story Micheline was recounting as Jean glanced over to get a glimpse of Marie. She took his breath away as she giggled at a joke one of the two men beside her had just delivered. He was grateful that she was having such a good time, though he wished he were the one beside her to enjoy her essence.

As dessert dishes were being cleared, Toussaint clinked his glass several times from the head of the table, cleared his throat, and stood. A silence fell over all in attendance.

"I want to thank you all for your presence this evening," Toussaint began, holding a crystal glass of red wine in his hand. "You are the wind behind the sails of our economy—though at times you may feel you are not as appreciated as you should be. Suzanne and I would like to take this opportunity to thank you for what you do, and show our appreciation by welcoming you to the house of our government."

He lifted his glass in a toast.

"Enjoy the festivities of the night—as it is still a young evening!"

"SALUT!" shouted the table in a cheerful, unified response.

String instruments began to play in the adjacent room and four elegantly dressed male servants rolled back the dining room doors to reveal that the *Grande Salle de Bal* - the ballroom - had been filled with 200 more guests who had arrived during the dinner. Toussaint walked to the other end of the table, outstretched his hand to Suzanne, and led her to the dance floor for the first waltz of the evening.

The two waltzed with the familiarity of a couple that had been together dancing for a lifetime. All eyes watched as they swayed together on the dance floor. Commissioner Julien Raimond, the second highest-ranking government guest, took his partner and joined Toussaint after a moment, signaling to the others that the dance floor was now officially open.

The guests at the dining table started to make their way toward the ballroom as those newly arrived eyed them with envy. Jean went to Marie, extended his hand, and slightly bowed his head.

"May I have this dance with the most beautiful woman of the colony?"

"Only if you promise to hold me tight and kiss me afterward," Marie replied with a smile.

"Your request is granted."

Jean led Marie onto the quickly-filling dance floor. Later that evening, while they were engrossed in a conversation with Henry and Marie-Louise Christophe, a soldier approached to whisper something in Henry's ear.

"You will please excuse me as I have been summoned by *Général* Louverture," he said before offering kisses to both Marie-Louise and Marie. "With him, I never know whether I will return within minutes or days—so these are precautionary."

As much as Jean wished to continue to dance with his wife, he would not abandon Marie-Louise until Henry returned or another familiar face joined them. The conversation turned toward Henry and Marie-Louise's children and how quickly they were growing. 15 minutes later, Henry returned to them and quietly pulled Jean aside.

"The Commander-in-Chief would like a word with you, Jean."

"Is that so? What about?"

"I'm not sure, but I know he admires and respects you."

"Well, lead the way," Jean said as they politely excused themselves from the women. Jean smiled as he glanced back to find two well-dressed gentlemen already sidling up to the ladies and begin conversing.

"Good," he thought. *"At least they will keep them company."*

Henry led Jean to a small, hidden living room three doors down from the ballroom. Here, he found Toussaint and his confidant, Commissioner Julien Raimond, seated and conversing with a gentleman who was rising to leave. The man nodded to Jean and Henry as he quickly exited the room.

"Ah, *Monseuir* Bayard. Come sit, please," Toussaint offered. "You as well, Henry."

Toussaint was seated on a bright red, plush Victorian couch. As Jean and Henry approached, the General gestured to the three chairs next to Raimond. An ornate oval cocktail table separated the group.

"Jean, I have long listened to Henry speak of you with the utmost admiration and respect," Toussaint began.

"He well knows the feeling is mutual," Jean responded.

"Have you met Commissioner Raimond, a loyal servant of France and my trusted advisor and confidant?"

"In passing at the hotel, but never formally," Jean responded, extending his hand. "Jean-Baptiste Bayard, Commissioner."

"A pleasure to meet you, Mr. Bayard" replied Raimond as they shook hands.

"Jean," Toussaint interjected, interrupting the socialization. "How is your business these days?"

"It continues to grow, *Général*. Your efforts have finally brought stability to the colony and we are all appreciative of that," Jean replied. "However the trade embargo imposed by the Americans has crippled business for many of us."

"How many ships do you have under sail, Jean?"

"Nine of my own, which I lease. I also subcontract 68 American vessels that ply the route from *Cap-Français* to Boston and my son manages the routes of 43 vessels from *Port Républicain* to New York," Jean replied.

"Your family business is more substantial than I'd imagined, Jean. Well done."

"The credit goes to my wife, Marie. I am simply a servant to her wishes."

"A humble man. I appreciate that," Toussaint replied with a knowing smile. "The colony requires some services which I feel you are well suited to administer. This will require some time and you will be duly compensated."

"I will attempt to live up to your expectations and do my best for the colony, but what may I ask, is it you require, *Général*?"

"You have been to America; you speak English well, and you fought in the American revolutionary war. The Americans would give you a warm reception, so I would hope."

"I indeed participated in the Battle of Savannah back in '79 with the Chasseurs Volontaires de Saint-Domingue, and I saw many of our patriots wounded or killed on their behalf. I would hope they would be grateful for our service and sacrifice," Jean agreed.

"I need an audience with their government. I wish to begin diplomatic relations with these United States," Toussaint said.

"Wouldn't that be administered from Paris, *Général*?" Jean inquired.

"The colony is progressing, Jean. It is time we begin speaking with our neighbors in this hemisphere from our own voice and not as a subject of France," Toussaint said, pausing to take a sip from his glass and leaning back on the couch. "I have spoken to Commissioner Raimond and he is in agreement—with most of my ideas at least."

He glanced toward Raimond who reluctantly nodded his agreement and interjected; "*Monsieur* Bayard, we are not talking of a break from France—but an informal engagement. As you know, the Americans and the French are, shall we say, of a different mindset nowadays?"

"In what capacity are you asking me to serve?" asked Jean.

"To act as my Diplomatic Trade Envoy to the United States," Toussaint responded.

"You mean an Ambassador?"

"No, not Ambassador—Diplomatic Trade Envoy," Raimond interrupted with a harsh and firm tone. "There is a crucial difference. We have no authority to appoint anyone to an official ambassadorial role; that is the sole right of France." Raimond firmly stated.

Jean continued to listen as Toussaint took over the conversation. Henry sat still and silent, monitoring the exchange.

"John Adams is a powerful man. He was the first Vice President under General George Washington. Now, he is the second President of the United States," Toussaint went on. "I have read about this man extensively from news reports. Many like him—but many do not. Those that do are aligned with emancipation. Those who do not are slavers. That tells me he is sympathetic to our cause and this is the perfect time to approach an American President."

"I can reach out to some contacts, but I do not have many inroads to the American government," replied Jean, somewhat apologetically. "What are you hoping to accomplish?"

"To open diplomatic channels and see how the United States and Saint-Domingue can benefit each other, as well as expand trade—among other things," Toussaint answered.

"Allow me time to speak with some colleagues before revisiting the subject with you, *Général*."

"Please do, Jean. Find out what they may require from us and I will in turn generate a list of services they could provide our colony."

He lifted his glass and the others instantly followed.

"An equal exchange for equal partners is what I seek," concluded Toussaint.

A few days later, Jean's brother Andre arrived back from one of his trips to Philadelphia. Andre had been traveling the route back and forth for over five years, spending months at a time in America. Jean quickly invited him to lunch. After some small talk, he steered the conversation to business.

"Tell me, brother, how is the new country, the United States of America?" asked Jean.

"Doing remarkably well, I'd say. Their economy is booming and within a few years should match the kinds of revenue we once enjoyed here," Andre replied.

"*Général* Louverture is keen to establish diplomatic channels with the country—and has asked me to be an envoy for trade," Jean said.

"I would decline that invitation, Jean," said Andre. "Two reasons: first, it would be extremely time-consuming and not worthwhile without substantial financial reward; and second, you are a *Gens de Couleur* and would not be accepted in many circles in that country."

"Are they openly prejudiced?"

"In some areas yes, and in others not. They do still legalize the slavery of Africans. To be effective, however, you would need to be white, Jean."

"I see. Who would you recommend for the position then, that is both white and loyal to our colony?" prodded Jean.

"Your man is Joseph Bunel," replied Andre without a moment's hesitation. "He is a white Frenchman married to a black Saint-Dominguen Creole named Marie Fanchette Estève. He is an abolitionist and very loyal to our colony."

"What does he do now?" asked Jean.

"He runs a plantation for an absentee owner in the *Plaine du Nord* and has an import and export business as well. They are quite well-run, I understand. I dealt with him as your sugar broker and can attest that he is solid of character and integrity."

"Can he negotiate? Is he political?"

Andre smiled.

"Oh, I had many a negotiation with him. I met my match, no doubt. As for politics, any good businessman can outmaneuver any politician, as you well know."

The two shared a hearty laugh.

Within the week, Jean and Andre made plans to visit Bunel at the *Labadie* plantation several miles away from *Cap-Français*. Jean was pleased to find he immediately liked the man. They conversed with him and his wife over the afternoon, dined with them that evening, and enjoyed an overnight stay in their home. Jean had confided the nature of the visit, and by the time he and Andre were preparing to leave the next morning, secured Bunel's cooperation should he pass muster with Toussaint.

Returning to *Cap-Français*, Jean sought an audience with Toussaint to convince him that he was not the best choice for the task. Instead, he made his recommendation that the General meets with Bunel. Andre, in the meantime, was on his way back to Philadelphia to explore a diplomatic channel with President John Adams.

Jean quickly arranged a lunch for Bunel, Toussaint, and Julien Raimond to have a preliminary meeting. After a short time, Toussaint officially appointed Joseph Bunel as his Diplomatic Trade Envoy to the United States and requested he depart to Philadelphia, the United States capital, as soon as possible.

Throughout November, Toussaint and Bunel met multiple times to reach an understanding of strategies and Toussaint's goals. Marie Fanchette prepared their plantation for an extended absence and by the end of the month, Jean received word from Andre of a connection with the Secretary of State's office and willingness to entertain a meeting.

Joseph and Marie Fanchette arrived in Philadelphia late that December, staying at the Morris House Hotel across from Washington Square. Snow had fallen the day before their arrival and Joseph and Marie strolled through the busy city, marveling at the snow-filled streets, albeit a stranger of cold weather.

Philadelphia, then capitol of the United States, was alive with vibrancy and life everywhere. Most hotels were filled with private and official balls hosted by foreign diplomats, local celebrities, and dignitaries—or had signs announcing upcoming events. Restaurants and pubs were overflowing with customers and laughter and amusement spilled onto the streets. During the day, newsboys selling competing papers would shout over each other to lure customers out of their coins, and cafes brimmed with patrons.

Andre had scheduled a meeting with Timothy Pickering, the Secretary of State, the day after Christmas; December 26, 1798. Pickering had been Secretary of State to George Washington and was kept on by the John Adams administration. The meeting was meant to be secret, as Pickering did not want Thomas Jefferson, Vice President, and a slave-holding planter, to catch wind.

Pickering's home was located in one of the fastest-growing areas of the city with neighbors consisting of congressmen, senators, artisans, businessmen, and even African Americans. As Bunel rounded the corner of Sixth Street onto Arch Street, he noticed the two-story home made of substantial brick was by far the most attractive on the block.

At 3:00 pm that Wednesday, Bunel knocked at the door. He was surprised to be greeted not by a butler or assistant but by Rebecca Pickering, wife of the secretary, in an elegant gown. Mrs. Pickering cheerfully asked whether his wife Marie Fanchette would be joining them. Marie however had previously insisted on declining the invitation so her black skin would not interfere in the delicate negotiations her husband was about to embark on.

Bunel, who had anticipated a private meeting with Secretary Pickering, was surprised to find other prominent guests of the American government also on hand for dinner. Among them was Congressmen Harrison Gray Otis from the state of Massachusetts, Robert Goodloe Harper of South Carolina, and even the Speaker of the House Jonathan Dayton from New Jersey.

The evening was lively and cordial and Bunel found himself the center of attention of his fellow diners—each wanting to extract information on the current circumstances in the rich and famous colony of Saint-Domingue. The participants discussed trade openly, going so far as to hint at the colony's possible independence from France. Pickering had anticipated the need to lead the conversations to obtain the best possible outcome in case Bunel was inexperienced in such matters. However, the island emissary surprised the gathering with his immense understanding of international trade, currency exchanges, commodities, and a host of other complex financial and supply chain topics. In fact, most of his positions on each mirrored Pickering's own.

Once the last guest departed, Rebecca approached the two.

"Tim, I have your brandy ready in your study."

She escorted the men to a room filled with books and manuscripts of politics and world affairs. Finding their seats in a small area of the study, Rebecca quickly poured two brandies into snifters, left the room, and shut the door.

"Thank you for your hospitality and audience, Mr. Secretary," Bunel began as they made themselves comfortable on two chairs near a warm fireplace. "I also extend greetings from the warm shores of Saint-Domingue and our Commander-in-Chief, *Général* Toussaint Louverture."

"It is an honor to receive you," Pickering replied. "Though we have conversed well throughout dinner, we still have much to discuss."

"Indeed," agreed Bunel. "*Général* Louverture greatly desires to foster a spirit of cooperation and trust between our two countries."

"Ah—but you do not represent a country," Pickering lightly scolded. "You are simply a colony of France."

The Secretary was cleverly testing the waters.

"Are you suggesting a separation from the homeland?" he continued.

Bunel parried the question with one of his own.

"Is France not a nation with which the United States is currently in an undeclared war, Mr. Secretary?"

"It is an unfortunate truth that the great nation of France and our United States do not agree on certain aspects of current affairs," Pickering allowed. "France believes our treaty reached with England—*the Jay Treaty*—violates some of our past agreements. We of course disagree."

"If we must discuss the Franco – American dispute, did it not begin with the United States' suspension of war debt payment obligations years ago?" asked Bunel, hoping to keep Pickering on the defensive.

"That debt was owed to King Louis the Sixteenth, not the new Republic that took over the country. Once the King was deposed—or should I say, murdered—the United States government considered such debt null and void."

"I am not a banker, Mr. Secretary, however, I understand that France, through surrogate privateers, has viciously attacked American trading vessels in the name of this undeclared Quasi War,"

Bunel pivoted.

"Yes. France cannot officially declare war as that would violate our treaties and officially void any debt they claim is still owed. As a result, they send their pirates to sink our merchant ships, steal their cargo and murder our citizens—all without claiming responsibility. Their pirates have already seized or sunken over 300 of these vessels."

"Is your navy not able to control this problem?" asked Bunel.

"After the revolution, our navy was dismantled and we became weakened on the seas due to budgetary constraints. We liquidated most of the ships to satisfy our short-term financing needs," admitted Pickering. "When we realized the danger in so doing, we quickly resumed rebuilding our navy. It has taken until now however to finally commission a few ships earlier this year."

Bunel nodded.

"We can only take care of some of the attacks around our shores; but not so much in the Caribbean. There they are launching raids from Tortuga, off your shores."

"If we could help take care of your French privateering problem—the pirates, that is…?" lead Bunel.

"We would be most grateful, of course," replied Pickering. "And in return?"

"The French Embargo Act passed this past June by your congress prohibits all trade with France and French colonies—which, as you pointed out, includes Saint-Domingue. This is crippling our ability to rebuild our economy after the ravages of war and unrest these past few years," stated Bunel. "Before this embargo, over 600 American ships routinely visited our ports and openly traded with our people. This current conflict has nothing to do with us but is devastating to our mutual commerce, all the same, hurting your people and ours."

Pickering looked over Bunel with admiration and respect. He quickly came to appreciate this man and the eloquence with which he approached matters. He also appeared to be a skillful negotiator.

"If we eliminated your pirate problem, would you consider

officially opening our trade routes?" Bunel offered, not disclosing the masterful scheme currently being played by Jean-Baptiste Bayard and some others by utilizing British vessels sailing cargo back and forth under British flags. "We respectfully request, that you make it legal for American vessels to trade with us."

"I am well aware of the Bayard family's vessels already trading in our ports," replied Pickering, surprising Bunel. "They are in a gray area as they ingeniously lease American vessels and brand them under the British flag, skirting the law. *Bravo.*"

He raised his glass while winking at Bunel. "It does benefit commerce though, eh?"

Pickering and Bunel were of equal minds and understood that the dinner they had conducted was the first step in the political lobbying necessary in Philadelphia. The next would be a proposition to President John Adams.

Pickering escorted Bunel to the front door where he was joined again by his wife, Rebecca. Bunel tipped his hat to the Secretary's wife and thanked her for a wonderful evening. She bid him good night and left once more. Pickering opened the door, letting in bitterly cold air, and they exchanged final words. As they shared a hearty handshake, both were in sincere hope of a successful outcome.

As Bunel exited the front door, a figure in the shadows across the street silently observed the two before disappearing under the cover of darkness.

Over the next several days Bunel was introduced to other members of Congress by selected friends of Pickering. As it could be claimed, Bunel was acting alone and in an unofficial capacity, the administration could plausibly deny any involvement in case negotiations backfired. However, unbeknownst to him, Bunel was being closely tracked by the same shadowy figure taking note of names, dates, and how long he spent with each lawmaker.

Even in the most tolerant of cities, like Philadelphia, the specter of race and slavery was not far from the central debate. Bunel and Marie Fanchette dined in the very best of restaurants and were treated with dignity and respect, albeit now and then they would catch awkward stares directed at the handsome White gentleman with the pretty negro woman by his side.

The Sunday afternoon following his dinner with Pickering, Bunel purchased the local newspaper, *The Pennsylvania Packet,* and encountered three articles of contrasting opinions that piqued his interest. They represented evidence of the day's variant positions on slavery and race relations. One reported the arrest of David Lewis under the provisions of the 1793 Fugitive Slave Law.

As quoted in the article, Lewis was a Mulatto man who confessed to 'being enslaved to Leany Jones of Richmond, Virginia.' Lewis was taken into custody and jailed awaiting 'his master to claim him and take him away.' This was occurring in Chester County—the county right next door to Philadelphia!

In the book reviews section of the tabloid was an excerpt from a popular book by Francis Stanislaus, *A Voyage to St. Domingo,* which extolled the virtue of 'the whip' as a remedy for the 'natural sloth and inactivity of black Dominguans.'

Interestingly, the same newspaper's international section included reports that Toussaint Louverture, 'beloved and respected for his talents, mild manners, and good faith, is the director in chief of that extensive, fertile, populous, and wealthy island of Saint-Domingue.' It also spoke of 'American disgrace' at the hands of French privateers, distinguishing the differences between condemnation of French aggression and the public approval of cooperation with the 'burgeoning Black-led government of Toussaint Louverture.'

Bunel knew navigating these conflicting attitudes and ideals would require careful crafting of public opinion and an innate understanding of which side the person with whom he was conversing fell as he navigated the halls of Congress.

The next day, December 31st, Pickering picked up Bunel at the hotel. After a brief carriage ride, they arrived on Market Street, between Fifth and Sixth Streets. Bunel admired the four-bay asymmetrical facade of the London-inspired three-story home in front of which they'd stopped. This was the city's largest private residence—The President's House.

The home had been occupied by George and Martha Washington from 1790-1797 during the former's presidency. In stark contrast to Adams, the first President had brought eight slaves from their Virginia mansion to serve them, whereas John Adams owned no slaves and employed only paid workers to go about servicing the home.

The Butler who greeted them with a genuine smile appeared happy and Bunel noticed the interracial staff treated him with a good amount of respect. The party was led to the third-floor office where Adams himself was waiting.

As the President stood from his desk and walked to greet them, he paused to warm his hands over the iron stove which heated the room. After the appropriate small talk, Bunel laid out Toussaint Louverture's proposal for bilateral relations, the re-opening of trade, and personal promises to protect American vessels from French privateers while respecting U.S. sovereignty. Secretary of State Pickering heartily endorsed the plan and assured the President he could shepherd the legislation through Congress.

Adams endorsed it in general and the men agreed to keep the meeting between them a secret until Pickering had the opportunity to shore up support.

President Adams invited Bunel to rejoin him for dinner in the formal state dining room in the new year on January 7, 1799. This would make history as the first official dinner between an American President and a representative of an African-led government.

Adams invited Pickering, as well as his closest advisors and several congressmen to dine with them. The conversation strategized the framework of a multicultural foreign policy for American

merchants and exporters. Discussions also centered on the need for a tripartite treaty involving the United States, Great Britain, and Saint-Domingue, and the final subject being an agreement on the need for U.S. representation in *Cap Français* and assured protection for American citizens.

The dinner exposed a striking difference in foreign policy in regards to the former President Washington, whose administration contributed money in U.S. support for Saint-Domingue's White planters in 1793 to help quash Toussaint Louverture and the revolutionary Blacks, fearing they would export the slave rebellion to American shores.

In contrast, President Adams now welcomed cooperation with the same revolutionaries—now leaders—to secure their future freedom in the world.

Bunel exited the dinner with an air of satisfaction, but as he was boarding the carriage, caught sight of a familiar shadow across the street. He had begun to see the man continuously after his first meeting with Pickering and decided the time had come to formally introduce himself and confront the man in the dark. As he crossed the street to accost the stranger, a passing carriage nearly ran him over. By the time it passed, the man had once again disappeared into the night.

A few blocks away, the shadowy figure slipped into the rear entrance of the two-story office and home of Philippe de Létombe, the powerful French consul to the United States. The man's feet traversed the familiar steps, stopping to knock on the door of the study. A voice inside the room called for him to enter.

"You have every reason to be concerned, your excellency," stated the shadow.

"Tell me—what have you learned Desbardes?" Létombe asked. Desbardes poured himself a large glass of cognac without being offered and immediately took a gulp.

"This envoy—Joseph Bunel, sent by Louverture—is making headway in gaining favor with the Americans, independent of France."

"In what sense?" prompted Létombe.

Desbardes took another swallow and continued.

"He and the Secretary of State are lobbying members of Congress to allow the President to decide whether to resume trade with Saint-Domingue—or any of our French colonies, for that matter—and offer protection from us."

"Has Bunel already met with the President?"

"Yes, this very evening! Someone I have well placed in the president's office who is familiar with this affair confirmed he is indeed warm to Louverture and the colony. Pickering appears to be at the forefront of the effort."

"Continue to report back all intelligence on this matter," Létombe stated. "*Au revoir*."

Desbardes guzzled the last of his cognac and began to leave, pausing for Létombe to stop him. He turned back.

"Are you not forgetting something, your Excellency?"

"On the side table, Desbardes. I wanted you to ask for it," said Létombe. "There is a difference between a patriot and a spy, you know. A patriot works for the love of France. A spy for the currency of any."

Desbardes looked at Létombe with barely concealed contempt before walking to the table and picking up an envelope. He quickly flipped his thumb through the paper currency within.

"There is no need to count Desbardes," Létombe said without looking up from his newspaper.

Desbardes turned and left the room.

Pickering led a host of allies in Congress lobbying the cause and soon executed a brilliant presentation to the full body arguing to establish a foreign policy that would increase American commercial coffers, provide bargaining leverage in Franco-American negotiations, and propel the United States past Great Britain in diplomacy with the Black-led government of Saint-Domingue.

Opponents of the arrangement included slaveholding planters in the South who feared potentially importing the colony's successful experiment in Black freedom to the United States. They argued the legislation violated the U.S. French Embargo Act passed in June of 1798, which prohibited trade with French-held possessions.

However, Pickering out-maneuvered them by attaching a key amendment to the existing act to quickly initiate the plan. The amendment authorized the president, at his sole discretion, to reopen or suspend trade with 'any persons, claiming, and exercising command and authority, in any island, port or place, belonging to the French Republic that guaranteed to stop privateering against U.S. merchant vessels.'

As the amendment was designed to benefit Toussaint Louverture and Saint-Domingue, the Southern lobby labeled it "Toussaint's Clause" and vowed to incorporate it as a negative campaign issue moving forward.

Politicians representing planters from the South howled at Pickering's successful gambit. Southern planters warned that before the embargo, American vessels were employing more and more Black seamen emanating from the newly freed Saint-Domingue.

These ex-slaves were arriving in American ports with money in their pockets and stories of a lush tropical paradise run by a free Black government existing just a few hundred miles south. This was riling up their local slaves as they pointed to the American Declaration of Independence wherein it stated, '*All men are created equal*'. The document was older than that of the French, however never implemented as intended.

On the final Friday of January, Bunel arrived at his hotel after a long day of talks with an assortment of congressmen. As he opened the door to his suite, he instantly felt something was wrong. He eyed the sofa and spotted a crumpled newspaper on one of the pillows. The bedroom of the luxurious suite was closed and his wife was nowhere to be found. He quickly approached the doors and flung them open.

Inside he found Marie in tears, lying on the bed. She looked up at him as he ran to comfort her.

"Why do you stay with me, Joseph? All I bring you is heartache and hardship," she sniffled.

"Nothing is further from the truth, Marie. I love you and I knew exactly what my future would be when we married. I did not regret it then and I do not regret it now!"

"Did you see what the newspaper wrote about me… about us?" asked Marie as she hid her swollen eyes filled with tears.

"Some racist senator spilling garbage into the streets," Bunel spat.

"They are talking about us, Joseph! It's in all the newspapers!" she cried, handing him one of the two papers on the bed. The headline read:

CONGRESSMAN GALLATIN CONDEMNS THE ENVOY OF SAINT-DOMINGUE FOR MISCEGENATION ON HOUSE FLOOR

Speech Proclaims Joseph Bunel Flagrantly Flaunts Negro Wife in Streets of Philadelphia

Bunel had already read the article earlier in the day. He had to look up 'miscegenation' in a dictionary to understand it referred to interbreeding between races. The article named him and his wife as the perpetrators of a crime. The article was pulling at straws in an attempt to excite the population against the legislation being proposed by Pickering.

Though he dismissed it as racist political propaganda, he knew the accusations were hard on her. They'd been in Philadelphia for a month and found it quite different than back home—where she was a highly-respected member of the community. Here, she felt like an outsider because of her skin color.

"I know it affects you terribly," Bunel comforted.

"They talk of me like I am dirty; as if I am an animal, not human!"

"It is they who should feel shame, Marie! I know this is difficult, but we are at war. This is a struggle for all Africans to regain their dignity after hundreds of years of bondage. *Général* Toussaint fought for it on the battlefield and we now fight it in the public forum. We must be strong," Bunel insisted.

"I do not know if I am strong enough, Joseph. I am not like you," Marie said, taking her kerchief and dabbing her eyes.

"You are indeed stronger than I, Marie. You are on the front lines. Tonight, we will go to war!"

"What do you mean?" asked a bewildered Marie.

"We will dine at the finest restaurant in Philadelphia and show all of them we are not hiding from the filth they wrote today. That it affects us not!"

"I cannot Joseph. Not after those newspapers!"

"You must! You are fighting for all of your people Marie—for your children. You are in the best position to resist this prejudice. It is not easy, but it is our duty."

"Even if I wanted to, I have nothing to wear. I have worn all of my garments already and must send them for cleaning."

"Come with me," Bunel said extending his hand for her to take.

Marie stood and followed him to the living room of the suite. Bunel went to the main door and knocked on it twice. In walked three White women with garment bags and suitcases.

"Good afternoon, Mrs. Bunel," one of them greeted in a cheery voice.

"We are here at your service," said another smartly-dressed blonde.

"Good afternoon, ladies. Joseph, what is the meaning of this?" asked Marie, flabbergasted.

"I wasn't sure what color or style of dress you would prefer tonight, so Valerie from the dress shop around the corner brought a half dozen selections to choose from."

He nodded to the first woman who had entered and the brunette standing next to her.

"Colleen is from the hair salon, and Kathleen does nails and cosmetics," smiled Joseph. "I will go and attend to restaurant reservations for, let's say 6:00? Does that give you enough time?"

Marie flew into his arms and hugged him tight. She looked at Joseph with loving eyes. It was all the answer he needed.

"Now get out of here as I have a wonderful husband to dress for!" she scolded, lovingly. Bunel turned and left the room, hearing the four women giggling behind him like schoolgirls on the playground.

He headed over to City Tavern, a favorite restaurant of President Adams, congressmen, and other notables of Philadelphia. The President had insisted he dine there while visiting the city. The eatery had opened in 1773 and had been famous for serving Philadelphia's best food for the past twenty-five years. The President had even procured a personally-signed note to give to the host on a busy night. He entered the establishment, asked for the manager, and deftly dropped the President's note to secure his reservation for the evening.

At 6:00 exactly, Joseph and Marie arrived and exited their coach in front of City Tavern. Marie Fanchette was ravishing in an emerald and white Victorian gown, adorned with a beautiful necklace of new shiny white pearls and a single encrusted diamond Joseph had just purchased for her on his way back from the restaurant.

As they entered, pairs of eyes peered toward them from every table as the congressmen's hateful and prejudiced speech was still fresh in the midst. A slight hush fell over the crowded eatery as the host cheeringly escorted them past, holding a chair for Marie to sit on and elegantly pushing her in as a show for the other diners.

A woman suddenly approached them and hissed, "I am shocked you would show your face here after what my husband said on the floor of Congress yesterday, Mr. Bunel."

Bunel stood and extended his hand. "I apologize madame—we have not been formally introduced. My name is Joseph Bunel, Diplomatic Envoy of Governor *Général* Louverture of Saint-Domingue."

"I know who you are, *Monsieur* Bunel," she shot back.

"And who are you, *Madame*?"

"Hannah Gallatin, wife of Congressman Albert Gallatin."

"I see. Allow me to introduce *my* wife, Marie Fanchette."

"I have no interest, *Monsieur*. What I am interested in is what you do in public—in public *with her!*"

"I was pleased to read your husband's comments in the newspapers," continued Bunel without missing a beat. "It has brought forth a flood of wonderful emotions which remind me of the love I enjoy with my wife."

He looked over at Marie with admiration and affection.

"We are here to celebrate just that actually. Is the congressman present, so I may thank him personally?"

"Whatever is it you are talking about?" replied a confused Hannah Gallatin.

"Your husband accurately pointed out how very special my Marie Fanchette is, *Madame*."

"Excuse me?" asked the woman, more confused than ever.

"Why it is as simple as the beautiful necklace Marie is now wearing. Don't you understand, *Madame*? Do I need to simplify it further for you?"

Hannah Gallatin was equally confused and appalled. "I am at a loss, *Monsieur* Bunel."

The pearl necklace she wears has many beautiful white faces on it, does it not?" prompted Bunel.

"So?"

"So, you could very well be one of those many, many same white faces. But notice the diamond centerpiece is dramatically different. That beautiful specimen is like my wife; surrounded by common white pearls, such as yourself, yet she is magnificently special. Your husband is brilliant to have pointed this out to everyone in Philadelphia—perhaps the entire nation!"

"How dare you!" Hannah Gallatin seethed.

"We are here, *Madame* to celebrate all of the wonderful publicity Congressman Gallatin has showered upon us in your American newspapers. Please do thank him on our behalf."

With that, Bunel turned his back on the red-faced woman and sat down across from Marie. Hannah Gallatin gasped at his gall, and Marie covered her smile with her kerchief and she picked up a menu. The woman snarled several choice words under her breath and stormed off.

Joseph and Marie had a wonderful dinner that evening, the latter even seeming to revel a bit in her new notoriety.

Pickering's plan proceeded well. By helping secure the passage of the amendment, Adams scored points with the fledgling country's business community, which had suffered huge losses under the current embargo. Newspapers were touting its benefits and the administration of Toussaint Louverture was looked upon with favor by the average American.

President Adams was now at liberty to act further. He required more than a consul for trade; he needed a man of action, whom he could trust to make appropriate decisions in a faraway land.

He summoned Alexander Hamilton, Inspector General of the United States Army to his office along with Secretary of State Pickering. Hamilton was familiar with the Caribbean, having grown up in Christiansted, St. Croix—a Danish colony. He was against slavery and of equal minds with Adams approximately half the time.

"Hamilton, I know you, and I do not see eye-to-eye on all things," Adams began. "But I trust your recommendation for a diplomatic trade envoy to Saint-Domingue, and require it post haste."

Adams laid out his strategy, being careful to caution against the appearance of backing any move that could be interpreted as supporting the colony's independence from France. Hamilton listened carefully but responded immediately.

"I have just the man for the job, Mr. President."

Twenty

THE BREAK OF TOUSSAINT
AND RIGAUD

Cap-Français
January 1799

In a span of only four years—from 1794 through 1798—Toussaint had driven out the British from Saint-Domingue, overseen the retreat of the Spanish, ousted virtually all French bureaucratic and militaristic authority from the colony, and become Commander-in-Chief and Governor-*Général* of a near autonomous Saint-Domingue.

As he saw it, there were now only three remaining challenges to his supreme authority—and he needed counsel from the only person he trusted: the love of his life, Suzanne.

The two were seated enjoying their morning coffee ritual on the veranda of Government House in early January of 1799. Suzanne had wrapped a blanket around her as the winter wind coming from the bay was chilly and moist, but she did so love the outdoors.

Toussaint fidgeted slightly before impatiently blurting out what was on his mind.

"Suzanne, I have three issues that I need your counsel on. First, the National Assembly in France believes I am not loyal to France and am secretly courting independence…"

"I have heard that quite a bit, Toussaint. So, are you?" Suzanne asked pointedly.

Toussaint continued without acknowledgment; "Second, *Général* André Rigaud and his Mulatto forces are a problem. Rigaud claims Hédouville has granted him autonomous authority in the South. He has written claiming that he is no longer subordinate to me."

"That is indeed a problem, Toussaint. I believed him an honorable gentleman when he came for a visit. And the third issue?"

"Spanish Santo Domingo must be turned French. Our current treaty with Spain ceded the colony to France. We must take control of it before the Spanish citizens there get used to ruling themselves."

"Toussaint, I so wish that you and Sonthonax, or even Hédouville had been able to get along. Sonthonax worked tirelessly to save the colony for France—and you worked to free the slaves, which he ended up making official in the eyes of the Government," Suzanne said. "Are you that much different?"

"Sonthonax is a scoundrel! He only freed the slaves because he had no other choice—he would have been killed by the Whites. It was inevitable that we would find ourselves in conflict, Suzanne."

"Well, you ultimately won and shipped Sonthonax back to France. However, the Commissioner assured his place in our history by abolishing slavery in Saint-Domingue."

"I also had Hédouville chased off; the people feared he would re-enslave them and undo all their beloved Sonthonax had accomplished" Toussaint added.

"I agree—Hédouville was up to no good," said Suzanne, nodding her head slightly. "You have been through a lot Toussaint. You fought against the French for the Spanish, came back to the

French, and ended up defeating not only the Spanish but driving the British out of Saint-Domingue."

She reached her hand over to grab his.

"I am so proud of you, my husband. I always hear how your soldiers and citizens adore and respect you for what you have done for them."

"Thank you Suzanne—but do not underestimate the delicate will of the people. They can turn within a day's notice if the right scoundrel motivates their emotions," he replied. "As for the French, that is another story altogether; they fear my growing power and suspect I have sentiments toward independence—which I do not right now."

"I know, my love. But if that is their perception, you will need to eliminate it," Suzanne said forcefully.

"I presume that is why they sent Hédouville in the first place— to save the colony from me. Unfortunately, he managed to drive a wedge between Rigaud and me before leaving. I suspect he is safely back home now, anxious to spread his venom and watch our conflict."

"Can you salvage the relationship with Rigaud, for the sake of the colony Toussaint?" Suzanne asked, almost pleading. "You have a history together. You together defeated the British. He dined at our home and appeared quite pleasant!"

"I do not know. I just don't know."

Toussaint rose from his seat and approached the veranda's guardrail.

"He is certainly stubborn and can have a foul and violent personality—which you did not experience—and I strongly believe he has his eyes on the ultimate rule of the South, perhaps even as an independent colony."

"And none of that applies to you, Toussaint?" she replied with a smile.

He ignored her comment and changed the subject. "What do we make of this new United States of America?" he asked of her. "Not only is the United States a newly free nation, but it could be a model we might follow. The Secretary of State, a man named Timothy Pickering, is presenting a friendly and supportive position with us in their capital."

"You may do well to align the colony with a small, fledgling country rather than with either the colonial aspirations of Britain or France," said Suzanne, thoughtfully. "The primary question is whether you'd have better trade deals with the United States? If so, can you still maintain good relations with Paris?"

"That is exactly why I sent Joseph Bunel as our Diplomatic Trade Envoy. He is making headway in Philadelphia on our behalf. We must get this embargo lifted—France and the United States are at odds because of the Americans' debt to them. France is punishing them for this, but we are the ones suffering."

"What about the landowners, Toussaint? Will they support you on this?"

"I am certain that they will. It is in their economic interests. Instead of dealing with France's *Exclusif* prices, they could make up lost revenue through trade with the United States and perhaps look favorably upon our government for ushering in new prosperity."

He turned back to his chair and strode back over to rejoin Suzanne.

"As it stands now, their crops are rotting and the salted fish, lumber, and iron from America are no longer being supplied."

"Toussaint, you cannot tell anyone of your plans to move away from France and closer to the United States. You must keep the appearance of loyalty to France. You need to make a statement of support," counseled Suzanne.

"My idea is to ask Philippe Roume to come back from Santo Domingo to *Cap-Français* and assume the duties previously held by Hédouville as France's representative. I shall be seen as pro-France for asking him to become the new French agent. I will also compose a letter to the French *Directorie* explaining that it was Hédouville alone who expedited his own departure owing to bad policies which caused our people to rise up against him."

Toussaint's loyalty to France was not purely posturing. There was an innate trust and loyalty to France among the *Gens de Couleur—the free people of color like him, whether Black or Mulatto,* particularly those freed before general emancipation. These citizens wished to separate themselves from the former slaves and had adopted French culture and customs as their identity—mostly scorning anything African. They spoke French, dressed in its fashion, practiced the Catholic religion, and idealized France. Toussaint also had a strong bond with France as his sons were currently studying there.

Both the North and South of the colony experienced relative calm after Hédouville's departure. An influx of white planters returned to their plantations, began a rebirth of agriculture, and rumors started to circulate of the soon-to-be-enacted *"Toussaint's Clause"* which would lift the trade embargo with the United States.

Toussaint welcomed back those who had fled during the conflict with open arms. He knew that being in power required guns, cannons, swords, soldiers, and ammunition—these essentials required money. Money was derived from sugar, coffee, and indigo which produced export duties and taxes. These required more White planters and their financial investments to join the Gens de Couleur planters as well as Cultivators to work the land.

Toussaint declared the enforcement of the work code Hédouville had initiated and justified it as law from France. The order stated that 'any man not in the army must stay on the land he had worked previously on as a slave, and contract himself for three years'. Most of the Cultivators were disgruntled by this, but fell short of dubbing it the practice of slavery, as they were being paid a wage. Toussaint's men soon came to be known as *soldiers of the gun* while the Cultivators became *workers of the hoe.*

Phillippe Roume arrived in *Cap-Français* from Santo Domingo later that January and immediately set out to calm the disagreements between Toussaint and Rigaud. Rigaud worried France because of his readiness to kill both Whites and Blacks when it served his purposes. Rigaud was also ruling a semi-independent colony in the South after the British were expelled.

Roume prepared for a trip to *Port Républicain* and asked Toussaint to meet him for the fifth-anniversary celebration of the 1794 official abolition of slavery on February 4th. The earlier August 1793 'Sonthonax liberation' had not been considered official by France and remained uncelebrated.

The celebration was attended by Toussaint, with his officers Mornet, and Laplume at his side. Rigaud was also in attendance with his officers, Beauvais and Pétion. The huge celebration featured dancing, drums, food, and plenty of rum. All hoped Rigaud and Toussaint would be able to reconcile and the colony would remain at peace.

After the celebration, Roume spoke to Rigaud privately. The Commissioner, the official replacement of Hédouville, wished to ensure that Rigaud understood he reported to Toussaint, regardless of Hédouville's letter. Rigaud was not pleased and demanded he be in charge of *Petit Goâve, Grand Goâve,* and *Léogâne*; towns located in the southern territory he had conquered from the British.

Hoping to settle the matter, Roume called a meeting to review the issues facing them. Toussaint arrived later than expected and found Roume and Rigaud conversing in a seated area on the veranda of the Commissioner's office.

Roume stood when Toussaint entered.

"Welcome Governor *Général* and thank you for coming. I assume you are familiar with *Général* Rigaud"

Toussaint stood at attention, giving Rigaud the French military salute as a sign of respect. Rigaud sat casually and looked up at Toussaint.

"Louverture, you can save your salute for your men. You are neither my superior nor subordinate."

Toussaint stood a while longer at attention to demonstrate to Roume how rude and unprofessional Rigaud was acting. After a few moments of complete awkward silence, Toussaint dropped his unanswered salute and extended his hand to Roume. The latter's eye contact revealed to Toussaint that Roume preferred him to Rigaud. Toussaint assumed Roume would likely report back to his superiors of this incident—citing Rigaud as unprofessional.

"Shall we have a conversation, then?" Roume asked—more an order than a request. The three men entered a comfortable and well-appointed library with couches and chairs for seating.

The meeting was tense with disagreements and accusations launched from both sides. Rigaud accused Toussaint of motivating the Black Cultivators against the Mulattos, making it increasingly difficult to oversee them on the plantations. Toussaint claimed Rigaud was applying laws more harshly to former Black slaves and imprisoning them without due process.

Back and forth the grievances went, eventually leading to the ongoing dispute concerning would rule *Petit* and *Grand Goâve*. Roume included the towns under Toussaint's authority, to which Rigaud vehemently objected.

"*Général* Rigaud, it is time to unite the colony for the good of all our peoples," stated Roume. "Do you not agree, gentlemen?"

"This colony will unite when all of us drop the past and commit to building the colony back to its former greatness," interjected Toussaint. "To accomplish this, Whites, Blacks, and Mulattos must live together in peace."

"Do not think I did not notice you listing the Mulattos last in your list, Louverture," Rigaud snapped with contempt. "Here is my list of demands should we wish to accomplish peace; first, Saint-Domingue belongs to the Mulattos."

Rigaud held up his fingers as he counted. "Second, France belongs to the Whites. Finally, Negros can go back to Africa!"

With that, Rigaud stood and walked out of the meeting, vowing to never give up his territory to Toussaint. Rigaud then departed Port Républicain for Jacmel alongside his officers and the 100 Mulatto soldiers who had arrived with him.

The town was abuzz with rumors and anxiety the following week. Roume and Toussaint thought it best to move the capital of the colony from *Port Républicain* to *Cap-Français* until further notice.

Toussaint put up signs for a general meeting of all Mulattos on the upcoming Sunday at the Catholic Church. When the time came, Toussaint walked slowly down the aisle to the front of the ornate church. As he looked left and right and met the eyes of the parishioners, each put their heads down. The clanging of his sword echoed throughout the church.

He approached the podium and slowly removed his tricorn hat. The participants gasped as they saw the mauve *mouchwa tèt* of war on the head of Toussaint as opposed to the yellow one of peace. The air was still and a swarm of flies had entered the church to eerily agitate those present.

Toussaint looked upon the crowd. There wasn't a sound to be heard but of the buzzing insects until he spoke.

"You Mulatto Gens de Couleur who have always betrayed the Blacks from the beginning of the revolution - what is it that you want today? There is no one who does not know that you want to be masters of the colony and exterminate the Whites and enslave the Blacks!"

People began nervously looking at one another, gasping and shaking their heads from side to side in disapproval.

"But perverse men that you are, you ought to consider that you are forever dishonored already by the deportation and the murder of those Black troops who fought with you many years ago that you betrayed. Why did you sacrifice them? Because they were Black!"

Toussaint's anger bubbled to the surface and an out-of-character roar exited his throat.

"Why! Why does Général Rigaud refuse to obey ME? ... Answer?... Because I am Black!

Why else should he refuse to obey a French Général like himself and one who has contributed more than anyone else to the expulsion of the English?

The parishioners began to whisper and grumble their

dissatisfaction towards Toussaint.

"You Mulattos—through your treachery and your insane pride— you have already lost the share of political power you once had. As for Général Rigaud, he is utterly lost. I see him before my eyes in the depths of the abyss. A rebel and traitor to his country. He will surely be devoured by the troops of liberty!

More gasps as their beloved protector and Mulatto brother Rigaud was being villainized. Shouts of '*NO!*' could be heard.

"You Mulattos—"

Toussaint raised his right hand high and brought it down hard in a fist on the pulpit which uttered a deep base sound against the wood that echoed for a moment throughout the church, catching everyone off-guard and resulting in utter silence.

"I see to the bottom of your souls; you are ready to rise against me. But although my troops are leaving, I leave here my eye to watch you, and my arm, which will always know how to reach and strike you."

The attendees sat in stunned silence as Toussaint marched down the corridor, with his sword loudly clanging as it dangled on his side, and out of the church where soldiers had prepared Bel Argent for his departure. He mounted the horse and galloped out of town with his honor guard close behind.

Having heard of Toussaint's fiery speech, Rigaud planned to publicly post Hédouville's letter relieving him from subordination to the Governor *Général*. Rigaud had become resolute against his foe.

Over the next several months, diplomatic letters and exchanges from Commissioner Roume continued to press Rigaud into accepting the territorial makeup that the French government had imposed. Toussaint had already a strong contingent in the towns of *Petit* and *Grand Goâves* on the coast of the southern peninsula. He sent warnings to be ready at all times for a possible attack and feared civil war was inevitable. Time would prove him correct.

Twenty-One

TOUSSAINT LOUVERTURE AND DR. STEVENS

Approaching Cap-Français
April 1799

Some years ago, along a long sandy beach on the island of St. Croix in the Danish West Indies colony, two young boys were taking turns diving under the azure blue Caribbean waters on the west side of Gallows Bay. One after the other, they would bring up conch shells and toss them on the rocks, adding to a growing pile already harvested.

"Alex, I think we've got enough now, don't you think?"

"Yeah, we've got a nice haul today, Ned! We did good, *Mon*!"

"Mama will be pleased. She loves lobster and conch," replied Ned. "Let's get a couple more bugs—more would be perfect for Sunday dinner. There are some in that hole down below."

"Beat you to it!" Alex smiled, taking a deep breath and disappearing under the surf. Ned filled his lungs with air and quickly followed with a lobster snare in his hand. He dove down, weighted by a belt of rocks hidden in pouches of cloth around his waist which his mother had sewn for him last Christmas. It helped him dive rapidly and fight his buoyancy on the surface.

Ned arrived on the ocean floor to find Alex already working the small cave, his arm deep within the cavity. The sand was jetting out of the cave's mouth and he knew instantly that Alex had snared a prize—and what a prize it was; a Caribbean lobster of at least four pounds!

The crustacean was fighting as hard as it could to remain in the safety of its hole as Ned kicked harder in Alex's direction to help. Ned grabbed onto Alex's snare, already lassoed to the creature, and the two yanked as hard as they could to dislodge the lobster's legs from the coral points to which it had anchored. It wasn't budging as it waited for the two boys to exhaust the oxygen in their lungs. Alex looked at Ned and held up three fingers—the sign of a secret maneuver they had executed many times before.

Three, two, then one finger—and the boys pushed the snare towards the bug—their name for Caribbean lobsters—giving the crustacean a false sense of victory. The crustacean temporarily dislodged its grip on the rocks and attempted to head backward. Just then, Ned and Alex gave a synchronized pull of the snare and the lobster lifted, legs scrambling to grab coral or rock, as the boys pushed off from the ocean bottom with their muscled legs.

They breached the surface gulping the salty air to refill their lungs. The two boys looked at each other and burst into laughter.

"She's the one Alex. She's the prize of the catch! Let's take a look to make sure she has no eggs. Would be a shame to throw her back."

The boys waded over to a huge black rock and threw the lobster upon it, holding the snare tight so it wouldn't wander back into the water. They flipped the bug onto its side, inspecting her bottom for any reddish eggs. Finding none, they looked at each other and laughed the childish, innocent laugh of twelve-year-olds and laid their backs on the huge sun-warmed rock, exhausted and panting after the ordeal.

Ned watched as pelicans dove after a school of fry, the small silvery main staple of Spanish Mackerel, Bonito, Barracuda, and

Tuna. He looked up at the sky; the sun was bright and hot, just how he liked it. He'd certainly burn under it if not for the smelly lard-based concoction his mother cooked up in the kitchen to protect his skin. He promised her to always wear it. Next to him, Alex suddenly sat up.

"Ned, promise you'll always stay here on St. Croix with me. We could sell our catches to the ships that visit. We could even salt some. We are good fishermen, you and me. We make a great team."

"I'll never leave this place. Alex," answered Ned. "There's nowhere else for me like this."

In the distance, the two boys could hear a voice calling.

"Masta Ned, Masta Ned, Masta Ned!"

Ned raised his hand and waived in acknowledgment.

"About that time. Seems they've sent Oliver to fetch us."

Alex and Ned placed their haul into two canvas bags; four lobsters, eight conchs, and two large Spanish mackerels.

"Our moms will be pleased, Ned," Alex said with excitement. "We will all eat well this day!"

As it was on every Sunday, their mothers would send the boys to hunt for seafood to bring back to the traditional Sunday supper attended by the Stevens and Hamilton clans. The slave Oliver arrived to retrieve the conch, lobster, and fish to begin the cleaning and filleting process.

"Masta Ned, you boys done good!" Oliver smiled large as he peered into the bags.

"That we did, Oliver. Here; Alex and I want you to have this for your family's supper today."

Ned held up a Spanish Mackerel and a two-pound lobster, thrusting them toward the slave.

"I cannot accept that *Mon*, you should know that by now. I would get a whipping if anyone caught me," Oliver said. "No slave is allowed to eat that good."

"It's always been our secret, Oliver. We've never been caught before—go ahead, take it," replied Ned.

"Yeah Oliver, take it why don't ya," Alex said.

"But I's a slave, Masta."

"Well, you're no slave to us. You're our friend. So take the food and keep it between us," Ned insisted. "If it were up to me and Alex, there would be no slaves."

Oliver smiled back as Alex and Ned both looked at him as a true friend and equal. Though only fifteen, Askel had a family of young brothers, sisters, and a mother to feed. His father had been senselessly killed by the hand of a ruthless drunk Danish sailor many years ago.

Ned looked across the beautiful beach, filled with coconut trees and sea grapes, and out towards the ocean. He took one deep breath, then another, as oxygen rushed into his lungs and refreshed him to the point of giddiness. On the horizon, a schooner was slowly sailing toward them. He loved the islands dearly. He closed his eyes—the constant lapping waves only broken by the sound of his name being called from a distance over and over again…

"Dr. Stevens… Dr. Stevens … Dr. Stevens?!"

Suddenly aware of the person speaking to him, Dr. Edward Stevens snapped himself out of his childhood daydream and looked over at the man standing next to him. The far-off schooner could still almost be seen in the distance as he realized his mind had wandered to his childhood in St. Croix and his beloved friend, Alexander Hamilton.

He was now aboard the schooner *Kingston*, an armed merchant ship under the able skipper Captain Elija Hodge and escorted by the *USS Ganges*, a U.S. Naval ship under the command of Captain Thomas Tingey. They had departed Philadelphia on the unusually frigid morning of March 17th and were now plying the waters of the warm South Atlantic, a day's sail away from *Cap-Français* in Saint-Domingue.

Traveling with Dr. Stevens were his wife Hester, Saint-Domingue Diplomatic Trade Envoy Joseph Bunel, and his wife

Marie-Françoise Fanchette. Also on board was Robert Ritchie—the new U.S. Consul to *Port-Républicain*—and Jacob Mayer, returning as the Consul in *Cap-Français*.

Charles Carre accompanied the party as his secretary and Carre's father, John—who owned property in Saint-Domingue, which had been confiscated under the French Émigré law when they fled to Philadelphia in 1793—was in hopes of accepting Toussaint Louvertures's offer for *Émigrés* to return to the island and resume cultivation.

Dr. Stevens was the highest-ranking American diplomat ever dispatched to the colony. President John Adams himself had gifted him a three-volume standard issue set of *Laws of the United States of America* and a letter containing *"Standing instructions to Consuls and Vice-Consuls of the United States."*

"Ned, you appeared to be in a rather deep daydream," the man who'd awoken him said as they stood on the bow where the occasional drop of spray would salt them before evaporating in the warm wind.

"I cannot tell you how much it pleases me to be returning to the Caribbean, Joseph," Stevens replied.

"Yes, you mentioned you were from the Danish West Indies; How long has it been, Ned?" asked Joseph Bunel.

"After getting my medical degree, I returned to begin a medical practice on St. Croix. I left over seven years ago, in '92, with my wife for Philadelphia. I was coaxed to come north by my childhood best friend Alexander Hamilton and university roommate William Thornton," Dr. Stevens explained. "He's now the chief architect of the new White House in Washington, D.C. We are all from the West Indies."

Well, it certainly beats that cold weather of Philadelphia," Bunel laughed. "I cannot imagine how people live there their entire lives. I almost froze to death! Far too cold for me. I'm a Caribbean son, myself."

"I didn't realize how I missed it so," said Dr. Edward *'Ned'* Stevens, wistfully.

"How did you find your way back here, may I ask?"

"When I came to Philadelphia, I worked for the Bush Hill Hospital. Alex, now Inspector General Alexander Hamilton, asked me to go on a mission to Spanish San Juan on the island of Puerto Rico. The American government needed someone who spoke fluent Spanish as well as French and was no stranger to the Caribbean. A French privateer, La Boudaine, had captured the *New Jersey*—a huge four-hundred-ton American merchant vessel—and asked me to negotiate her release."

"That is a tall and dangerous order in this neighborhood," whistled Bunel.

"Indeed it was," agreed Dr. Stevens. "When I couldn't secure her release in San Juan, I traveled to Saint-Domingue to seek the assistance of French agent Hédouville. I also met with the Commissioner, Phillippe Roume. I hoped they would help influence La Boudaine, whom I assumed was in collaboration with them. I eventually bribed Hédouville and that is how I got the ship released."

"That's rather extraordinary," Bunel said with gaining interest.

"Oh yes. While in *Cap-Français* I also became friends with a few of Louverture's officers; Captains, and Lieutenants. While drinking rum one afternoon, one of them discloses that Hédouville had plans to invade the southern states of America and was mobilizing a Black army composed of some of Louverture's men without his knowledge. Hédouville planned to neutralize Louverture and take over his army and eventually the colony. A French *Général*, through and through," Dr. Stevens said as he looked into Bunel's eyes to gauge the reception of his barb. Bunel remained steady-faced.

Dr. Stevens turned and looked out over the ocean for several moments. He then turned back to Bunel and continued.

"When Toussaint Louverture heard of the plot, he was angered beyond reproach. I believe this is one of the reasons he conspired against Hédouville—and we know how that turned out; gone— thrown out of the colony! It seems Toussaint has no stomach for the complications of invading America."

"I can promise you the *Général* has no intentions of that sort.

Good diplomatic relations with the United States is paramount to his mission," Bunel stated. "He is committed to the rebuilding of his home of Saint-Domingue."

"You asked how I obtained this position. My successful release of the *New Jersey*, uncovering and reporting on Hédouville's plot, and my relationships with many in the government and business community of Saint-Domingue," finished Dr. Stevens.

"Well earned, it would appear," Bunel nodded his head.

"Alexander Hamilton recommended me and put in a good word as well—and what about you, Joseph?" asked Dr. Stevens. "What is your stake in all of this?"

"My wife is black and our children live in this world. Maybe I can help shape what it will look like for them; we may not be able to persuade all Americans of the equality of blacks, but we can build a stronger Saint-Domingue, a free Saint-Domingue, where blacks, whites, and mulattos can live and prosper in harmony if that is possible," replied Bunel. "That is my hope at least—I know it is idealistic."

"Is *Général* Louverture the right man to lead the colony to this future?" probed Dr. Stevens.

"In America, token notice is given to former slaves. Abolitionists view people from Africa as poor Negros, seeking charity from inhumane White masters. They pity them and provide charity through housing, food, and other benefits. This could be a devastating long-term addiction of subservience for an entire population. Toussaint has no tolerance for that. I believe he despises the thought of prolonged charity to the Africans as repayment for their past bondage."

"Explain?" pressed Dr. Stevens.

"The Governor *Général* did not send me, hat in hand, to approach the American government seeking charity. He did not send me asking your government to bless our anti-slavery stance or petition on its behalf. He did not send me to beg America to lift the current trade embargo. The Governor *Général* sent me to meet American officials and present an opportunity for our two countries to benefit equally. He proposes an equal or higher value from Saint-Domingue for an equal or higher value from the United States."

Dr. Stevens smiled despite himself. The man before him was certainly not lacking in spirit.

"Toussaint Louverture does not see himself as a black man dealing with President Adams as a white man, but rather as a head of state dealing with a peer, and allowing each other equal standing."

"This is entirely new to Atlantic diplomatic relations, Bunel," Dr. Stevens replied. "You and I are going to make history together."

That evening, Captain Hodge had several formal dinner tables set on the top deck for all passengers on board. To this point, each had been dining in small groups in rotation in the dining room below. This however was to be the customary 'Captain's Dinner' on the final evening of the voyage, where all were welcome to meet and dine together on the top deck.

The stars glittered in the night sky as guests arrived on deck, introducing themselves to those they were not yet familiar with. Joseph and Marie Bunel knew almost all attendees and quickly sought to formally and cordially introduce themselves to those they did not.

Two men who had been watching the ocean from the starboard side of the ship turned suddenly and nearly bumped into them. Bunel expertly initiated an introduction.

"Gentlemen, allow me to introduce myself; my name is Joseph Bunel, Diplomatic Trade Envoy of Saint-Domingue to the United States of America. This is my lovely wife Marie-Françoise Fanchette."

Bunel waited as one of the men looked at the other before addressing him.

"A pleasure. My name is Ricardo Desbardes, and this is my associate, Reginald Luterne."

The hairs on the back of Bunel's neck suddenly shot up as he recognized Desbardes as the man who'd been following him from the shadows in Philadelphia. Unsure whether the fiend had figured out that Bunel had made him, he cautiously extended his hand.

As the two continued past them to their table on the far end of the deck, Bunel vowed to return the favor and have them tailed during their stay in Saint-Domingue. The colony was his territory, not theirs.

The following morning, the Stevens, Bunels, and most of the other passengers and seamen aboard awaited on the starboard side as Captain Hodge expertly navigated the *Kingston* toward the *Cap-Français* harbor. Dr. Stevens marveled at the size of the bay and the number of houses behind the many grand vessels anchored at the wharf.

Within a couple of hours, the *Kingston* was tied to the dock and dockworkers busied themselves purposefully on shore. The sounds of a productive marina could be heard as men went about loading and unloading cargo to their awaiting land transportation.

Once disembarked Dr. Stevens and his entourage bid farewell to Bunel and boarded a carriage to the *Hôtel de la Couronne*. During the ride, Hester Stevens excitedly pointed out the straight and mostly paved roads, fine squares, parks, schools, churches, hospitals, and City Theater.

She was surprised to learn *Cap-Français* had a population approximate to Boston. Her husband reminded her that this was the richest city in the new world and was granted the label the *'Paris of the Caribbean'* and the island itself the *'Pearl of the Antilles'*.

Shortly after checking into the hotel, a note was delivered to their room with greetings from Henry Christophe, commanding *Général* of *Cap-Français*, along with an invitation to dine that evening. Dr. Stevens was elated to be making inroads with people in the government. From his previous visit to the colony, he knew, now Colonel Christophe, was a well-respected and connected leader.

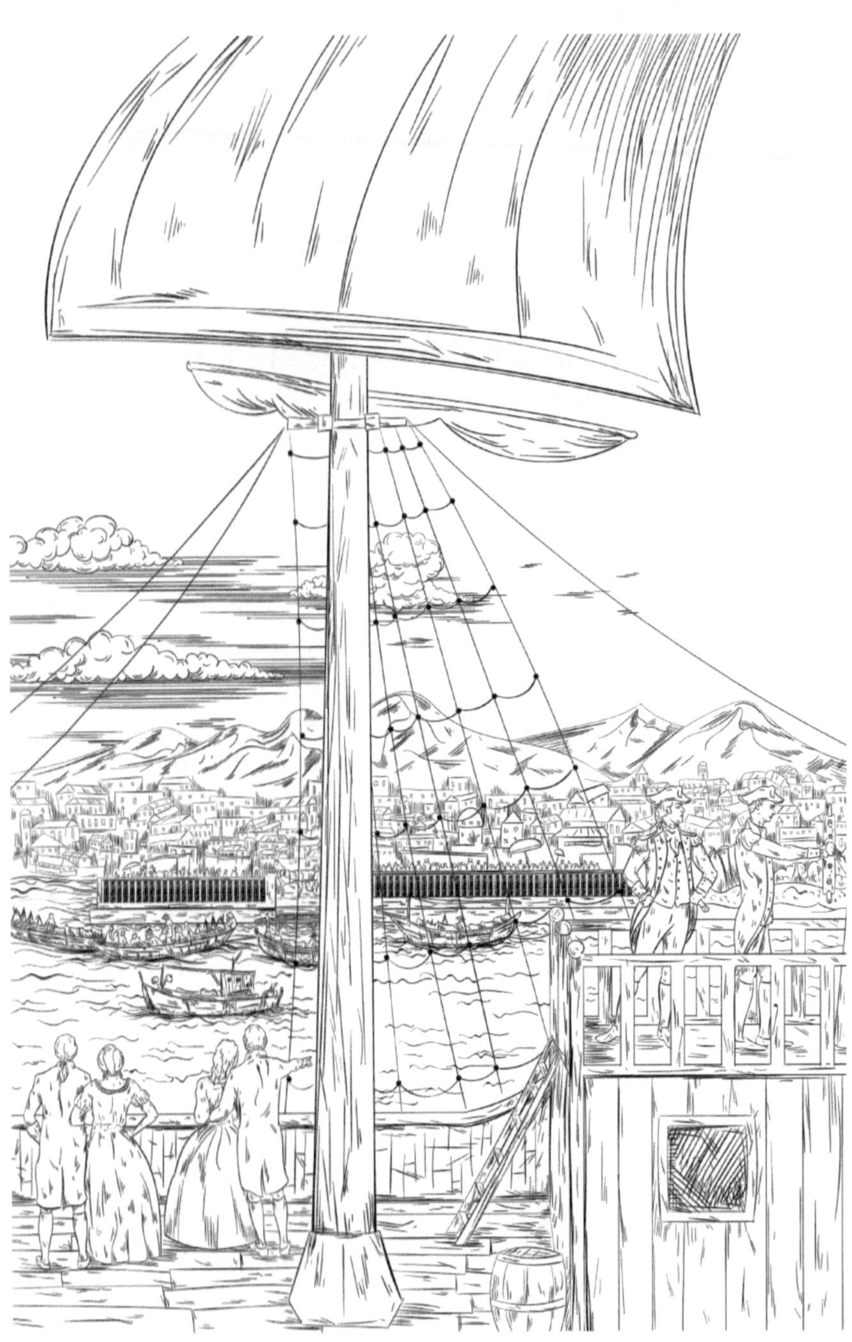

Dinner that evening was a lavish event. Hester marveled at the chic restaurant and incredible cuisine at *La Couronne*; a mixture of French and Creole. Henry and his wife Marie-Louise were impeccable hosts and had invited the hotel's co-owners, Marie and Jean-Baptiste Bayard, to dine with them as well. The Stevens were captivated by stories of the islands, their connections in France, and Jean and Henry's service in Savannah during the fight for America's independence. Neither had any idea that soldiers from the colony had fought in the American Revolution.

Henry informed Dr. Stevens that the Governor *Général* had anticipated their arrival, but was in *Gonaïves* at present. However, Henry had sent word the moment he learned of their arrival.

Toussaint had been meeting with agents from Jamaica at the time but cut short the talks and hurried back to *Cap-Français* once he heard the new diplomat had arrived. He came into town late the following afternoon and immediately set up a meeting for the morning.

The next day, Dr. Stevens and his secretary, Charles Carre, were escorted by Joseph Bunel to Government House. As he entered the palatial building, Dr. Stevens took notice of the fine appointments throughout. In his previous travels to the colony, he'd appreciated the pretense of luxury but was still surprised by the white marble floors, ornate columns, and King Louis XVI-style furnishings of the conference room.

Toussaint Louverture greeted them himself, ever cordial, smiling, and dressed in a plain uniform. He introduced the *Directoire's* agent from France, Phillippe Roume, and the colony's French budget directors—Dumaine and Idlinger.

Dr. Stevens produced the official letter from President John Adams outlining his confidence and offering Toussaint cordial correspondence as equals—even quoting Toussaint's earlier letter speaking of good sense, boldness, and candor.

Dr. Stevens then informed the party that the United States had sent, as a gift of goodwill, sixty thousand U.S. dollars and a shipload of dried and salted meats, flour, and goods for the army.

Toussaint's government was in dire financial condition from the ravages of war. He'd funded the government and military through a barter system, securing goods and services from merchants in exchange for agricultural products. To raise cash, he borrowed money from local banks and creditors with risky debt schemes, often approaching from one and months later another to pay the first. This gift was a God-send.

The meeting proceeded well, with Toussaint enthusiastically leading the conversation. Dr. Stevens later recounted in a report that the Governor *Général* was a seasoned negotiator and did so with zeal—often anticipating the formers' remarks throughout their talks. They were of the same mindset that a proclamation should be published immediately, in which the essential points required by the Government of the United States would be acceded to.

"I object," Roume said, suddenly interrupting the proceedings. "The American government cannot mandate that we disallow French military vessels in *Port-Républicain* and *Cap- Français!* Furthermore, why are they inserting the British into this agreement?"

"The British rule the seas surrounding Saint-Domingue through our eastern seaboard" countered Dr. Stevens. "They demand respect and until you and we have a navy capable of confronting them, they have the ability to seriously damper our trade."

The negotiations continued with Toussaint holding back and allowing the participants to exhaust themselves into a stalemate.

"I move to adjourn this meeting until 3:00 pm this afternoon," said Toussaint, raising his hand after yet another fiery exchange. "Commissioner Roume and I will work on a suitable response to this dilemma."

Toussaint looked at Bunel and gave a nod toward Carre as a signal to Bunel to separate him from Stevens. Bunel understood this and invited Carre to walk with him and as a pretense offered to show him the office of the Governor *Général*. As they exited, Toussaint could hear Bunel expertly distracting the secretary so Toussaint could have a private conversation with Dr. Stevens.

"Let me show you the way out," Toussaint said, gesturing to Dr.

Stevens. "This house is so large that sometimes I even wander down the wrong corridor and find it difficult to find my way back."

"Thank you, *Général*. Gentlemen; I bid you *au revoir*," Dr. Stevens said to the three other men as they left out the far door.

Toussaint waved his open palm forward and put a light touch to Stevens' shoulder with his other to guide him. Dr. Stevens felt a warmth and a sort of calm emanating from Toussaint's touch—much needed after the intensity of negotiations with the three hard-headed Frenchmen.

"Your Secretary Pickering would have been quite impressed with your response to Roume's proposals in the meeting, Dr. Stevens," began Toussaint. "The difference between Roume and I is my interests are for the citizens of this colony while his are exclusively for the French Government. I assure you that I will persuade Commissioner Roume that the proclamation will be modeled with most of your suggestions—and if he fails to agree, I will have him exit the colony," he said with a smile on his face.

"I beg you not to proceed to extremities on our behalf, Governor," replied Dr. Stevens. He was concerned the General might act rashly, but quickly realized he'd misinterpreted Toussaint's humor.

"I have asked Bunel to host a lunch in your honor. We will reconvene this afternoon," Toussaint said as the two men reached the front of Government House. Outside, the sun was bright and Dr. Stevens found a carriage waiting with Carre and Bunel, which whisked them off to *Hôtel de la Couronne*.

Before Dr. Stevens had left for his meeting that morning, Marie Bayard called upon his wife, Hester. They had hit it off the evening prior and unearthed a fast and fond friendship. He found them both conversing with Marie-Louise Christophe and Marie-Françoise Bunel after concluding a tour of the local dress shops of *Cap-Français*. Hester Stevens had been introduced to many fresh local French Caribbean designs and the packages on a chair adjacent to her demonstrated her enjoyment and approval by way of an open wallet.

Bunel, Stevens, and Carre excused themselves from the ladies to dine separately and review acceptable counter-options should Roume insist on his changes. After completing their lunch, they rode back to Government House and were ready and waiting in the ornate conference room by 2:45 pm.

Twenty minutes later, the door opened and Roume and Toussaint entered.

"Great news, gentlemen. Commissioner Roume has agreed to the proclamation as it is written," Toussaint stated before even sitting. Roume looked quiet, reserved, and in submission to the Governor *Général*.

Dr. Stevens sent a dispatch to Secretary Pickering and informed him of the agreement with the Louverture administration and to seek the President's approval. He further wrote,

"*...it is evident that the whole power of the Dominguan government is in the hands of Toussaint Louverture, who knows how to exercise it when it is necessary.*"

Dr. Stevens further went on to say,

"*...this colony cannot remain long as an appendage of France. The period is not far distant when it must be forever separated from the Mother Country.*"

Dr. Stevens also wrote to Alexander Hamilton, informing him that Commissioner Roume was,

"*...a mere cipher. He suffered to maintain the appearance of authority only from political motives Toussaint Louverture's power is supreme.*"

The American understanding early in the relationship was that Toussaint was the premier power broker of the colony. With Roume's signature included on all documents between Toussaint and the U.S. Government, it also signified to world audiences that all actions were initiated and endorsed by France.

The tabloids of both Saint-Domingue and the United States were reporting on these developments, and the private sector viewed them as a potential new era of prosperity. In Saint-Domingue, agricultural products were being harvested at a feverish pace to be among the first exported. In America, ships were being loaded with goods to sell to the colony. Every shipyard was ordered to build ships as quickly as workers could be found and hired for the task.

Everywhere, *Émigrés* who had left Saint-Domingue were making plans to return, reclaim their land and renew cultivation. Even before the agreement was signed by President Adams, ships crammed the harbor with cargo with those who decided not to wait. The casual eyes of onlookers knew it was all in preparation for the soon-to-be-canceled U.S. embargo.

In correspondence between Pickering, Toussaint, and Dr. Stevens, the Secretary spoke of President Adams' desire to include the British in trade negotiations. As the British navy had the superior force in the Caribbean, he'd secured assurances they would engage with any French privateers attacking U.S. vessels.

Toussaint was wary of the arrangement, but upon learning that General Thomas Maitland, who he now considered a friend and ally, would lead the talks, his mind was put at ease. After all, General Maitland had successfully negotiated the removal of all British troops from the colony and had offered Great Britain's support should Toussaint ever wish to free the colony from France and seek independence.

In June, Dr. Stevens, Toussaint, and Maitland met in the western town and former British stronghold of *L'Archaie.* Here, a secret tripartite treaty was agreed upon; this stated that French naval vessels would be barred from Dominguen ports. Toussaint pledged in part,

"...there would be no expeditions against any possessions of His Majesty or the United States of America by the troops of Saint-Domingue and further that I will defend British and American ships from all French privateers arriving in Saint-Domingue."

In exchange, Toussaint insisted that all allied ships—

commercial or military—enter the ports of *Cap-Français* or *Port Républicain* to be registered, be assessed import and export duties, and be issued a visa before proceeding to other ports of the colony. Toussaint however also provided a list of ports controlled by the renegade *Général* Rigaud which were not to be visited as protection could not be offered or guaranteed by Toussaint

Under the authority vested in him by the Intercourse Act *(the so-called Louverture Clause)*, President Adams was encouraged to proclaim that Dominguen-American commercial trade lanes were officially open for commerce as of August 1, 1799.

Dr. Stevens remained in Saint-Domingue to assist in trade matters and set up consulate offices in both *Port-Républicain* and *Cap-Français*. He and his family rented one of Toussaint's homes in the heart of *Cap-Français*—a solid two-story structure of European-hewn stone with a gilded wrought iron balcony.

The home also served as a diplomatic base where Dr. Stevens conducted much of his business and hosted foreign guests, local businessmen, and visiting U.S. ship captains.

Dr. Stevens would also frequently travel with Toussaint to all areas of Saint-Domingue. These trips yielded the American invaluable intelligence regarding the social and agricultural conditions well beyond the capital city.

On one particular visit to Toussaint's Sansay home at Ennery, after Toussaint and Stevens had consumed their fair share of a fine bottle of Tennessee whiskey that Dr. Stevens had received as a gift from an American named Captain Stillwell several weeks back during a port visit, Toussaint awkwardly stood and asked Stevens to follow him into his study.

He walked to a safe hidden under his desk, opened it, pulled out a canvas file, and handed it to Stevens. In it were detailed plans authored by the French to invade the southern United States through Louisiana. The plan had been authored by French Agent Hédouville, who had gone so far as to clandestinely recruit a dozen of Toussaint's junior officers to help execute it.

Toussaint explained that when he caught wind of the plan, he had it immediately shut down and had a dozen officers thrown out of the army before he expelled the French agent from the colony for good. He had kept it secret to not bring suspicion of ill-intent to his administration.

When Dr. Stevens confessed that he had known of the plan and already reported it to President Adams, Toussaint was shocked and suddenly burst into a deep-hearted laugh as if the American diplomat had just uttered the finest of jokes, causing Stevens to begin to laugh uncontrollably himself. Was it that funny or was it the vintage Tennessee whiskey at work? Maybe a little of both.

In the weeks that came, when French privateers sailed their prize vessels into the colony's ports, Toussaint was immediately notified and the army would be dispatched to kill, capture or chase away the pirates, retake possession of, and release the vessels back to their captains or owners through the auspices of Dr. Stevens and the American contingent in Saint-Domingue. This gesture from Toussaint to Stevens was designed to bolster Stevens' reputation as a man of action in the colony as Toussaint wanted him to stick around for quite some time.

In a report to Secretary Pickering, Dr. Stevens wrote,

"I have the most perfect confidence in the attachment of Toussaint to the government of the United States."

On a personal level, both men enjoyed each other's company and Toussaint found that his new relationship with Dr. Stevens rivaled his previous friendship with the sorely missed Etienne Laveaux.

By late June, Bunel returned home to the plantation he and Marie-Françoise managed in the *Plaine du Nord.* They were enjoying a summer of leisure and relaxation together after the months they'd spent in the United States followed by weeks of negotiations back in Saint-Domingue.

On this particular day, he was in his study reviewing some correspondence when Marie-Françoise entered the room.

"He's here," she said.

"Send him in and have Thomas bring a flask of rum and two glasses. I prefer you not be here," Bunel said to his wife who nodded and smiled in understanding as she left the room. Moments later, a man stepped in with his butler, Thomas.

"Have a seat," Bunel said as he waited for Thomas, the servant, to pour two glasses of rum and exit the room. The two men engaged in light small talk but soon arrived on the subject of Ricardo Desbardes.

"And what have you learned?" asked Bunel.

The spy proceeded to account for every person, place, gathering, and meal the man named Desbardes had met with or participated in from the day after they'd arrived back in the colony.

After a brief inspection, one common name became glaringly familiar to Bunel: Phillippe Roume, the French Commissioner. What on earth did Desbardes have in common with Roume, though? His informant's log chronicled no less than seven meetings between the two over the past three weeks.

Bunel furrowed his brow and took another sip of rum. This would require further investigation, of that he was sure.

Twenty-Two

THE CLASH OF TOUSSAINT AND RIGAUD

Jacmel
June 1799

On the warm, star-filled Saturday night of June 15th,1799 a lone rider quickly galloped his steed out of *Jacmel,* racing through the southern territory towards Toussaint's military headquarters in *Gonaïves*.

Toussaint had anticipated the necessity for rapid travel across the colony. To that end, he'd paid families in several local villages along main routes to maintain one of the fastest horses from his stable and have it ready at a moment's notice.

Gonaïves was 250 kilometers north of *Jacmel* and each station was 25 kilometers apart. At a full run, riders could cover the 25 kilometer distance between each in one hour—including time spent transitioning to the next pony. There was no need for saddles as the expert horsemen rode best without them.

The rider rode past *Port-Républicain, Archaie, Saint-Marc,* and *L'Estère*—finally arriving in *Gonaïves* before 9:00 am the following day. The lone horseman barreled into the military compound and was immediately surrounded by armed soldiers with rifles pointed before they could positively confirm his identity. Once the commander heard what the breathless rider had to say, he immediately dispatched four men to Toussaint's Sansay plantation in the town of *Ennery*, 30 kilometers east.

The four soldiers arrived at the plantation by noon to learn Toussaint was attending mass with his wife at *Ennery's* main chapel. The horsemen swiftly made their way to the center of town just as the church bells were tolling and the congregation was exiting the church. They charged into the square as parishioners and passersby looked on, intrigued by the spectacle. Something was amiss.

The horsemen dismounted as Toussaint walked briskly across the road to meet them, leaving his entourage with Suzanne and little St. Jean. As Toussaint approached, he returned the soldiers' salutes. The leader stepped forward and handed Toussaint a leather pouch;

"Dispatch from *Jacmel, Mon Génerál*."

Toussaint opened the pouch, scanned the letter, and crumpled it in his hand.

"Ride to Sansay and await my return there," Toussaint ordered as he turned and returned to Suzanne and the group.

"Friar, I am afraid that I must cancel our bible study and lunch plans," he said, addressing the priest. "There is some pressing business I must attend to. Suzanne, I will need your counsel; let us depart for Sansay immediately."

Suzanne looked at her husband, reading his disposition. She understood this was serious. They mounted the carriage with St. Jean and Toussaint ordered the driver to make haste for home, a short distance away. Upon their arrival, he was pleased to find the staff had fed the horsemen as he needed them ready for their imminent missions.

The dispatch Toussaint had received contained two messages; the first was a letter from Marie-Jeanne Lamartiniére, his spy in *Jacmel*, informing him that Génerál Rigaud had concluded a meeting with his field commanders and they were preparing for war. It read that he had published his letter of authority from Gabriel, comte d'Hédouville in the local newspaper and had posted copies in all towns and cities of the South.

The second document was a published copy of the Hédouville letter itself—which Toussaint had not seen until right then. Its contents officially released Rigaud from Toussaint's authority and appointed Rigaud the sole and supreme commander of the Southern Department.

Hédouville had purposefully conjured up the scheme to drive a wedge between Rigaud and Toussaint as revenge for the Governor General expelling him from the colony.

Increasing the tensions, Rigaud had accused Toussaint of a secret alliance with the white *Émigré* planters who had returned to the colony and Rigaud criticized his policy of forced labor which was managed under the watchful eye of the latter's army. Rigaud said this stood as the first step back to slavery.

Toussaint shook with rage but sought to contain his anger in the presence of his wife. He and Suzanne entered the study so she could begin to assist in preparing dispatches to his commanders in the field, including Laplume, Dessalines, Christophe, Vaublanc, and Moyse advising them to be on high alert for a pending attack.

They then drafted a letter to Commissioner Roume advising him of these new developments, including excerpts from Hédouville's letter as well as communication to Joseph Bunel and Edward Stevens urging them to coordinate a communique with the American government as he feared Rigaud would try to destabilize the newly reopened trade agreement.

One by one, he sent the four horsemen to different parts of the island to deliver the dispatches and prepared himself for travel to *Gonaïves*. In the communications, he summoned Dessalines, Vaublanc, and Moyse to meet him at *Port-Républicain* and to bring with them every able-bodied soldier ready to march.

The situation deteriorated rapidly. On June 18th, only two days later, Rigaud launched an open rebellion attacking the towns of *Petit-*

Goâve and *Grand-Goâve*. Laplume was quickly overrun and driven out with his army scattering under the onslaught. Without any protection, the Mulatto forces massacred the white *Émigrés* along with landowners of any color who had sided with either the British or Toussaint.

By noon of the fifth day of the rebellion, Toussaint and a force of 20,000 reached *Léogâne*. Once there, he learned the Mulatto Alexandre Pétion, who served under Laplume, had defected to Rigaud—taking with him several capable young officers and soldiers including Jean-Pierre Boyer.

Toussaint had always considered Pétion the more capable commander over Laplume and reprimanded himself for not having put the former in the top position. Perhaps he would have retained his loyalty. That he would never know.

After demoting Laplume, Toussaint placed his army under the command of Jean-Jacquess Dessalines. Soon after, he received word of coordinated Mulatto rebellions elsewhere in *Môle-Saint-Nicolas* and many towns in the *Artibonite* Valley. Toussaint led his army from town to town suppressing the skirmishes, and handing out swift justice by eschewing elongated trials and military tribunals in favor of executions for the insurrectionists.

A brief attempt at a rebellion in *Cap-Français* was quickly snuffed out by Henry Christophe. Those involved were arrested and jailed to await trial. When Commissioner Roume received Toussaint's dispatch recounting the events over the prior days, he quickly declared Rigaud an outlaw and issued a warrant for his arrest.

As Toussaint swept the south, he called the Cultivators to arms, who quickly retrieved the muskets previously gifted by him and Sonthonax. 8,000 peasant soldiers were mobilized under the claim that the Mulattos would re-enslave them if victorious. He sent them further south to join with Dessalines. Toussaint then turned back north to *Môle-Saint-Nicolas* with Moyse's forces following.

In *Grand-Goâve*, Rigaud had assembled his war counsel and was preparing to begin a meeting when Alexandre Pétion suddenly entered the room with Boyer in tow. Rigaud stood and enthusiastically welcomed Pétion with a warm embrace.

"You have chosen well Alexandre. You are fighting with me and for your people."

"I am with you, *mon Général*. Tell me what you need and I will do it."

Rigaud then strode over to a map on the wall.

"Gentlemen, we have captured this town here, *Grand-Goâve*. We have also secured *Petit-Goâve*—here. We own *Jacmel*, here. The enemy is in *Léogâne* 25 kilometers north—less than a 5-hour march from here.

He continued, "I have secretly sowed rebellions in many towns from the *Artibonite* north to *Môle-Saint-Nicolas;* a distance of 300 kilometers. Toussaint will be forced to split his army to quell the various insurrections across a vast swath of the colony."

"I also sent our two strongest insurgents to *Môle-Saint-Nicolas* and *Port-de-Paix,* further splitting Toussaint's forces in the north."

The men in the room listened in rapt attention, nodding along.

"I know the *Génerál*. He will rush to the rescue of Jacques Maurepas at *Port-de-Paix* while simultaneously attacking *Môle-Saint-Nicolas*. He has an emotional attachment to the people of that town—remember he was nearly knighted King there by the British."

The men chuckled heartily, bringing a smile across Riguad's face.

"With Toussaint bogged down in the north, we will launch a coordinated attack on Dessalines in *Léogâne* before he has the opportunity to render aid. Toussaint has also sent 8,000 Cultivators—who just dropped their hoes for gifted muskets and with little to no training—marching north. Though they outnumber us three to one, one of our men is worth five of theirs, so in battle *we* effectively outnumber *them*."

"And what of Louis-Jacques Beauvais in *Jacmel, mon General*? He has declared his forces neutral. How do we proceed?" asked a senior officer.

"Let him babysit the town. We will take it when necessary. *Jacmel* is key as we will resupply ourselves from her port."

President John Adams and his wife Abigail were at his 11-room summer home in Peacefield, Massachusetts on a sweltering July day awaiting a special guest. The man they were expecting would prove key to his Dominguan diplomacy and an essential enforcer of the fledging international trade agreements that had already shown signs of enormous promise and prosperity.

The President had already decided that if the man could not meet him at his home, he would travel nearly anywhere to make the engagement happen. The reason being, his guest—Silas Talbot, the Captain of the U.S. Frigate *Constitution*—had recently been slighted by the Secretary of the Navy, Benjamin Stoddert.

Talbot was previously promised the most senior officer position of the American Navy, but the Secretary had instead awarded it to Captain Thomas Truxtun, Talbot's junior who had become an instant hero after his capture of the French privateer *L'Insurgente* a few months prior. Truxtun leveraged his newfound fame, by threatening to resign, to win the promotion.

The Department of the Navy had only been established—under Adams' insistence—one year prior. There were only six ranked Captains with Talbot by far the most experienced. The President was privy to a letter Talbot had written the Secretary of Navy, writing:

"*...I will freely relinquish my present station and retire to private life if there is a desire, from political or any other motives, to place Captain Truxtun over me.*"

This presented Adams with a major problem, as his Dominguan diplomacy required a Naval component to complement the State Department's initiatives. Adams had committed the majority of these forces to the West Indies trade effort, and Talbot was quite familiar with the West Indies, and Saint-Domingue in particular, from past assignments. He was incredibly qualified for this initiative.

Talbot did arrive at the Massachusetts mansion, appearing in a dazzling uniform consisting of a bright navy blue jacket with two gold epaulets on his shoulders and formal tails trailing behind, complimented by a double row of shiny gold buttons and bright white breeches. His Captain's hat was under his arm as he gave the door 3 solid knocks with his knuckles covered in crisp white gloves.

The President greeted him personally and led Talbot to his study where they would await Abigail's call for dinner. An amicable conversation flowed between them as both men were born New Englanders.

"Captain, I want to impress upon you the importance of the mission I am about to confide in you," President Adams began.

"As you may know Mr. President, I am on the verge of retirement," Talbot countered.

"You do not wish to retire any more than I want you to leave office, Silas—may I call you Silas?"

"But of course, Mr. President. It is not news to you that I have been wronged by the Secretary of the Navy, and the time has come to simply explore my other options," Talbot replied.

"You are a warrior, Silas. What are you going to do—run merchant ships with sugar cane, molasses and rum out of the West Indies?"

Talbot shrugged, hoping not to give away too much before he better understood what the President had in mind.

"I want you to accept this new mission and remain in the Navy," Adams offered.

Talbot could sense the desperation in the President's demeanor and decided to take a gamble.

"What of my promotion and rank if I should accept, Mr. President?"

"You will be given the top spot, Captain Talbot."

"The Secretary of the Navy has already given that spot to Captain Truxtun."

"I am the President—not Secretary Stoddert. Leave that matter to me. Now, are you ready for your mission?"

"With your assurance, I am at your service, Mr. President."

"I have received an urgent communique from Dr. Edward Stevens that our fledging diplomacy is at risk in Saint-Domingue. It seems a rebel, a General in the army by the name of André Rigaud is waging a civil war against the legitimate government of General Toussaint Louverture."

"Do you plan to enter this war, Mr. President?"

"Not officially. That would require approval from Congress and I had a hard enough time getting the so-called *'Toussaint's Clause'* portion of our new trade legislation through."

"How then do you intend to execute this…*assistance*…to General Louverture?"

"Rigaud and his *Rigaudins*, as his army called themselves, have threatened American vessels sailing in and out of Saint-Dominguen ports. That is an interruption of our trade initiatives. Our agreement limits Toussaint's ability to maintain a navy of his own as congressmen, mostly those in the South, feared he might invade and emancipate their slave-holding states."

"Do you believe Toussaint is that much a threat, Mr. President?"

"No, I do not. Dr. Stevens is on the ground in *Cap-Français* and has developed a trusting relationship with the General. He assures me that Louverture is only interested in the development of the colony and has no stomach, time, or resources for such ventures."

"Do you trust Dr. Stevens is reading this man accurately?"

"General Louverture has shared military intelligence with Dr. Stevens regarding the French agent Hédouville's plot to invade our country through the French colony of New Orleans. He provided documentation to prove the claim. Once the General learned of the plot, he outmaneuvered Hédouville, ejecting him from the colony and punishing the officers involved," stated the President.

"He sounds like a solid ally, Mr. President," agreed Talbot. "So what is my mission?"

"You will assist and protect our vessels, keeping the shipping lanes open by any means necessary," said Adams, looking squarely into Talbot's eyes.

"Any means, Mr. President?"

"Any and all, Silas. You will work in concert with Dr. Stevens on the ground—he is extremely well connected."

"Mr. President, I will require total authority to make decisions on the spot and without your approval, as things can change quickly in a faraway land."

"Indeed. You and Dr. Stevens will share this joint authority. But you must both agree together on any move that we make within the colony."

"Is the ultimate objective Saint-Domingue's independence from France, Mr. President?"

"Not at this time. However, an independent Saint-Domingue free of French influence would certainly be a winning bet for the United States. After all, we cannot have a powerhouse managed by France with an army larger than ours only several hundred miles south of our shores—and one can never know who will be in charge of France next, given their recent revolution."

"Where does Toussaint Louverture stand on his colony's independence?"

"No one knows. He claims loyalty to France yet acts independently from her. He plays the British, and the Spanish, and I believe us as well to get his most desirable results—and he is brilliant at it."

"Do you fault him for that, Mr. President?"

"Not at all. He is shrewd and intelligent. He understands that he is only one election away from a change in U.S. policy. My predecessor, President Washington, backed his enemies and supplied weapons and funding to the planters trying to oust him. Now, the United States supports him. Should I lose the next election and that fool Thomas Jefferson ascends, he will turn America's back on Saint-Domingue. Louverture knows that and understands he is in a tough predicament, and is looking for any allies he feels might be necessary."

"Tell me about Dr. Stevens."

"A solid diplomat. He has opened up Saint-Domingue's treasure chest for our countrymen. I predict over 1,000 ships will be trading with the colony by year's end. Many Americans will become rich as a result."

"I accept your mission providing I can rely on my judgment in conjunction with Dr. Stevens to keep the shipping lanes open and provide assistance to General Louverture."

"John… *John!*" he heard Abigail calling from the hallway. "Dinner is served!"

The two shook hands. In less than half an hour John Adams had re-secured his vision for Saint-Domingue.

Two weeks later, Adams sat to compose a difficult letter to Secretary of the Navy, Benjamin Stoddert. He was essentially defying his Secretary's pronouncement of Captain Truxtun as the Navy's highest officer—instead inserting Captain Talbot.

He rose from his desk and walked to the window. Presidents are required to make tough and unpopular decisions. Beyond the glass in front of him, Adams caught sight of the U.S. *Constitution* heading out of the Boston harbor towards the open ocean and on its way to become the flagship of America's naval presence in Saint-Domingue. The wind was propelling the two-hundred-foot frigate's topsails 225 feet in the air as the vessel began its voyage to the Caribbean waters under the guidance of his handpicked captain, Silas Talbot.

Rigaud's Mulatto forces had taken *Môle-Saint-Nicolas* and had besieged *Port-de-Paix*. Toussaint moved his army under the cover of darkness each night, leading them northwest. The men walked silently, keeping their horses as quiet as possible to avoid attacks from pockets of *Rigaudian* forces.

They eventually reached a crossroad north of *Le Borgne*. They elected the west road and continued. However, less than a kilometer further the horses became agitated, knowing instinctively that something was amiss.

A flare suddenly shot in the sky, illuminating their presence like a torch in the night. A cannon blast erupted from the road ahead and rifle fire crackled from all directions, mowing down soldiers before they could assume a defensive position.

Over a fifteen-minute blitzkrieg, a dozen men and four horses lay dead on the ground. The rest had found their way out of the firefight but remained shocked by the ferocity of the attack.

"Keep cover!" Toussaint ordered as his commanders passed the word down the line. "No more movement tonight!"

As morning broke, three more men had succumbed to their injuries. Toussaint was well aware of how close he had come to being killed himself.

Just as Rigaud had accurately predicted, Toussaint decided to split his force, sending Moyse to *Port-de-Paix* to rescue Maurepas, and Augustin Clervaux—a Mulatto officer still loyal to Toussaint,—to *Môle-Saint-Nicolas* to retake the town.

In a daring assault on *Port-de-Paix*, Moyse drove the *Rigaudins* into a retreat to the town of *Jean Rabel*. Moyse turned over the prisoners captured in the battle to Maurepas, who spared no mercy. In a ritual taught to them by the honorable British General Maitland, the prisoners were tied to the mouths of cannons and blown out to sea.

Moyse left Maurepas in *Port-de-Paix* to chase the *Rigaudins* to *Jean Rabel*. From there, the rebels were forced to flee into the mountains. Successful, Moyse, headed towards *Môle-Saint-Nicolas* to rejoin Clervaux.

Clervaux had already begun bombarding *Môle-Saint-Nicolas* with cannons. When bolstered by the addition of Moyse, a week of steady barrages made the *Rigaudins* defenses weak. Before the victors could enter the town, however, Rigaud's commanders ransacked the local treasury and paddled south out of the harbor to rejoin Rigaud.

In *Cap-Français*, the firing squad assembled every hour. Three men, and in some cases women, would become the targets of the squad of six soldiers who carried out the executions. The prisoners would receive a speedy trial, perhaps of two or three minutes to legitimize their death sentences from a military judge appointed by General Henry Christophe.

This was the part of warfare Henry detested. These prisoners had fought for what they believed in but were simply on the wrong side of history. Not all of the Mulatto *Gens de Couleur* was of ill mind; in fact, many still fought alongside Henry. Only the *Rigaudins* mulattos were in the wrong—they believed Saint-Domingue was only for them; that the Whites should go back to France and the Blacks back to Africa. This infuriated Henry. What the heck would any of them do in Africa, a land about which they knew nothing?

In the Saint-Domingue Toussaint envisioned, Whites, Blacks, and Mulattos would live in peace. The *Géneral* insisted the proof that they could exist together was found in the very rebels who were now traitors. The Mulattos themselves were the product of White and Black men and women. How could they cast the very people who'd conceived them aside?

Henry could hear the executioners' rifles from the docks. He was supervising a gang of soldiers unloading an American merchant vessel that had just arrived from Philadelphia.

As the first crate was coming off the gangplank, he ordered the soldiers to open it. It contained new muskets, American made of the finest quality. He scanned the bill of lading to find the shipment contained 2,800 of them in 120 crates.

The same unloading of muskets from American ships was also taking place in *Gonaïves* and *Port Républicain*, courtesy of President John Adams. Not only the muskets—but powder and shot as well. When the ship's Captain came down the gangplank, he informed Henry he would also be leaving much of the ballasts on the ship. They were made of lead after all, and could be melted down to manufacture more musket balls locally.

When Toussaint marched into *Cap-Français* in late August, he brought with him over 600 prisoners he'd captured in various battles, nearly all men, walking with their hands tied behind their backs. They were escorted to the main town square, the *Place d'Armes*, and told to wait there until further notice. It was late on a Saturday afternoon and the prisoners were certain they would receive a mass trial and execution the following day. They were provided with no food or water. The following morning the prisoners still stood; fatigued, hungry, and exhausted, many falling to the ground. Soldiers would rush to administer a swift kick until they rose again. Many defecated or urinated on themselves for relief.

At 11:00 am a group of children, ages eight to twelve years old, arrived for their first communion. They were comprised of Black, White, and Mulatto boys and girls dressed in their best clothes. They walked into the square to see the hundreds of prisoners gathered, with many crying, some wailing, but most bowing their heads and saying their final prayers before death.

When the children reached the Catholic Church across the street from the square, they were ordered to stand on the wide stairs and turn toward the prisoners. The group of youths numbered so many they flowed across the sidewalk and onto the street. Toussaint rode up in full uniform atop Belle Argent and dismounted. A soldier took the reins and walked the horse to the side of the road.

A four-foot podium had been erected between the church and the town square. Toussaint walked up the podium and turned toward the children, his back to the prisoners in the square.

He addressed the children politely and quizzed them on their knowledge of catechism, smiling broadly when they would yell out the correct answers in unison. Satisfied with their preparation and knowledge, Toussaint nodded to the archbishop to begin an outdoor mass for all present. The many prisoners looked on in grave despair, realizing that their last rites were about to be administered.

It was a hot summer afternoon and the sun shone high in the sky.

A faint breeze blew salty air in from the ocean.

When it was time for the homily, Toussaint went back to the podium and began a speech on Catholic faith and duty. He expounded on the obligations of mercy and the duty of compassion. He turned to the prisoners then and announced,

"You Mulatto *Gens de Couleur* have sinned. You have abandoned your faith. You have killed and maimed. You have not been compassionate. You have not shown mercy. You have lost faith in your fellow man."

The crowd of nearly 1,000 remained utterly silent.

"Rigaud is driven by deadly passions. He has dug a gulf at your feet; he has laid snares you could not avoid. He wished you as partisans in his revolt; and to succeed in his objective, he has employed falsehood and seduction."

A *malfini* could be heard cawing in the sky as it glided around the square. It looked down curiously at the crowd and Toussaint at it; admiring its freedom and grace. The hawk would dart in and out of an incoming flock of griffon, chasing away the nasty buzzards that were eyeing the pathetic bunch of prisoners and eagerly anticipating their next meal.

The prisoners waited for Toussaint to put them out of their misery with an order of execution. Their leader, Rigaud, would certainly do the same to their enemy.

"Today, my children of the first communion, we will show these sinners what it is to be a Christian. To be Catholic. These Mullatos have suffered enough. They have been punished by the fate of God. According to the duty of mercy of which I have just spoken, I hereby make an example for you today. One of forgiveness, which you must live with every day forward."

Toussaint then turned to face the prisoners.

"Mulatto prisoners: you are hereby released with no further punishment. You will be provided with new clothes. You will be nourished with food, water, and given medical attention. You will be allowed to return home with safe passage papers and neither violence nor interference by any of my soldiers or any citizen of our colony will befall you."

The crowd of onlookers remained silent. Some were stunned, others wrestling with confusion or joy, and others with anger, seeking revenge for a loved one who may have been harmed by the revolt of the *Rigaudins*.

"Any that attempts to harm you will risk arrest. You will be treated as the brothers and sisters of Saint-Domingue that you are. Take this message of the mercy and forgiveness of Governor-*Génerál* Toussaint Louverture back to your towns."

The prisoners could scarcely believe their ears. Many refused to lift their heads, terrified they were being tricked.

"Tell your brothers and sisters that I am kind and forgiving, I am humane. I open my arms to you. Come, all of you; I will receive you all—no less those of the South than those of the West, and of the North—come to me, and then return to the children, wives, and homes you abandoned."

It was the children who broke the silence, clapping with enthusiasm as the nuns quickly began leading them in songs. The soldiers marched the prisoners to a large empty field nearby where caldrons of cornmeal and beans were already prepared. Barrels of water to drink and bathe were brought in. One by one, they received their meals, and new clothes, and then began to depart *Cap-Français* for their homes.

By September, Toussaint was on the march south after briefly stopping at his headquarters in *Gonaïves*, and in *Saint-Marc* to assure all was in order. He arrived at *Sources Puantes*, a dozen kilometers or so north of his destination of *Port-Républicain*.

To address the enormous amount of bureaucratic colonial paperwork that had been piling up, he traveled from *Gonaïves* in the carriage he normally reserved for him and Suzanne. Comfortable enough with room for four, he interchanged different secretaries who would take dictation of the correspondence for orders and other official business that was backlogged.

He arrived on a Wednesday morning at a plantation that functioned as a collection point for the hundreds of horses being brought in for the war effort from the *Artibonite* Valley and the Spanish side of the island. He'd appointed Joseph Bunel as his paymaster for the horses as he trusted him with the sparse government funds available from the depleted treasury. Although Toussaint preferred to pay for the horses through barter, the farmers didn't consider agricultural products a valid source of payment.

When the carriage finally came to rest near the midsized farmhouse, Toussaint exited to stretch his stiff arms and legs and take a few deep breaths.

Bunel greeted him and reported that the plantation had only accumulated 600 of the 1,000 horses they sought. Furthermore, they only had enough capital for another 50 or so. Again, the sellers preferred money to sugar, coffee, and rum.

Toussaint walked to the nearest paddock and recognized one of the handlers longing a young stallion. The horse was traveling along the outside edge of the large ring while the handler held the line from the center. He was training the horse to respond to commands through the pressure and release of the line as well as a longing whip. This process built trust and respect with the beast, and soon it would be ready for mounting by a soldier.

Toussaint could see soldiers all around him working diligently with their horses and applying the same technique. From station to station he went, pleased with the activity. He eventually reached a paddock where his most experienced trainers were breaking in the wildest of stallions who had never been ridden before.

He watched awhile before one of the men awaiting his turn with a horse recognized him. He called for the others to stop what they were doing and offered a salute.

"Bon jour, Mon Général!"

Toussaint returned the salute, but his interest was quickly pulled to what appeared to be an experienced trainer suffering grave difficulties with a huge Spanish Andalusian stallion—nearly 1,000 pounds by his estimate.

Throughout history, Andalusians were known for their prowess as war horses; originally brought to the island during the colonial conquests of Christopher Columbus. Most were imported by noblemen who came seeking land and increases in their fortunes. For 300 years, escaped Andalusians would make it out to the plains or into the mountains and live in the wild. These horses were plentiful—but difficult to capture.

Toussaint watched and admired the skilled trainer until the horse bucked a final time, throwing him to the floor. The man landed hard but got up and limped out of the paddock.

"That was a valiant effort," offered Toussaint. The man looked up, recognized the général, and immediately saluted.

"*Mon Général.*"

"How long have you been trying to break him?" continued Toussaint. "Magnificent animal."

"I'm the third to try, *Général*. I am at my wit's end and I have no more time to devote to him. We have other difficult horses to break and this one is taking too much time and resources. We will soon slaughter him for meat."

"Allow me to try," Toussaint said to the obvious surprise of the trainer.

"*Non, Mon Général*! We need you too much. I would be devastated if something happened to you or if you were injured somehow."

"Nonsense," said Toussaint with finality as he entered the paddock. The horse immediately sensed his presence and angrily turned toward him. Toussaint proceeded slowly, well aware of the air aggressively being snorted out of its nostrils. He paused, turned, and walked away.

The stallion looked curiously at Toussaint, confused as to why he was retreating, and began to follow. The animal suddenly bolted for Toussaint in an attempt to intimidate him only turning to brush past his right shoulder at the last moment and come to a stop at the other side of the paddock.

Toussaint turned again to calmly walk in the opposite direction. The stallion shook its head, growled loudly, and repeated the charge, passing Toussaint from behind on his left this time.

Toussaint had employed this maneuver numerous times on other wild horses. On the stallion's fifth charge, he approached the horse and stopped 10 feet away. The stallion hoofed the ground with aggression and Toussaint turned again and walked away. This ritual went on with Toussaint rewarding good behavior by walking toward the animal and reprimanding bad behavior by walking away.

Finally, the horse walked to Toussaint rather than charge and followed him around the pen. Toussaint stopped, produced a crystal sugar cube from his pocket, and held it for the stallion to lick. He then began to pet the animal affectionately on his face and mane.

Toussaint suddenly mounted the stallion, which snorted and took several steps backward, then to the side before reluctantly accepting the human on top of him. Toussaint let the animal move as he wanted for several minutes before taking the reins and teaching it the guiding commands of right, left, forward, and back with awards of affection for compliance to commands.

The number of onlookers had now increased to over 50 trainers marveling at Toussaint's mastery of the horse. In only half an hour, the General had the beautiful Andalusian turning, running, stopping, cantering, and performing all manner of advanced maneuvers.

Toussaint was impressed by this horse's intelligence and ability to learn. He stopped, dismounted, and pulled out another cube of sugar for it to enjoy. He guided the horse to water and allowed him to drink. Within an hour, the horse was totally submissive to him.

The crowd had swelled to nearly one hundred by this time. It dawned on Toussaint that he had just conducted a mass training exercise without realizing it. As he exited the paddock, the other trainers clapped and saluted him.

Toussaint decided to keep the Andalusian under his purview to be gifted to a loyal confidant at a later date. He hosted a dinner that evening for the trainers and officers wherein he expressed his appreciation for them. He emphasized the importance of training the horses properly for the battles soon to come.

The following day, Toussaint sent his carriage carrying three of his secretaries and escorted by twelve of his honor guard to *Port-Républicain* to complete copies of correspondences and file them in the records. An hour after their departure, he mounted the Andalusian and led the remainder of his honor guard out of *Sources Puantes* to follow. He enjoyed being out of the carriage and in the saddle again. He smiled at his men and all could see he was in good spirits and enjoying himself.

Only two miles into their ride, the crackling of gunfire exploded ahead of them. With his command, the detachment rushed half a mile up the road to the fight.

When they arrived, his carriage had been turned on its side with two of his secretaries dead inside—the other was pinned underneath and four of his honor guard lay dead on the ground beside it. The carriage itself was the obvious target of the attack.

Toussaint surveyed the scene. This was no random attack, but a targeted assassination attempt on his life. He was now convinced he was also the target of the previous attack in *Le Borgne*. Just as he had spies in the vicinity of Rigaud, so must Rigaud have equal assets watching him.

The deaths of these innocents irrevocably changed the rules of engagement. Rigaud had made this war personal. By targeting him, nothing was safe or sacred anymore. What if Suzanne had been riding with him—or his son Saint-Jean? Rigaud had been invited to his home, they had dined together, and Toussaint had introduced him to his wife and child. Yet it was clear this man had no boundaries.

The Honor Guard Commander appeared before him.

"It is you they were after, *Mon Général*. We must be sure to increase our security measures to keep you safe."

Toussaint looked around him, then at the distant mountains. A beautiful green valley lay in front of him bathed in bright sunshine. It was surreal.

What had this colony become? How long would it remain like

this? Would it get worse or better—and when? Toussaint felt betrayed. More than Rigaud's insubordination, the publishing of the Hédouville letter, and ongoing rebellion; this was a betrayal of trust.

"Yes, Commander. I have been stabbed in the back by a sharp stiletto," he replied to the guard.

"It is time for us to destroy them all, *Mon Général*—no mercy! I knew these men laying on the ground before us. All good men, every one of them. All with family and children. I will avenge their death and protect you with my life, *Mon Général*."

Toussaint looked directly into the strong and solid eyes of the Commander, who could not hide the hints of moisture forming in their corners.

"God, who knows our thoughts and who sees all, is witness to the purity of my principles. They are not founded on this barbarous ferocity that takes pleasure in shedding human blood. From here on, I call this war *La Guerre des Couteaux – 'The War of Knives'*."

Toussaint turned and looked towards the mountains.

"You shall have your vengeance, Commander."

A malfini cawed high above in the sky, the same hawk thought Toussaint that had observed over the procession in the square at *Cap Francais*. As it glided through the sky, it maintained its cry— seemingly desperate to communicate a message Toussaint could not yet interpret. He stared and admired the majestic bird—so comfortable and free in the sky, commanding respect and attention from both humans and prey. The Honor Guard Commander eyed him anxiously, awaiting his next order.

"Will I one day be as free as the malfini?" Toussaint thought to himself. *"Will this colony find a peace equal to its beauty, one it so rightlyfully deserves? Can I achieve the same respect and attention this bird commands of me?"*

With a final loud caw, the hawk departed, disappearing high into the blue sky. The message had suddenly become quite clear. Toussaint closed his eyes and breathed in deeply.

There was no other option; Andre Riguad had to be eliminated for the good of the colony, no matter the cost.

TO BE CONTINUED.

Subscribe to our Newsletter
For updates on future books in the saga.

www.TriumphToTragedy.com

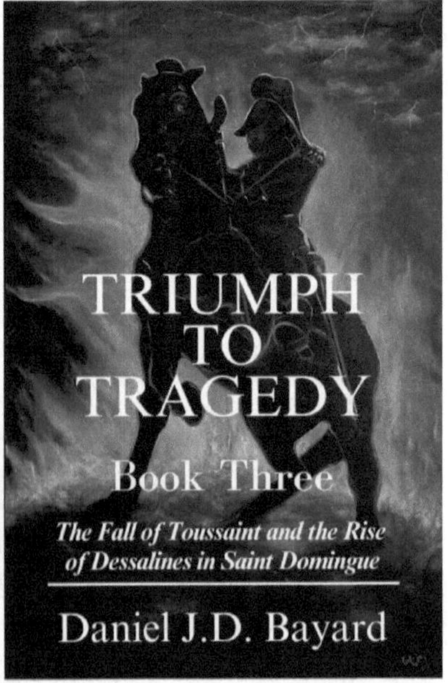

Epilogue

A multitude of obstacles and challenges lay ahead, which threatened to fracture the fragile peace and burgeoning economy of the colony.

The Rigaudins had their interpretation of how the colony should look and who was entitled to live there. Rigaud's vision was one only for Mulattos, with the Whites packing up and returning to France and the Blacks loaded onto ships and sent back to Africa—free to roam with the wild animals and fight amongst themselves.

The freed Black slaves' idea of a free Saint-Domingue eliminated the plantation system and organized work. They desired a simplistic life with perhaps a small plot of land, a hut, and a life of leisurely farming, feeding their family, dancing, practicing their voodoo, and lounging in their free time.

The Bosals—newly arrived slaves born in Africa—were angry. They'd been kidnapped from their country, beaten and thrown onto cramped slave ships, sailed halfway around the world, and chained and whipped into servitude or death. If they survived the initial few months, they were at risk of sickness from diseases to which their bodies had no immunity. Those slaves born in the colony faired better but at the price of losing their souls. They were nothing but livestock and in some cases worth even less. Women, either imported or born on the island, were subject to rape, forced breeding, or both.

The Whites required rehabilitation from slavers to employers.

Their investments and expertise were desperately needed to restore the economy to the former wealth and splendor it enjoyed prior to the wars and destruction caused by the British, Spanish, French, and slave rebellions.

Toussaint's belief and hope was that blacks, whites, and mulattos could coexist in peace. The former slaves would willingly be employed by property owners of any color and granted a living wage to cultivate the plantations and restore the economy. Ex-slaves would be provided their precious piece of land to farm and sell the surplus—carving out a better life for they and their fmilies.

He planned to build schools and healthcare facilities and assure the Catholic religion was practiced in place of the voodoo which was so pervasive in the mountains. He would fund and maintain the trained, disciplined, and well-equipped army required to keep the imperialistic nations away and preserve internal stability.

The recent diplomatic treaties with the United States and Britain were a good start but the various factions could not all share a common vision.

The weak and feeble revolutionary government in France was alternately dysfunctional, incompetent, and inept. Rumors ran rampant of a powerful General by the name of Napoleon Bonaparte who was threatening to implement order on his own terms—through force if necessary. Bonaparte had aligned himself with the *Grands Blancs* to seize power. Toussaint feared the exchange for this support, would mean a return to the practice of slavery.

A peaceful and prosperous future would indeed be a challenge to achieve. More immediate, however, was the prospect of civil war; *La Guerre des couteaux – The War of Knives*. By its end, the colony would bow in unison to an ultimate ruler.

But first, either Toussaint or Riguad would have to die.

The Story Continues in Book Three…

Toussaint has been challenged by fellow General André Rigaud in a bid to create an autonomous Mulatto controlled state in the colony's south. Book Three will begin with the civil war called *La Guerre des Couteaux* (War of Knives) in late 1799.

Although Louverture did not completely sever ties with France after defeating rival leaders among the Haitian revolutionary population and wrestling control from the French bureaucrats, he promulgated an autonomous constitution for the colony in 1801 which named himself Governor-General for Life—against Napoleon Bonaparte's prior knowledge or wishes.

Realizing that France had lost operational control and a solid tax revenue base, Napoleon Bonaparte launched The Saint-Domingue expedition underthe command of his brother-in-law, General Charles Victor Emmanuel Leclerc, in an attempt to regain French control of the Caribbean colony, reinstitute slavery throughout all of their Caribbean holdings and later strengthen their control over the Louisiana territories. Their initial successes, due to overwhelming military manpower and assets will pressure Toussaint Louverture to enter retirement.

In 1802, Toussaint will be invited to a parley by French Divisional General Jean-Baptiste Brunet but was arrested upon arrival. He was deported to France and jailed at the Fort de Joux prison, a bitterly cold institution in the French Alps. He died as a prisoner in 1803 of exposure to the bitter cold and lack of medical treatment.

The Haitian Revolution continued under Louverture's lieutenant, Jean-Jacquess Dessalines. Although Louverture died before the later and most violent stages of the war, his achievements set the ground for the Haitian army's final victoriy at the Battle of Vertières.

Suffering massive losses in multiple battles at the hands of the Haitian army and losing thousands of men to yellow fever, the French capitulated and withdrew permanently from Saint-

Domingue in November of 1803, ironically the same year of Toussaint's death. Toussaint's lieutenant, Jean-Jacquess Dessalines, declared independence on January 1, 1804, establishing the sovereign state of Haiti.

AUTHORS NOTES
In Order of Appearance
in the Triumph to Tragedy Series

HENRY CHRISTOPHE

Christophe (1767 – 1820) began his military career as a drummer boy in the famed Chasseurs-Volontaires de Saint-Domingue and reportedly worked at the Hotel la Couronne, albeit for an unknown period of time. As an adult, he became a key leader in the Haitian Revolution and ascended to be a monarch of the Kingdom of Haiti by proclaiming himselfe king. Christophe set out to improve all aspects of life in the Northern Province focusing on building defense mechanisms for his country, expanding agricultural production and educating his people.

JEAN BAPTISTE CHARLES HENRI HECTOR, COMTE D'ESTAING

d'Estaing (24 November 1729 – 28 April 1794) was a French general and admiral. Following France's entry into the American War of Independence in 1778, d'Estaing led a fleet to aid the American rebels and participated in the failed attempt to oust British troops from the city of Savannah, Georgia. He was executed by guillotine during the Reign of Terror. Before his execution, d'Estaing wrote, "After my head falls off, send it to the British as they will pay a good deal for it!"

GEORGES BIASSOU

Biassou (1741 – 1801) was an early leader of the 1791 slave uprising in Saint-Domingue. Although I place him as part of the Maréchaussée of Saint-Domingue, though there is no evidence he served in that force. He withdrew from Santo Domingo in 1795 to St. Augustine, Florida and at one time owned the historic Salcedo House. There he served as a Spanish general, fought Indians, owned a plantation, retired, and died at age 60 in 1801 during a drunken bar brawl. He was buried with honors by the Spanish military.

Daniel J.D. Bayard

CÉCILE FATIMAN

Fatiman (1771-1883), was a Haitian voodoo priestess, a mambo. She is famous for her participation in the voodoo ceremony at Bois Caïman along with Dutty Boukman which prompted the slave revolt that is considered to be one of the starting points of the Haitian Revolution.

TOUSSAINT GUINO (BREDA) LOUVERTURE

Also known as Toussaint L'Ouverture or Toussaint Bréda; (1743 – 1803) was a Haitian general and the most prominent leader of the Haitian Revolution. During his life, Louverture first fought against the French, then for them, and then finally against France again for the cause of Haitian independence. As a revolutionary leader, Louverture displayed military and political acumen that helped transform the fledgling slave rebellion into a revolutionary movement. Louverture is now known as the "Father of Haiti".

In 1802, Toussaint was captured and deported to France on the 74-gun French ship the Créole. He warned his captors that the rebels would not repeat his mistake, "In overthrowing me you have cut down in Saint-Domingue only the trunk of the tree of liberty; it will spring up again from the roots, for they are numerous and they are deep."

During his imprisonment at the frigid Fort-de-Joux in Doubs, France, Louverture, who was a bona fide French General, attempted to gain an audience with Napoleon who refused. He wrote a memoir and died in prison on April 7, 1803, at the age of 60.

He was reported to have buried a treasure near his plantation in Ennery, which Napoleon had men hunt for but was never found.

SUZANNE SIMONE BAPTISTE LOUVERTURE

Suzanne Louverture (1742 – 1816) was the wife of Toussaint Louverture. When in 1801 the constitution appointed Toussaint as governor of Saint-Domingue, she received the title of "Dame-Consort."

In 1802, Charles Leclerc's troops captured her along with her husband and the rest of her immediate family and shipped them to France. Madame Louverture survived her husband, who died in a French prison the following year. She was the mother of three boys, the youngest of which, Saint-Jean, died in 1804 in Agen, France. She died in 1816, in the arms of her sons, Placide and Isaac in Agen as well.

FRANÇOIS ANTOINE BAYON DE LIBERTAT

Libertat (1732 - 1802) was believed to be the one who freed Toussaint Louverture as the head manager of the Breda Plantation in Saint-Domingue. It is also believed that he developed a strong bond with Toussaint and assisted him in launching his own plantation business.

MOYSE (MOYSE, MOÏSE, MOISE) LOUVERTURE

Most commonly "Moise" (1773 - 1801) was a military leader and one of the most ardent leaders of the first uprising in 1791 and acted as the second-in-command to Toussaint. There is universal agreement that Toussaint Louverture adopted Moise as his nephew. Originally allied with Toussaint, Moise grew disillusioned with the minimal labor reform and land distribution for Black former slaves under the Louverture administration and lead a rebellion against Toussaint in 1801. Though executed on order of L'Ouverture, the insurrection he directed highlighted the failure of the Haitian Revolution in creating real revolutionary labor change and ignited the movement that eventually contributed to driving Louverture from office.

PLACIDE LOUVERTURE

Placide (1781 – 1841) was born before his mother's marriage in 1782 to Toussaint Louverture, who accepted the boy as his legitimate son. He was sent to school in France under scholarship granted by Napoleon Bonaparte. Placide and his brother Isaac were charged with delivering a letter to their father from First Consul Napoleon Bonaparte strongly suggesting he retire as Governor General of the colony and cede his power to General Leclerc, his designated replacement.

Upon returning to Saint-Domingue, he sided and fought with his father against the French government. When Toussaint was arrested and deported on June 8, 1802, by order of Napoléon Bonaparte, so was the entire family along with his mother and his brothers—Saint-Jean and Isaac.

ISAAC LOUVERTURE

Isaac (1786 - 1854) was the son of Toussaint and Suzanne Louverture. He and his half-brother Placide were sent to France in 1797 to be educated. They both returned with General Charles Leclerc to Saint-Domingue in the failed expedition to seize control and re-establish slavery in the colony. Placide and Isaac were charged with delivering a letter to their father from First Consul Bonaparte.

MATÍAS DE ARMONA

de Armona (1731 – 1796) was a governor of Las Californias, serving from 1769 to 1770, during the Spanish Empire's colonial rule of New Spain. While in Santo Domingo, he negotiated the recruitment of the Black slave army to fight under the Spanish Colonial army as the Black auxiliaries.

JEAN-JACQUESS DESSALINES

Dessalines (1758-1806) was a leader of the Haitian Revolution and on January 1, 1804, became the first ruler of an independent Haiti soon after he enacted the 1805 constitution. Under Dessalines, Haiti became the first country to permanently abolish slavery. Initially regarded as governor-general, Dessalines was later named Emperor of Haiti as Jacques I (1804–1806) by generals of the Haitian Revolution Army and ruled in that capacity until being assassinated near the capital of Port-au-Prince in October of 1806. He has been referred to as the father or one of the founding fathers of the nation of Haiti.

GENERAL CHARLES BELAIR

Belair (1760–1802) was Aide-de-Camp and lieutenant of Toussaint Louverture, Head of the 7th demi-brigade, Commandant of l'Archaie and Former lieutenant of Biassou. He was also said to be a nephew of Toussaint Louverture. In 1796, he married Sanite Belair, a female hero of the revolution.

SANITE 'SUZANNE' BÉLAIR

Sanite Bélair, (1781 –1802) was a Haitian revolutionary and lieutenant in the army of Toussaint Louverture. Born free from affranchi parents in Verrettes, Haiti, she married Brigade commander and later General Charles Bélair in 1796. She was an active participant in the Haitian Revolution, became a sergeant, and later a lieutenant during the conflict with French troops of the Saint-Domingue expedition. Her portrait appears on the Haitian 10 gourdes banknote.

MARIE LOUISE COIDAVID

Coidavid (1778 - 1851), was the Queen of the Kingdom of Haiti from 1811–1820 as the spouse of Henri Christophe. She was born into a free family; her father was the owner of Hôtel de La Couronne in Cap Francais, Saint-Domingue. Henri Christophe was a slave purchased by her father and he supposedly earned enough money in tips from his duties at the hotel that he was able to purchase his freedom before the Haitian Revolution.

They married in Cap-Francais in 1793, having had a relationship with him from the year prior. They had four children: François Ferdinand, Françoise-Améthyste, Athénaïs, and Victor-Henri. She was exiled for 30 years after Christophe's death. Shortly before her death, she wrote to Haiti for permission to return, however, died in Italy.

FRANÇOIS-THOMAS GALBAUD DU FORT

du Fort (1743 – 1801) was a French general who was briefly governor-general of Saint-Domingue and exiled by the authorities from there. When Galbaud reached Paris in the spring of 1794 he was at once arrested and thrown into Abbaye prison. In 1799 he was released and rejoined the army, assigned to Egypt, with the rank of brigadier-general but died of the plague in 1801 in Cairo.

BENOIT JOSEPH ANDRÉ RIGAUD

Rigaud (1761 – 1811) was the leading mulatto military leader during the Haitian Revolution and the civil war in the colony. Among his protégés were Alexandre Pétion and Jean-Pierre Boyer, both future presidents of Haïti. Rigaud, like many mulatto's of the day, was a racist who hated the Black population of the island. He returned to Saint-Domingue in 1802 with the expedition of General Charles Leclerc to unseat Toussaint and re-establish French colonial rule and slavery in Saint-Domingue

ALEXANDRE PÉTION

Pétion (1770 – 1818) was the first President of the Republic of Haiti from 1807 until his death in 1818. He is acknowledged as one of Haiti's founding fathers; a member of the revolutionary quartet that also includes Toussaint Louverture, Jean-Jacquess Dessalines, and his later rival Henri Christophe.

Pétion distinguished himself as an esteemed military artillery officer and commander with experience leading both French and Haitian troops. The 1802 coalition formed by he and Dessalines against French forces led by Charles Leclerc would prove to be a watershed moment in the decade-long conflict, eventually culminating in the decisive Haitian victory at the Battle of Vertières in 1803

NAPOLEON BONAPARTE

Napoleon (1769 – 1821) and later known by his regnal name Napoleon I, was a French military and political leader who rose to prominence during the French Revolution and led several successful campaigns during the Revolutionary Wars. He unsuccessfully attempted to re-enslave the most valuable of the French possessions, Saint-Domingue, from 1801 to 1803.

CHARLES VICTOIRE EMMANUEL LECLERC

Leclerc (1772 – 1802), of small stature, was a French Army general who served under Napoleon Bonaparte during the French Revolution. He was husband of Pauline Bonaparte, sister to Napoleon. In 1801, he was sent to Saint-Domingue (Haiti), where an expeditionary force under his command captured and deported the Haitian leader Toussaint L'Ouverture, in an unsuccessful attempt to reassert full imperial control and slavery over the Saint-Domingue. Leclerc died of yellow fever during the failed expedition.

COLONEL CHARLES HUMBERT MARIE VINCENT

Vincent (1753 – 1831) entered the French military service in 1773. In 1801, he delivered the new constitution established by Toussaint Louverture to First Consul, Napoleon Bonaparte in France. Vincent warned against making the doomed Saint-Domingue expedition, but his advice was not heeded. First Consul, Napoleon Bonaparte, exiled him to the island of Elba. After his exile in 1803, Vincent went on to serve a brilliant military career until his retirement in 1815 at age 62.

PAULINE BONAPART

Bonaparte (1780–1825), the youngest of Napoleon's three sisters, was the most frivolous one. She possessed magnetic beauty and charm. Whenever she went, the eyes of men turned after her. Men loved her and she loved them. Pauline was a nymphomaniac and much to Napoleon's chagrin, she made it very public.

LOUIS DAURE LAMARTINIÈRE

Lamartinière (1771 - 1802) was a participant in the Battle of Crête-à-Pierrot. Lamartiniere was a small, thin, man of thirty years during the battle who by all appearances was. He was the illegitimate son of a White father and a sacratras - a quadroon - mother. Lamartiniere's father owned a sugar plantation and refinery near Léogane. He had recognized his mulatto son but left his property to his legitimate, White son. He was the husband of Marie-Jeanne Lamartinière.

MARIE-JEANNE LAMARTINIÈRE

"Marie-Jeanne" (unknown - 1802), was a Haitian soldier and reportedly a "dazzling beauty." She served in the Haitian army during the Haitian Revolution and in at the Battle of Crête-à-Pierrot (March 1802) with her husband Louis Daure Lamartinière. She fought in a male uniform standing along the fort's ramparts bearing both a rifle and a sword.

CATHERINE FLON

Flon (unknown birth-death) was a Haitian seamstress, patriot, and national heroine. She is regarded as one of the symbols of the Haitian Revolution and independence. She is celebrated for tearing off the White portion of the French flag and then sewing the first Haitian flag in May 1803 and maintains an important place in Haitian memory of the Revolution to this day.

MARIE SAINTE DÉDÉE BAZILE

Bazile (unk. birth-death), known as Défilée and Défilée-La-Folle, is a figure of the Haitian Revolution. She is remembered for retrieving and burying the mutilated body of Emperor Dessalines after his assassination at Pont Rouge, at the northern entrance to Port-au-Prince. Dédée Bazile was born near Cap-Français to enslaved parents and made a living serving as a sutler to the army of Dessalines.

EMPRESS
MARIE-CLAIRE HEUREUSE FÉLICITÉ BONHEUR

Félicité (1758 - 1858) became Empress of Haiti (1804–1806) as the spouse of Jean-Jacquess Dessalines and they had seven children together. During the siege of Jacmel in 1800, she was applauded for her work with the wounded and starving. She managed to convince Dessalines, besieging the city, to allow roads to be opened for food, clothes, and medicine which she personally delivered.

She is also credited for saving many French colonists by hiding them under her bead during the revolutionary war.

FRANÇOIS CAPOIS

Capois (1766 – 1806) military career began in 1793 after a visit with independence leader Toussaint Louverture. Capois is mostly known for his extraordinary courage and especially his herculean bravery at the Battle of Vertières in which the French general Viscount of Rochambeau, commander of Napoleon's army even called a brief cease-fire to congratulate him.

He was nicknamed "Capois la Mort" for his numerous episodes of defying death during battles.

JEAN-PIERRE BOYER

Boyer (15 February 1776 – 9 July 1850) was one of the leaders of the Haitian Revolution, and President of Haiti from 1818 to 1843. He reunited the north and south of the country into the Spanish Haiti (Santo Domingo), which brought all of Hispaniola under one Haitian government by 1822. Boyer managed to rule for the longest period of time of any of the revolutionary leaders of his generation.

BATTLES OF THE REVOLUTIONS

The Battle of Vertières
(in Haitian Creole Batay Vètyè)
The Battle that Ended the Revolution
November 17th - 18th, 1803

The last major battle of the Haitian Revolution was fought 0n November 18, 1803, between the Saint-Domingue Revolutionary army and Napoleon's French expeditionary forces. Vertières is situated a few miles south of Cap-Français.

General Rochambeau sent Duveyrier to negotiate the French surrender and was given ten days to embark the remainder of his army and leave Saint-Domingue. The battle occurred less than two months before Dessalines' proclamation of the independent Republic of Haiti on January 1, 1804, in the town of Gonaïves.

Daniel J.D. Bayard

The Other Major Battles of the Haitian Revolution

Battle of Croix-des-Bouquets – March 1792

Siege of Port-au-Prince – January 1793

Battle of Cap-Français – June 1793

Capture of Fort-Dauphin – January 1794

Battle of the Acul – February 1794

Battle of Gonaïves – April 1794

Battle of Port-Républicain - May 1794

Battle of Jean-Rabel – April 1797

Battle of Ravine-à-Couleuvres – February 1802

Battle of Crête-à-Pierrot – March 1802

Siege of Port-au-Prince – October 1803

Battle of Vertières – November 1803

Siege of Santo Domingo – March 1805

ABOUT THE AUTHOR

Daniel Jean-Dominique Bayard

Mr. Bayard was born in Port-au-Prince, Haiti, and raised in the United States when his parents moved to New York in 1958. He returned to Haiti for the first time at 18 and has been fascinated with Haiti's culture, people, and historical significance ever since. He lived and owned a business in Haiti for a short period of time and came to love it.

While researching his family's ancestors dating back to the 17th century, he became intrigued with the complexities and drama of Saint-Domingue, the colonial precursor to the Republic of Haiti. In-depth research into all aspects of the period's history and aspects of colonial society led him to write this thrilling, enlightening, and entertaining story.

Mr. Bayard is a Chief Marketing Officer for a major company, married with 4 children, blessed with 5 grandchildren, and resides in South Florida.

Daniel J.D. Bayard

Ancestors of the Author

Philippe Bayard (Lille, France DOB 1689)
(Arrived in Saint-Domingue circa 1710)
Married Marie Debreuse

Jean-Philippe Bayard (Son) 1725
Married Jeanne Guillemette Bachelier

Jean-Baptiste Hyppolite Bayard (Son) 1750
Married Marie Jasmine

Jean-Baptiste Bayard (Son) 1775
Married Marie Victoire Georges

Achilles Othello Bayard (Son) 1823
Married Elizabeth Pressoir

Georges R. Bayard (Son) 1850
Married Marianne Clerie

Thomas Bayard (Son) 1879
Married Alzire Sansaricq 1881

Daniel Thomas Bayard (Son) 1912
Married Marcelle Elisabeth Oriol 1921

The Author:
Daniel Jean-Dominique Bayard (Son) 1957
Married Lily Anne Marie LaPlace 1957

THE REPUBLIC OF HAITI

Haitian Creole: Ayiti

The country of Haiti is located in the Caribbean on the western third of the island of Hispaniola. It is bordered by the Dominican Republic to the east, the Caribbean Sea, and the Atlantic Ocean.

Haiti's terrain consists mainly of rugged mountains interspersed with small coastal plains and river valleys. The government system is a republic; the chief of state is the president, and the head of government is the prime minister.

Haiti has a largely traditional economic system in which most of the economy relies on subsistence farming, and government regulation is widely constrained. Haiti is a member of the Caribbean Community (CARICOM)

In color, the flag of Haiti's top section is Blue and the bottom section is Red. The inserted image in the center of the flag consists of Blue, Red and Green in a White background.

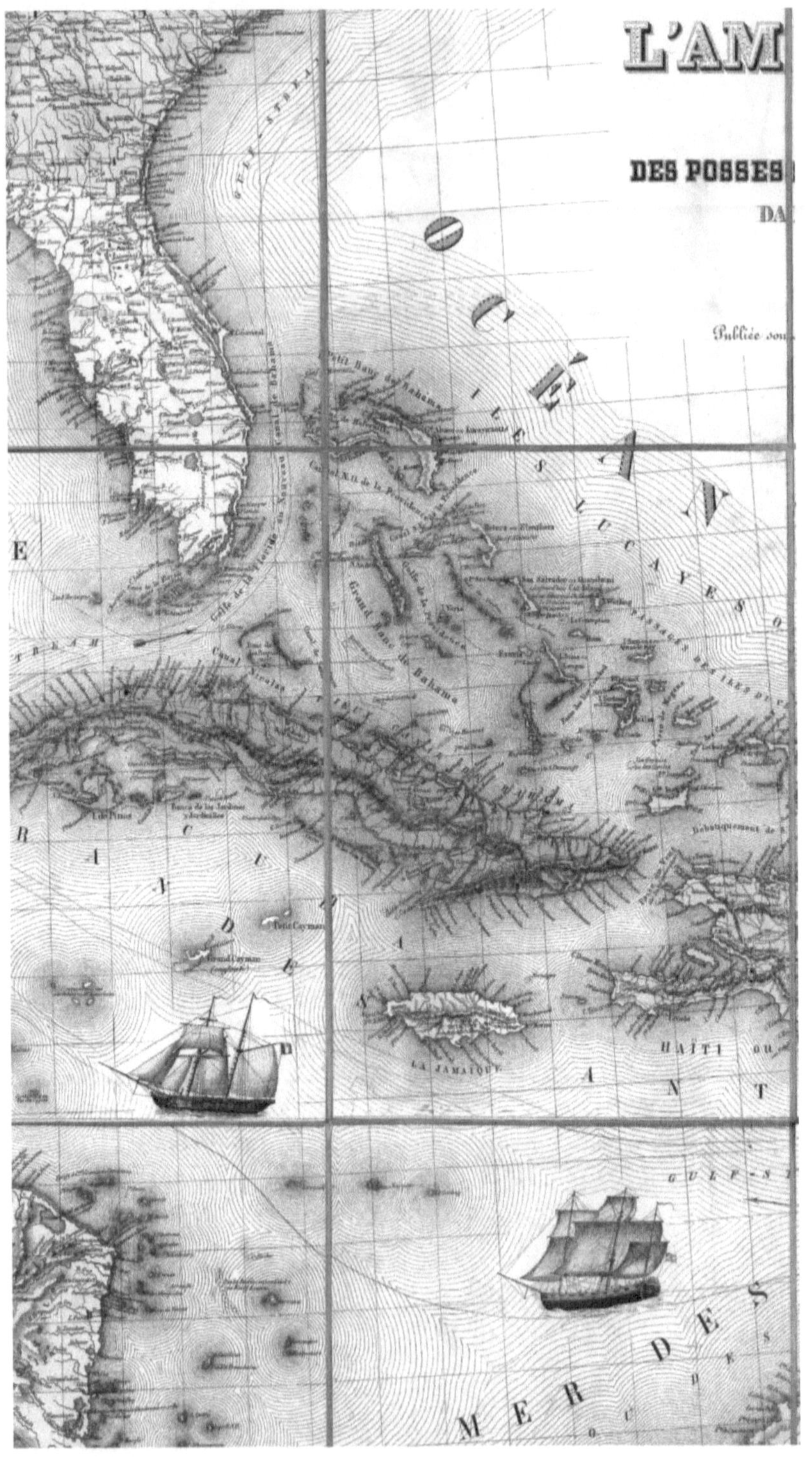
L'AM
DES POSSES
DA
Publiée sou
OCÉAN
ILES LUCAYES
MER DES
GULF-S

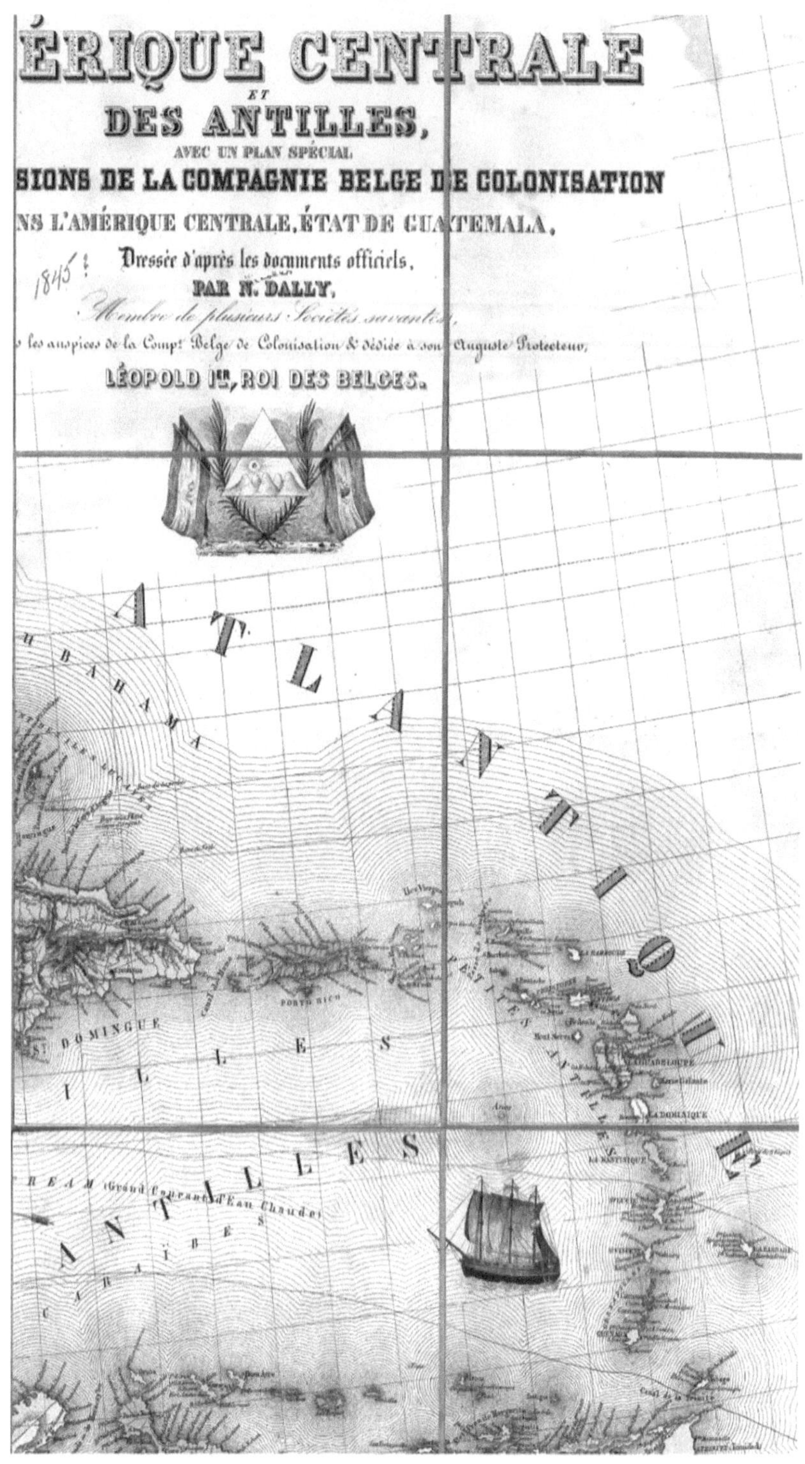
ÉRIQUE CENTRALE
ET
DES ANTILLES,
AVEC UN PLAN SPÉCIAL
SIONS DE LA COMPAGNIE BELGE DE COLONISATION
NS L'AMÉRIQUE CENTRALE, ÉTAT DE GUATEMALA,
Dressée d'après les documents officiels,
PAR N. DALLY,
Membre de plusieurs Sociétés savantes,
les auspices de la Comp.e Belge de Colonisation & dédiée à son Auguste Protecteur,
LÉOPOLD Ier, ROI DES BELGES.
1845
ATLANTIQUE
BAHAMA
ST DOMINGUE
PORTO RICO
ILES
ANTILLES
CARAÏBES